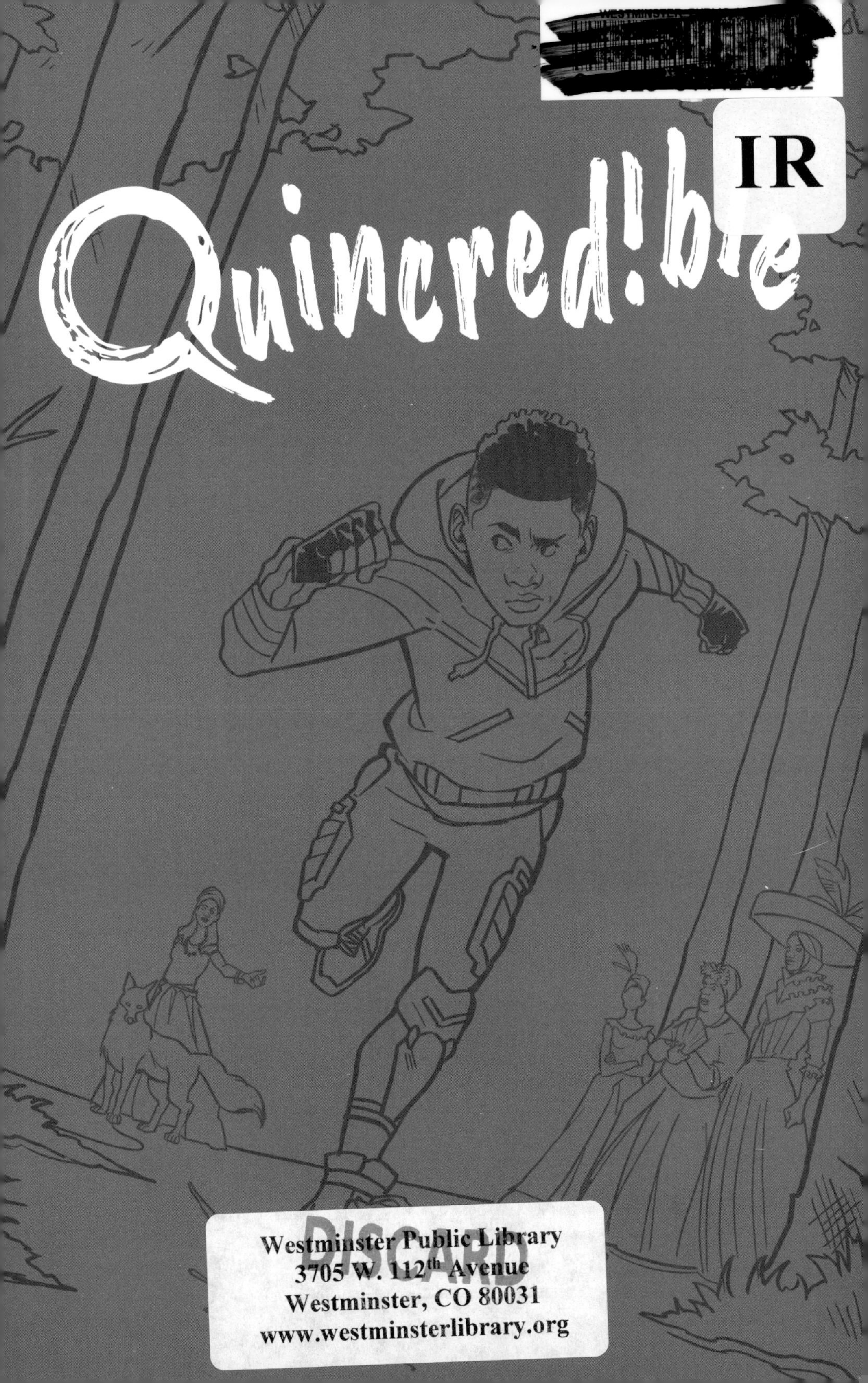
Quincred!ble

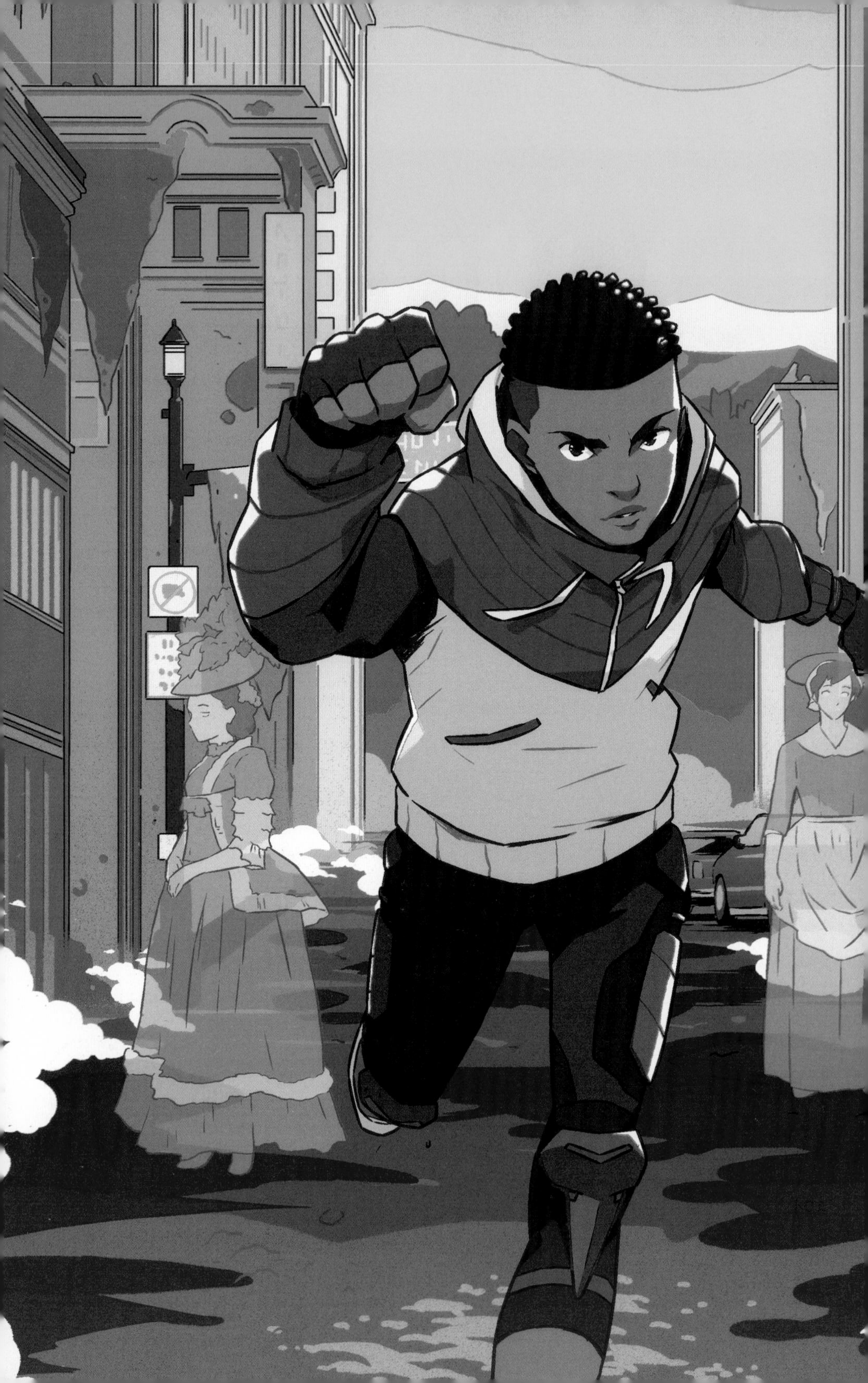

P9-EAY-171

CATALYST
PRIME

Quincred!ble

THE HERO WITHIN

created by **ISAAC REED**
written by **RODNEY BARNES**
illustrated by **SELINA ESPIRITU**
colored by **KELLY FITZPATRICK**
lettered by **AW'S TOM NAPOLITANO**
cover by **SELINA ESPIRITU**

STEENZ AND DESIREE RODRIGUEZ · editors
ZOE MAFFITT AND KAT VENDETTI · assistant editors
ANDWORLD DESIGN • designer

LCCN: 2020919620
ISBN: 978-1-62010-936-6
eISBN: 978-1-62010-949-6

Quincredible: The Hero Within, released JULY, 2021. Published by Oni-Lion Forge Publishing Group, LLC, 1319 SE Martin Luther King Jr. Blvd., Suite 240, Portland, OR 97214. © 2018 and 2019 Illustrated Syndicate, LLC. QUINCREDIBLE™, CATALYST PRIME™, and their associated distinctive designs, as well as all characters featured in this book and the distinctive names and likenesses thereof, and all related indicia, are trademarks of Illustrated Syndicate, LLC. All Rights Reserved. Oni Press logo and icon artwork created by Keith A. Wood. The events, institutions, and characters presented in this book are fictional. No similarity between any of the names, characters, persons, or institutions in this issue with those of any living or dead person or institution is intended, and any such similarity which may exist is purely coincidental. No portion of this publication may be reproduced, by any means, without the express written permission of the copyright holders. Printed in Canada.

CHAPTER ONE

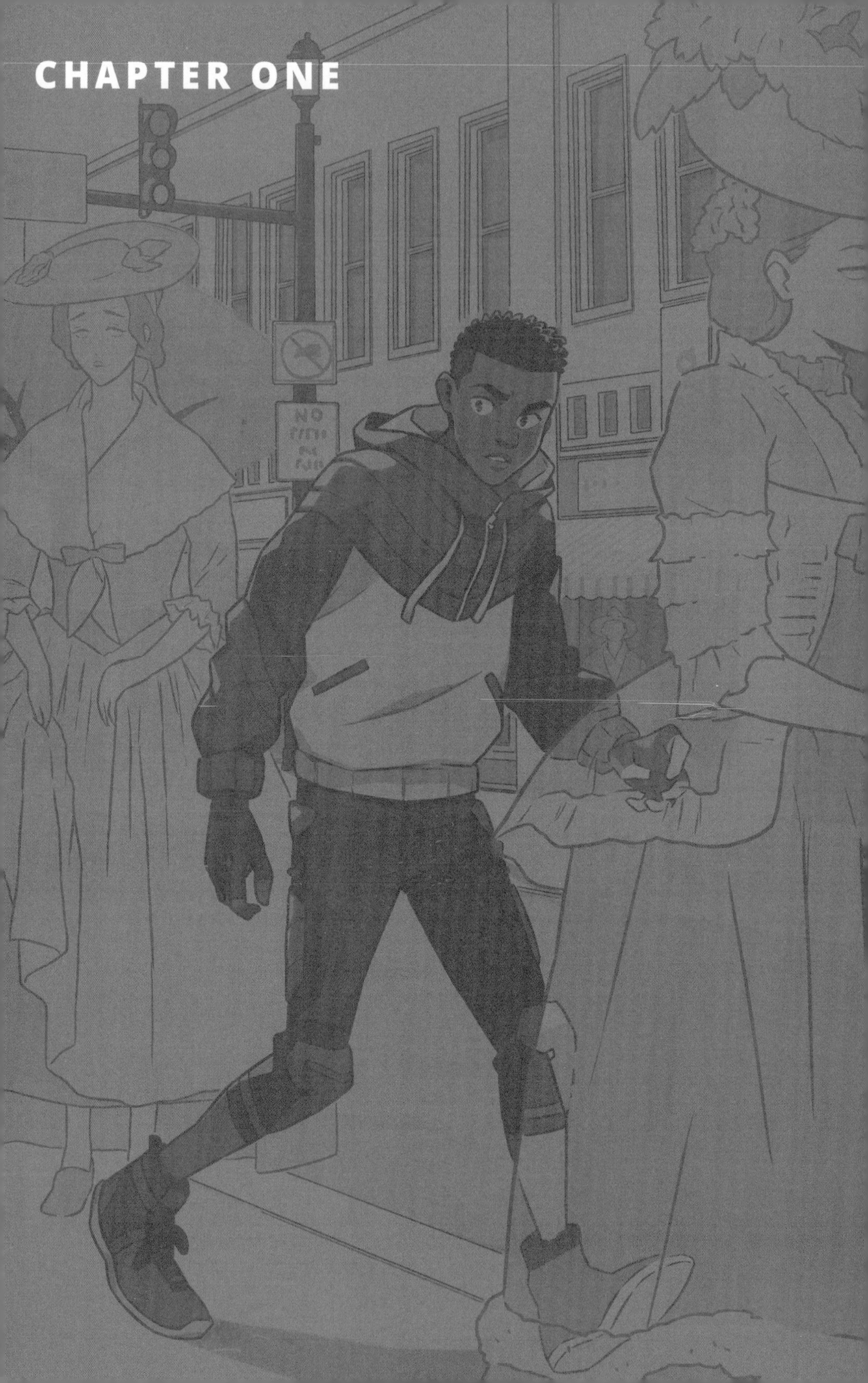

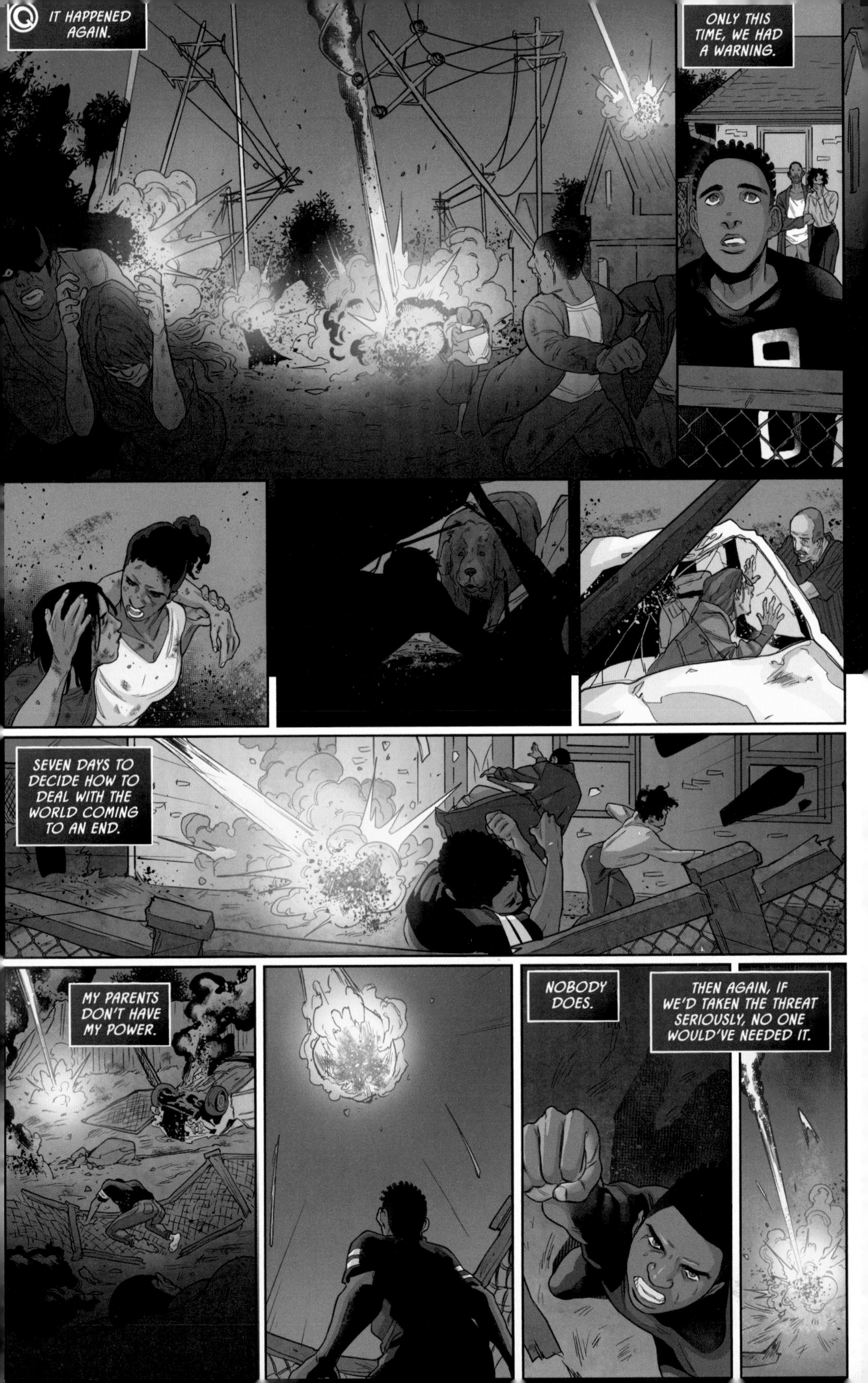
IT HAPPENED AGAIN.
ONLY THIS TIME, WE HAD A WARNING.
SEVEN DAYS TO DECIDE HOW TO DEAL WITH THE WORLD COMING TO AN END.
MY PARENTS DON'T HAVE MY POWER.
NOBODY DOES.
THEN AGAIN, IF WE'D TAKEN THE THREAT SERIOUSLY, NO ONE WOULD'VE NEEDED IT.

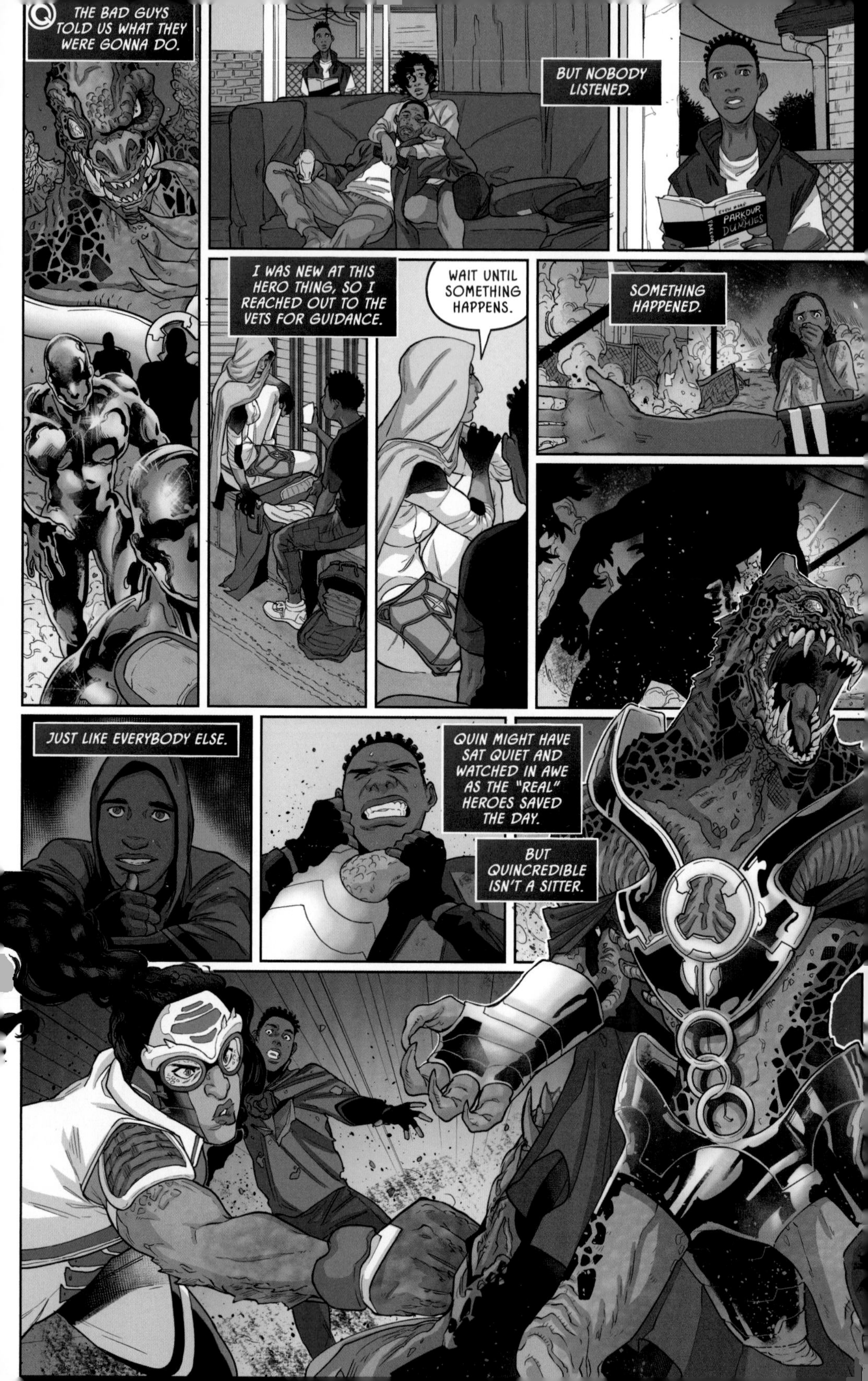
THE BAD GUYS TOLD US WHAT THEY WERE GONNA DO.
BUT NOBODY LISTENED.
PARKOUR DUMMIES
I WAS NEW AT THIS HERO THING, SO I REACHED OUT TO THE VETS FOR GUIDANCE.
WAIT UNTIL SOMETHING HAPPENS.
SOMETHING HAPPENED.
JUST LIKE EVERYBODY ELSE.
QUIN MIGHT HAVE SAT QUIET AND WATCHED IN AWE AS THE "REAL" HEROES SAVED THE DAY.
BUT QUINCREDIBLE ISN'T A SITTER.

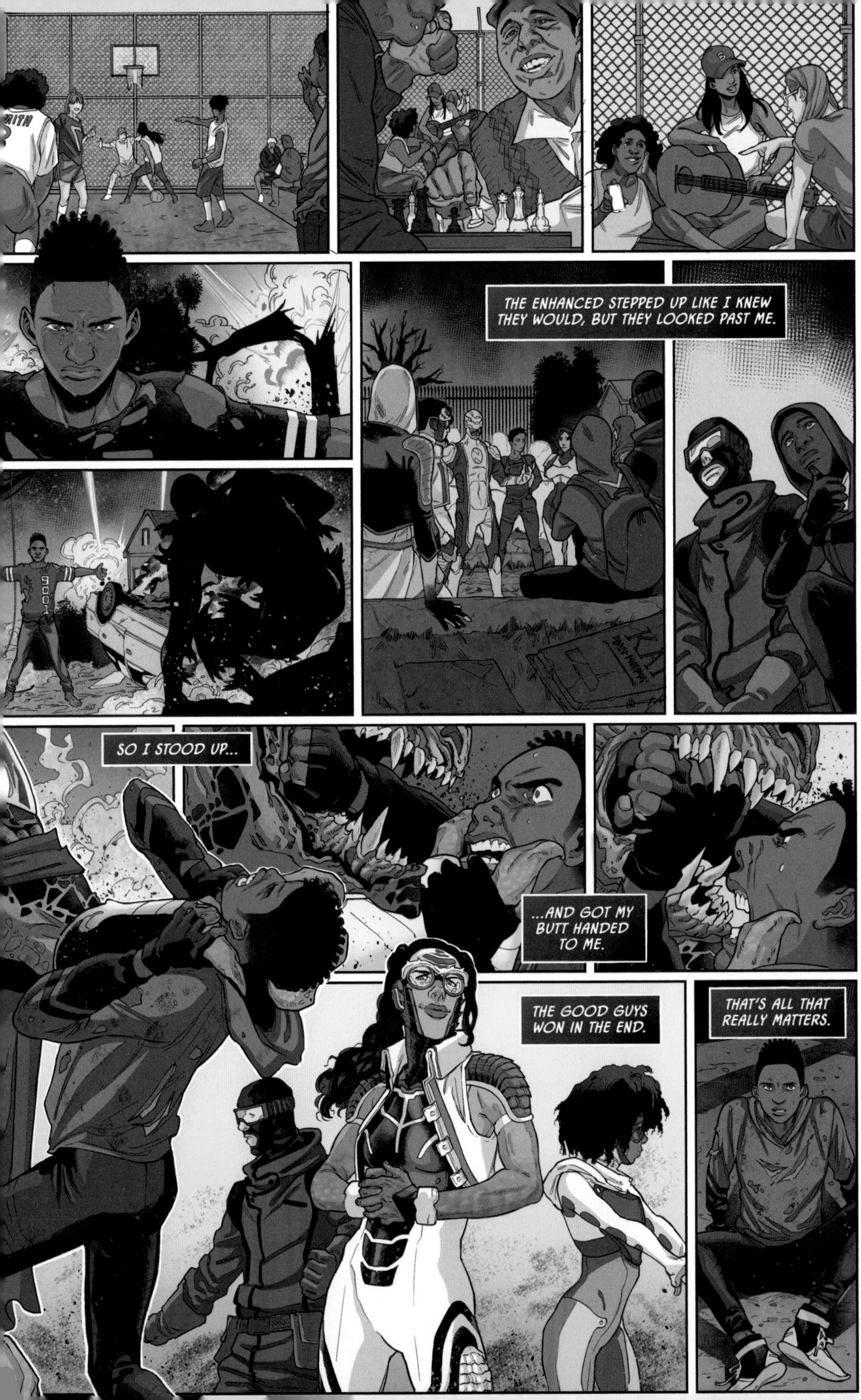
THE ENHANCED STEPPED UP LIKE I KNEW THEY WOULD, BUT THEY LOOKED PAST ME.
SO I STOOD UP...
...AND GOT MY BUTT HANDED TO ME.
THE GOOD GUYS WON IN THE END.
THAT'S ALL THAT REALLY MATTERS.

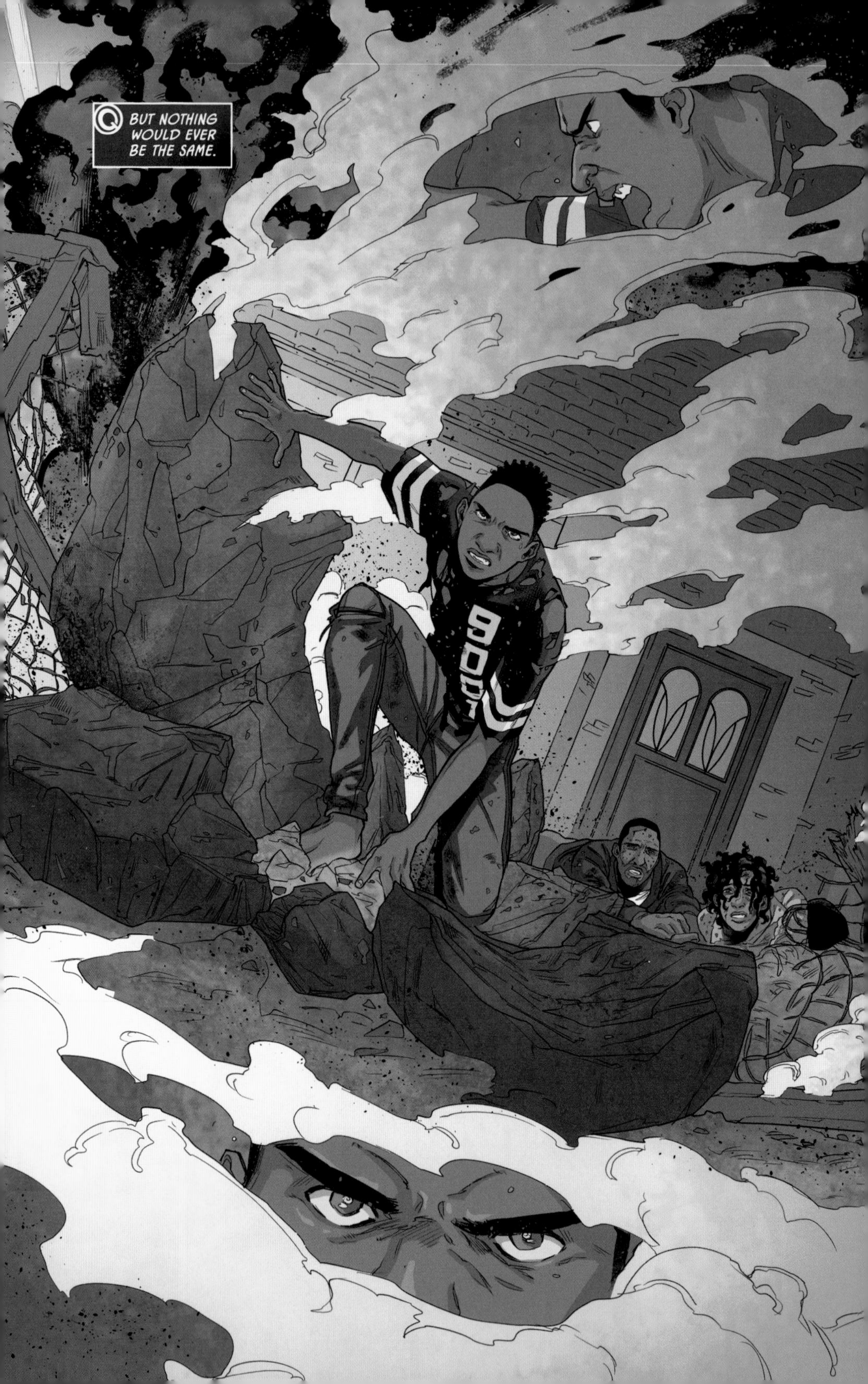
BUT NOTHING WOULD EVER BE THE SAME.

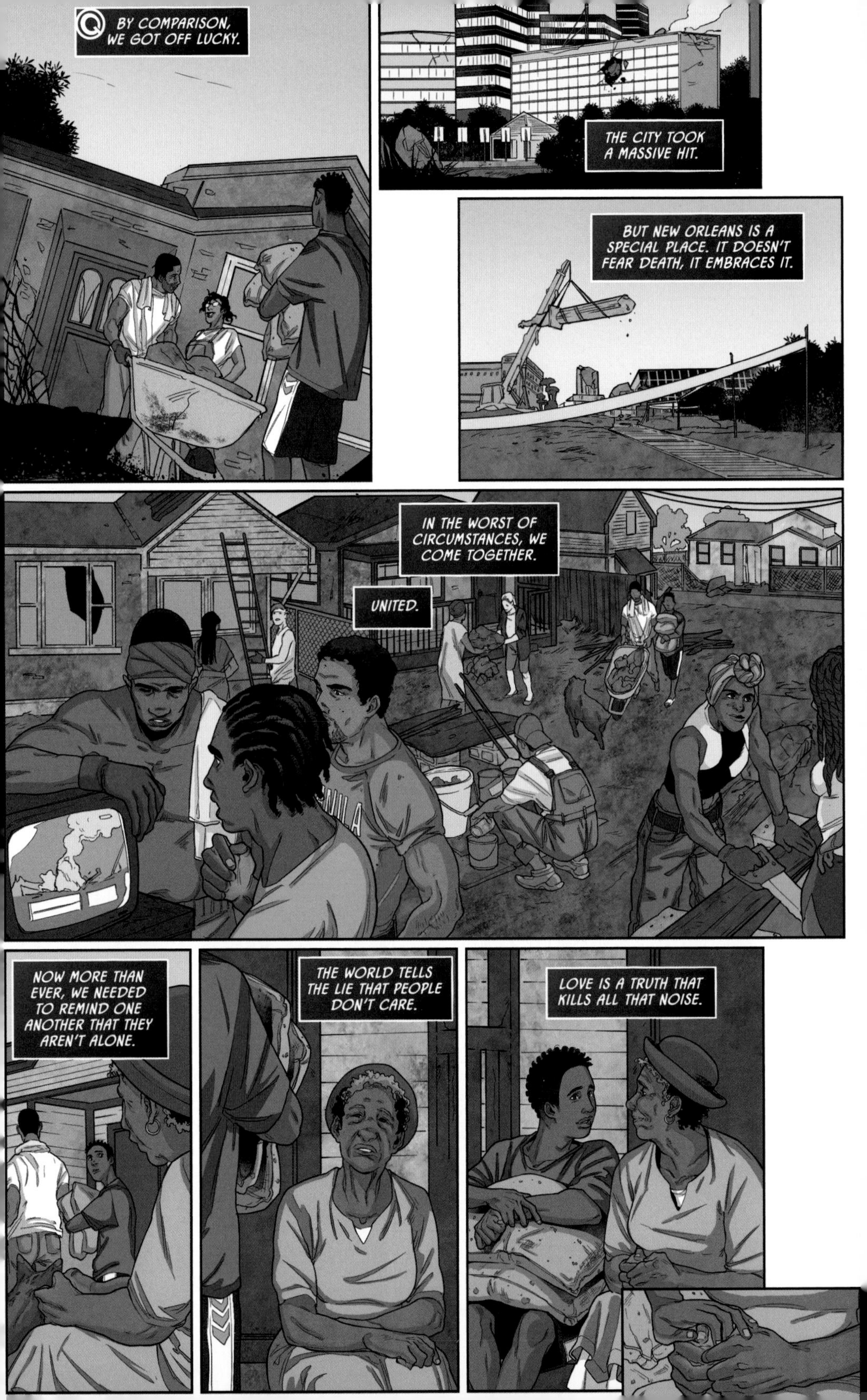
BY COMPARISON, WE GOT OFF LUCKY.
THE CITY TOOK A MASSIVE HIT.
BUT NEW ORLEANS IS A SPECIAL PLACE. IT DOESN'T FEAR DEATH, IT EMBRACES IT.
IN THE WORST OF CIRCUMSTANCES, WE COME TOGETHER.
UNITED.
NOW MORE THAN EVER, WE NEEDED TO REMIND ONE ANOTHER THAT THEY AREN'T ALONE.
THE WORLD TELLS THE LIE THAT PEOPLE DON'T CARE.
LOVE IS A TRUTH THAT KILLS ALL THAT NOISE.

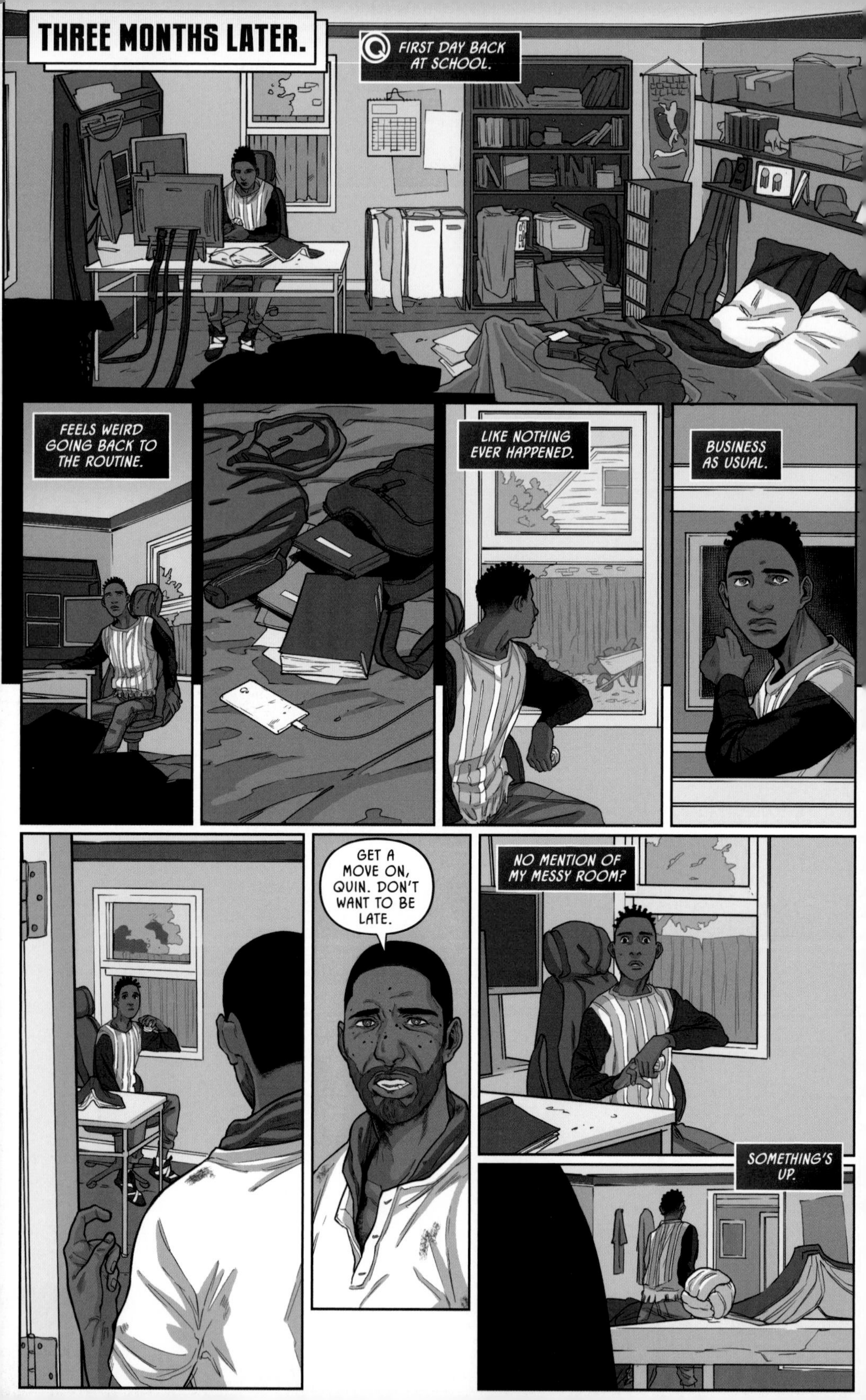
THREE MONTHS LATER.
FIRST DAY BACK AT SCHOOL.
FEELS WEIRD GOING BACK TO THE ROUTINE.
LIKE NOTHING EVER HAPPENED.
BUSINESS AS USUAL.
GET A MOVE ON, QUIN. DON'T WANT TO BE LATE.
NO MENTION OF MY MESSY ROOM?
SOMETHING'S UP.

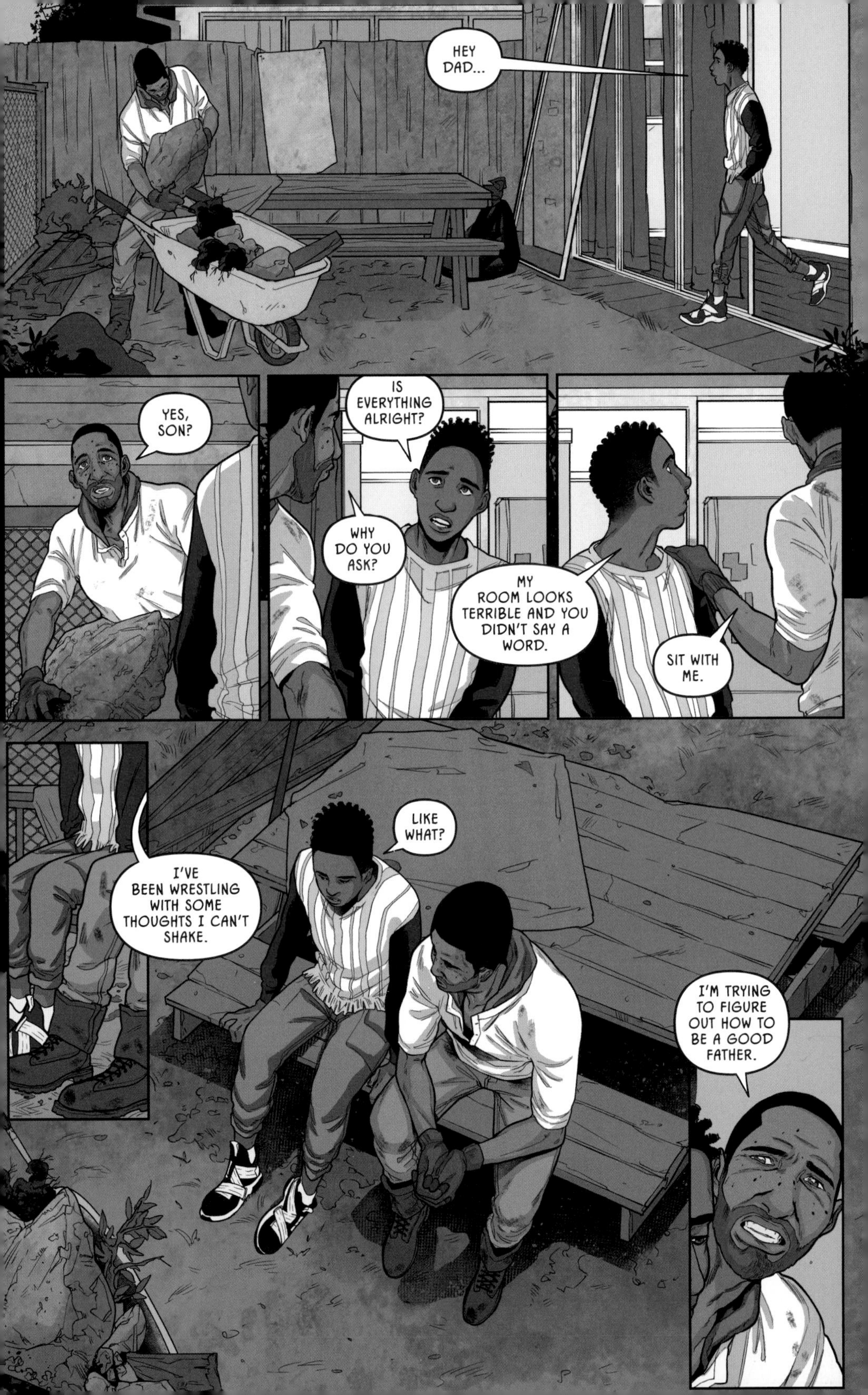
HEY DAD...
YES, SON?
IS EVERYTHING ALRIGHT?
WHY DO YOU ASK?
MY ROOM LOOKS TERRIBLE AND YOU DIDN'T SAY A WORD.
SIT WITH ME.
I'VE BEEN WRESTLING WITH SOME THOUGHTS I CAN'T SHAKE.
LIKE WHAT?
I'M TRYING TO FIGURE OUT HOW TO BE A GOOD FATHER.

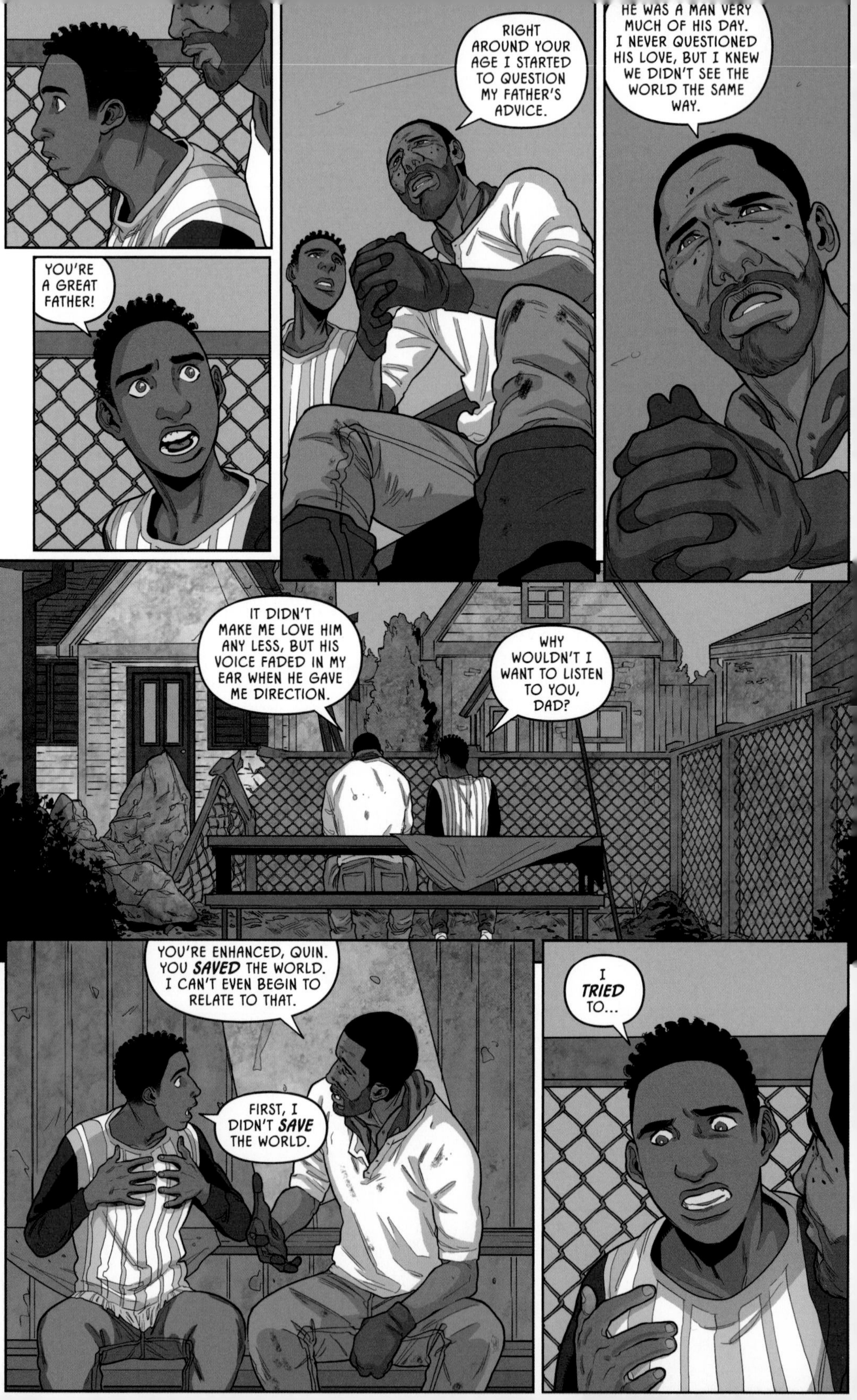
RIGHT AROUND YOUR AGE I STARTED TO QUESTION MY FATHER'S ADVICE.
HE WAS A MAN VERY MUCH OF HIS DAY. I NEVER QUESTIONED HIS LOVE, BUT I KNEW WE DIDN'T SEE THE WORLD THE SAME WAY.
YOU'RE A GREAT FATHER!
IT DIDN'T MAKE ME LOVE HIM ANY LESS, BUT HIS VOICE FADED IN MY EAR WHEN HE GAVE ME DIRECTION.
WHY WOULDN'T I WANT TO LISTEN TO YOU, DAD?
YOU'RE ENHANCED, QUIN. YOU SAVED THE WORLD. I CAN'T EVEN BEGIN TO RELATE TO THAT.
FIRST, I DIDN'T SAVE THE WORLD.
I TRIED TO...

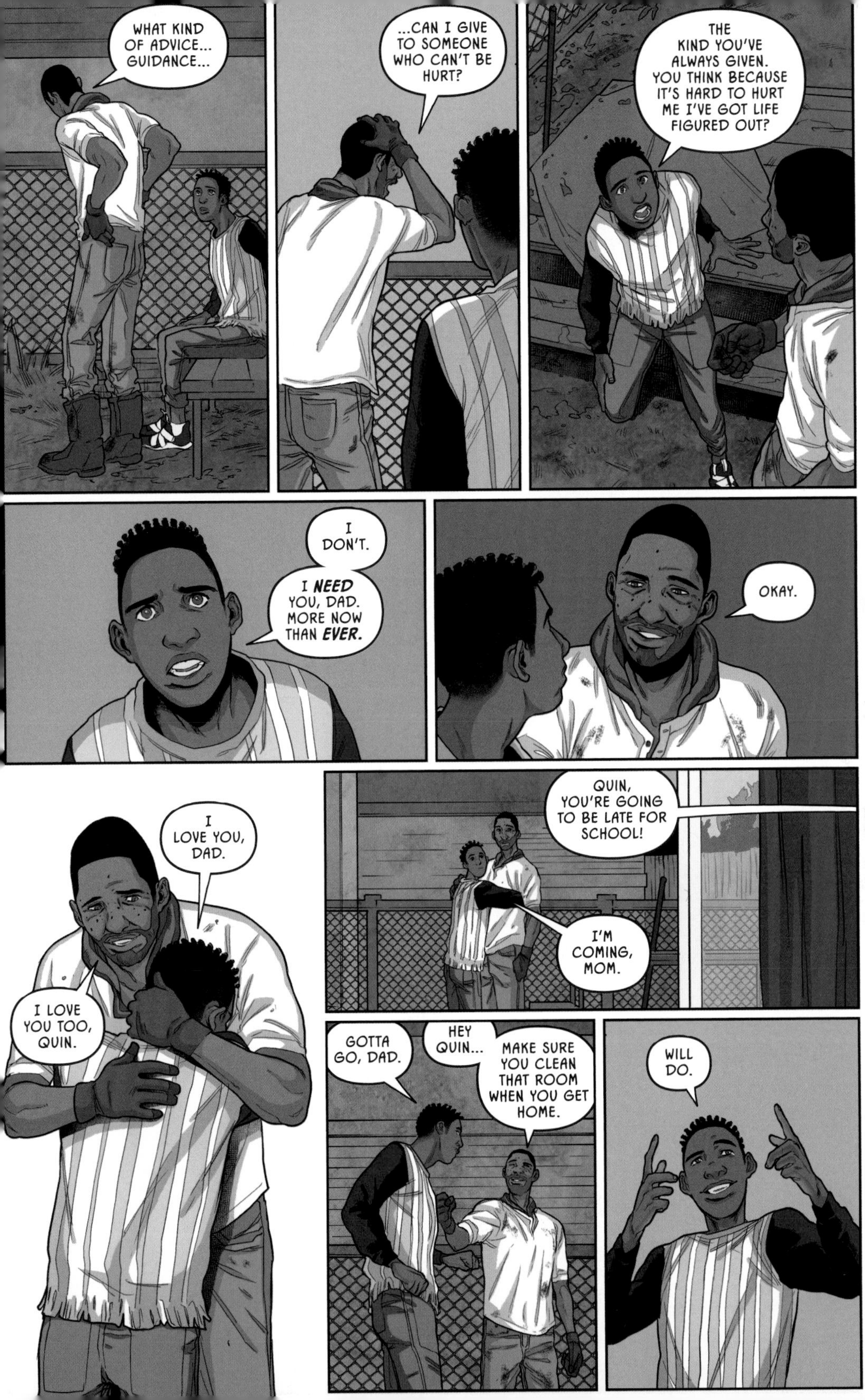

WHAT KIND OF ADVICE... GUIDANCE...
...CAN I GIVE TO SOMEONE WHO CAN'T BE HURT?
THE KIND YOU'VE ALWAYS GIVEN. YOU THINK BECAUSE IT'S HARD TO HURT ME I'VE GOT LIFE FIGURED OUT?
I DON'T.
I **NEED** YOU, DAD. MORE NOW THAN **EVER.**
OKAY.
I LOVE YOU, DAD.
I LOVE YOU TOO, QUIN.
QUIN, YOU'RE GOING TO BE LATE FOR SCHOOL!
I'M COMING, MOM.
GOTTA GO, DAD.
HEY QUIN...
MAKE SURE YOU CLEAN THAT ROOM WHEN YOU GET HOME.
WILL DO.

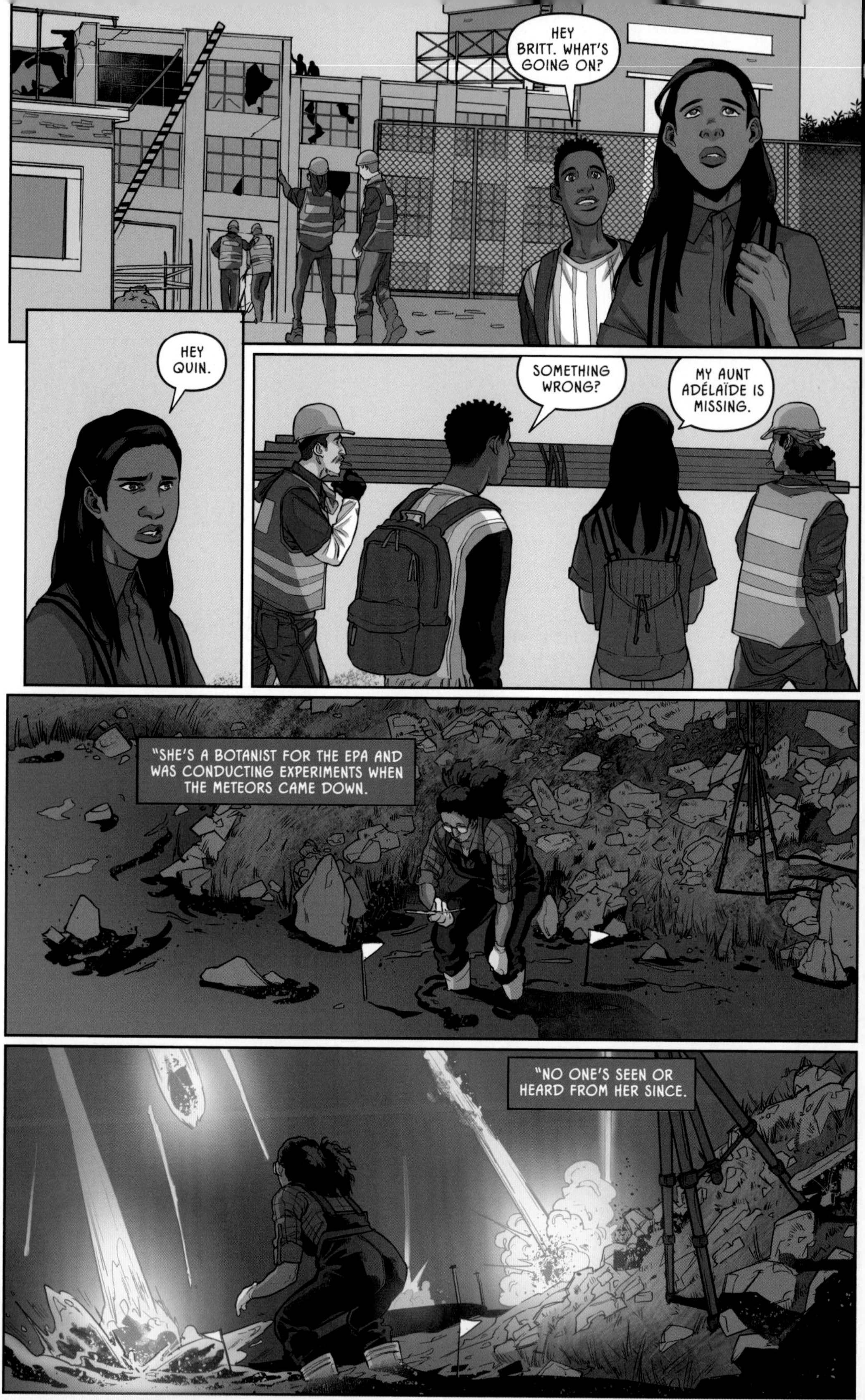
HEY BRITT. WHAT'S GOING ON?
HEY QUIN.
SOMETHING WRONG?
MY AUNT ADÉLAÏDE IS MISSING.
"SHE'S A BOTANIST FOR THE EPA AND WAS CONDUCTING EXPERIMENTS WHEN THE METEORS CAME DOWN.
"NO ONE'S SEEN OR HEARD FROM HER SINCE.

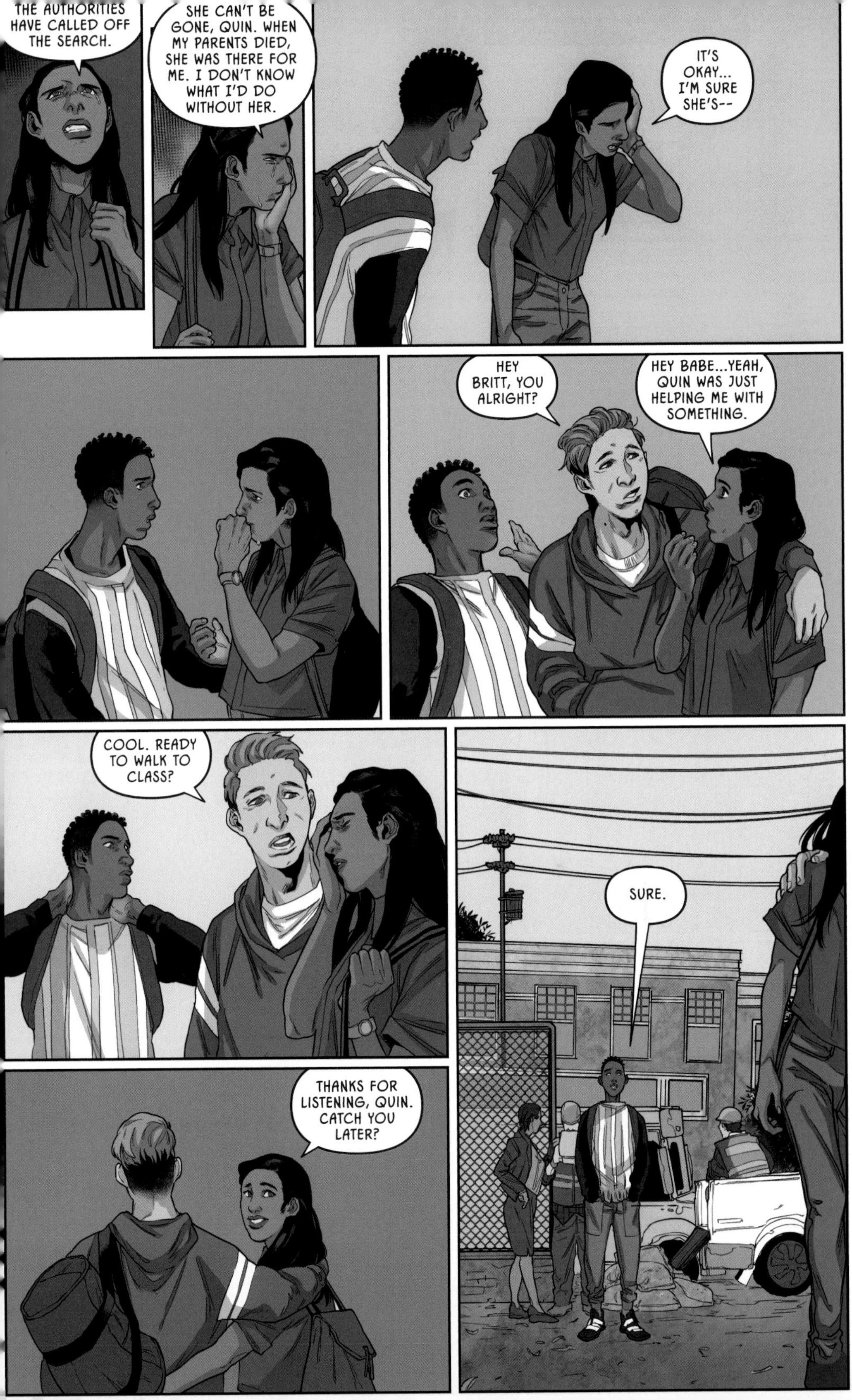
THE AUTHORITIES HAVE CALLED OFF THE SEARCH.
SHE CAN'T BE GONE, QUIN. WHEN MY PARENTS DIED, SHE WAS THERE FOR ME. I DON'T KNOW WHAT I'D DO WITHOUT HER.
IT'S OKAY... I'M SURE SHE'S--
HEY BRITT, YOU ALRIGHT?
HEY BABE...YEAH, QUIN WAS JUST HELPING ME WITH SOMETHING.
COOL. READY TO WALK TO CLASS?
THANKS FOR LISTENING, QUIN. CATCH YOU LATER?
SURE.

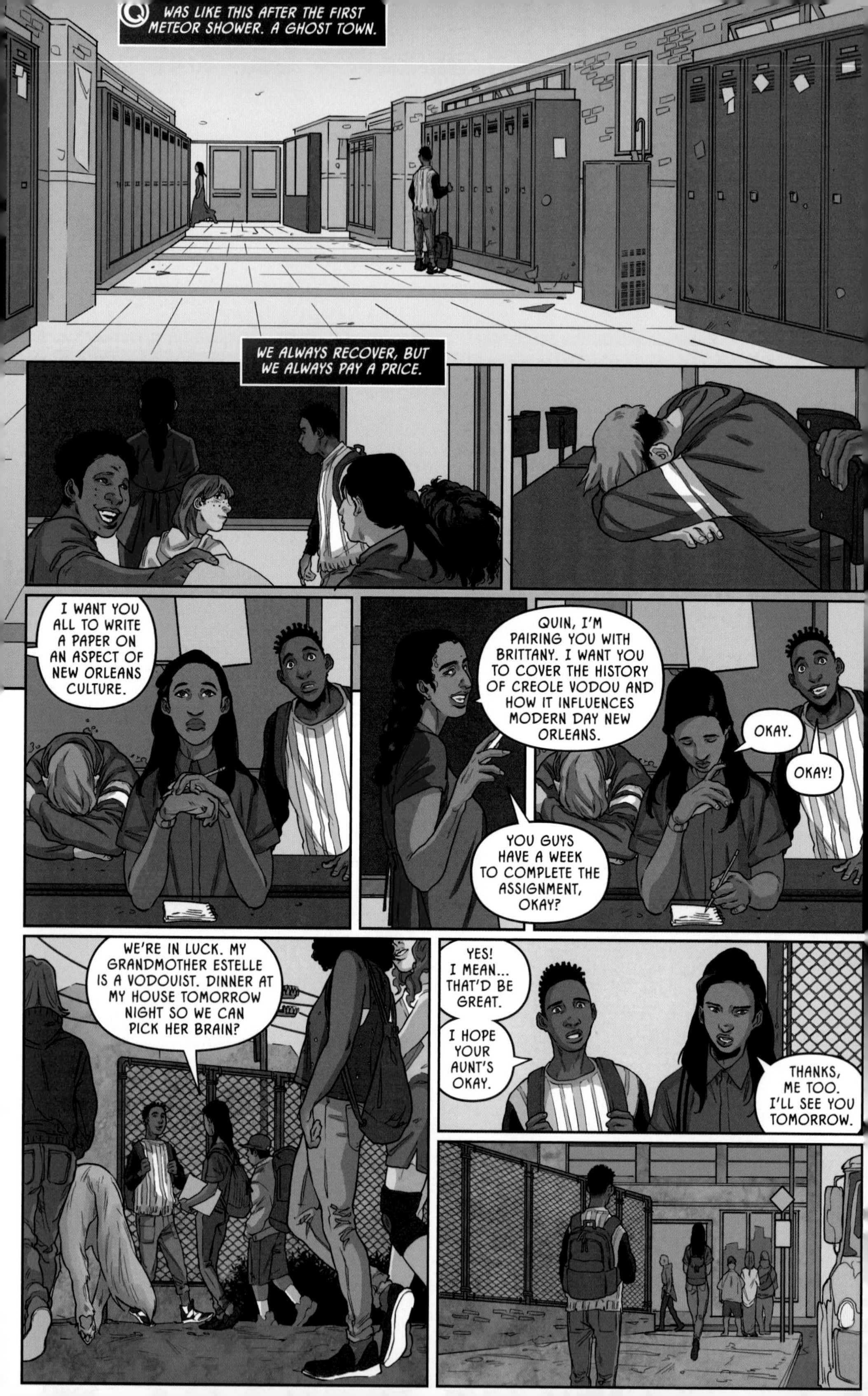
Q WAS LIKE THIS AFTER THE FIRST METEOR SHOWER. A GHOST TOWN.
WE ALWAYS RECOVER, BUT WE ALWAYS PAY A PRICE.
I WANT YOU ALL TO WRITE A PAPER ON AN ASPECT OF NEW ORLEANS CULTURE.
QUIN, I'M PAIRING YOU WITH BRITTANY. I WANT YOU TO COVER THE HISTORY OF CREOLE VODOU AND HOW IT INFLUENCES MODERN DAY NEW ORLEANS.
YOU GUYS HAVE A WEEK TO COMPLETE THE ASSIGNMENT, OKAY?
OKAY.
OKAY!
WE'RE IN LUCK. MY GRANDMOTHER ESTELLE IS A VODOUIST. DINNER AT MY HOUSE TOMORROW NIGHT SO WE CAN PICK HER BRAIN?
YES! I MEAN... THAT'D BE GREAT.
I HOPE YOUR AUNT'S OKAY.
THANKS, ME TOO. I'LL SEE YOU TOMORROW.

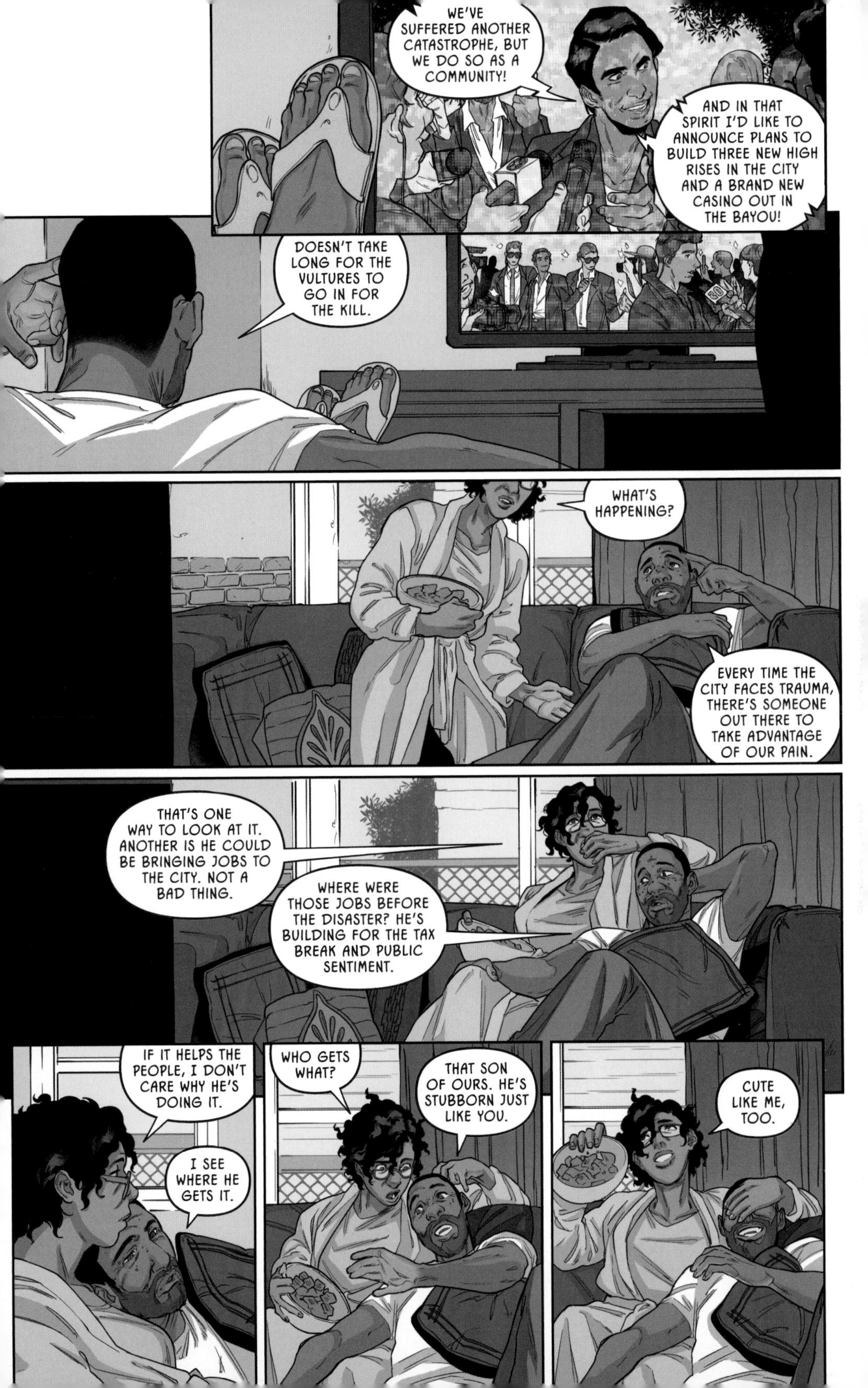
WE'VE SUFFERED ANOTHER CATASTROPHE, BUT WE DO SO AS A COMMUNITY!
AND IN THAT SPIRIT I'D LIKE TO ANNOUNCE PLANS TO BUILD THREE NEW HIGH RISES IN THE CITY AND A BRAND NEW CASINO OUT IN THE BAYOU!
DOESN'T TAKE LONG FOR THE VULTURES TO GO IN FOR THE KILL.
WHAT'S HAPPENING?
EVERY TIME THE CITY FACES TRAUMA, THERE'S SOMEONE OUT THERE TO TAKE ADVANTAGE OF OUR PAIN.
THAT'S ONE WAY TO LOOK AT IT. ANOTHER IS HE COULD BE BRINGING JOBS TO THE CITY. NOT A BAD THING.
WHERE WERE THOSE JOBS BEFORE THE DISASTER? HE'S BUILDING FOR THE TAX BREAK AND PUBLIC SENTIMENT.
IF IT HELPS THE PEOPLE, I DON'T CARE WHY HE'S DOING IT.
I SEE WHERE HE GETS IT.
WHO GETS WHAT?
THAT SON OF OURS. HE'S STUBBORN JUST LIKE YOU.
CUTE LIKE ME, TOO.

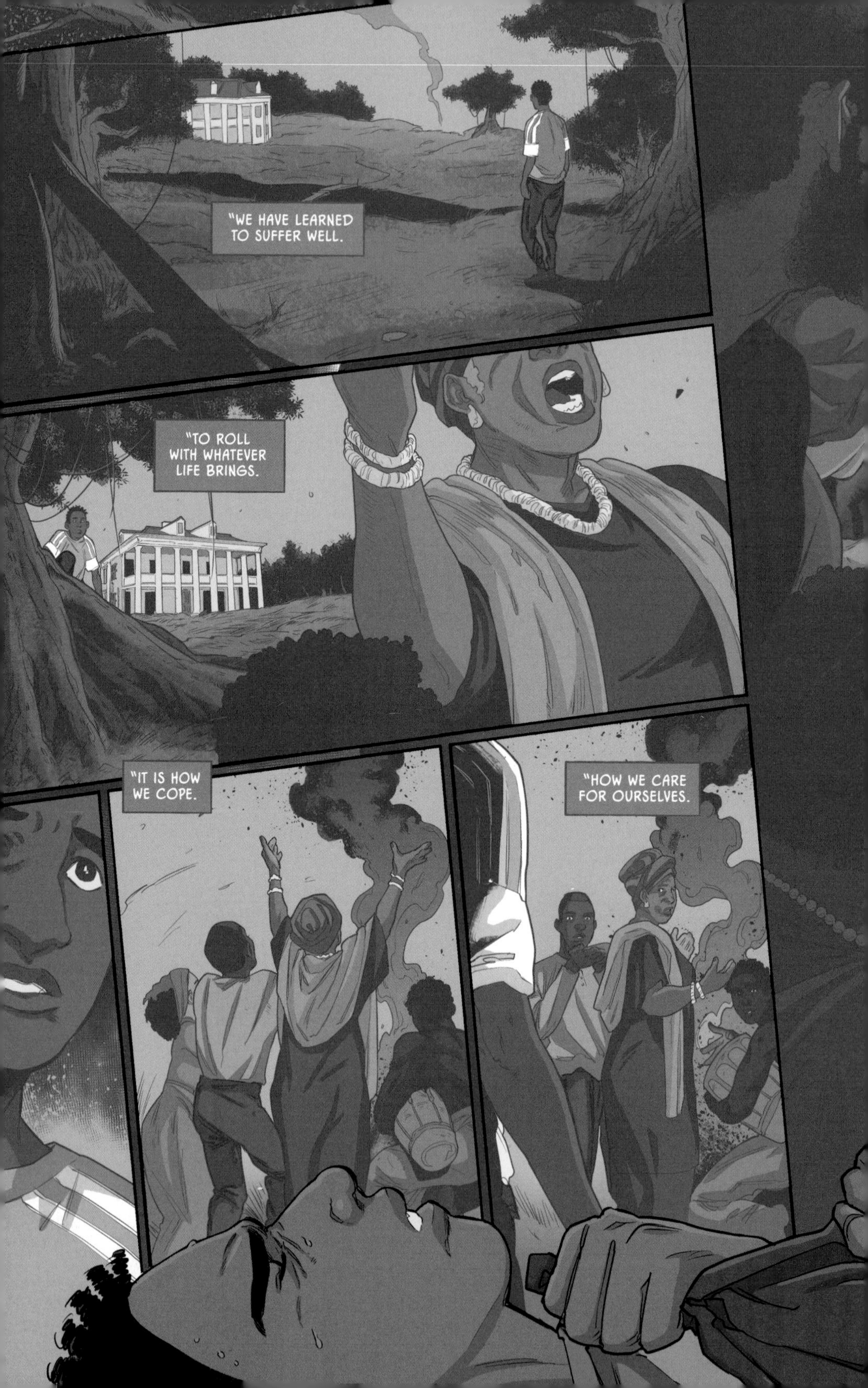
"WE HAVE LEARNED TO SUFFER WELL.
"TO ROLL WITH WHATEVER LIFE BRINGS.
"IT IS HOW WE COPE.
"HOW WE CARE FOR OURSELVES.

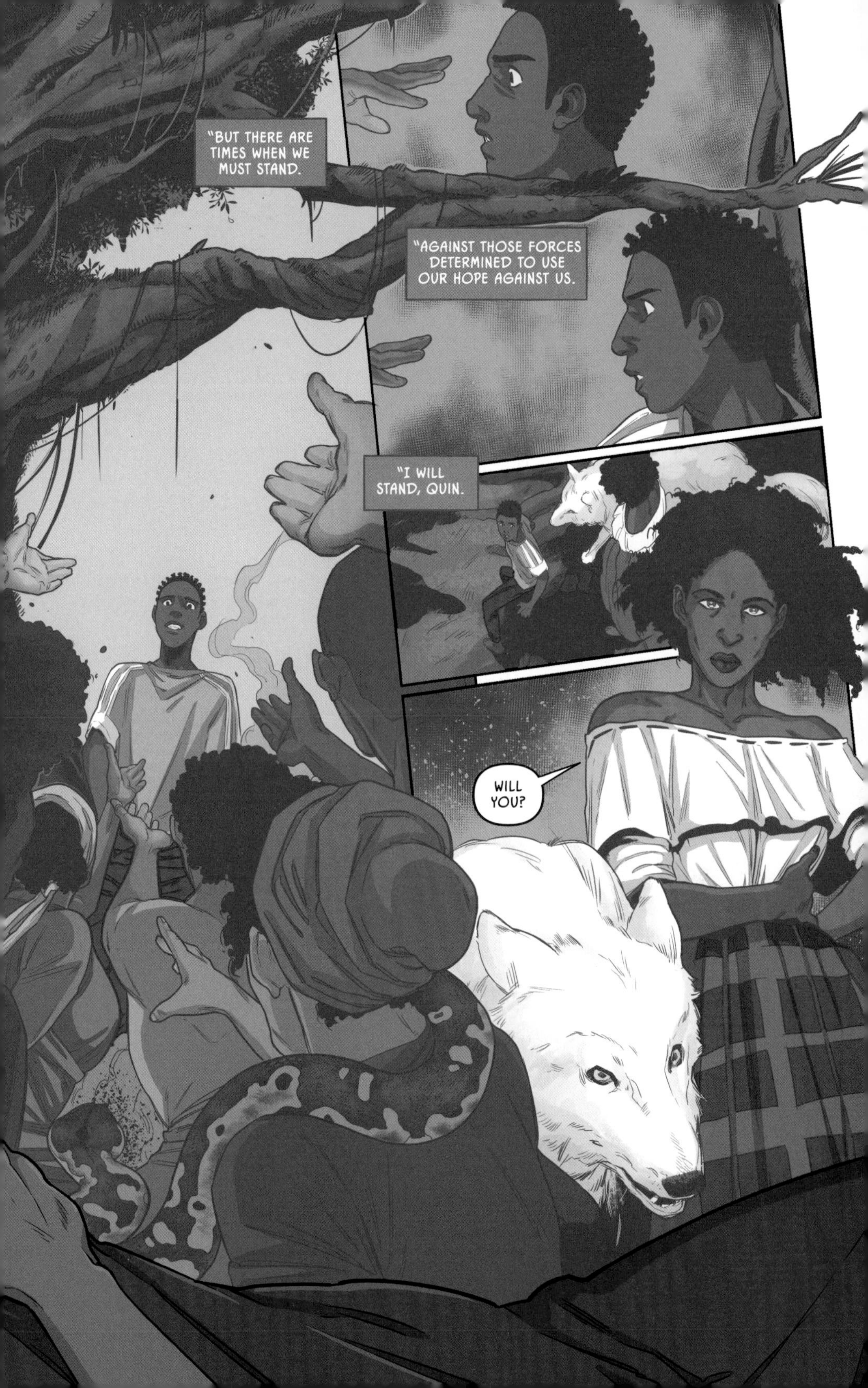
"BUT THERE ARE TIMES WHEN WE MUST STAND.
"AGAINST THOSE FORCES DETERMINED TO USE OUR HOPE AGAINST US.
"I WILL STAND, QUIN.
WILL YOU?

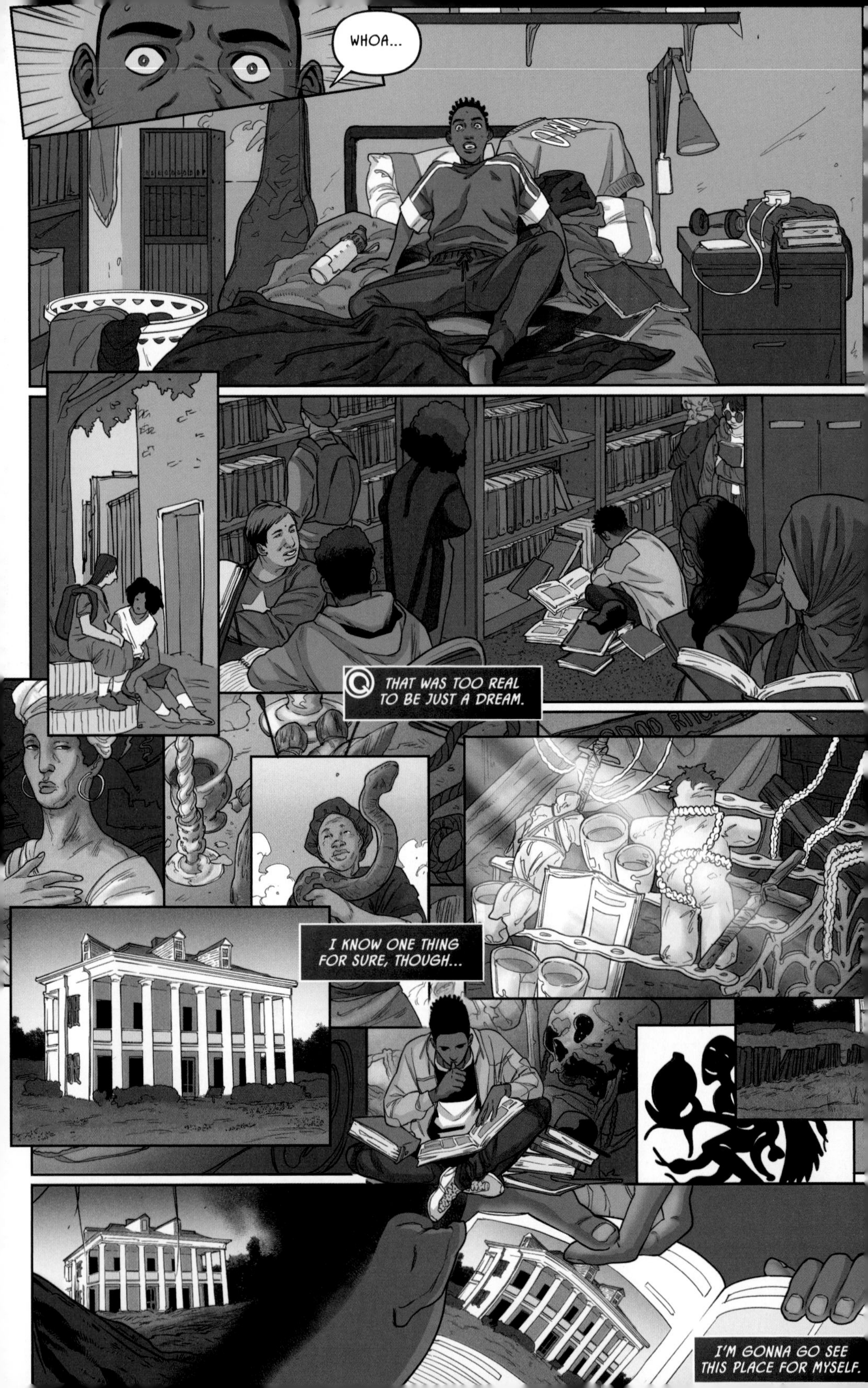
WHOA...
THAT WAS TOO REAL TO BE JUST A DREAM.
I KNOW ONE THING FOR SURE, THOUGH...
I'M GONNA GO SEE THIS PLACE FOR MYSELF.

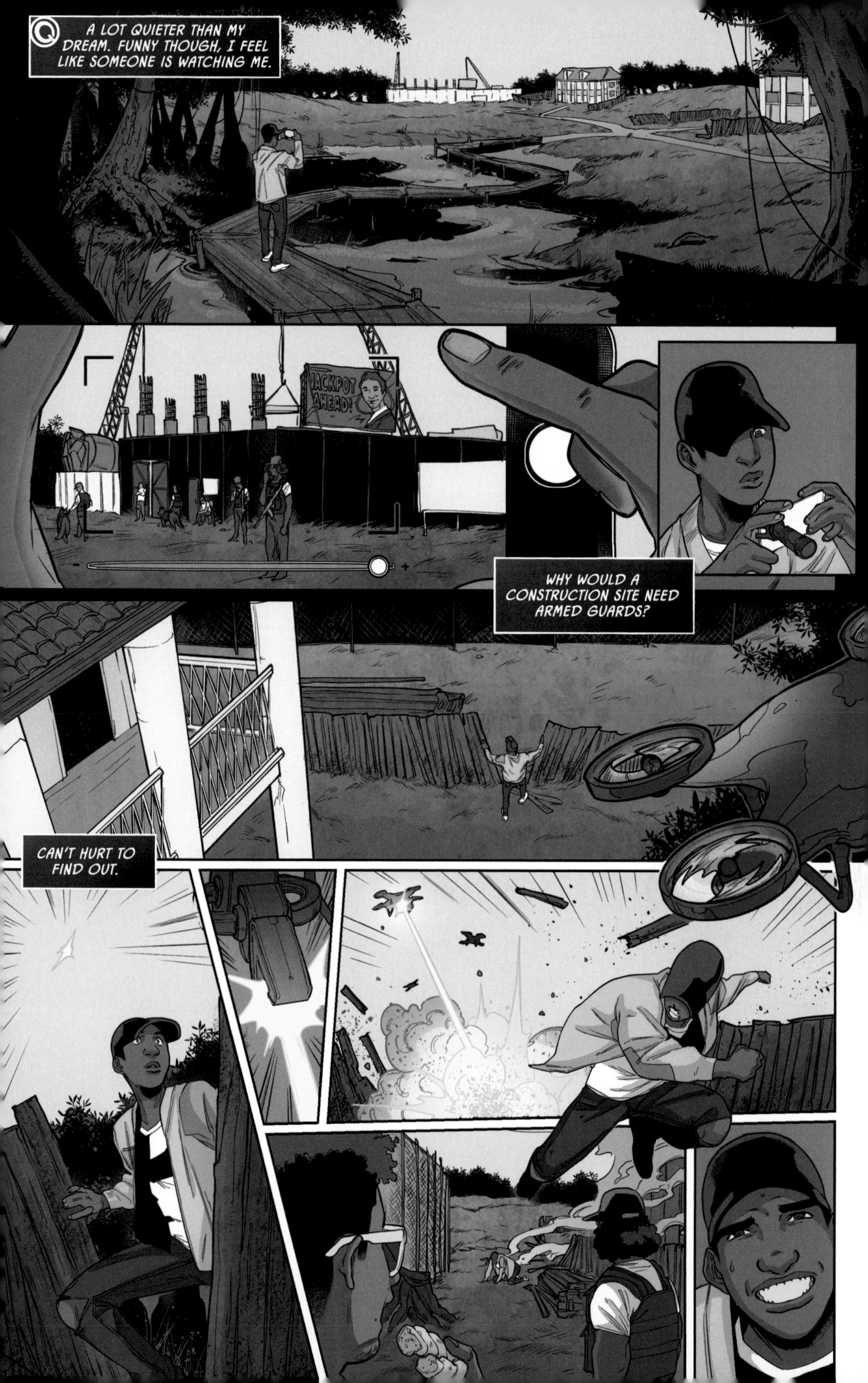
A LOT QUIETER THAN MY DREAM. FUNNY THOUGH, I FEEL LIKE SOMEONE IS WATCHING ME.
JACKPOT AHEAD!
WHY WOULD A CONSTRUCTION SITE NEED ARMED GUARDS?
CAN'T HURT TO FIND OUT.

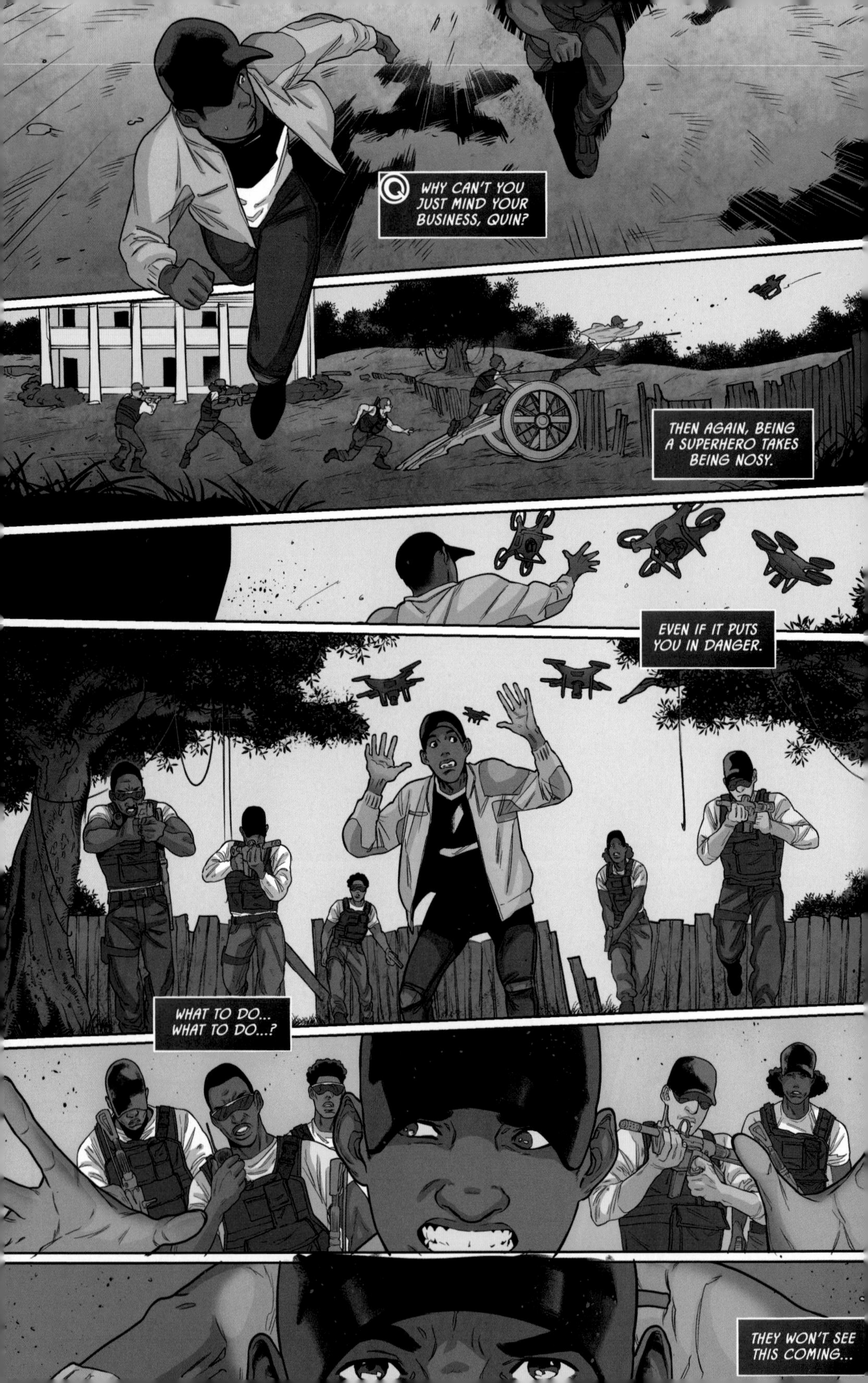
WHY CAN'T YOU JUST MIND YOUR BUSINESS, QUIN?
THEN AGAIN, BEING A SUPERHERO TAKES BEING NOSY.
EVEN IF IT PUTS YOU IN DANGER.
WHAT TO DO... WHAT TO DO...?
THEY WON'T SEE THIS COMING...

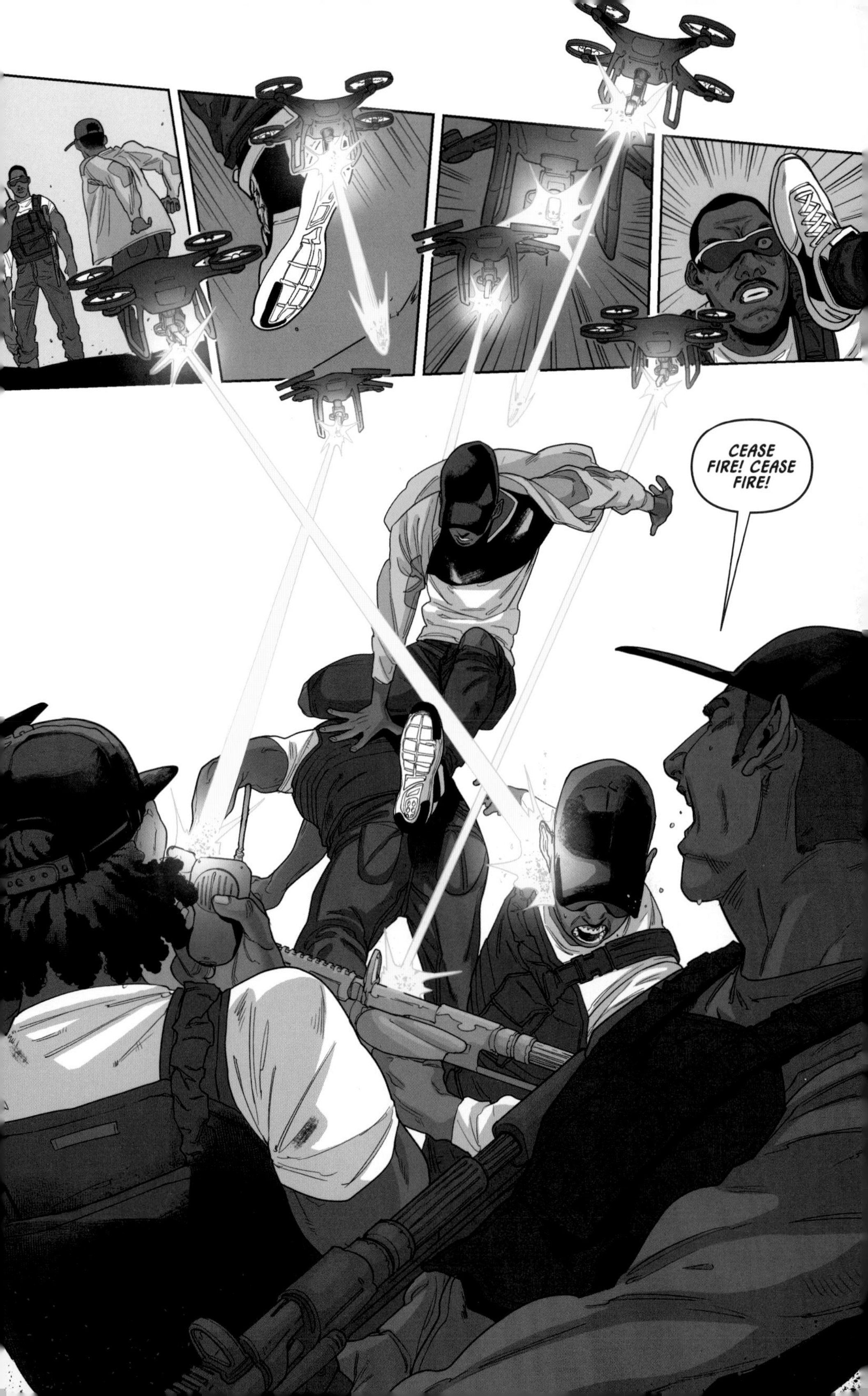
CEASE FIRE! CEASE FIRE!

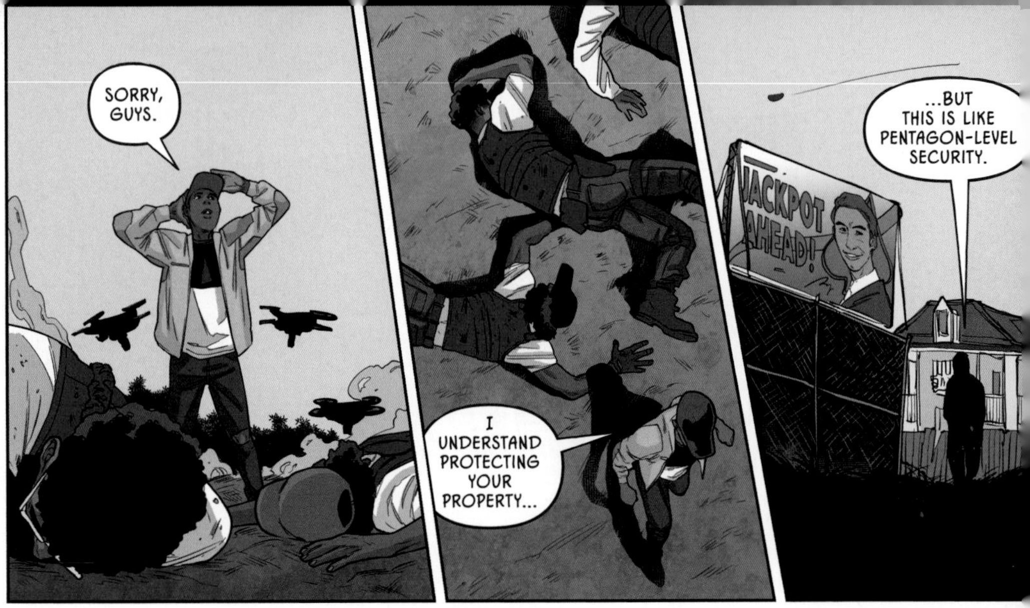
SORRY, GUYS.
I UNDERSTAND PROTECTING YOUR PROPERTY...
...BUT THIS IS LIKE PENTAGON-LEVEL SECURITY.
JACKPOT AHEAD!

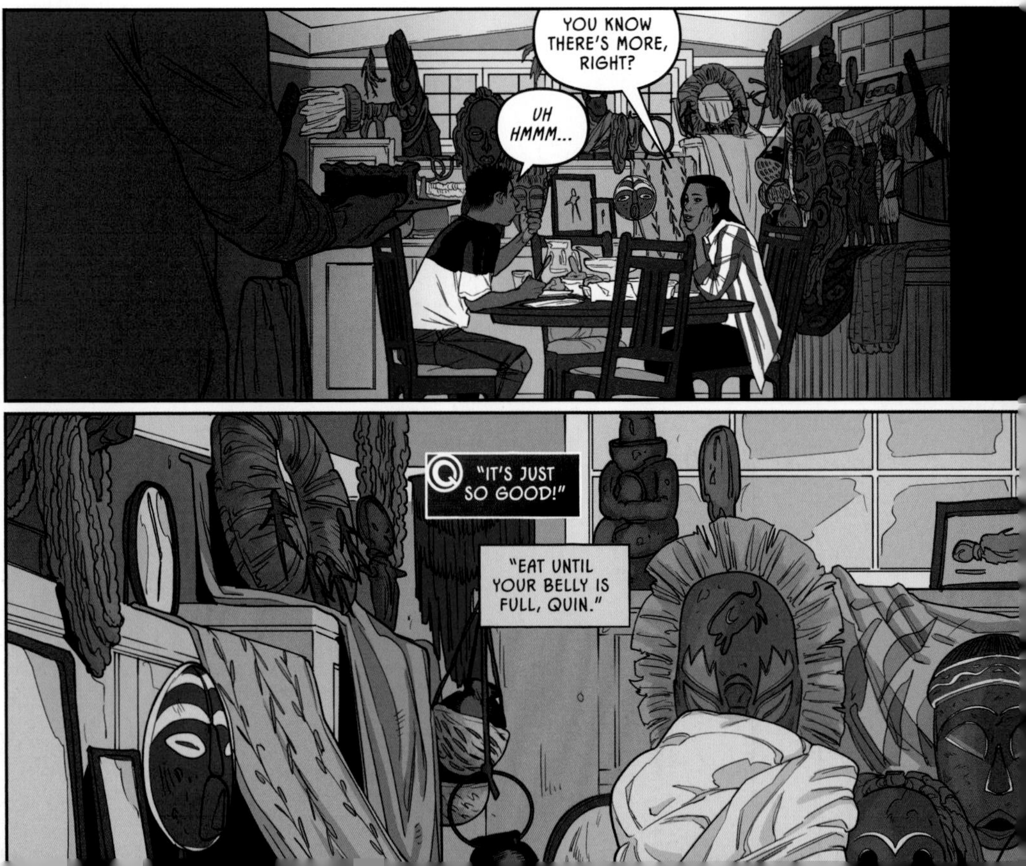
YOU KNOW THERE'S MORE, RIGHT?
UH HMMM...
"IT'S JUST SO GOOD!"
"EAT UNTIL YOUR BELLY IS FULL, QUIN."

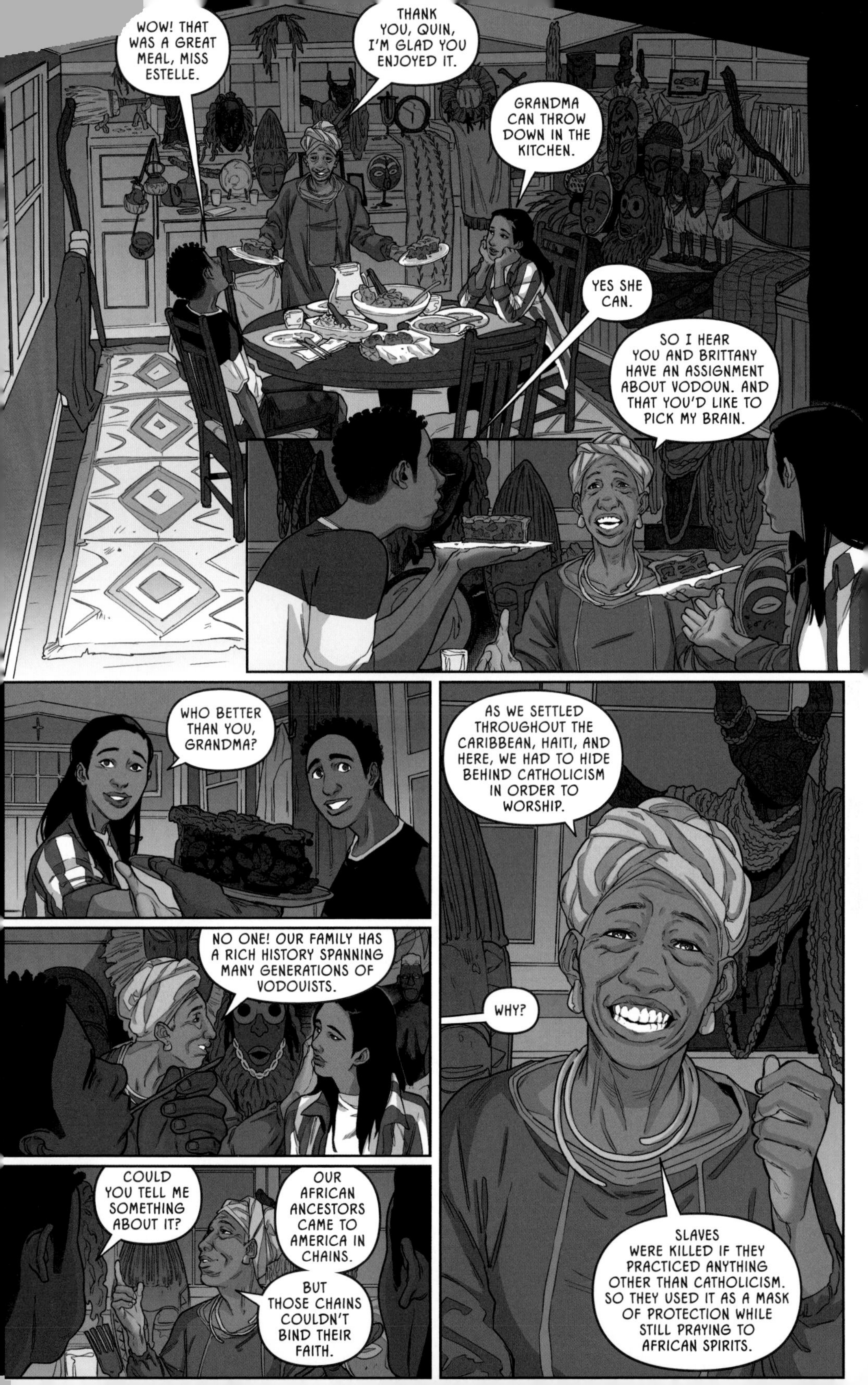
WOW! THAT WAS A GREAT MEAL, MISS ESTELLE.
THANK YOU, QUIN, I'M GLAD YOU ENJOYED IT.
GRANDMA CAN THROW DOWN IN THE KITCHEN.
YES SHE CAN.
SO I HEAR YOU AND BRITTANY HAVE AN ASSIGNMENT ABOUT VODOUN. AND THAT YOU'D LIKE TO PICK MY BRAIN.
WHO BETTER THAN YOU, GRANDMA?
NO ONE! OUR FAMILY HAS A RICH HISTORY SPANNING MANY GENERATIONS OF VODOUISTS.
COULD YOU TELL ME SOMETHING ABOUT IT?
OUR AFRICAN ANCESTORS CAME TO AMERICA IN CHAINS.
BUT THOSE CHAINS COULDN'T BIND THEIR FAITH.
AS WE SETTLED THROUGHOUT THE CARIBBEAN, HAITI, AND HERE, WE HAD TO HIDE BEHIND CATHOLICISM IN ORDER TO WORSHIP.
WHY?
SLAVES WERE KILLED IF THEY PRACTICED ANYTHING OTHER THAN CATHOLICISM. SO THEY USED IT AS A MASK OF PROTECTION WHILE STILL PRAYING TO AFRICAN SPIRITS.

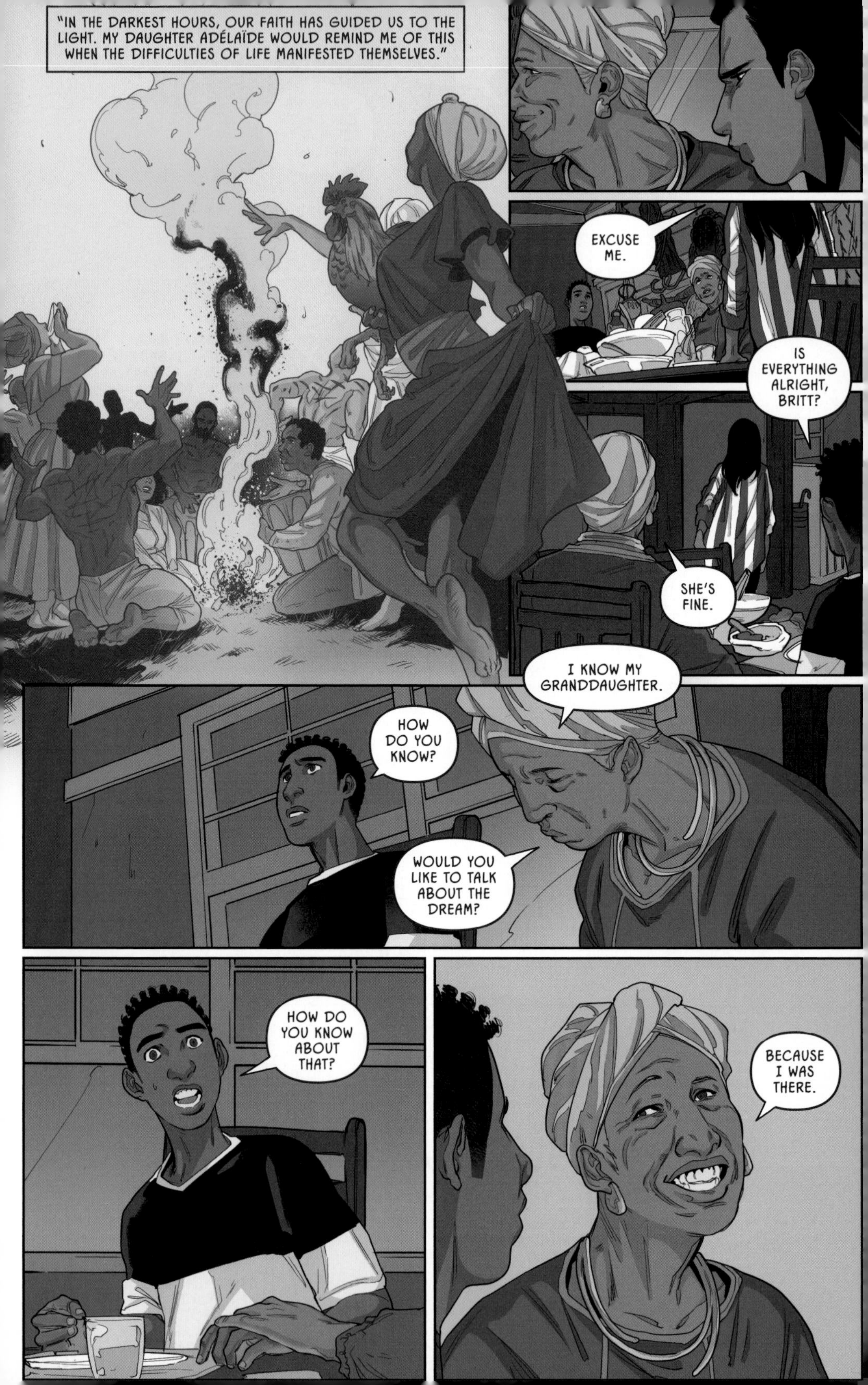
"IN THE DARKEST HOURS, OUR FAITH HAS GUIDED US TO THE LIGHT. MY DAUGHTER ADÉLAÏDE WOULD REMIND ME OF THIS WHEN THE DIFFICULTIES OF LIFE MANIFESTED THEMSELVES."
EXCUSE ME.
IS EVERYTHING ALRIGHT, BRITT?
SHE'S FINE.
I KNOW MY GRANDDAUGHTER.
HOW DO YOU KNOW?
WOULD YOU LIKE TO TALK ABOUT THE DREAM?
HOW DO YOU KNOW ABOUT THAT?
BECAUSE I WAS THERE.

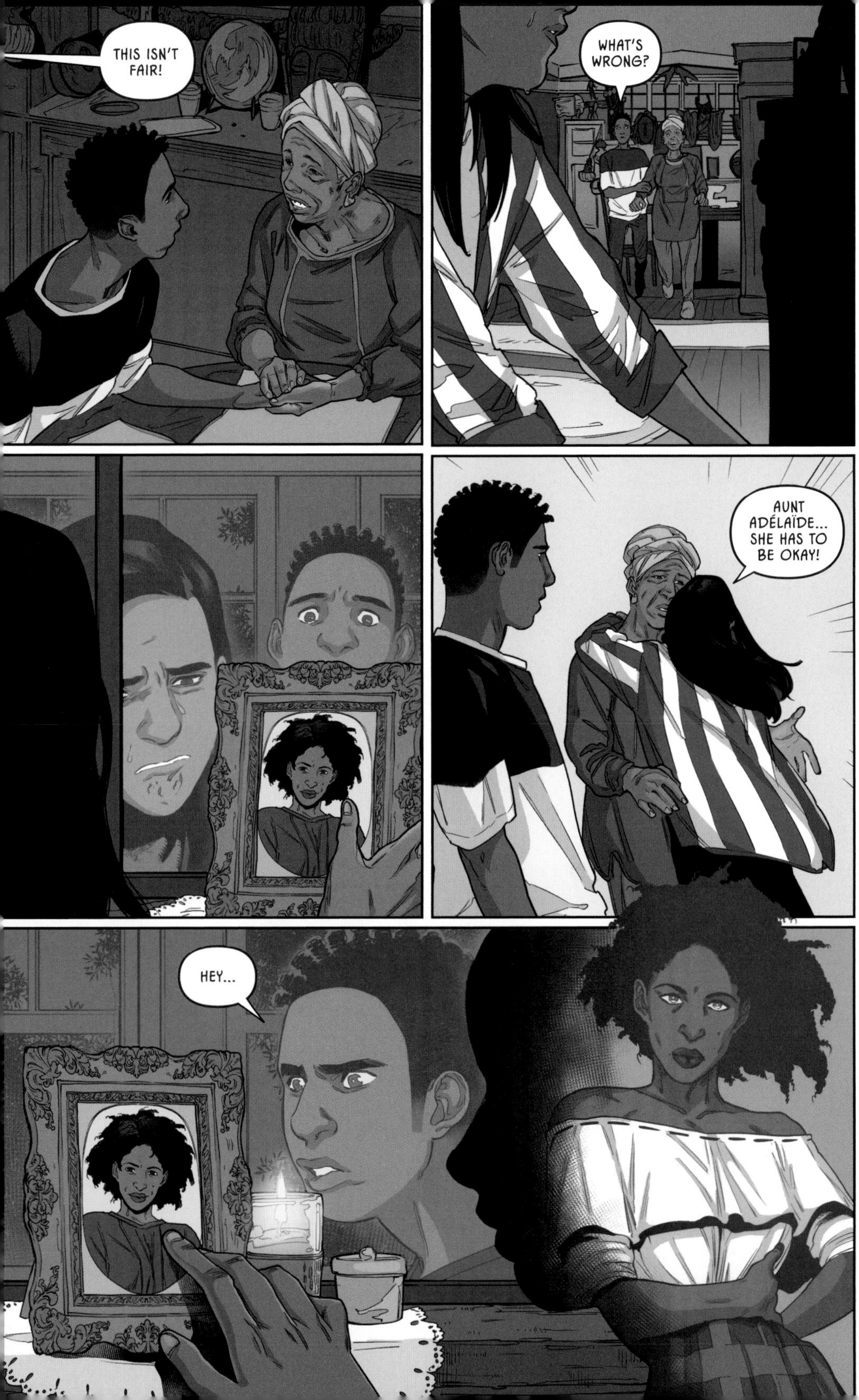
THIS ISN'T FAIR!
WHAT'S WRONG?
AUNT ADÉLAÏDE... SHE HAS TO BE OKAY!
HEY...

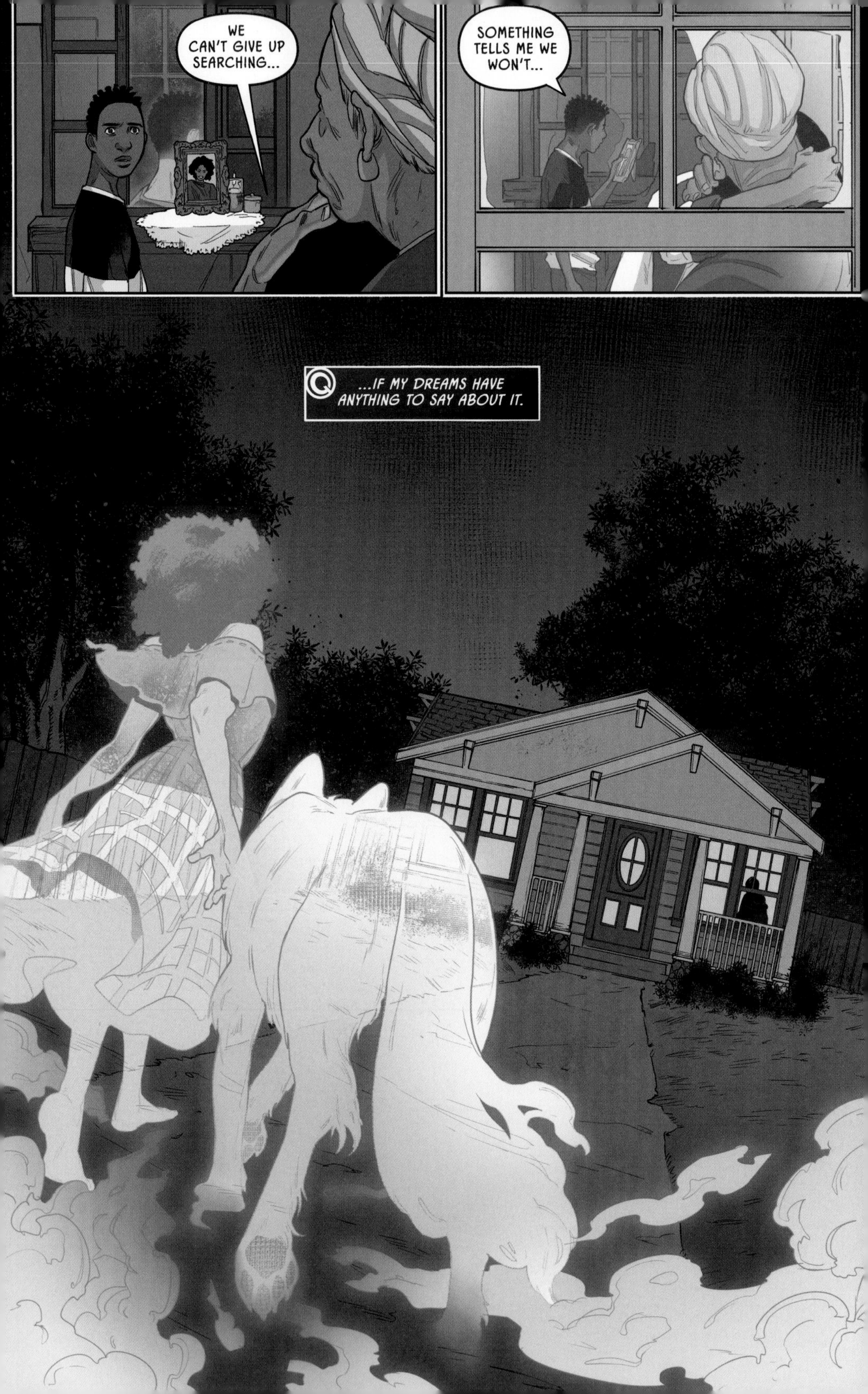
WE CAN'T GIVE UP SEARCHING...
SOMETHING TELLS ME WE WON'T...
...IF MY DREAMS HAVE ANYTHING TO SAY ABOUT IT.

CHAPTER TWO

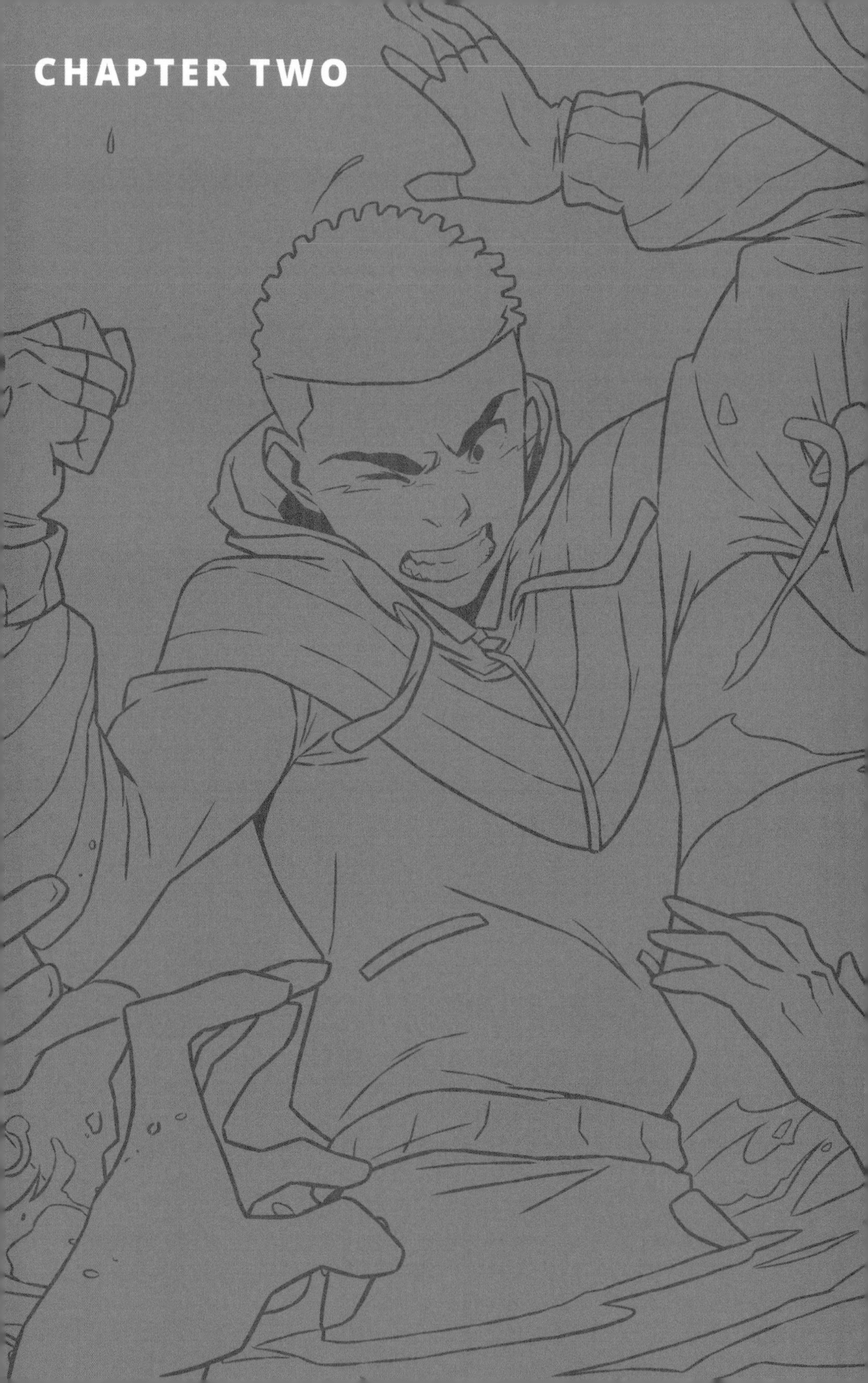

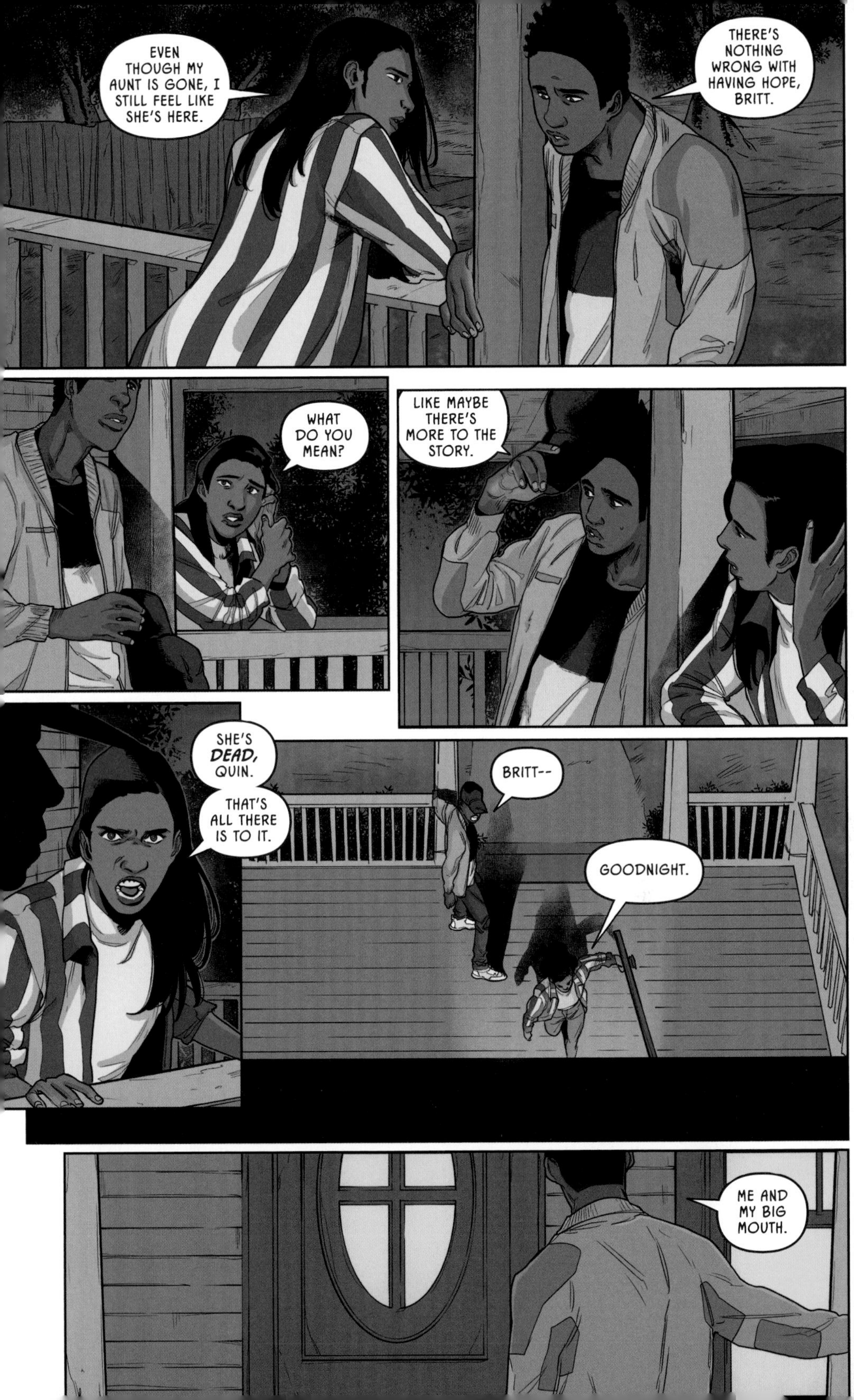
EVEN THOUGH MY AUNT IS GONE, I STILL FEEL LIKE SHE'S HERE.
THERE'S NOTHING WRONG WITH HAVING HOPE, BRITT.
WHAT DO YOU MEAN?
LIKE MAYBE THERE'S MORE TO THE STORY.
SHE'S *DEAD,* QUIN.
THAT'S ALL THERE IS TO IT.
BRITT--
GOODNIGHT.
ME AND MY BIG MOUTH.

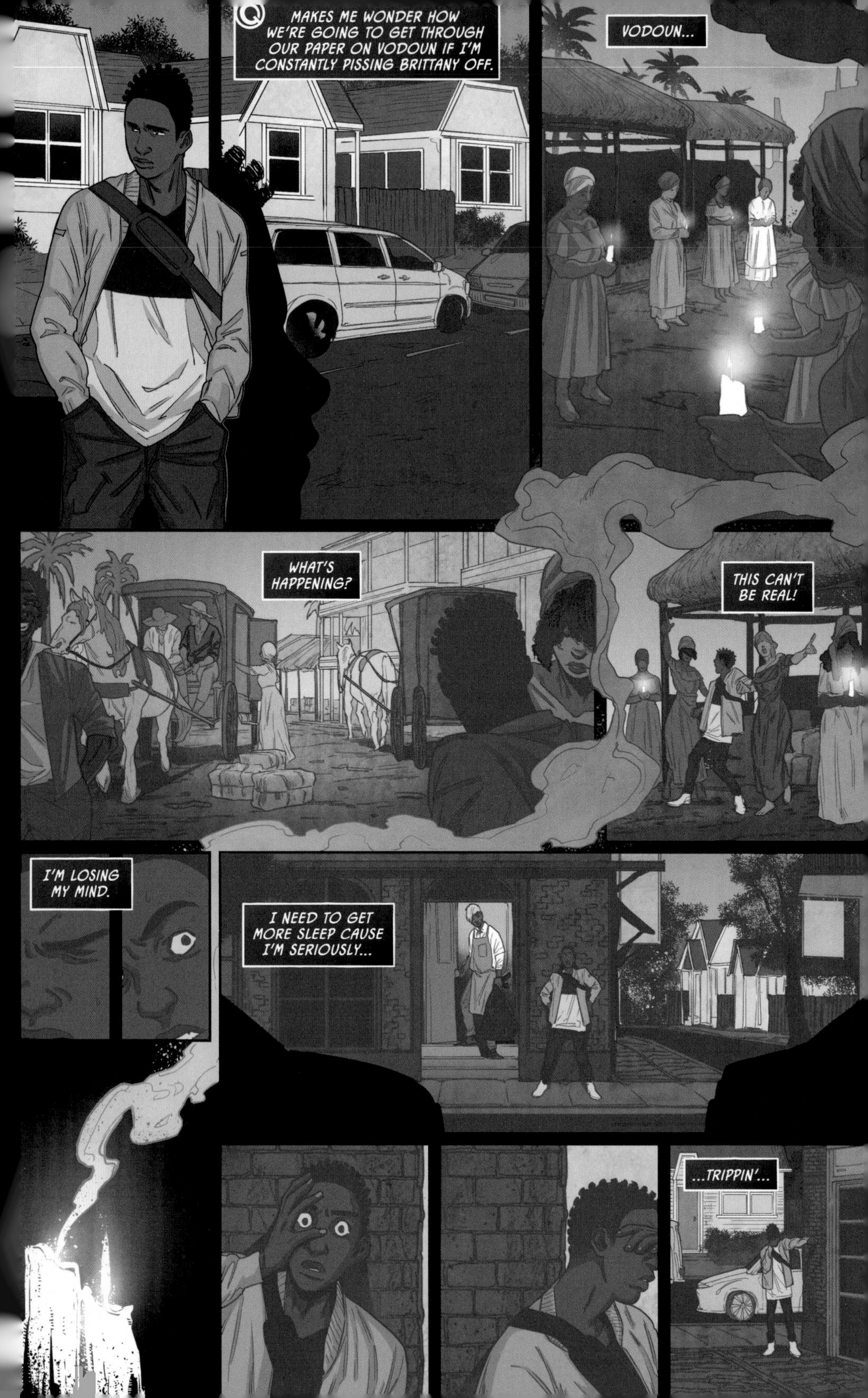
MAKES ME WONDER HOW WE'RE GOING TO GET THROUGH OUR PAPER ON VODOUN IF I'M CONSTANTLY PISSING BRITTANY OFF.
VODOUN...
WHAT'S HAPPENING?
THIS CAN'T BE REAL!
I'M LOSING MY MIND.
I NEED TO GET MORE SLEEP CAUSE I'M SERIOUSLY...
...TRIPPIN'...

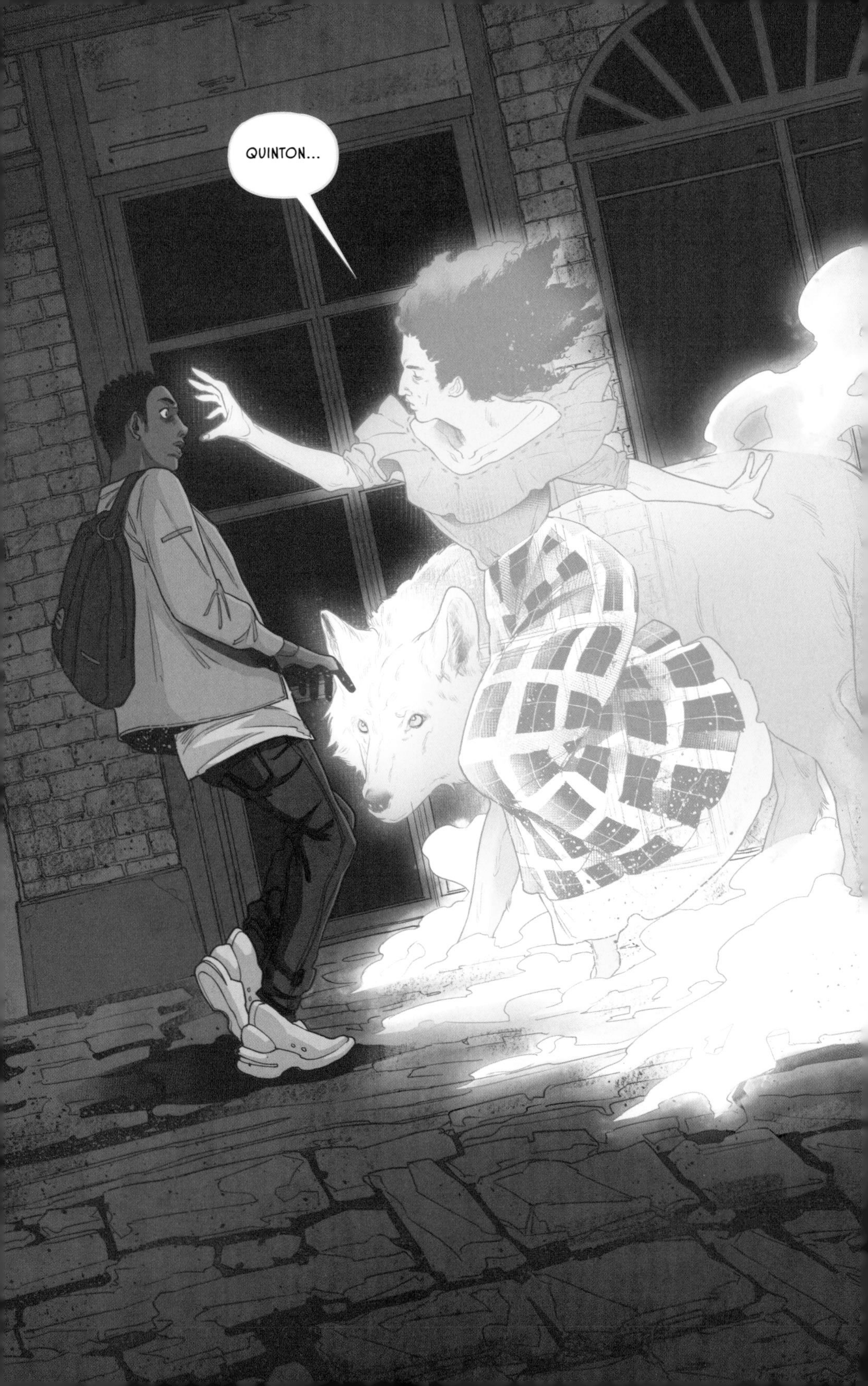
QUINTON...

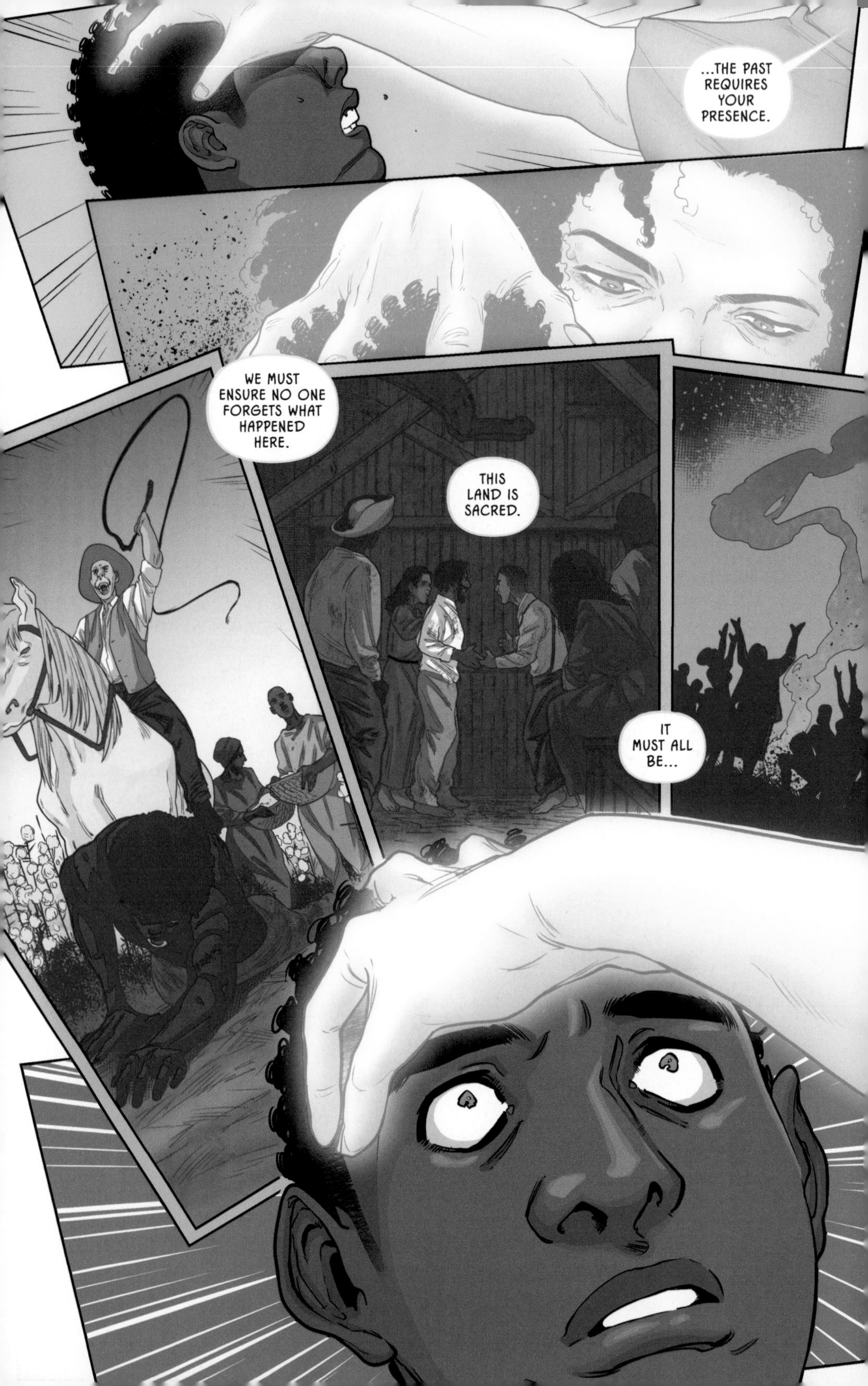
...THE PAST REQUIRES YOUR PRESENCE.
WE MUST ENSURE NO ONE FORGETS WHAT HAPPENED HERE.
THIS LAND IS SACRED.
IT MUST ALL BE...

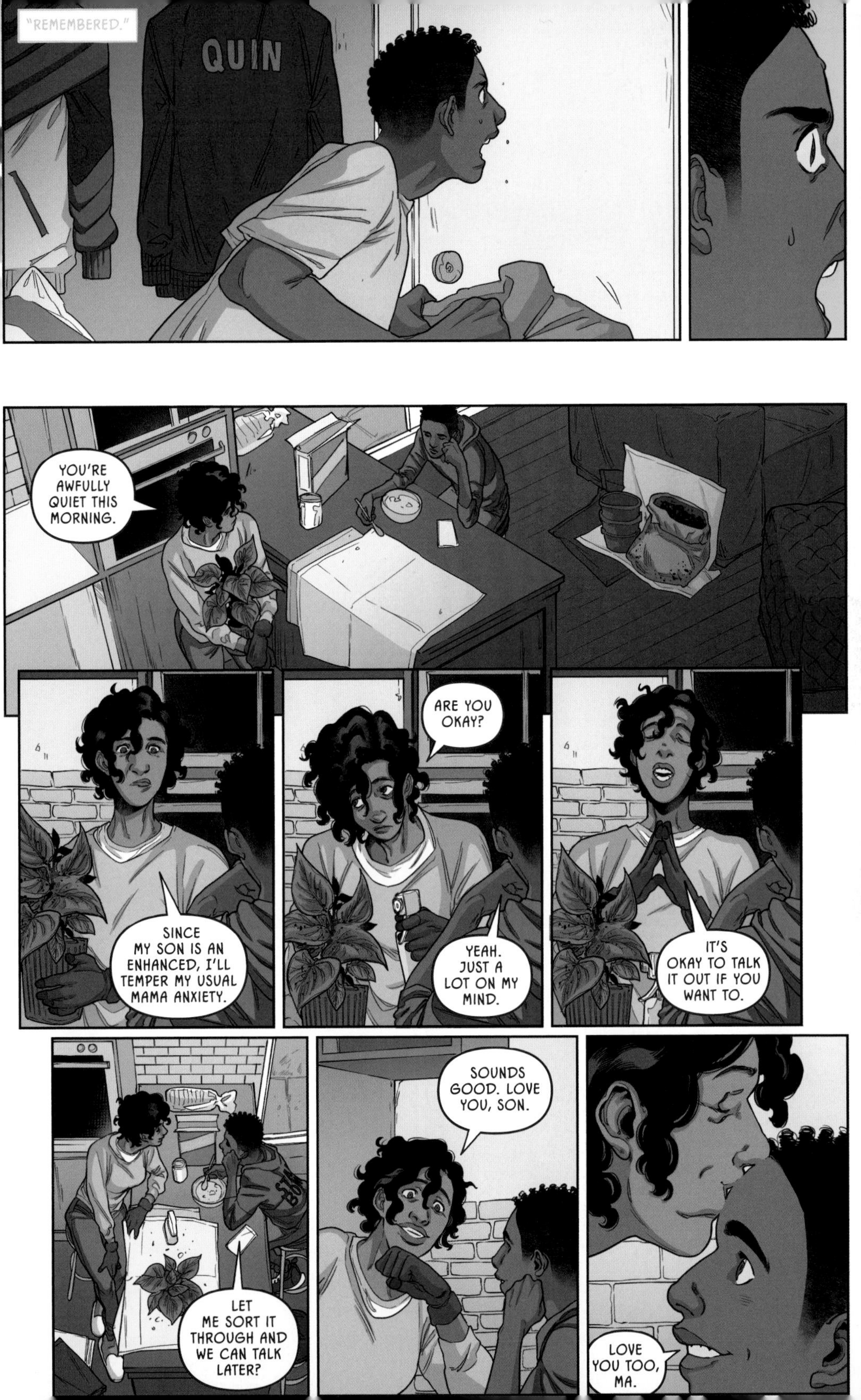
"REMEMBERED."
QUIN
YOU'RE AWFULLY QUIET THIS MORNING.
SINCE MY SON IS AN ENHANCED, I'LL TEMPER MY USUAL MAMA ANXIETY.
ARE YOU OKAY?
YEAH. JUST A LOT ON MY MIND.
IT'S OKAY TO TALK IT OUT IF YOU WANT TO.
LET ME SORT IT THROUGH AND WE CAN TALK LATER?
SOUNDS GOOD. LOVE YOU, SON.
LOVE YOU TOO, MA.

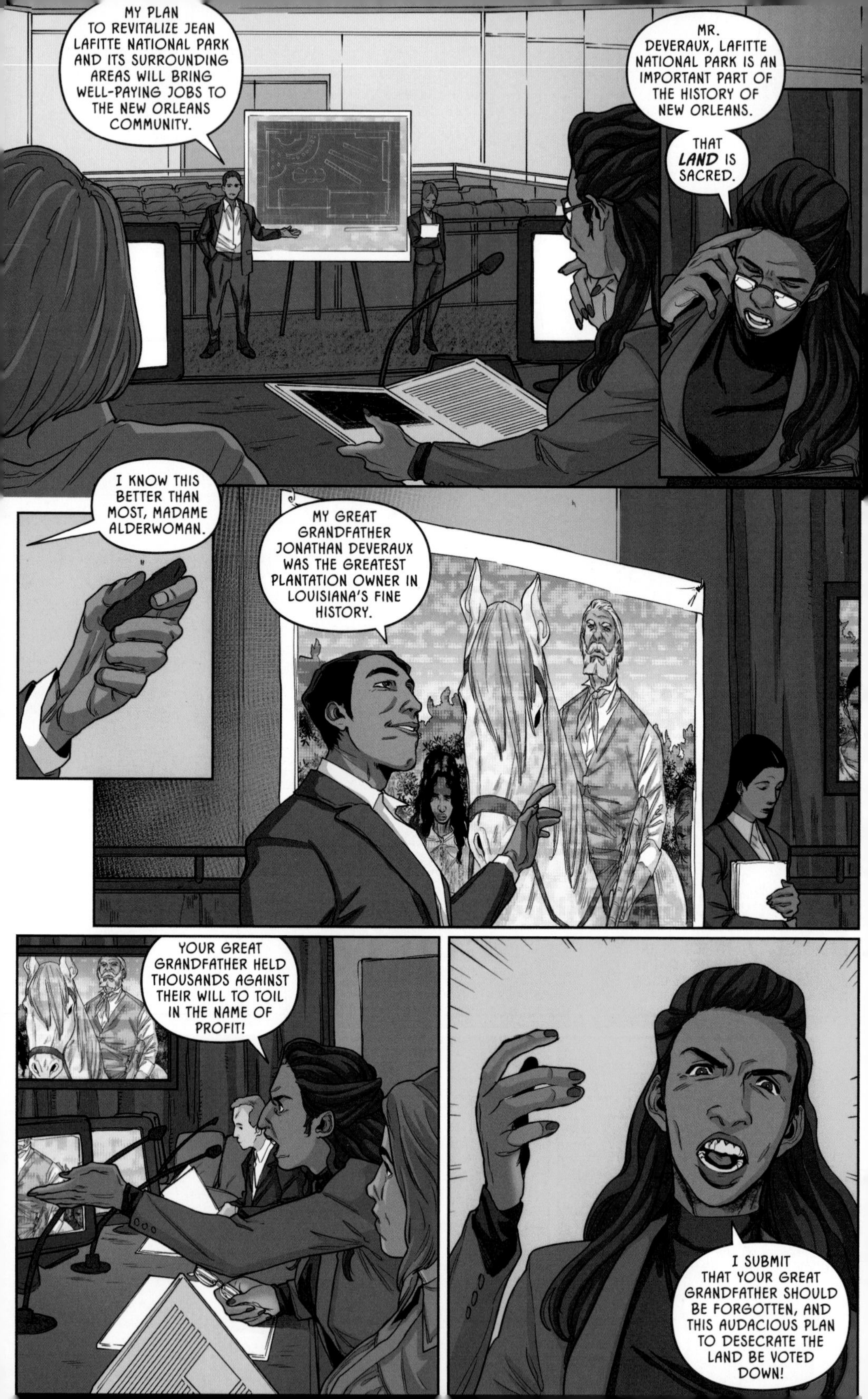
MY PLAN TO REVITALIZE JEAN LAFITTE NATIONAL PARK AND ITS SURROUNDING AREAS WILL BRING WELL-PAYING JOBS TO THE NEW ORLEANS COMMUNITY.
MR. DEVERAUX, LAFITTE NATIONAL PARK IS AN IMPORTANT PART OF THE HISTORY OF NEW ORLEANS.
THAT **LAND** IS SACRED.
I KNOW THIS BETTER THAN MOST, MADAME ALDERWOMAN.
MY GREAT GRANDFATHER JONATHAN DEVERAUX WAS THE GREATEST PLANTATION OWNER IN LOUISIANA'S FINE HISTORY.
YOUR GREAT GRANDFATHER HELD THOUSANDS AGAINST THEIR WILL TO TOIL IN THE NAME OF PROFIT!
I SUBMIT THAT YOUR GREAT GRANDFATHER SHOULD BE FORGOTTEN, AND THIS AUDACIOUS PLAN TO DESECRATE THE LAND BE VOTED DOWN!

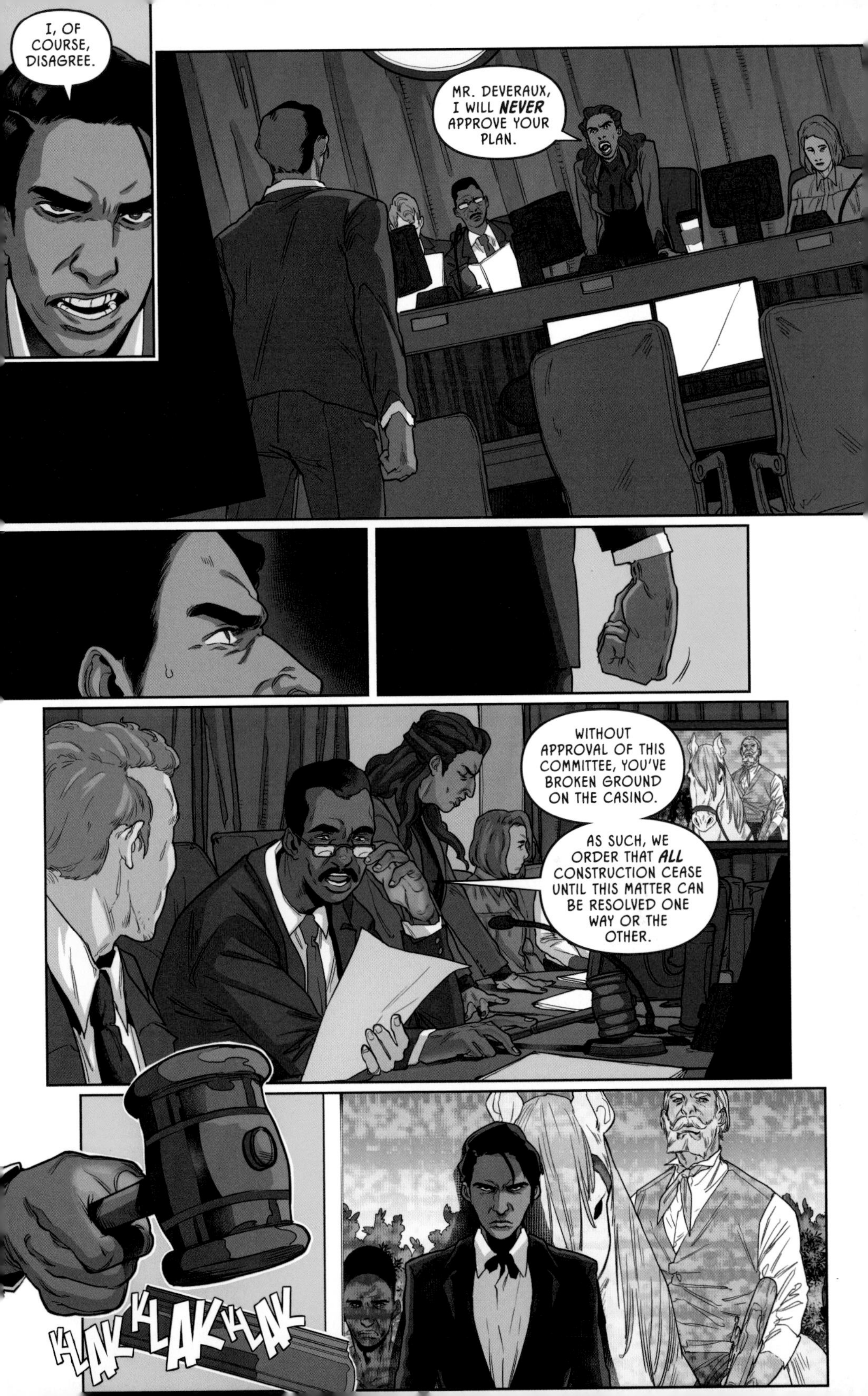
I, OF COURSE, DISAGREE.
MR. DEVERAUX, I WILL NEVER APPROVE YOUR PLAN.
WITHOUT APPROVAL OF THIS COMMITTEE, YOU'VE BROKEN GROUND ON THE CASINO.
AS SUCH, WE ORDER THAT ALL CONSTRUCTION CEASE UNTIL THIS MATTER CAN BE RESOLVED ONE WAY OR THE OTHER.
KLAK KLAK KLAK

HEY QUIN.

HEY.

I'M SORRY FOR LAST NIGHT. I KNOW YOU WERE JUST TRYING TO HELP.

IT'S OKAY. I CAN'T IMAGINE LOSING SOMEONE SO CLOSE TO ME.

I GOT USED TO HER BEING THERE FOR ME. LOVING ME.

MY GRANDMOTHER SAYS, "DEATH IS JUST THE BEGINNING OF LIFE."

WISH I COULD UNDERSTAND WHAT SHE MEANS.

SOUNDS LIKE *HOPE.*

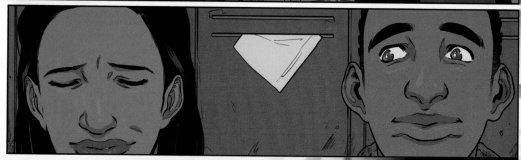

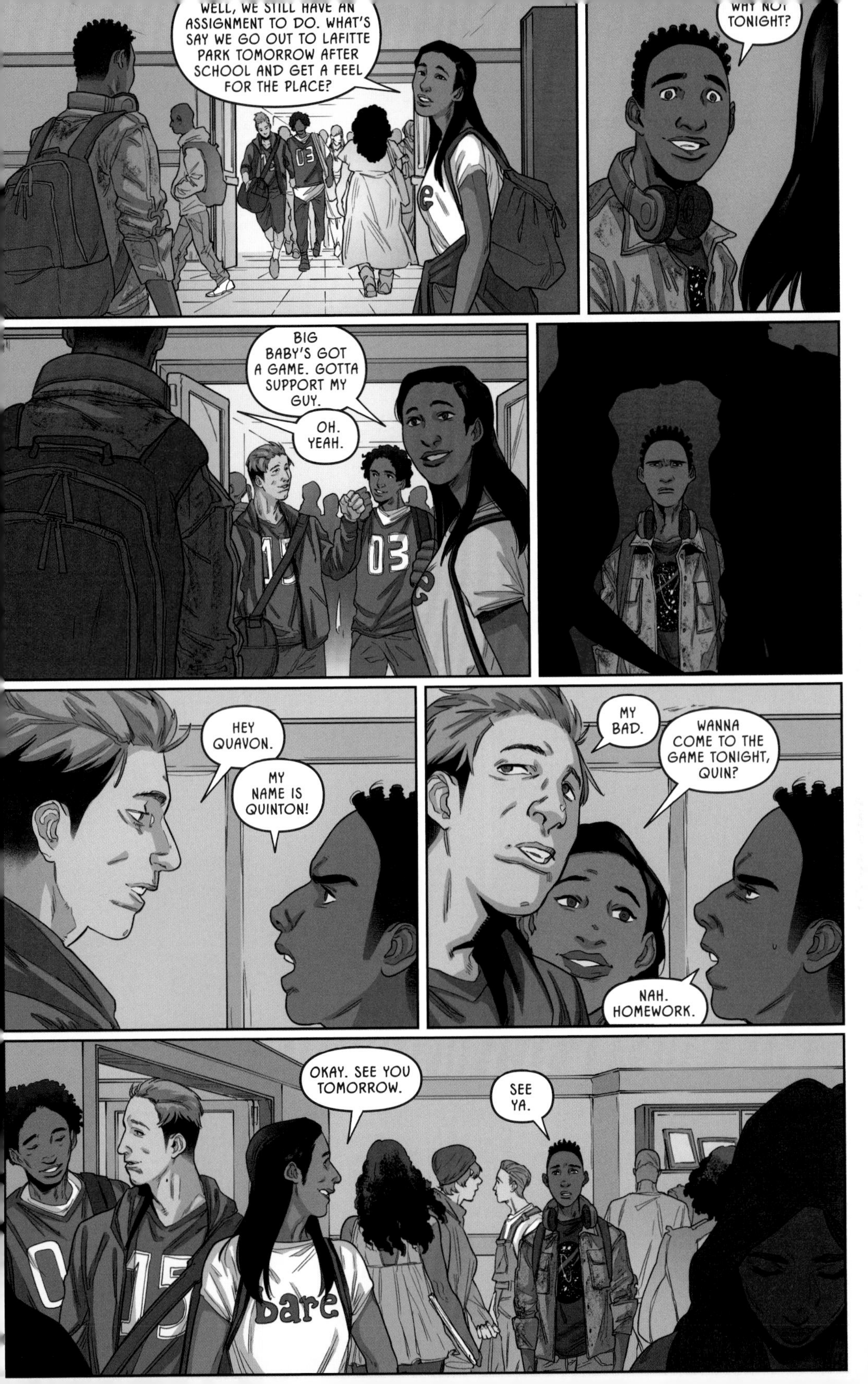
WELL, WE STILL HAVE AN ASSIGNMENT TO DO. WHAT'S SAY WE GO OUT TO LAFITTE PARK TOMORROW AFTER SCHOOL AND GET A FEEL FOR THE PLACE?
WHY NOT TONIGHT?
BIG BABY'S GOT A GAME. GOTTA SUPPORT MY GUY.
OH. YEAH.
HEY QUAVON.
MY NAME IS QUINTON!
MY BAD.
WANNA COME TO THE GAME TONIGHT, QUIN?
NAH. HOMEWORK.
OKAY. SEE YOU TOMORROW.
SEE YA.

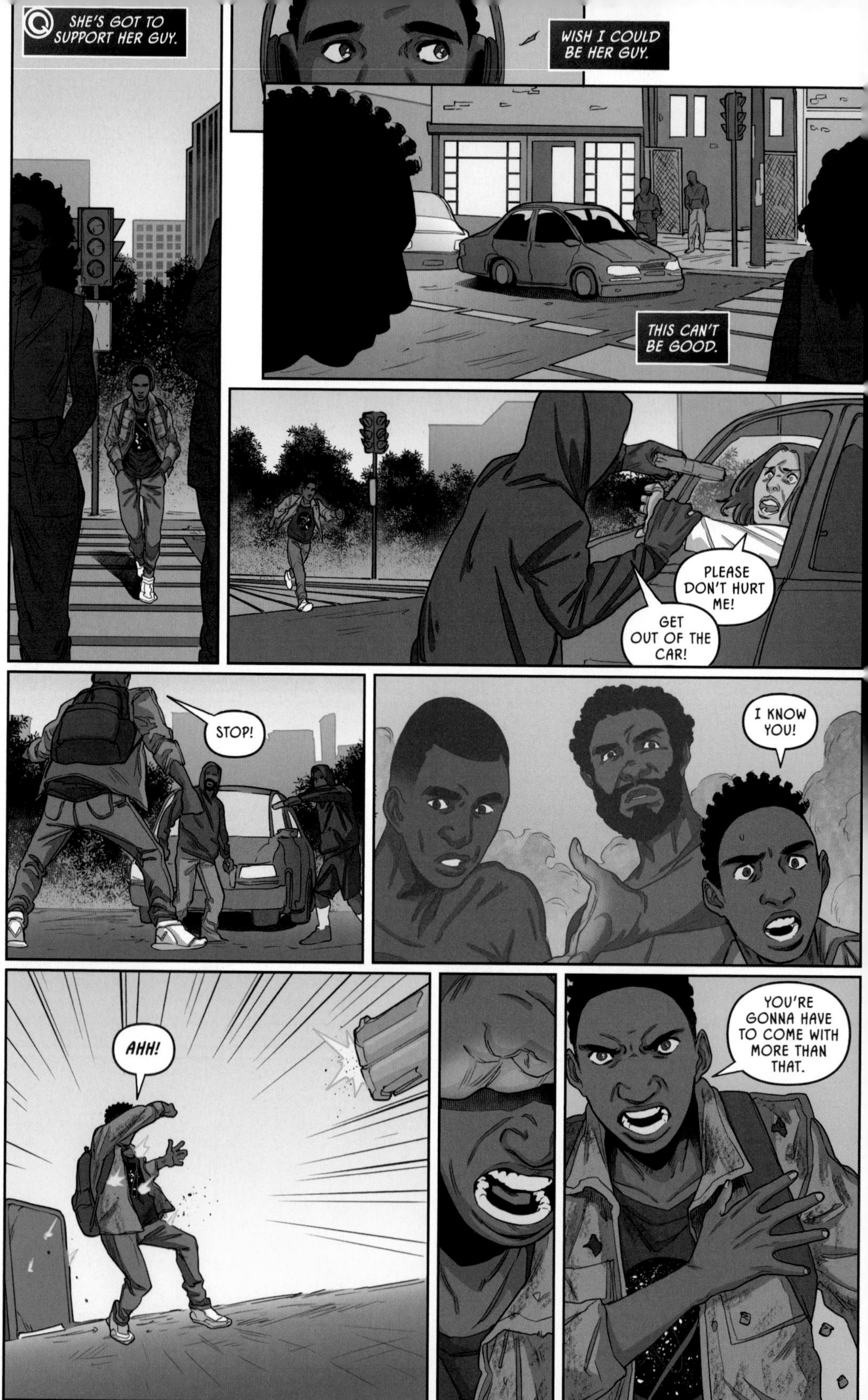
SHE'S GOT TO SUPPORT HER GUY.
WISH I COULD BE HER GUY.
THIS CAN'T BE GOOD.
GET OUT OF THE CAR!
PLEASE DON'T HURT ME!
STOP!
I KNOW YOU!
AHH!
YOU'RE GONNA HAVE TO COME WITH MORE THAN THAT.

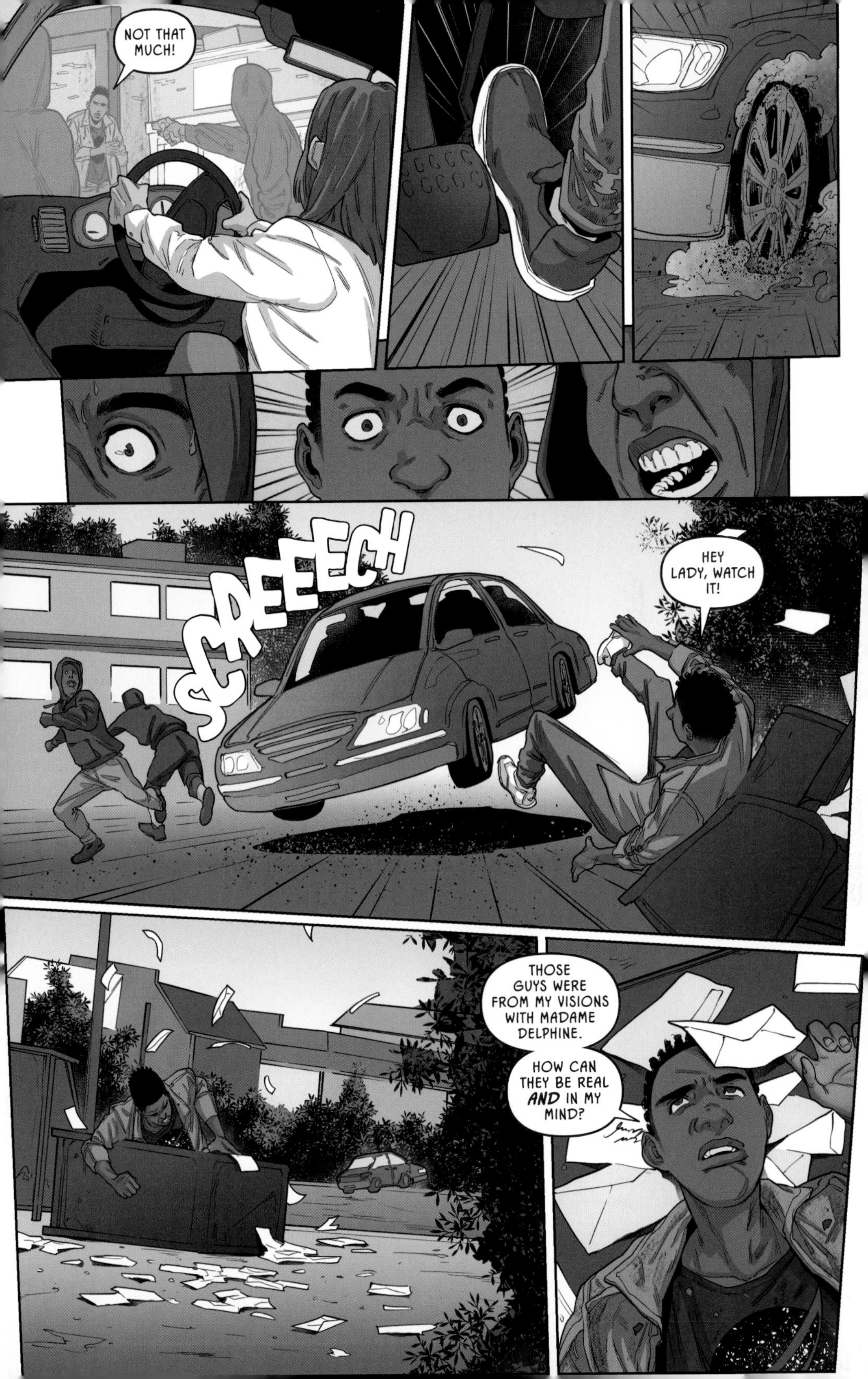
NOT THAT MUCH!
SCREEECH
HEY LADY, WATCH IT!
THOSE GUYS WERE FROM MY VISIONS WITH MADAME DELPHINE.
HOW CAN THEY BE REAL AND IN MY MIND?

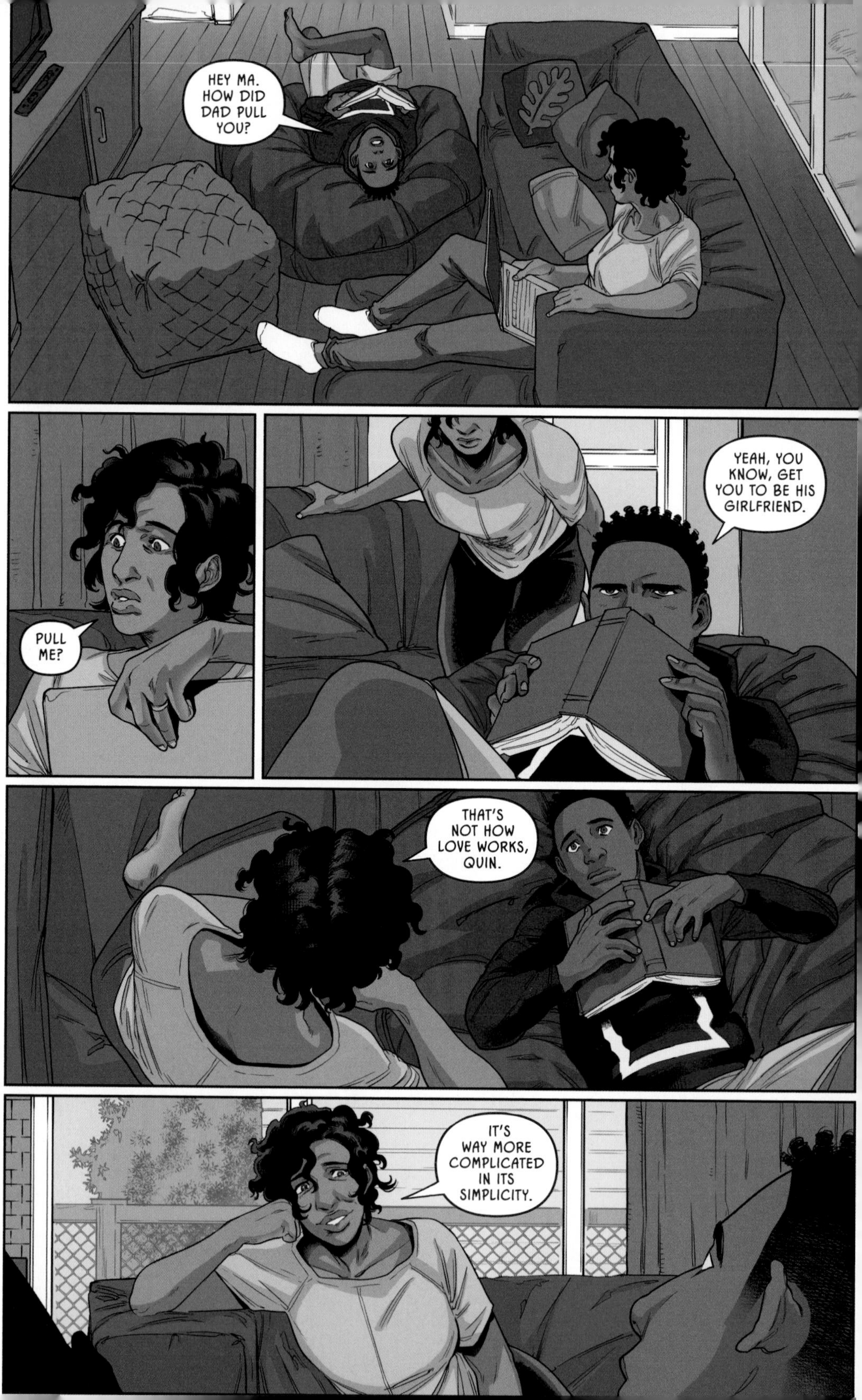
HEY MA. HOW DID DAD PULL YOU?
PULL ME?
YEAH, YOU KNOW, GET YOU TO BE HIS GIRLFRIEND.
THAT'S NOT HOW LOVE WORKS, QUIN.
IT'S WAY MORE COMPLICATED IN ITS SIMPLICITY.

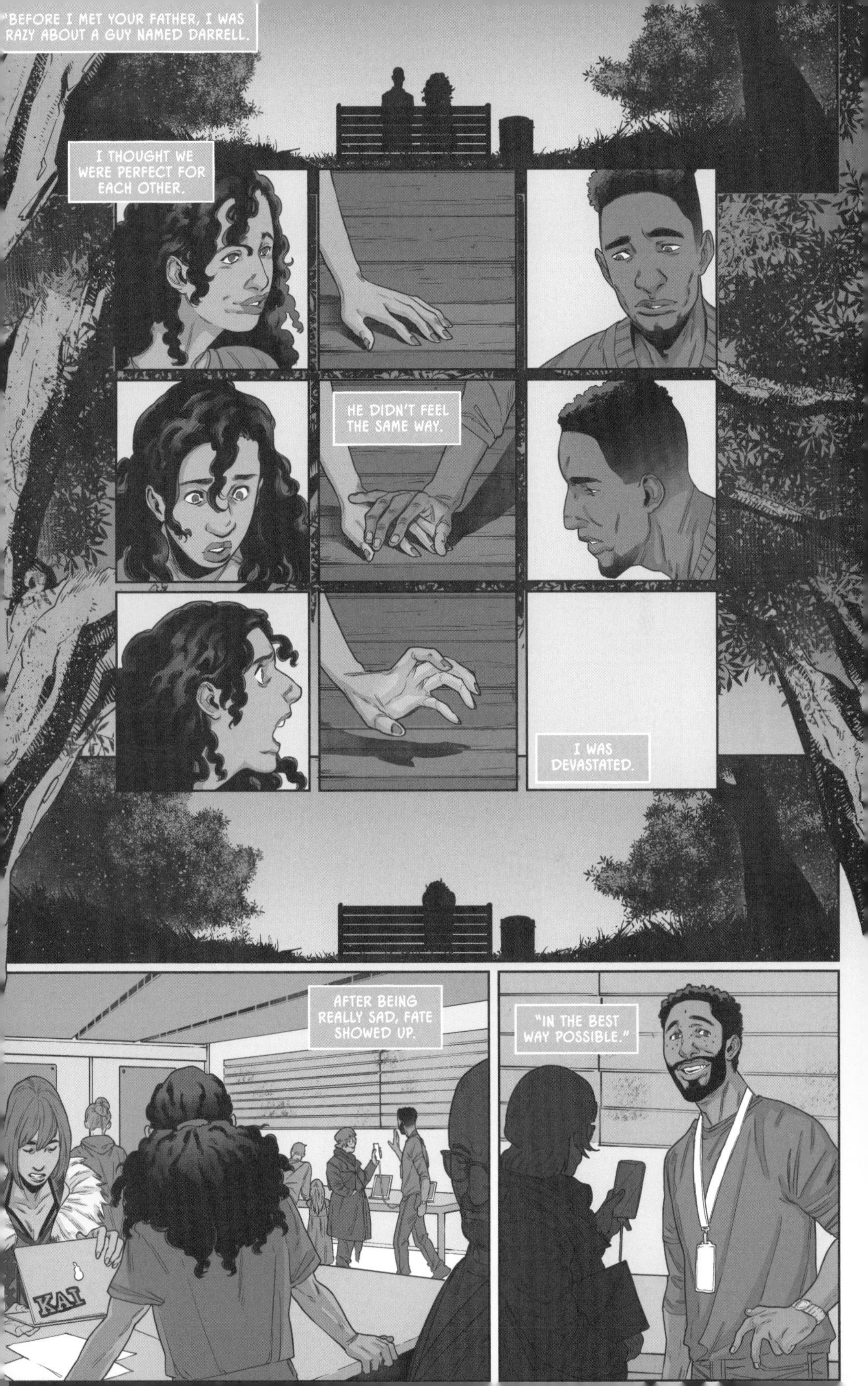
"BEFORE I MET YOUR FATHER, I WAS
RAZY ABOUT A GUY NAMED DARRELL.
I THOUGHT WE WERE PERFECT FOR EACH OTHER.
HE DIDN'T FEEL THE SAME WAY.
I WAS DEVASTATED.
AFTER BEING REALLY SAD, FATE SHOWED UP.
"IN THE BEST WAY POSSIBLE."
KAI

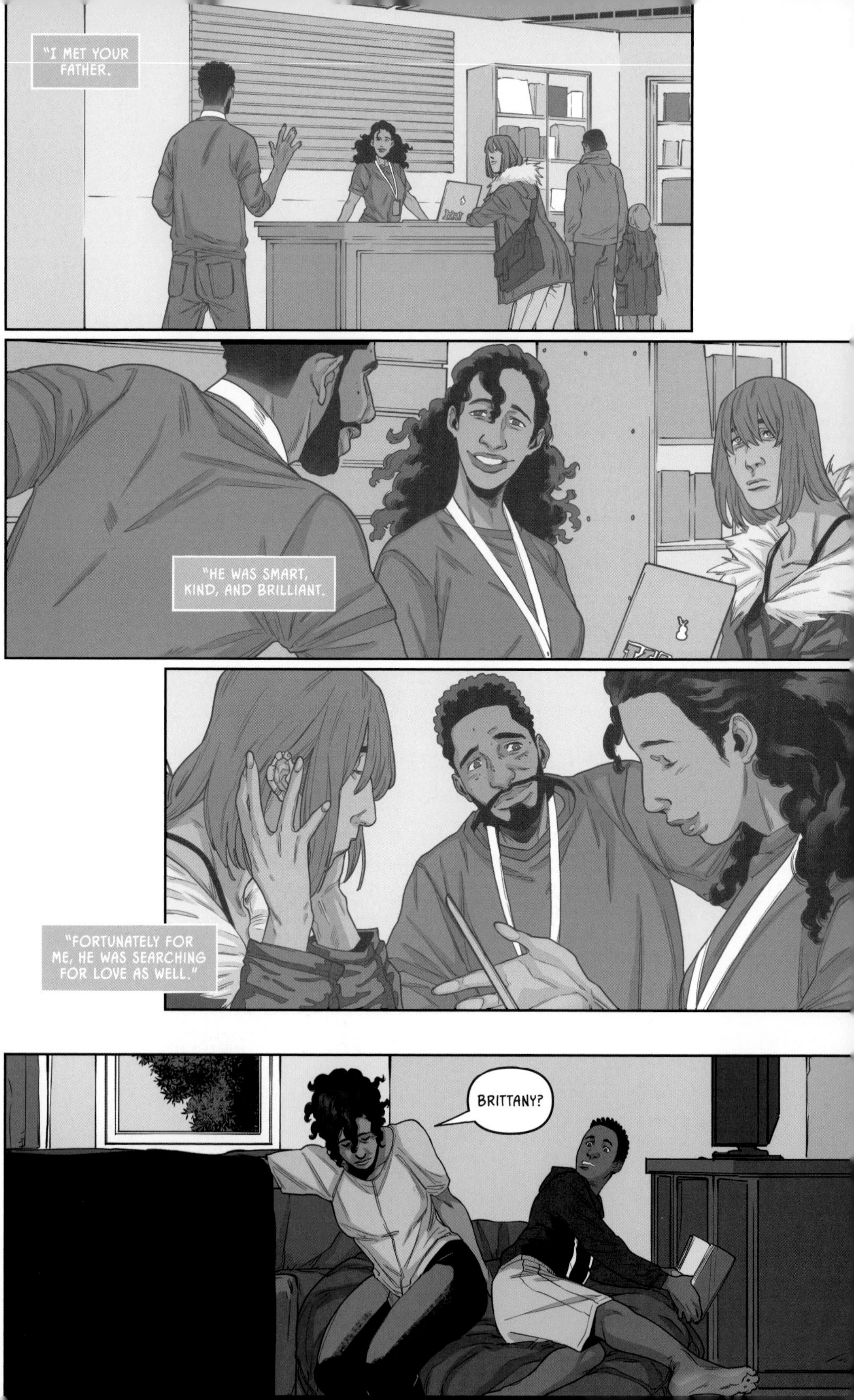
"I MET YOUR FATHER.
"HE WAS SMART, KIND, AND BRILLIANT.
"FORTUNATELY FOR ME, HE WAS SEARCHING FOR LOVE AS WELL."
BRITTANY?

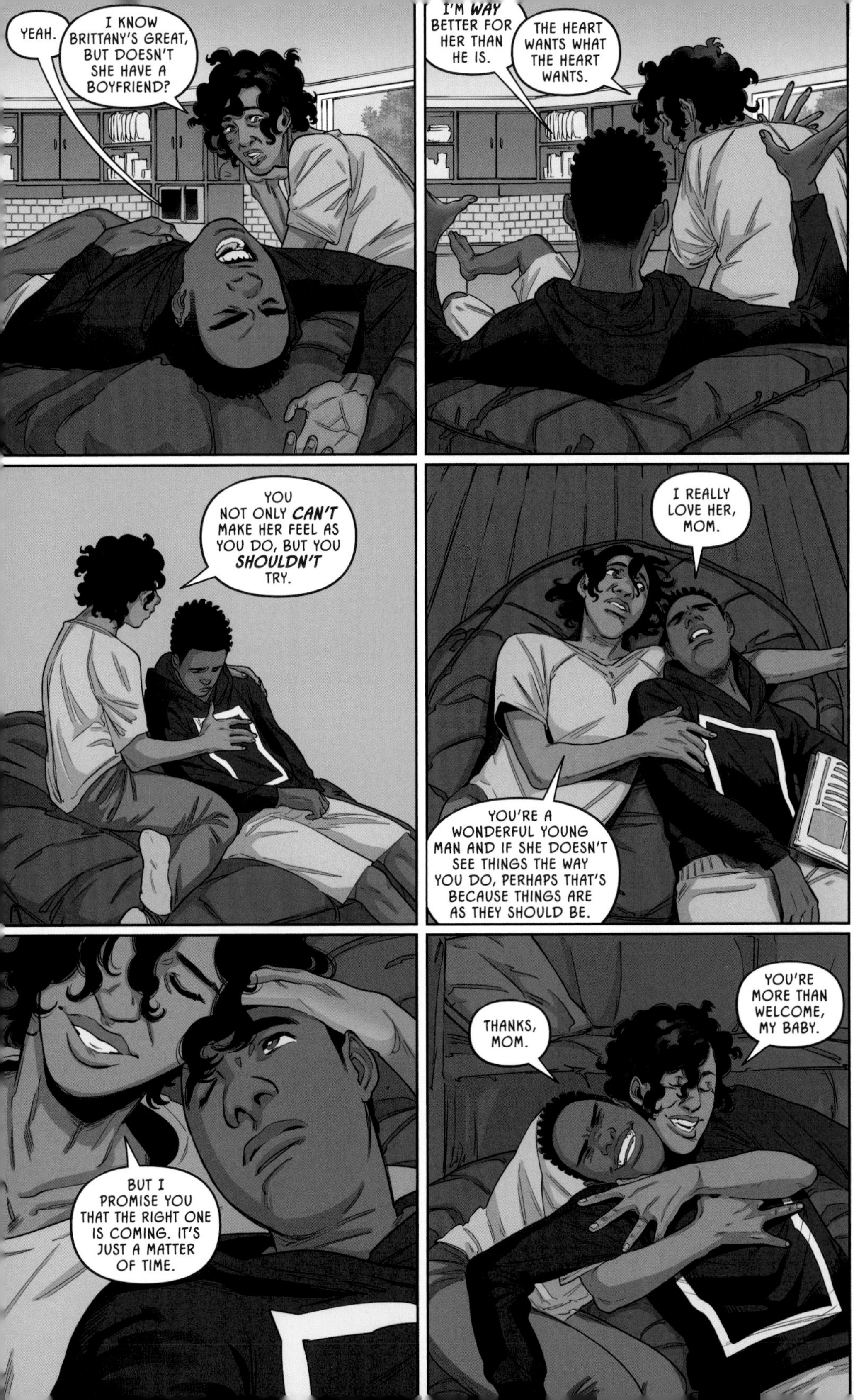
YEAH.
I KNOW BRITTANY'S GREAT, BUT DOESN'T SHE HAVE A BOYFRIEND?
I'M *WAY* BETTER FOR HER THAN HE IS.
THE HEART WANTS WHAT THE HEART WANTS.
YOU NOT ONLY *CAN'T* MAKE HER FEEL AS YOU DO, BUT YOU *SHOULDN'T* TRY.
I REALLY LOVE HER, MOM.
YOU'RE A WONDERFUL YOUNG MAN AND IF SHE DOESN'T SEE THINGS THE WAY YOU DO, PERHAPS THAT'S BECAUSE THINGS ARE AS THEY SHOULD BE.
BUT I PROMISE YOU THAT THE RIGHT ONE IS COMING. IT'S JUST A MATTER OF TIME.
THANKS, MOM.
YOU'RE MORE THAN WELCOME, MY BABY.

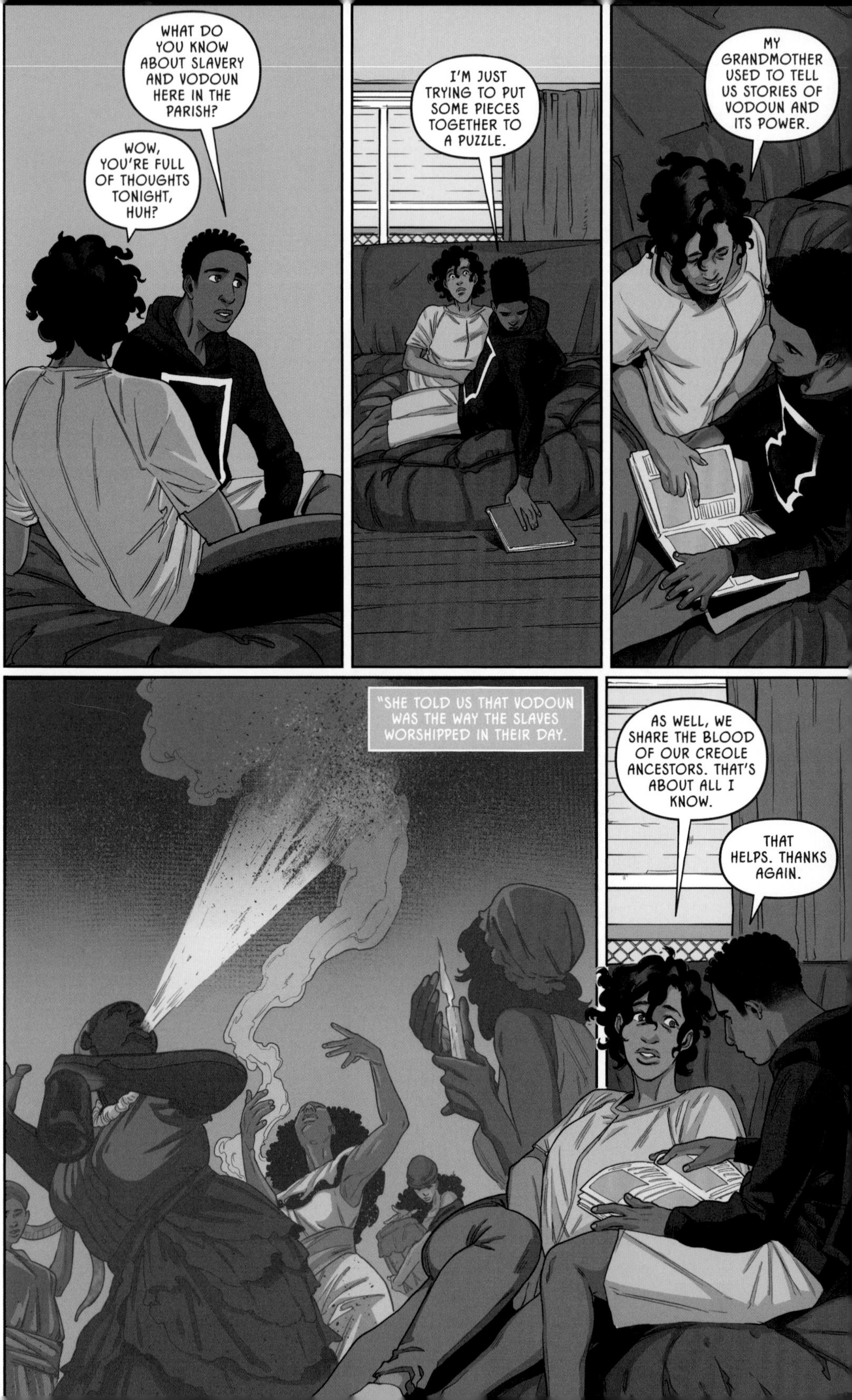
WHAT DO YOU KNOW ABOUT SLAVERY AND VODOUN HERE IN THE PARISH?
WOW, YOU'RE FULL OF THOUGHTS TONIGHT, HUH?
I'M JUST TRYING TO PUT SOME PIECES TOGETHER TO A PUZZLE.
MY GRANDMOTHER USED TO TELL US STORIES OF VODOUN AND ITS POWER.
"SHE TOLD US THAT VODOUN WAS THE WAY THE SLAVES WORSHIPPED IN THEIR DAY.
AS WELL, WE SHARE THE BLOOD OF OUR CREOLE ANCESTORS. THAT'S ABOUT ALL I KNOW.
THAT HELPS. THANKS AGAIN.

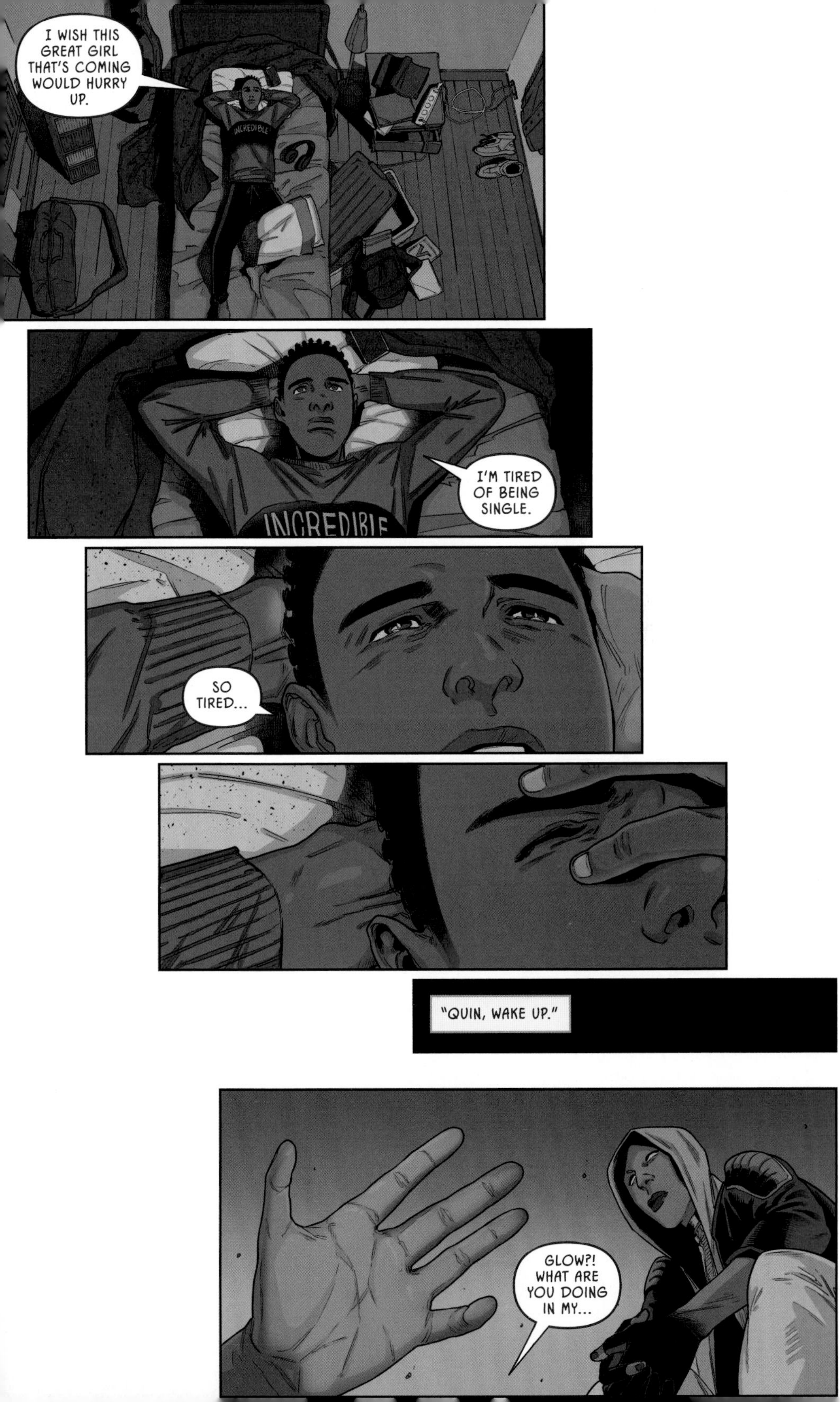
I WISH THIS GREAT GIRL THAT'S COMING WOULD HURRY UP.
INCREDIBLE
I'M TIRED OF BEING SINGLE.
SO TIRED...
"QUIN, WAKE UP."
GLOW?! WHAT ARE YOU DOING IN MY...

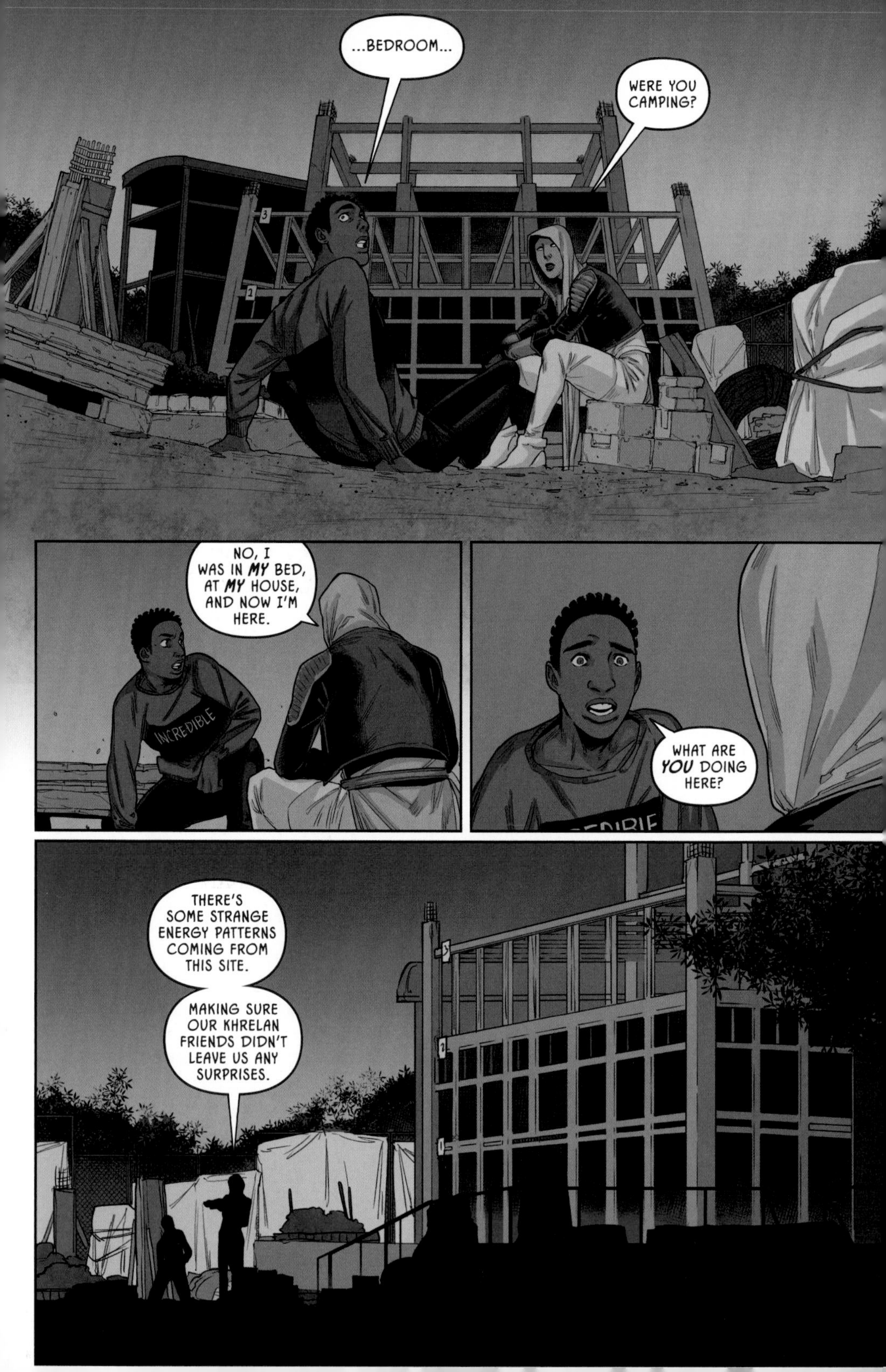
...BEDROOM...
WERE YOU CAMPING?
NO, I WAS IN MY BED, AT MY HOUSE, AND NOW I'M HERE.
INCREDIBLE
WHAT ARE YOU DOING HERE?
THERE'S SOME STRANGE ENERGY PATTERNS COMING FROM THIS SITE.
MAKING SURE OUR KHRELAN FRIENDS DIDN'T LEAVE US ANY SURPRISES.

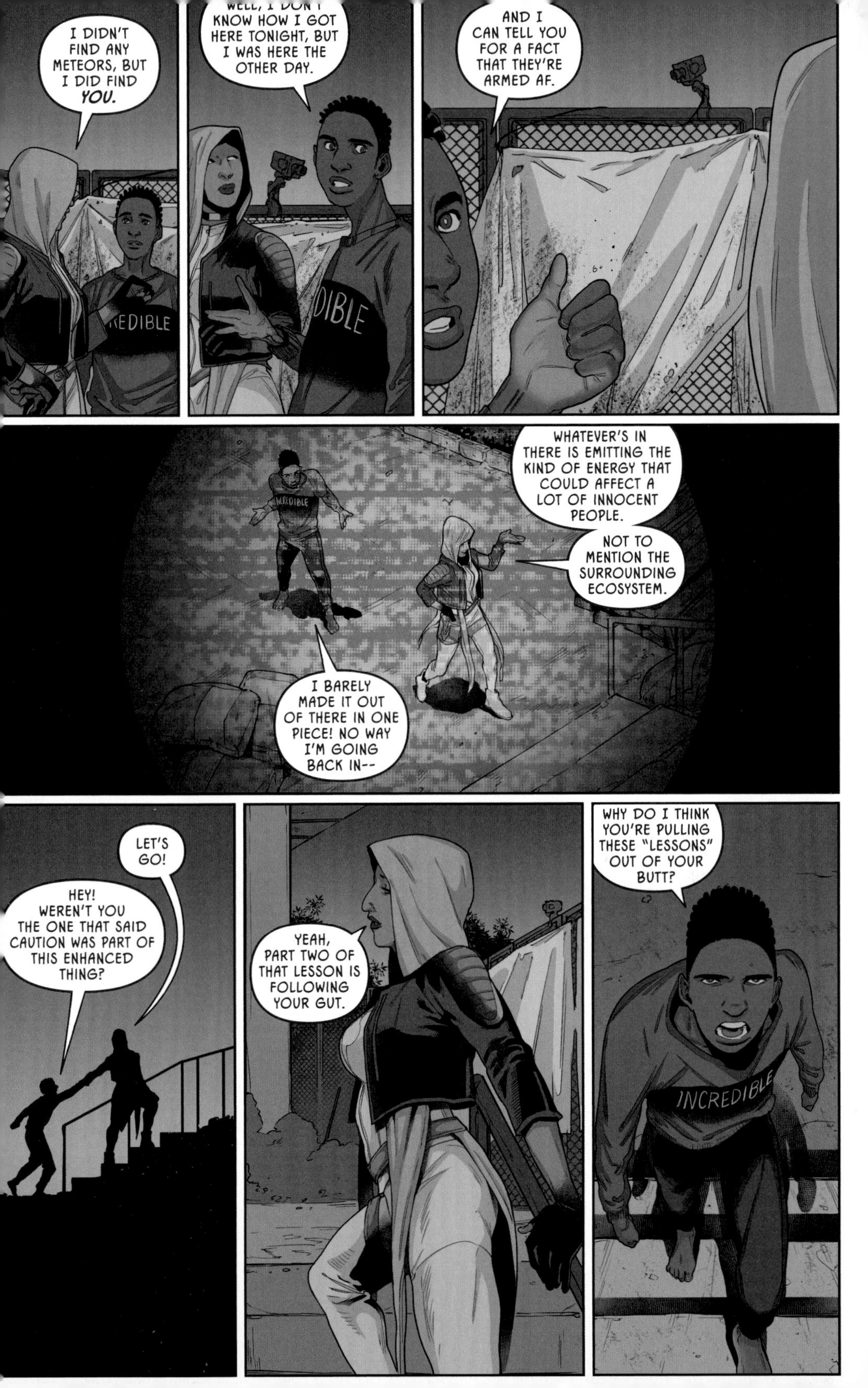
I DIDN'T FIND ANY METEORS, BUT I DID FIND *YOU.*
WELL, I DON'T KNOW HOW I GOT HERE TONIGHT, BUT I WAS HERE THE OTHER DAY.
AND I CAN TELL YOU FOR A FACT THAT THEY'RE ARMED AF.
WHATEVER'S IN THERE IS EMITTING THE KIND OF ENERGY THAT COULD AFFECT A LOT OF INNOCENT PEOPLE.
NOT TO MENTION THE SURROUNDING ECOSYSTEM.
I BARELY MADE IT OUT OF THERE IN ONE PIECE! NO WAY I'M GOING BACK IN--
LET'S GO!
HEY! WEREN'T YOU THE ONE THAT SAID CAUTION WAS PART OF THIS ENHANCED THING?
YEAH, PART TWO OF THAT LESSON IS FOLLOWING YOUR GUT.
WHY DO I THINK YOU'RE PULLING THESE "LESSONS" OUT OF YOUR BUTT?
INCREDIBLE

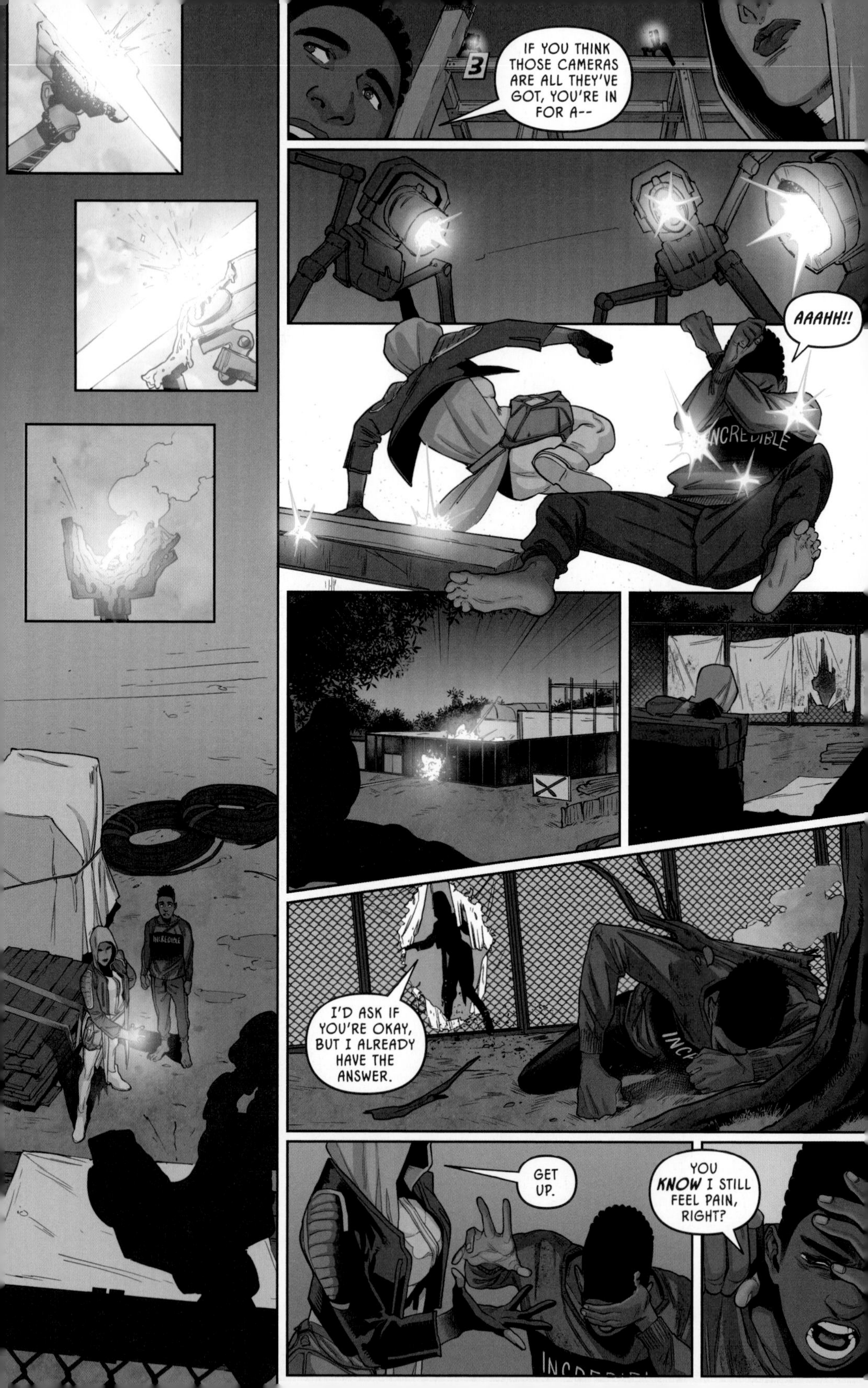

3
IF YOU THINK THOSE CAMERAS ARE ALL THEY'VE GOT, YOU'RE IN FOR A--
AAAHH!!
INCREDIBLE
I'D ASK IF YOU'RE OKAY, BUT I ALREADY HAVE THE ANSWER.
GET UP.
YOU **KNOW** I STILL FEEL PAIN, RIGHT?

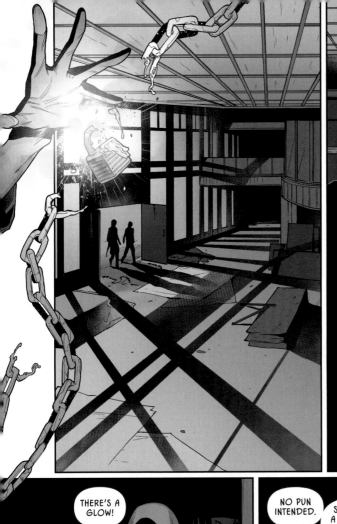

THERE'S A GLOW!

NO PUN INTENDED.

SEE THERE'S A GLOW AND *YOUR* NAME IS GLOW--

I GOT IT.

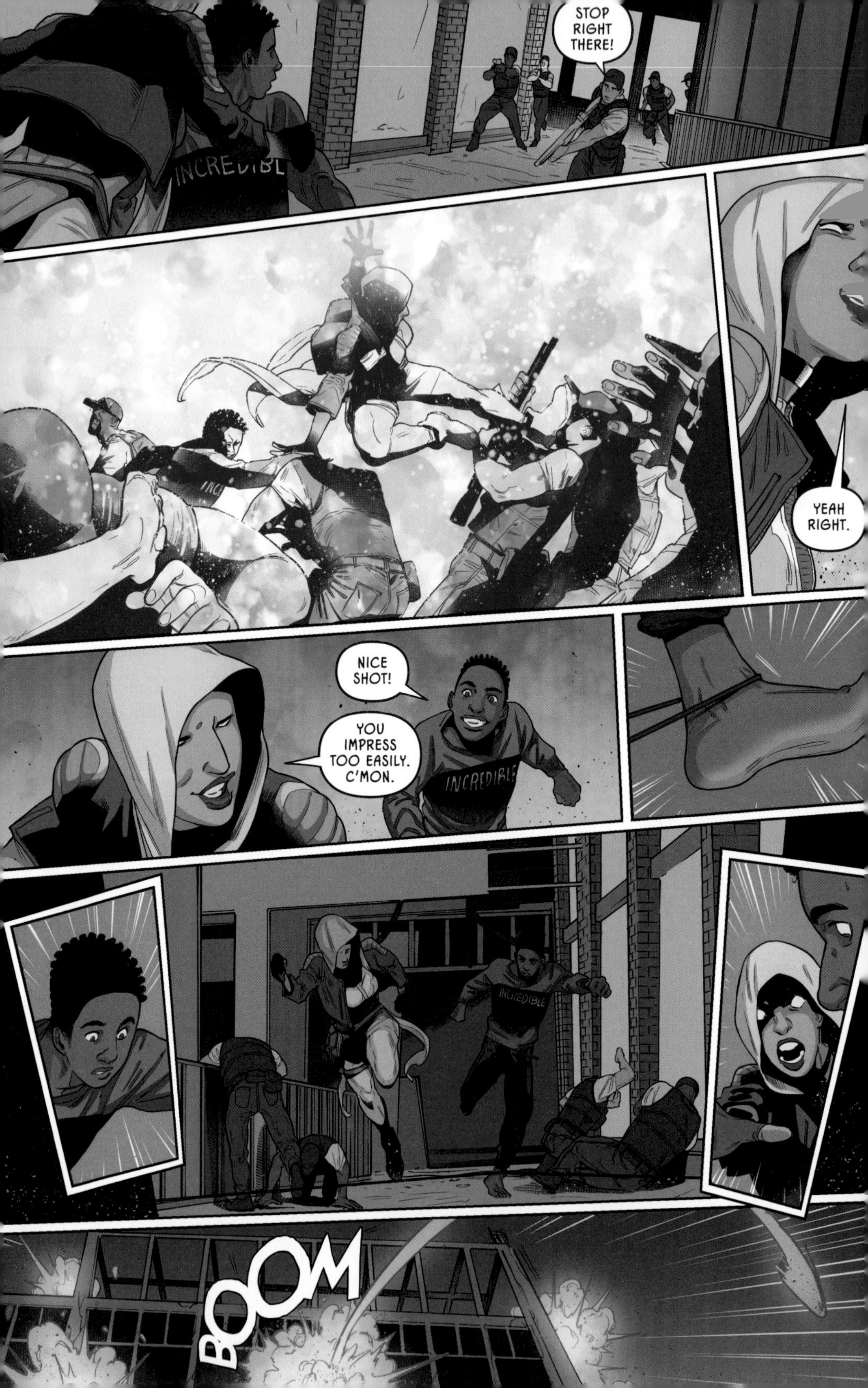
STOP RIGHT THERE!
INCREDIBLE
YEAH RIGHT.
NICE SHOT!
YOU IMPRESS TOO EASILY. C'MON.
INCREDIBLE
INCREDIBLE
BOOM

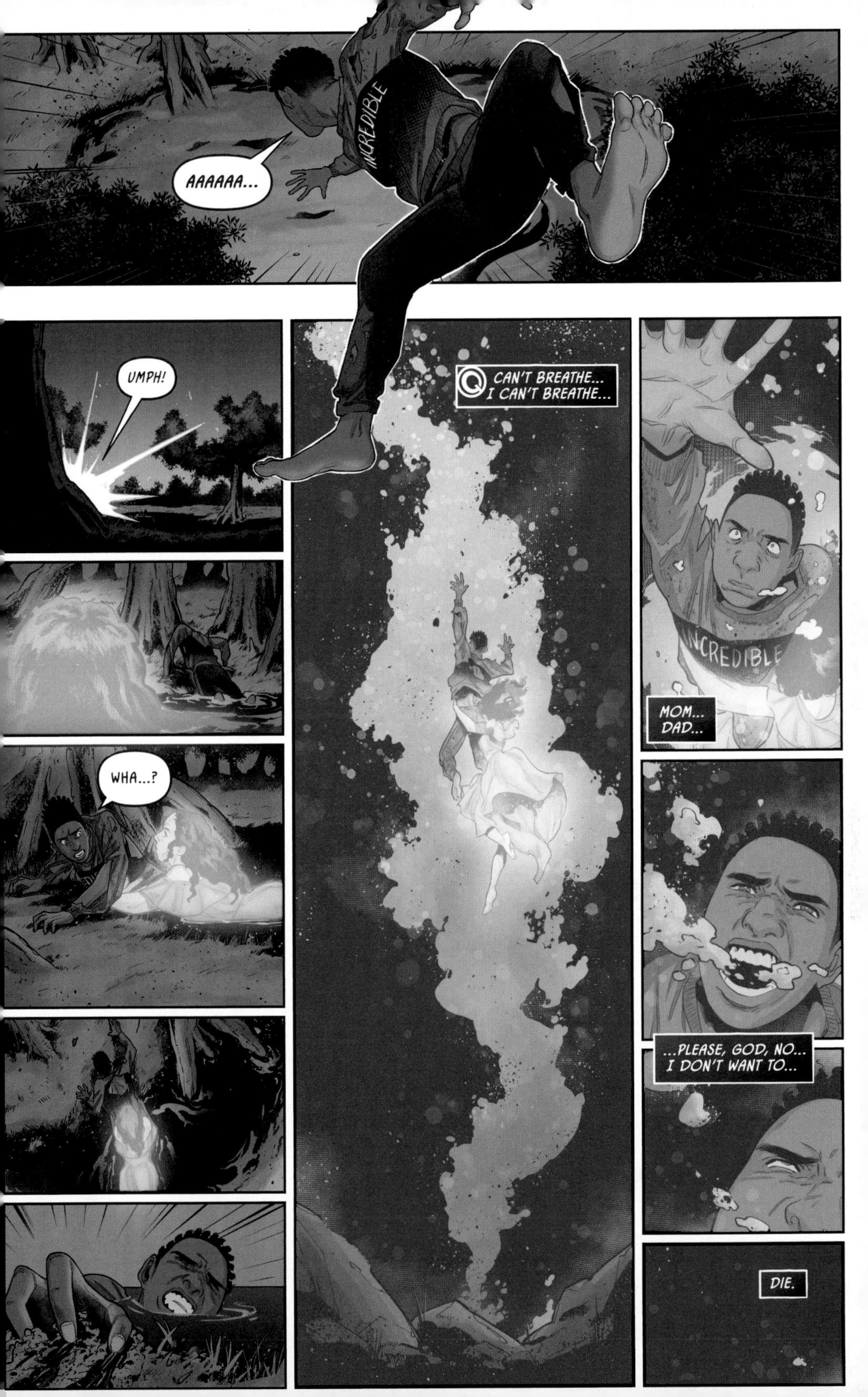
AAAAAA...
UMPH!
WHA...?
CAN'T BREATHE...
I CAN'T BREATHE...
INCREDIBLE
MOM...
DAD...
...PLEASE, GOD, NO...
I DON'T WANT TO...
DIE.

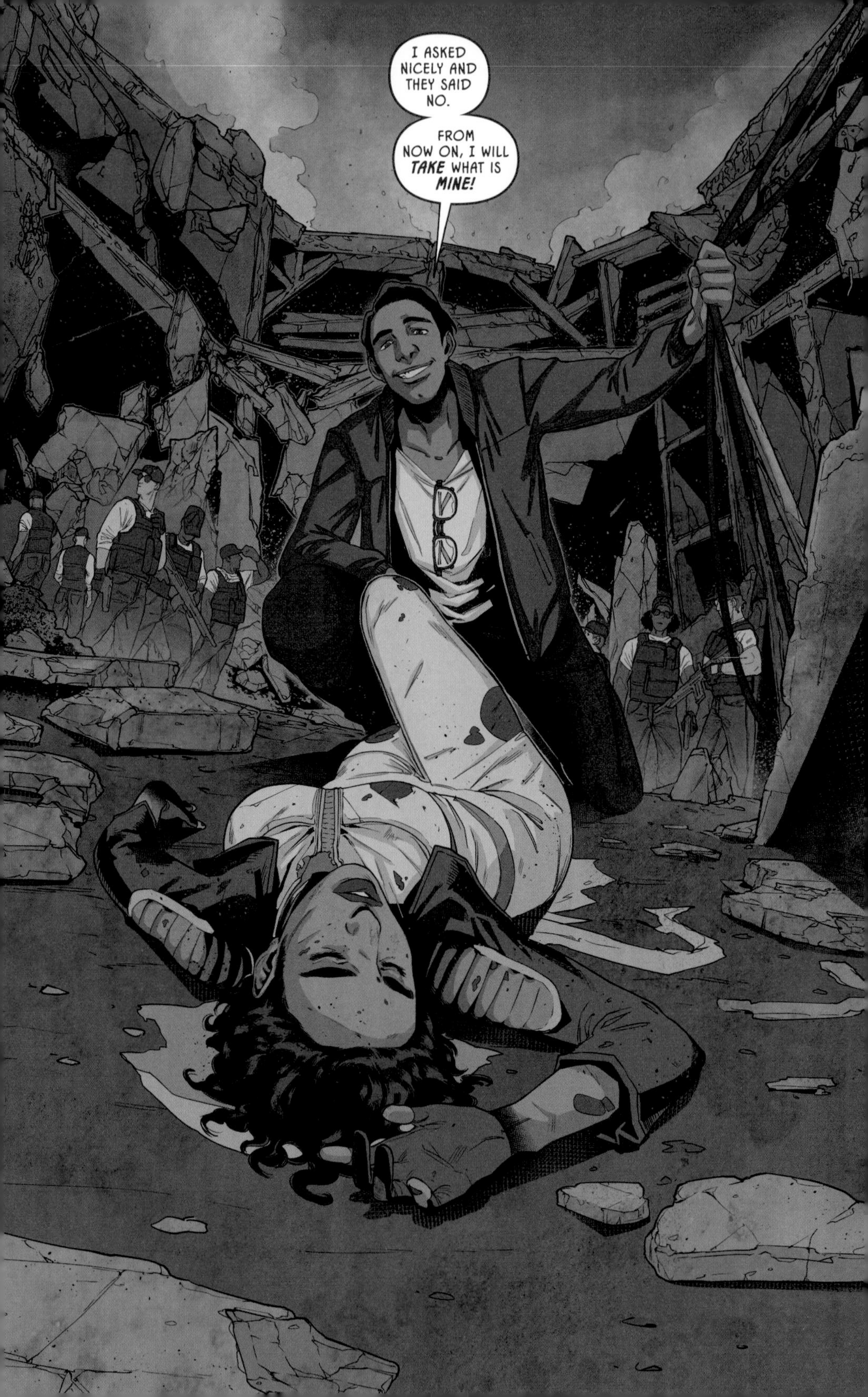
I ASKED NICELY AND THEY SAID NO.
FROM NOW ON, I WILL *TAKE* WHAT IS *MINE!*

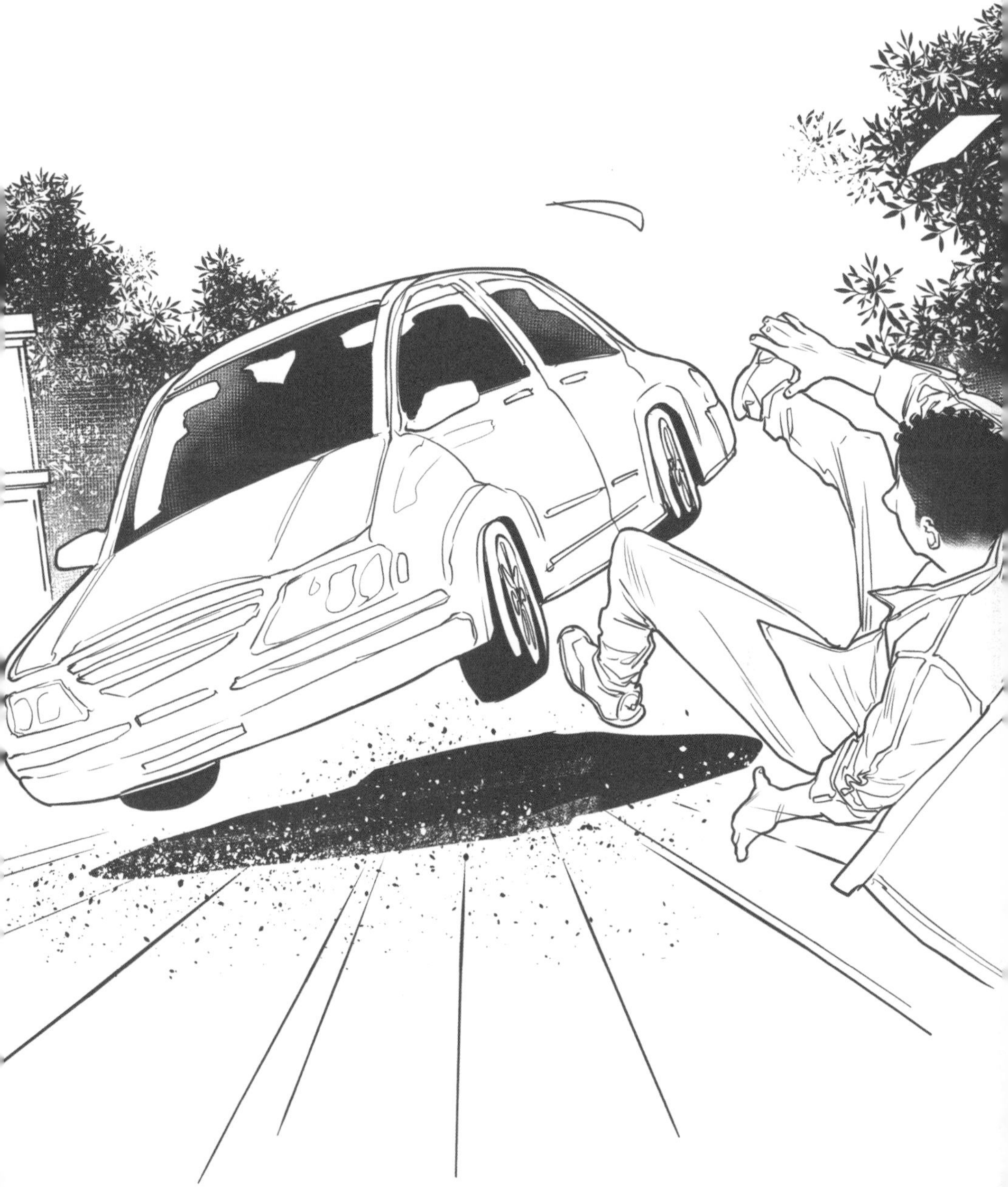

CHAPTER THREE

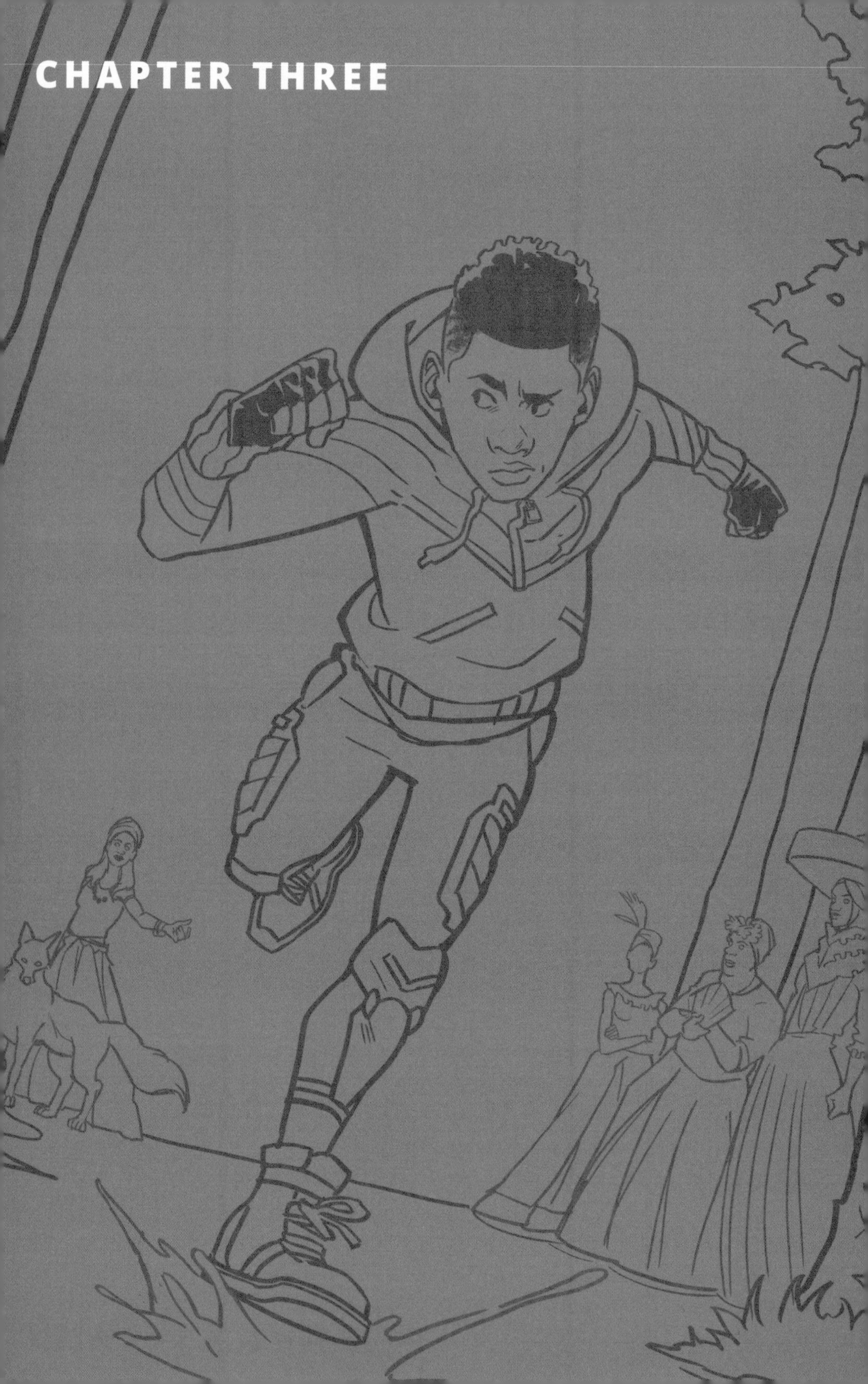

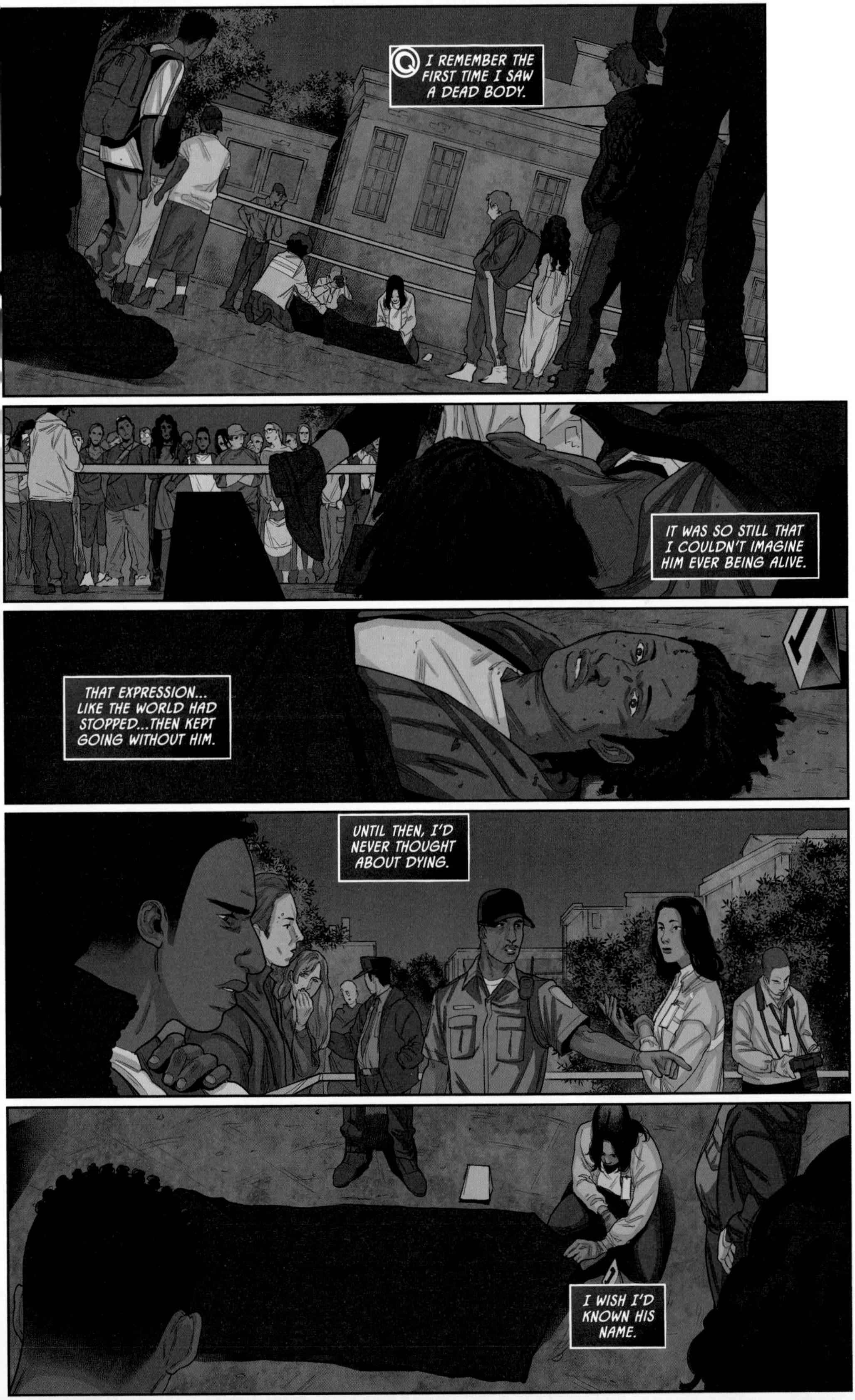
I REMEMBER THE FIRST TIME I SAW A DEAD BODY.
IT WAS SO STILL THAT I COULDN'T IMAGINE HIM EVER BEING ALIVE.
THAT EXPRESSION... LIKE THE WORLD HAD STOPPED...THEN KEPT GOING WITHOUT HIM.
UNTIL THEN, I'D NEVER THOUGHT ABOUT DYING.
I WISH I'D KNOWN HIS NAME.

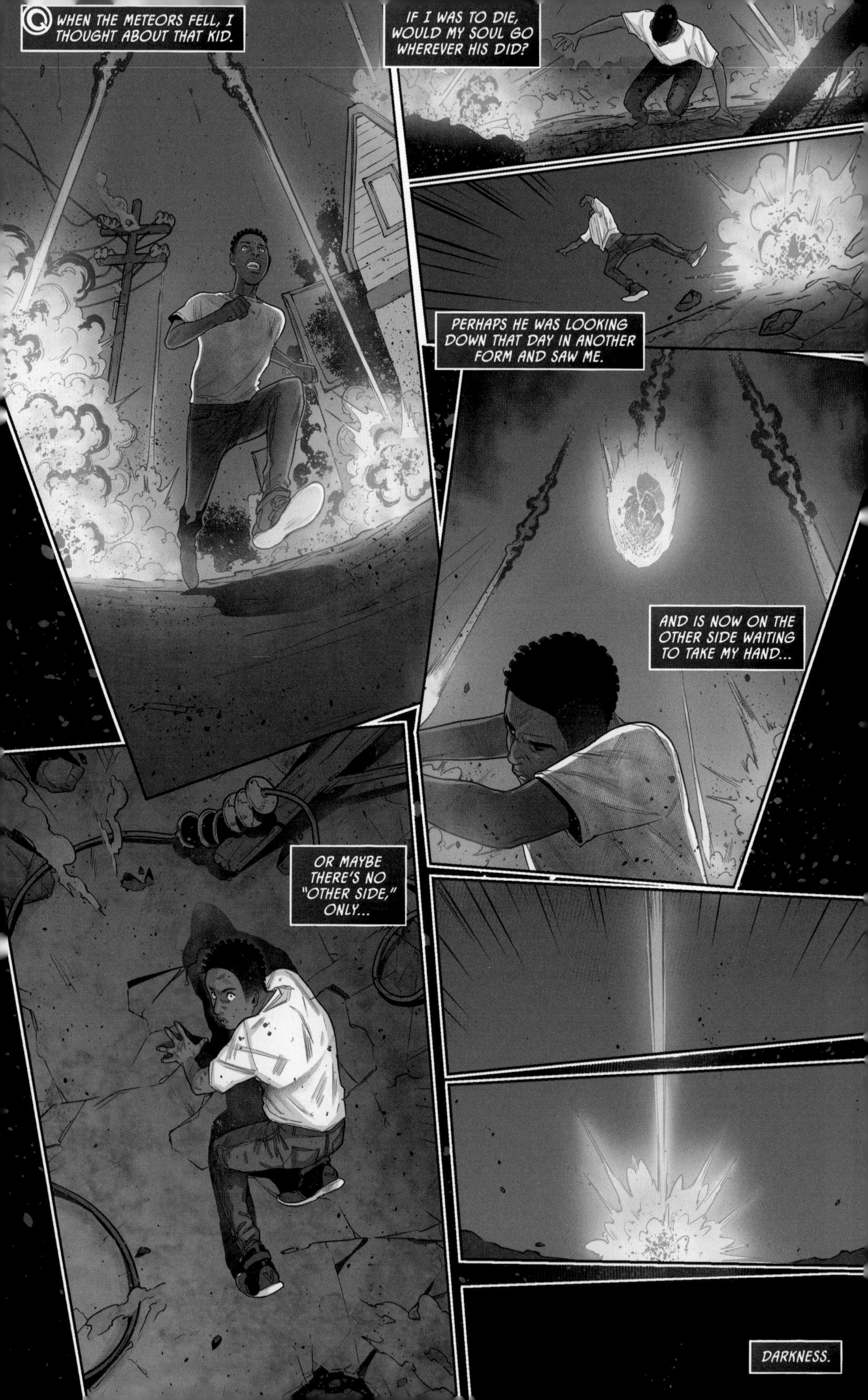
WHEN THE METEORS FELL, I THOUGHT ABOUT THAT KID.
IF I WAS TO DIE, WOULD MY SOUL GO WHEREVER HIS DID?
PERHAPS HE WAS LOOKING DOWN THAT DAY IN ANOTHER FORM AND SAW ME.
AND IS NOW ON THE OTHER SIDE WAITING TO TAKE MY HAND...
OR MAYBE THERE'S NO "OTHER SIDE," ONLY...
DARKNESS.

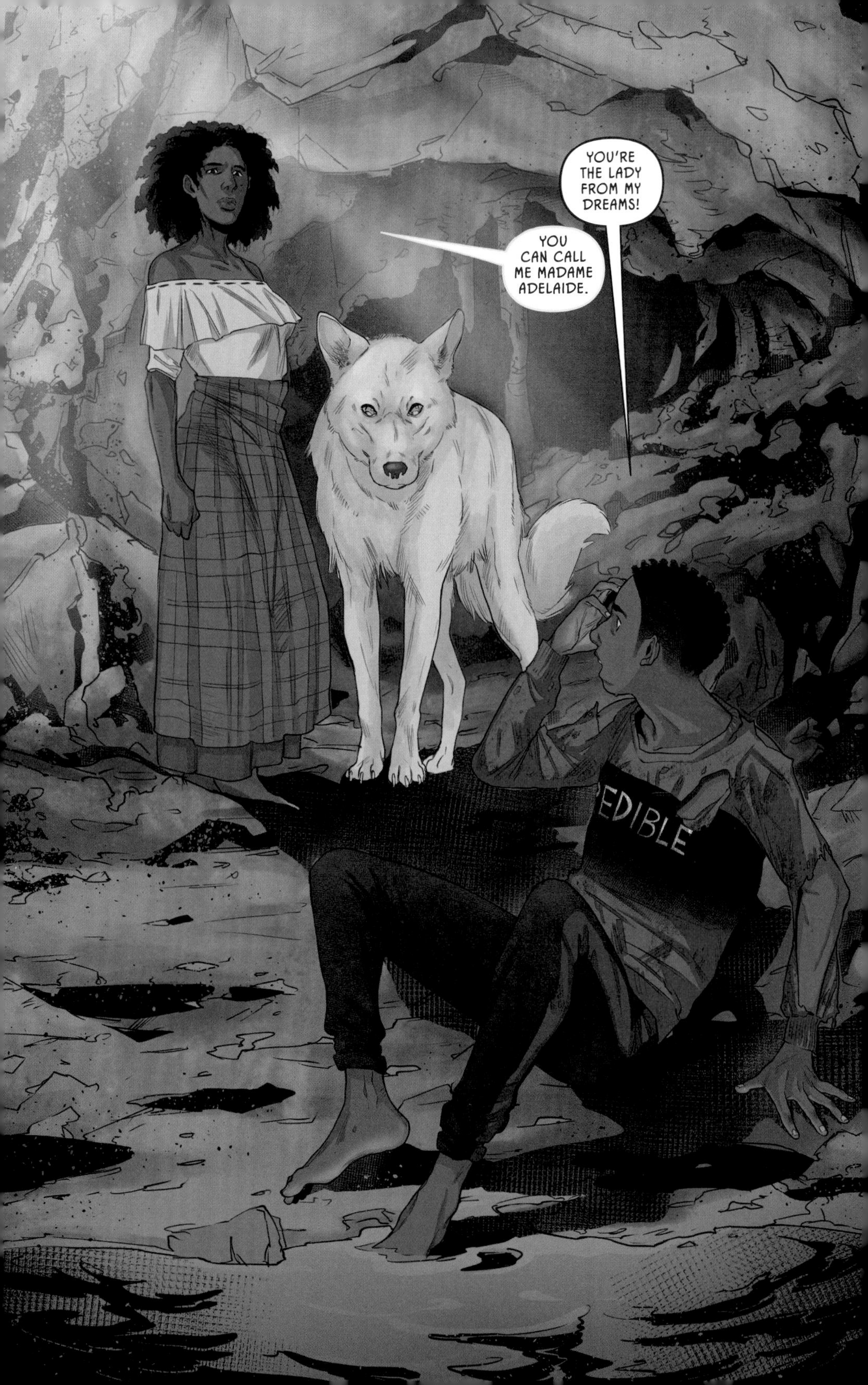
YOU'RE THE LADY FROM MY DREAMS!
YOU CAN CALL ME MADAME ADELAIDE.
EDIBLE

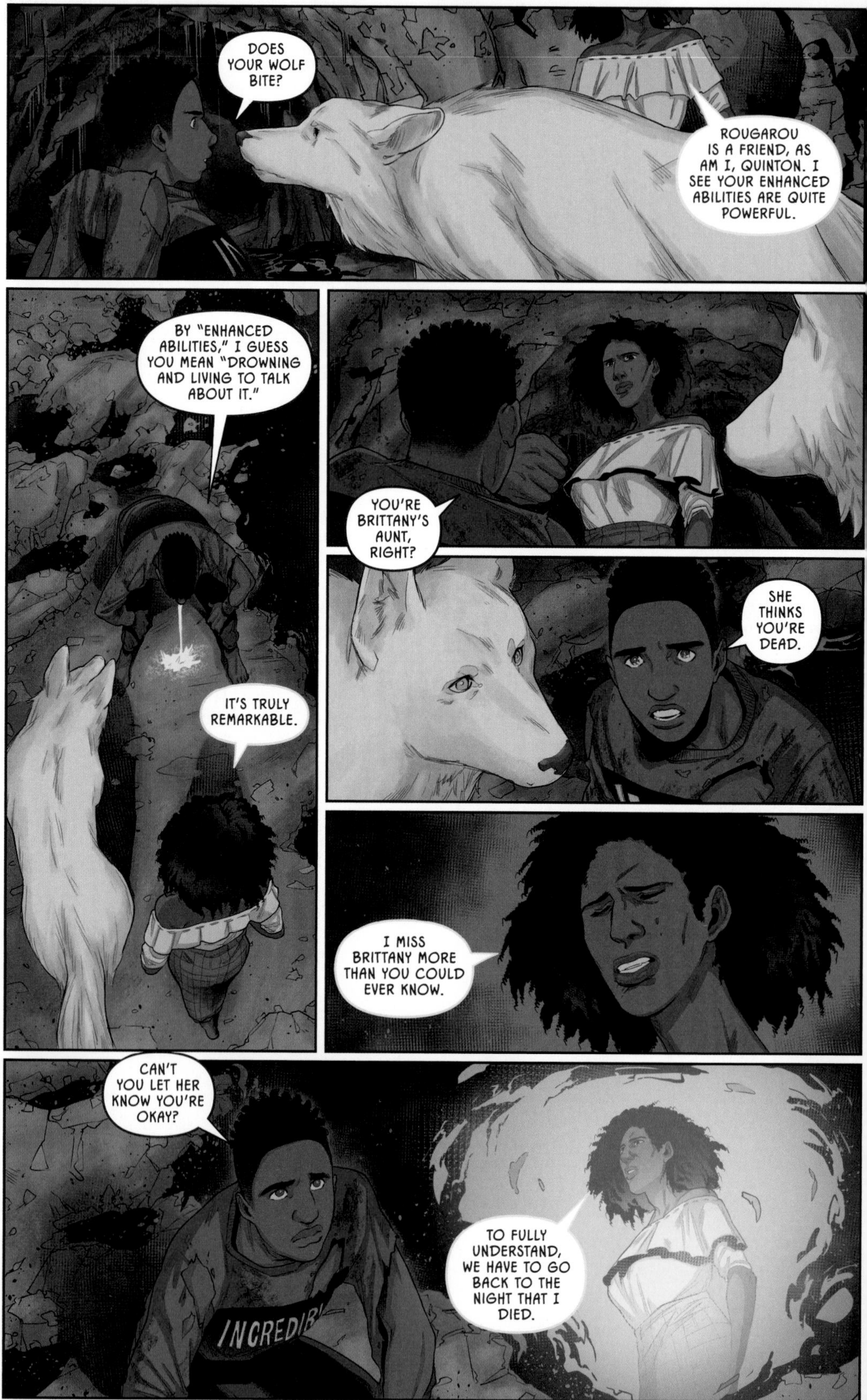
DOES YOUR WOLF BITE?
ROUGAROU IS A FRIEND, AS AM I, QUINTON. I SEE YOUR ENHANCED ABILITIES ARE QUITE POWERFUL.
BY "ENHANCED ABILITIES," I GUESS YOU MEAN "DROWNING AND LIVING TO TALK ABOUT IT."
IT'S TRULY REMARKABLE.
YOU'RE BRITTANY'S AUNT, RIGHT?
SHE THINKS YOU'RE DEAD.
I MISS BRITTANY MORE THAN YOU COULD EVER KNOW.
CAN'T YOU LET HER KNOW YOU'RE OKAY?
TO FULLY UNDERSTAND, WE HAVE TO GO BACK TO THE NIGHT THAT I DIED.
INCREDIB

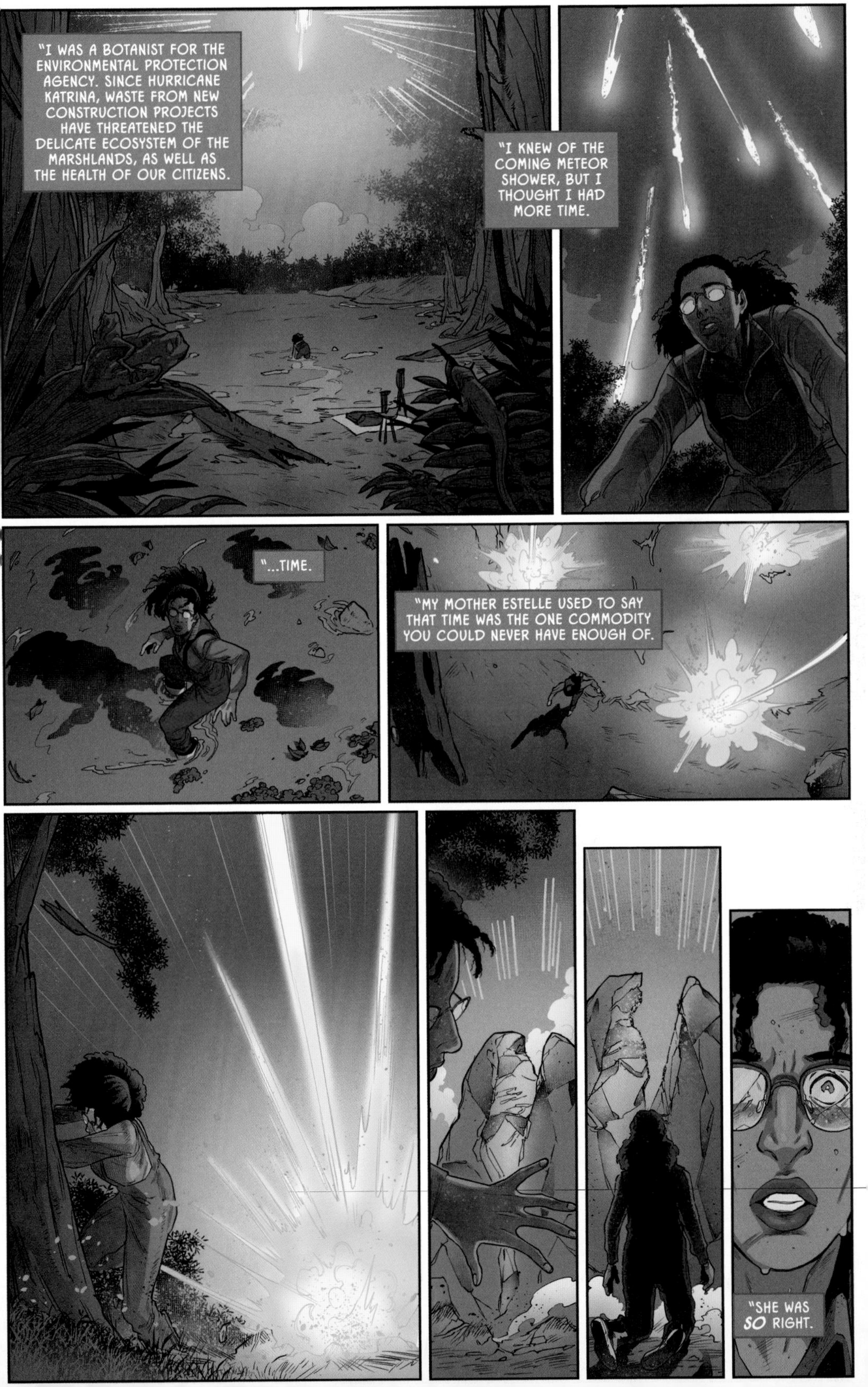
"I WAS A BOTANIST FOR THE ENVIRONMENTAL PROTECTION AGENCY. SINCE HURRICANE KATRINA, WASTE FROM NEW CONSTRUCTION PROJECTS HAVE THREATENED THE DELICATE ECOSYSTEM OF THE MARSHLANDS, AS WELL AS THE HEALTH OF OUR CITIZENS.
"I KNEW OF THE COMING METEOR SHOWER, BUT I THOUGHT I HAD MORE TIME.
"...TIME.
"MY MOTHER ESTELLE USED TO SAY THAT TIME WAS THE ONE COMMODITY YOU COULD NEVER HAVE ENOUGH OF.
"SHE WAS *SO* RIGHT.

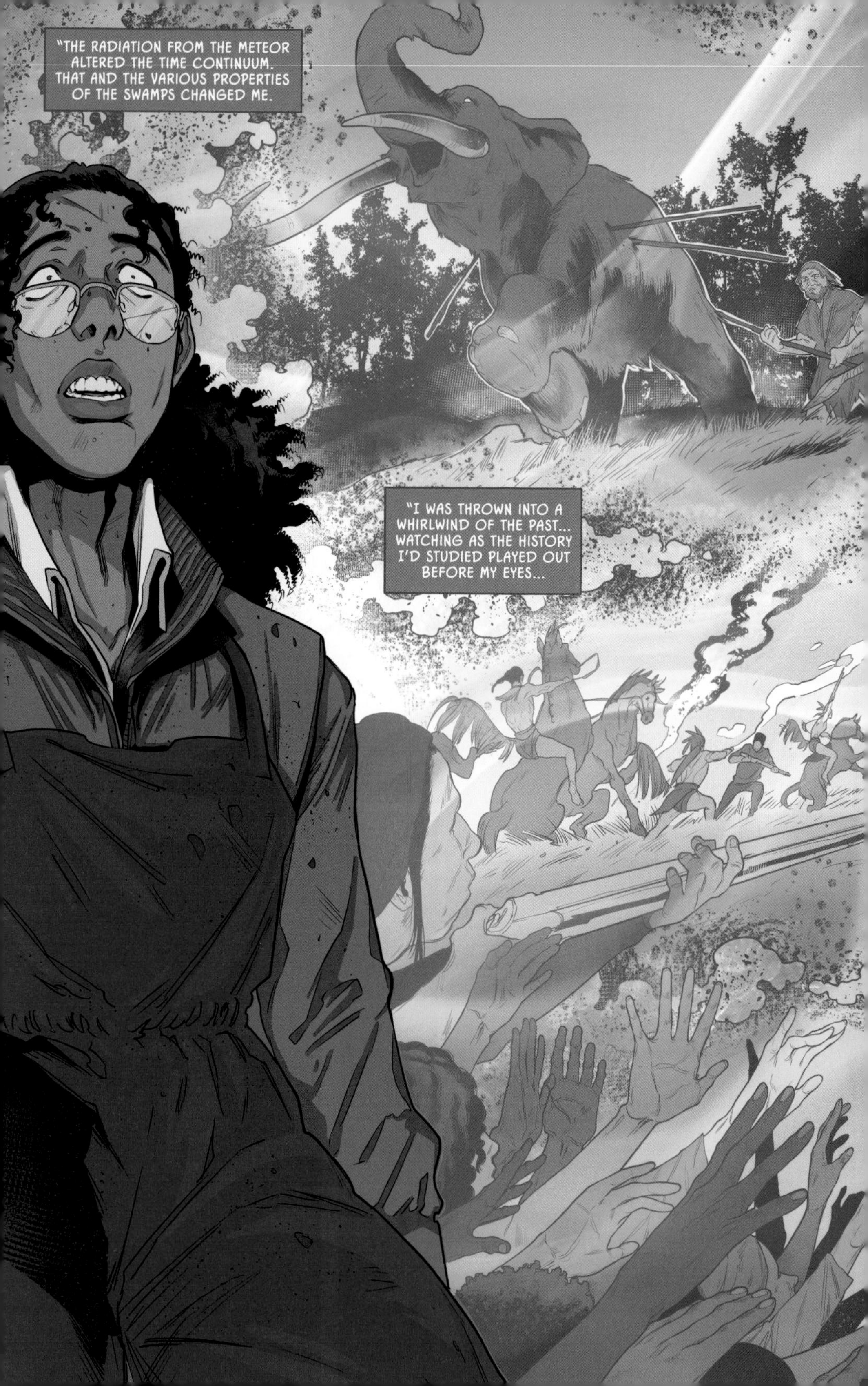
"THE RADIATION FROM THE METEOR ALTERED THE TIME CONTINUUM. THAT AND THE VARIOUS PROPERTIES OF THE SWAMPS CHANGED ME.
"I WAS THROWN INTO A WHIRLWIND OF THE PAST... WATCHING AS THE HISTORY I'D STUDIED PLAYED OUT BEFORE MY EYES...

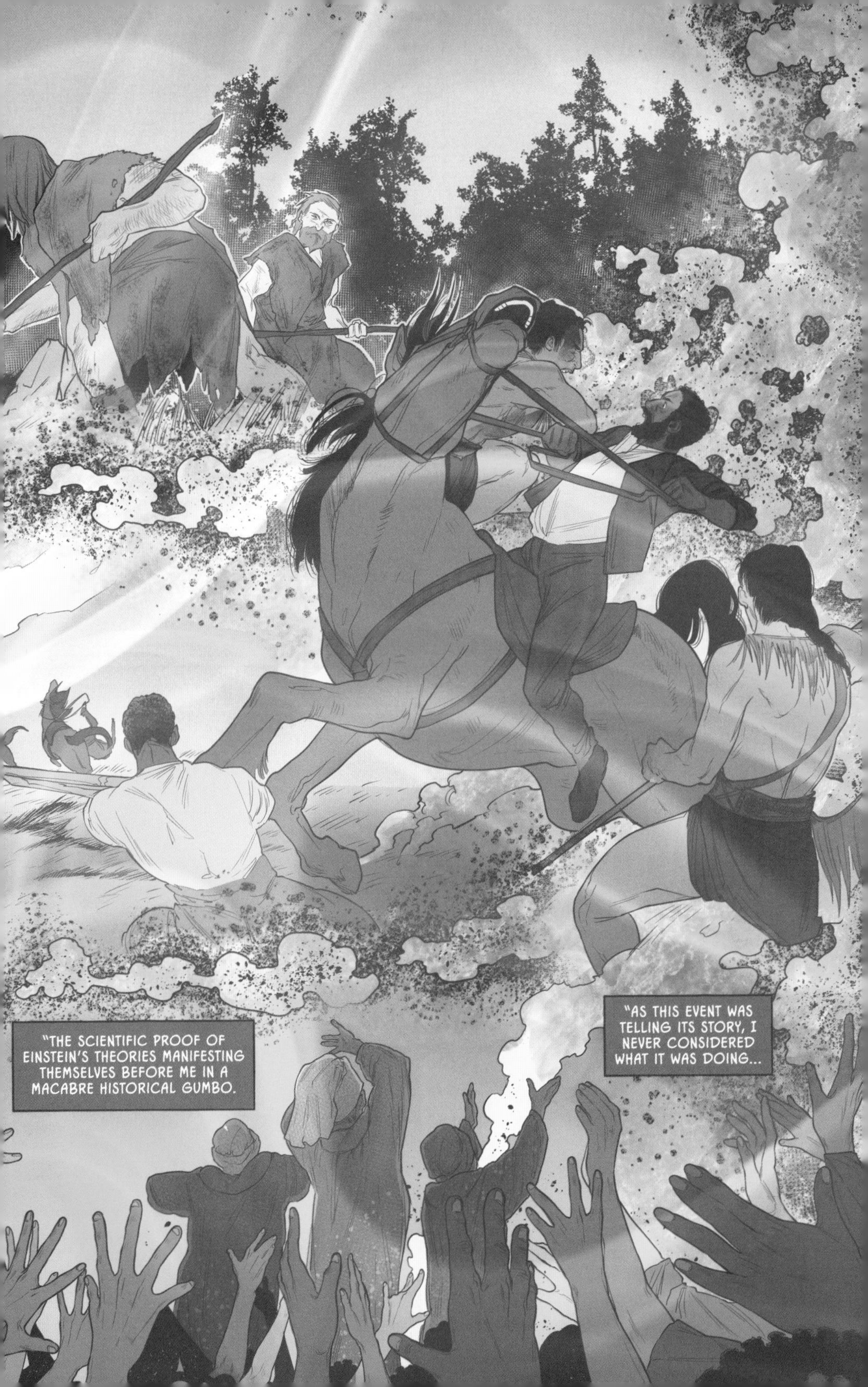
"THE SCIENTIFIC PROOF OF EINSTEIN'S THEORIES MANIFESTING THEMSELVES BEFORE ME IN A MACABRE HISTORICAL GUMBO.
"AS THIS EVENT WAS TELLING ITS STORY, I NEVER CONSIDERED WHAT IT WAS DOING...

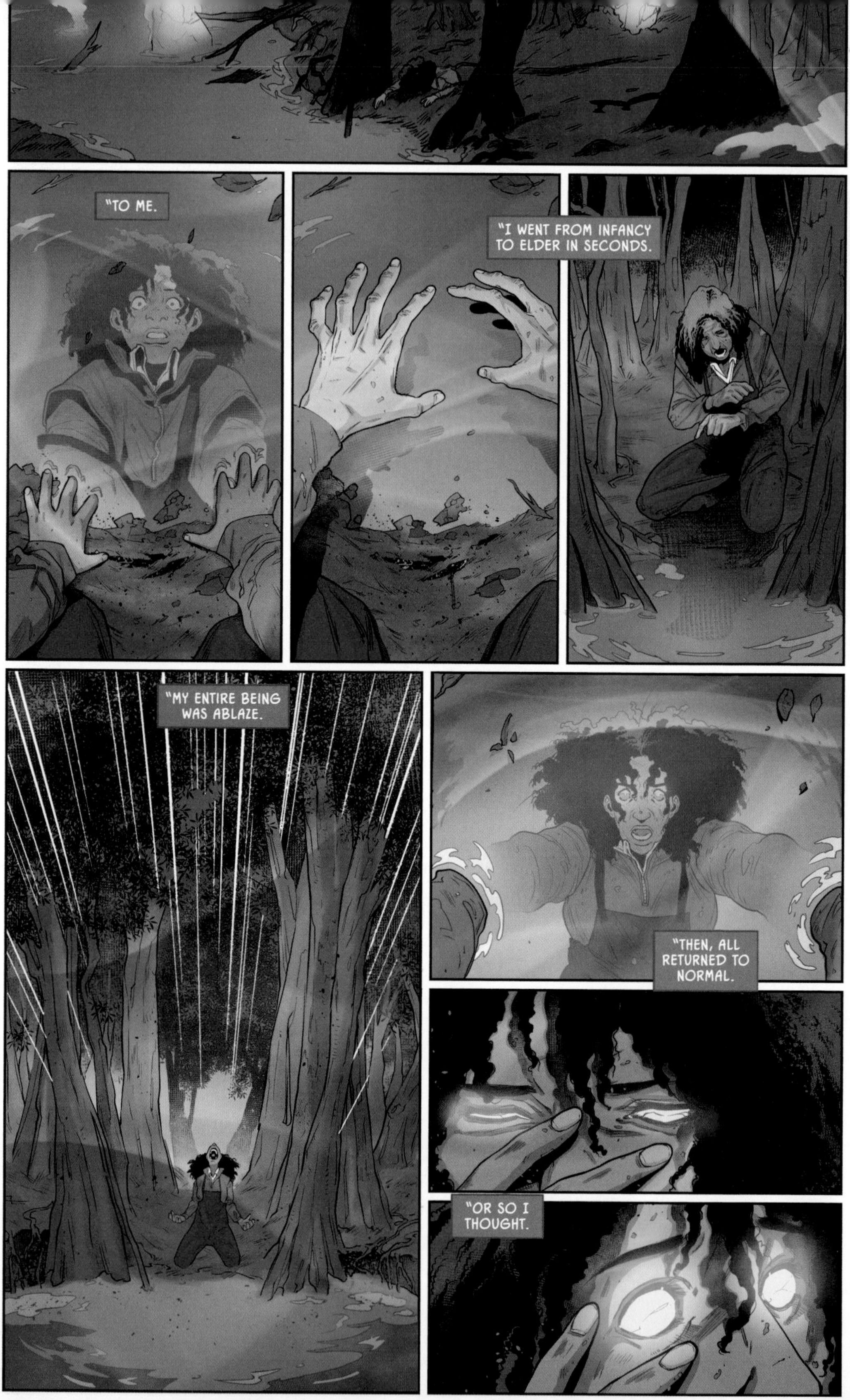
"TO ME.
"I WENT FROM INFANCY TO ELDER IN SECONDS.
"MY ENTIRE BEING WAS ABLAZE.
"THEN, ALL RETURNED TO NORMAL.
"OR SO I THOUGHT.

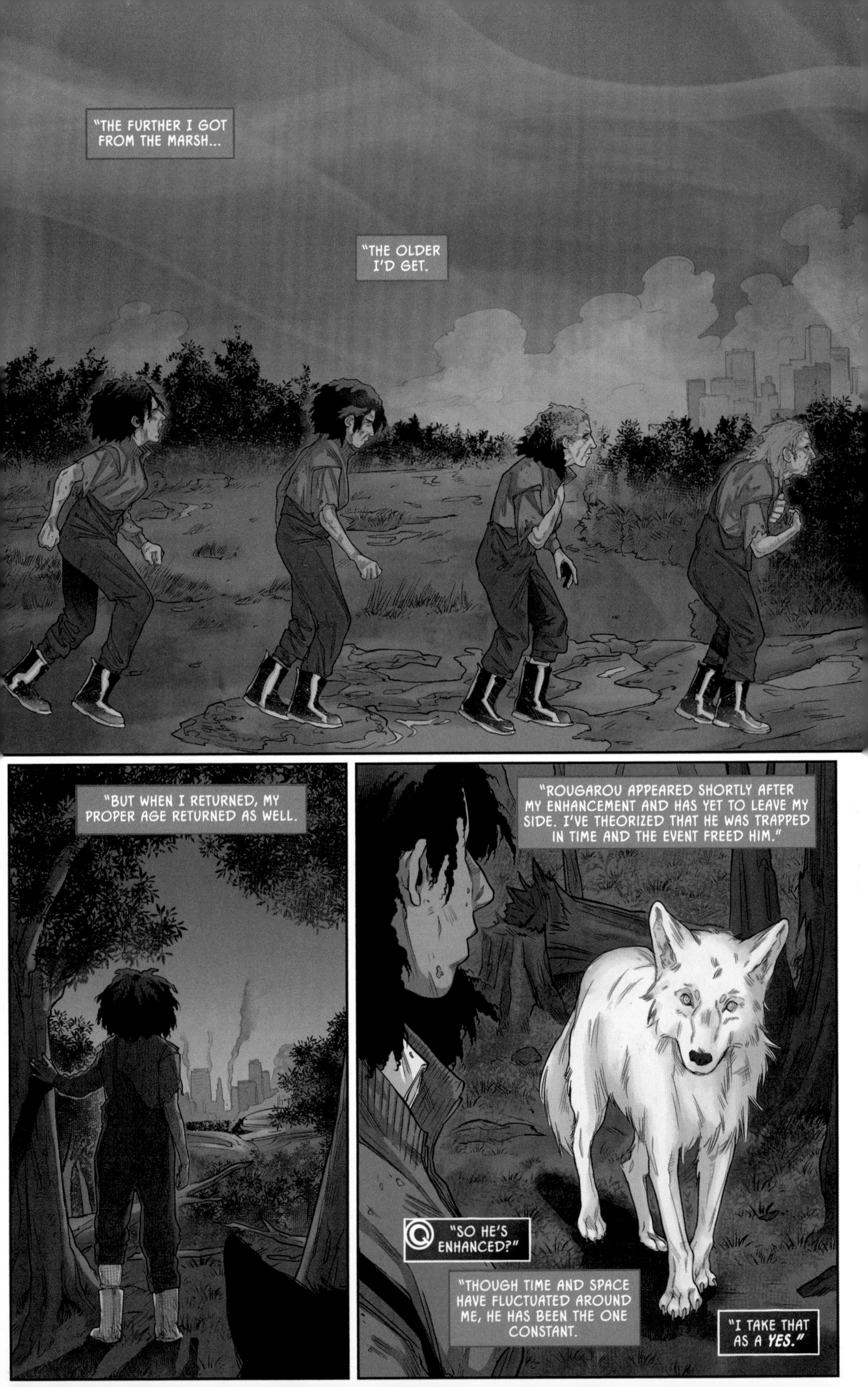
"THE FURTHER I GOT FROM THE MARSH...
"THE OLDER I'D GET.
"BUT WHEN I RETURNED, MY PROPER AGE RETURNED AS WELL.
"ROUGAROU APPEARED SHORTLY AFTER MY ENHANCEMENT AND HAS YET TO LEAVE MY SIDE. I'VE THEORIZED THAT HE WAS TRAPPED IN TIME AND THE EVENT FREED HIM."
"SO HE'S ENHANCED?"
"THOUGH TIME AND SPACE HAVE FLUCTUATED AROUND ME, HE HAS BEEN THE ONE CONSTANT.
"I TAKE THAT AS A *YES.*"

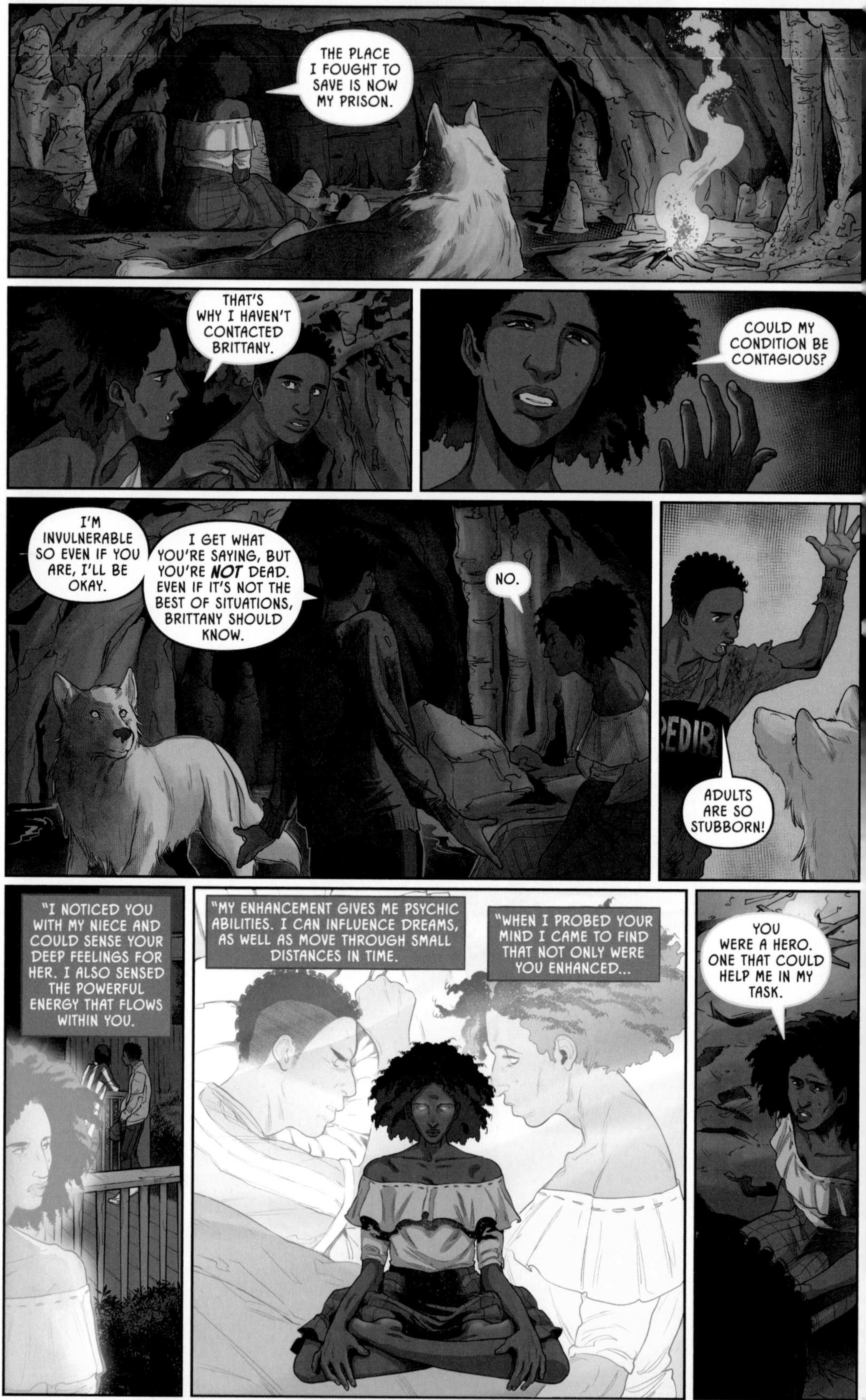
THE PLACE I FOUGHT TO SAVE IS NOW MY PRISON.
THAT'S WHY I HAVEN'T CONTACTED BRITTANY.
COULD MY CONDITION BE CONTAGIOUS?
I'M INVULNERABLE SO EVEN IF YOU ARE, I'LL BE OKAY.
I GET WHAT YOU'RE SAYING, BUT YOU'RE NOT DEAD. EVEN IF IT'S NOT THE BEST OF SITUATIONS, BRITTANY SHOULD KNOW.
NO.
ADULTS ARE SO STUBBORN!
"I NOTICED YOU WITH MY NIECE AND COULD SENSE YOUR DEEP FEELINGS FOR HER. I ALSO SENSED THE POWERFUL ENERGY THAT FLOWS WITHIN YOU.
"MY ENHANCEMENT GIVES ME PSYCHIC ABILITIES. I CAN INFLUENCE DREAMS, AS WELL AS MOVE THROUGH SMALL DISTANCES IN TIME.
"WHEN I PROBED YOUR MIND I CAME TO FIND THAT NOT ONLY WERE YOU ENHANCED...
YOU WERE A HERO. ONE THAT COULD HELP ME IN MY TASK.

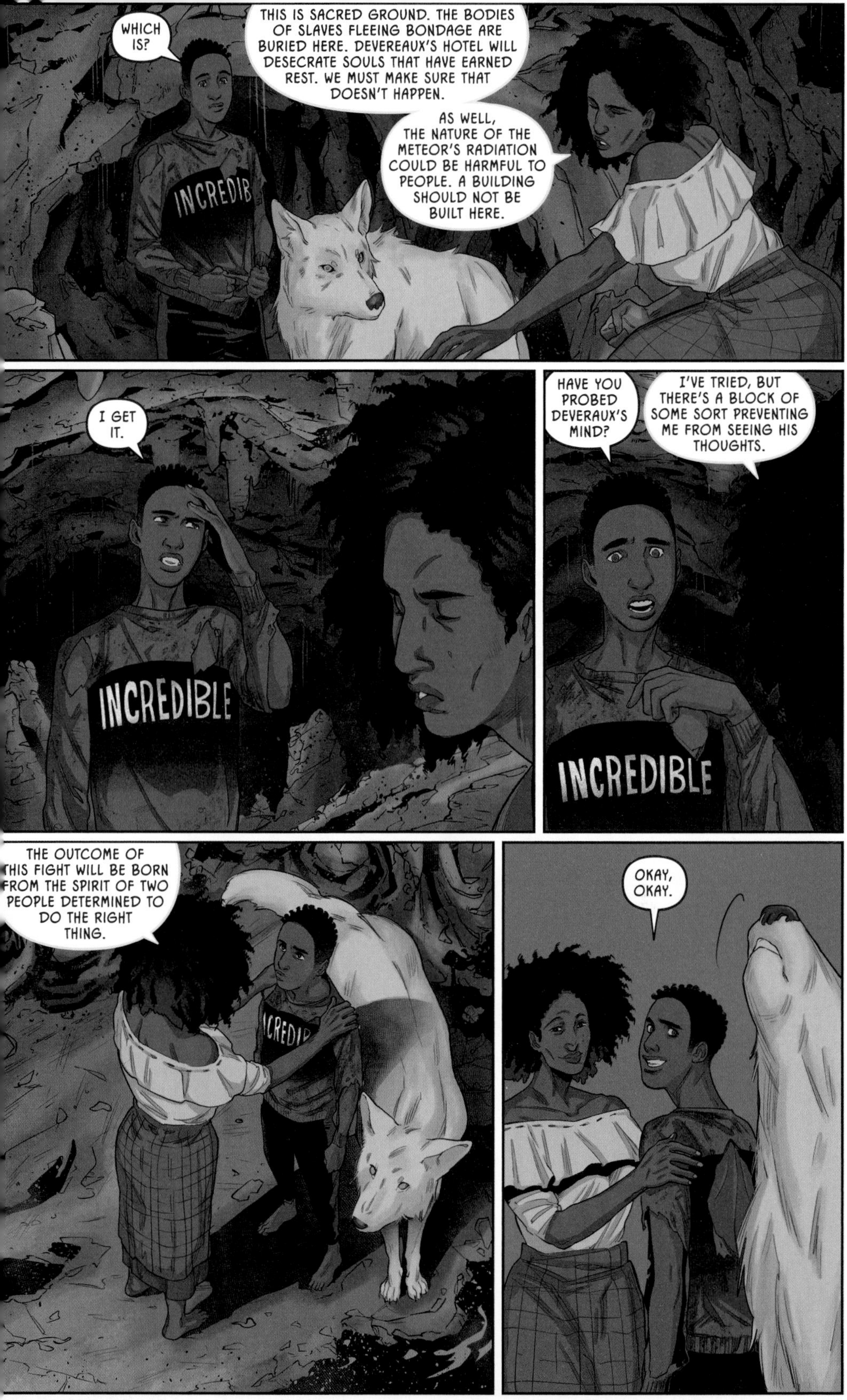
WHICH IS?
THIS IS SACRED GROUND. THE BODIES OF SLAVES FLEEING BONDAGE ARE BURIED HERE. DEVEREAUX'S HOTEL WILL DESECRATE SOULS THAT HAVE EARNED REST. WE MUST MAKE SURE THAT DOESN'T HAPPEN.
AS WELL, THE NATURE OF THE METEOR'S RADIATION COULD BE HARMFUL TO PEOPLE. A BUILDING SHOULD NOT BE BUILT HERE.
INCREDIB
I GET IT.
INCREDIBLE
HAVE YOU PROBED DEVERAUX'S MIND?
I'VE TRIED, BUT THERE'S A BLOCK OF SOME SORT PREVENTING ME FROM SEEING HIS THOUGHTS.
INCREDIBLE
THE OUTCOME OF THIS FIGHT WILL BE BORN FROM THE SPIRIT OF TWO PEOPLE DETERMINED TO DO THE RIGHT THING.
CREDIB
OKAY, OKAY.

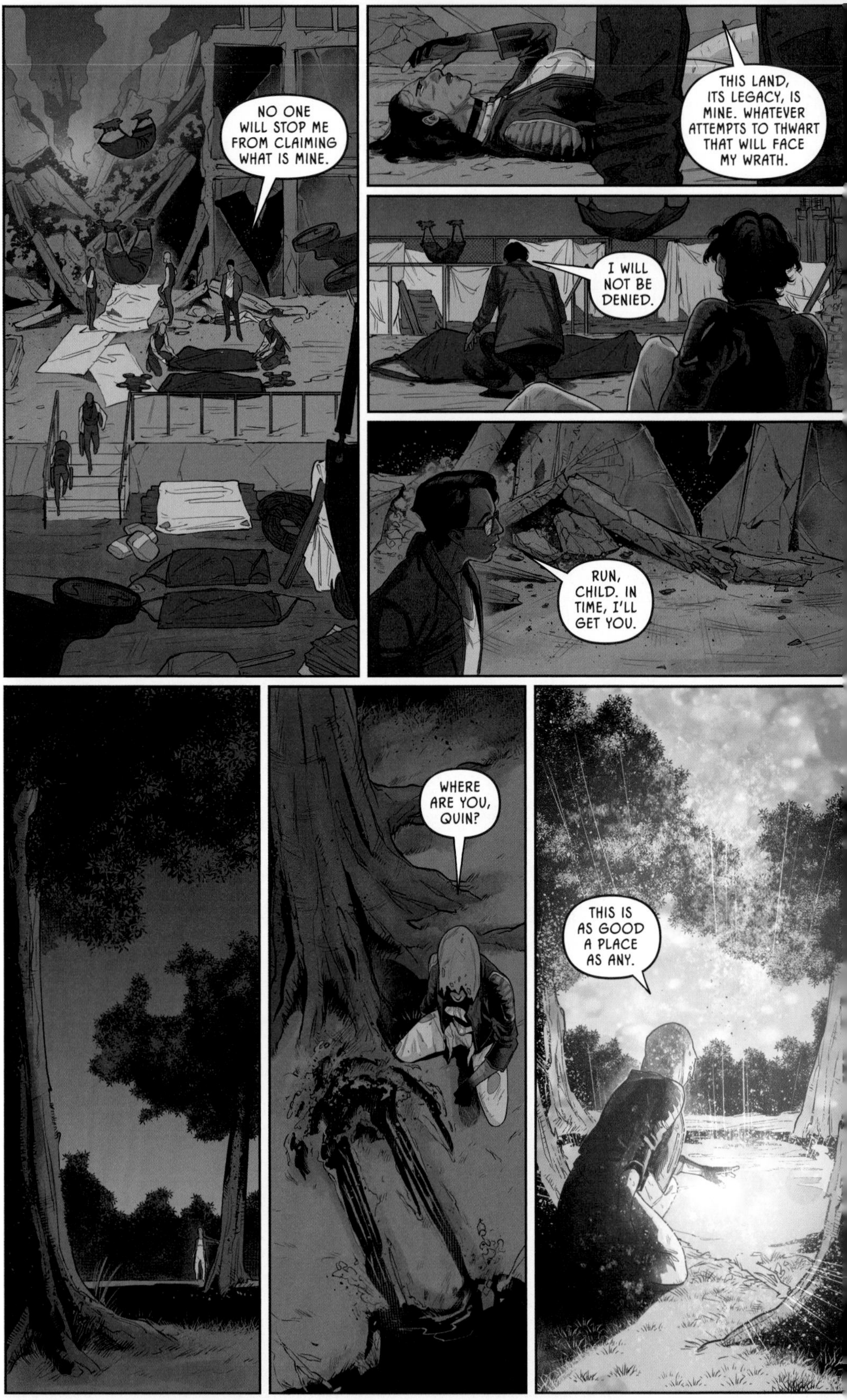
NO ONE WILL STOP ME FROM CLAIMING WHAT IS MINE.
THIS LAND, ITS LEGACY, IS MINE. WHATEVER ATTEMPTS TO THWART THAT WILL FACE MY WRATH.
I WILL NOT BE DENIED.
RUN, CHILD. IN TIME, I'LL GET YOU.
WHERE ARE YOU, QUIN?
THIS IS AS GOOD A PLACE AS ANY.

DEVERAUX?

NO, THAT'S MY FRIEND GLOW.

I HAVE TO GO. ONCE I GET MY HEAD TOGETHER I'LL COME BACK. BUT PLEASE, THINK ABOUT TALKING TO BRITTANY.

I WILL.

LATER, ROU.

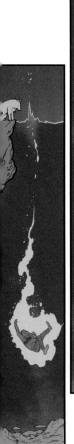

YOU OKAY?

YEAH. BUT I HAVE TO GET HOME.

THERE'S WORK TO DO.

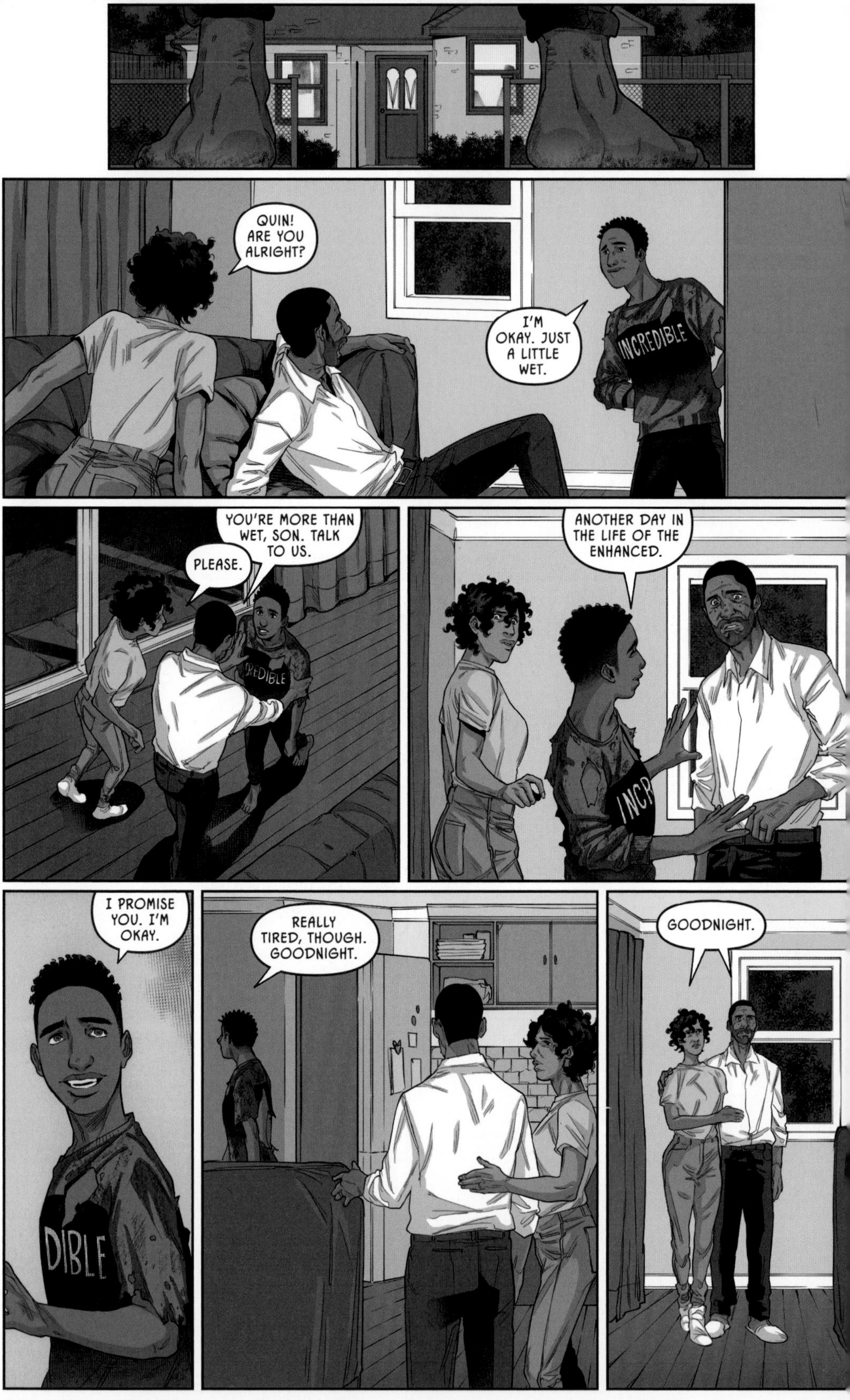
QUIN! ARE YOU ALRIGHT?
I'M OKAY. JUST A LITTLE WET.
INCREDIBLE
YOU'RE MORE THAN WET, SON. TALK TO US.
PLEASE.
ANOTHER DAY IN THE LIFE OF THE ENHANCED.
I PROMISE YOU. I'M OKAY.
DIBLE
REALLY TIRED, THOUGH. GOODNIGHT.
GOODNIGHT.

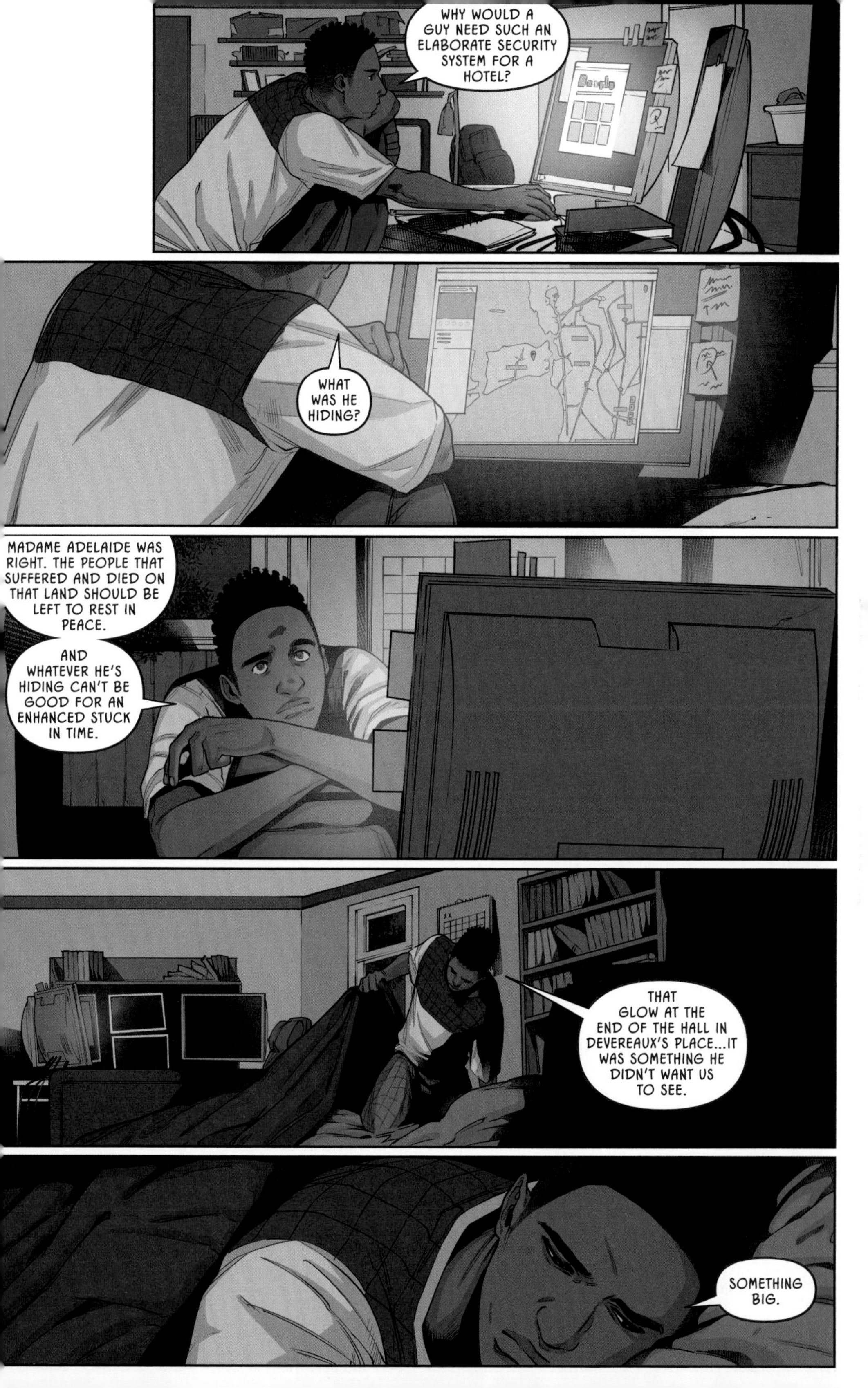
WHY WOULD A GUY NEED SUCH AN ELABORATE SECURITY SYSTEM FOR A HOTEL?
WHAT WAS HE HIDING?
MADAME ADELAIDE WAS RIGHT. THE PEOPLE THAT SUFFERED AND DIED ON THAT LAND SHOULD BE LEFT TO REST IN PEACE.
AND WHATEVER HE'S HIDING CAN'T BE GOOD FOR AN ENHANCED STUCK IN TIME.
THAT GLOW AT THE END OF THE HALL IN DEVEREAUX'S PLACE...IT WAS SOMETHING HE DIDN'T WANT US TO SEE.
SOMETHING BIG.

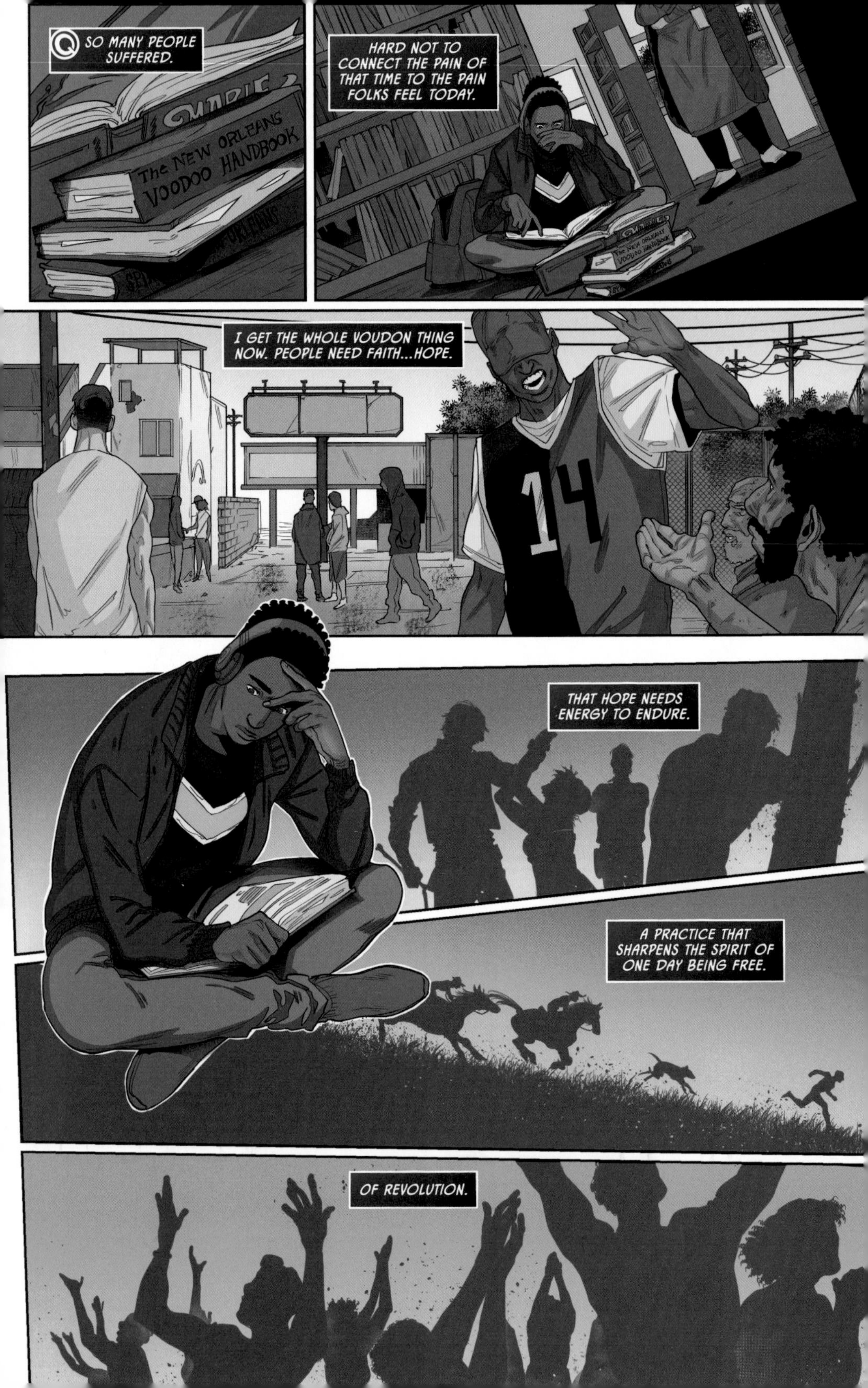
SO MANY PEOPLE SUFFERED.
The NEW ORLEANS VOODOO HANDBOOK
HARD NOT TO CONNECT THE PAIN OF THAT TIME TO THE PAIN FOLKS FEEL TODAY.
I GET THE WHOLE VOUDON THING NOW. PEOPLE NEED FAITH...HOPE.
14
THAT HOPE NEEDS ENERGY TO ENDURE.
A PRACTICE THAT SHARPENS THE SPIRIT OF ONE DAY BEING FREE.
OF REVOLUTION.

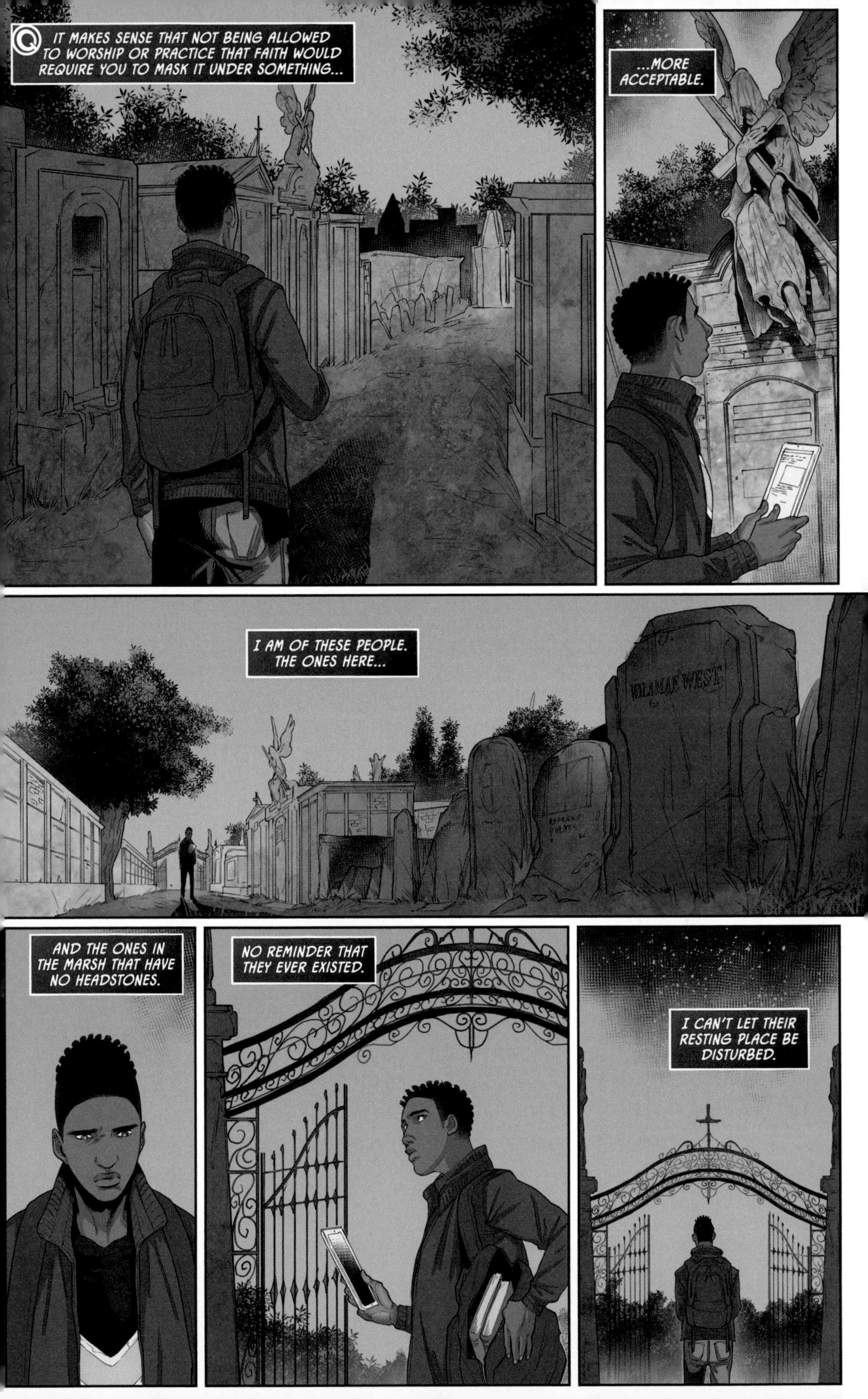
IT MAKES SENSE THAT NOT BEING ALLOWED TO WORSHIP OR PRACTICE THAT FAITH WOULD REQUIRE YOU TO MASK IT UNDER SOMETHING...
...MORE ACCEPTABLE.
I AM OF THESE PEOPLE. THE ONES HERE...
AND THE ONES IN THE MARSH THAT HAVE NO HEADSTONES.
NO REMINDER THAT THEY EVER EXISTED.
I CAN'T LET THEIR RESTING PLACE BE DISTURBED.

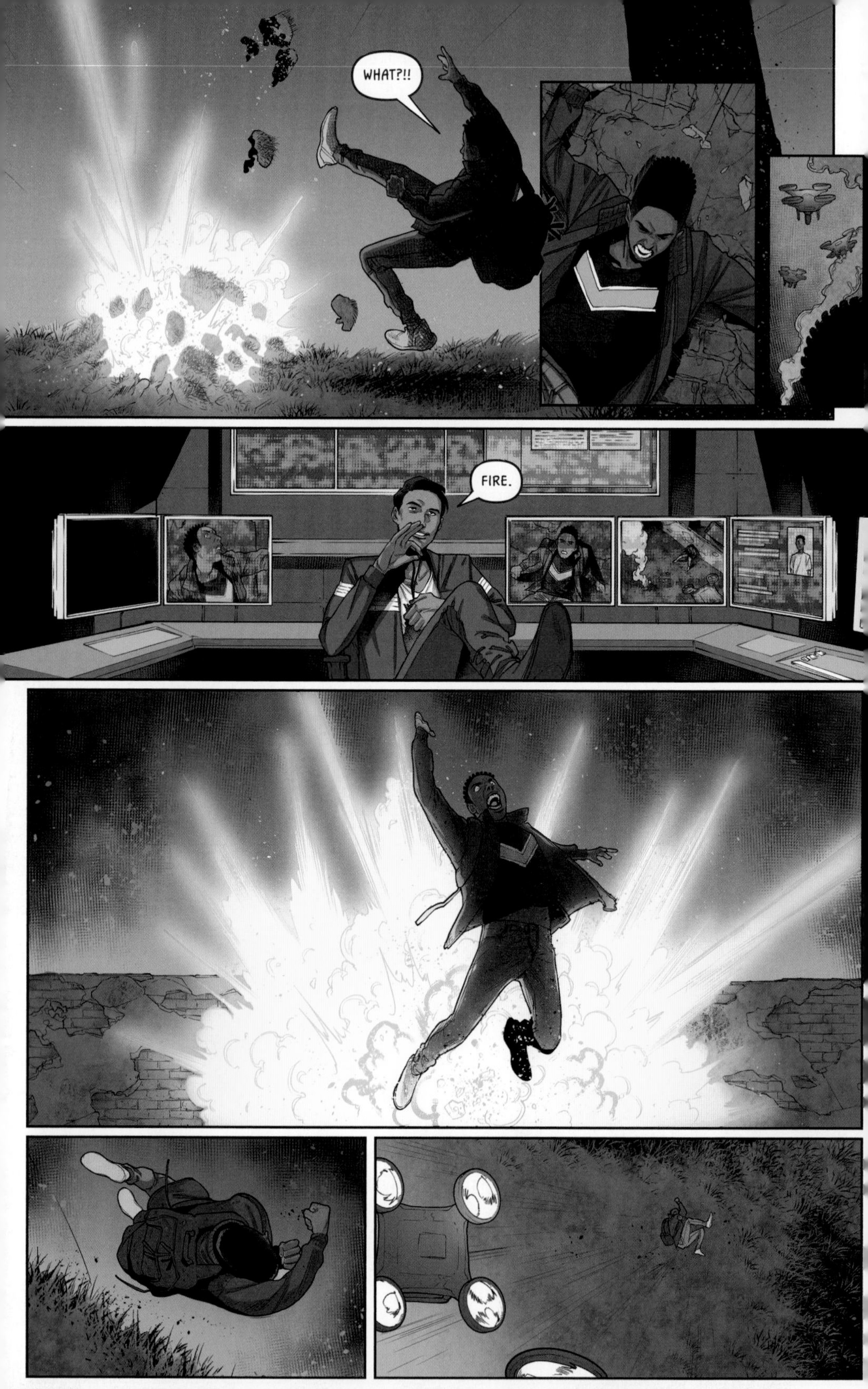
WHAT?!!
FIRE.

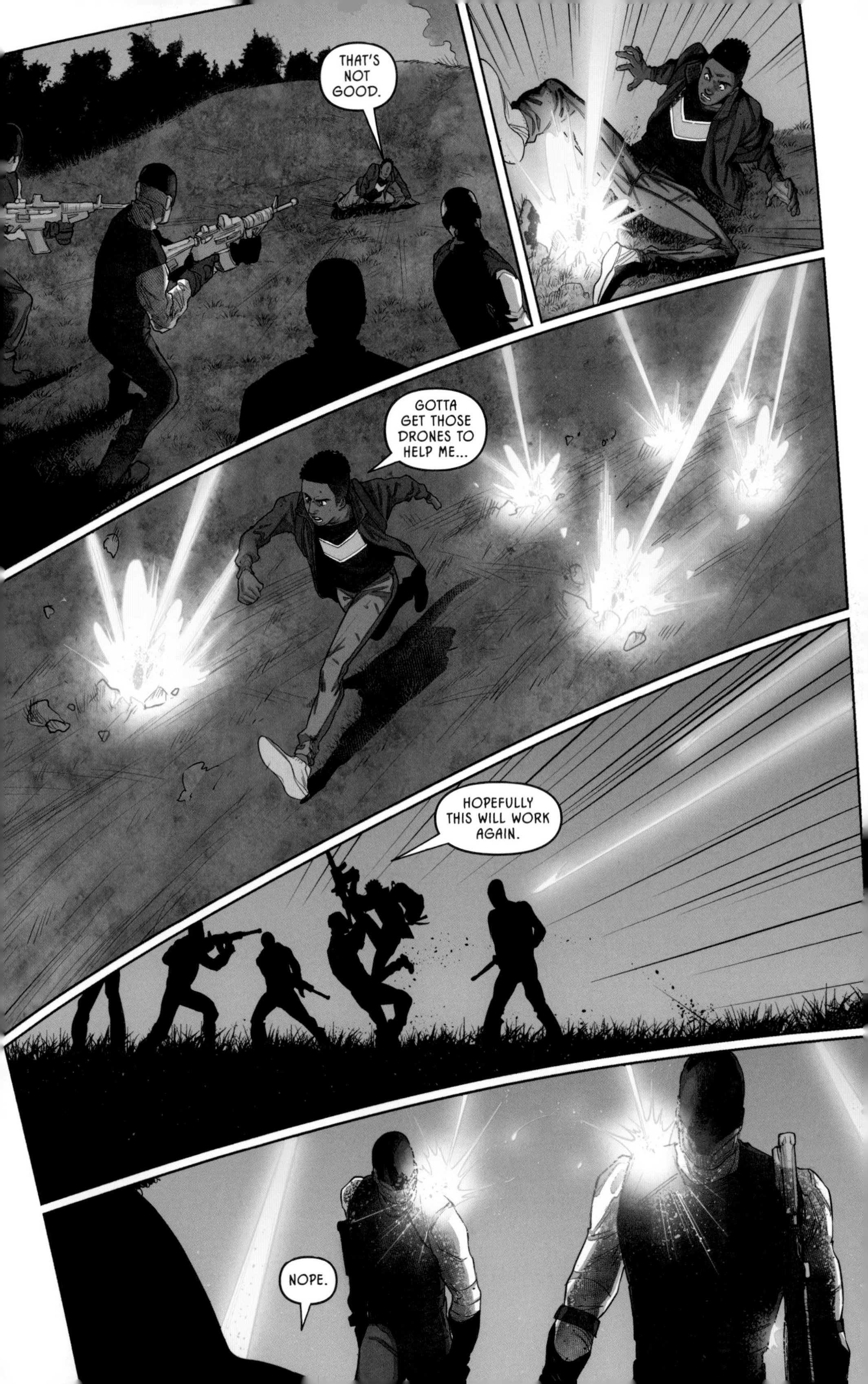
THAT'S NOT GOOD.
GOTTA GET THOSE DRONES TO HELP ME...
HOPEFULLY THIS WILL WORK AGAIN.
NOPE.

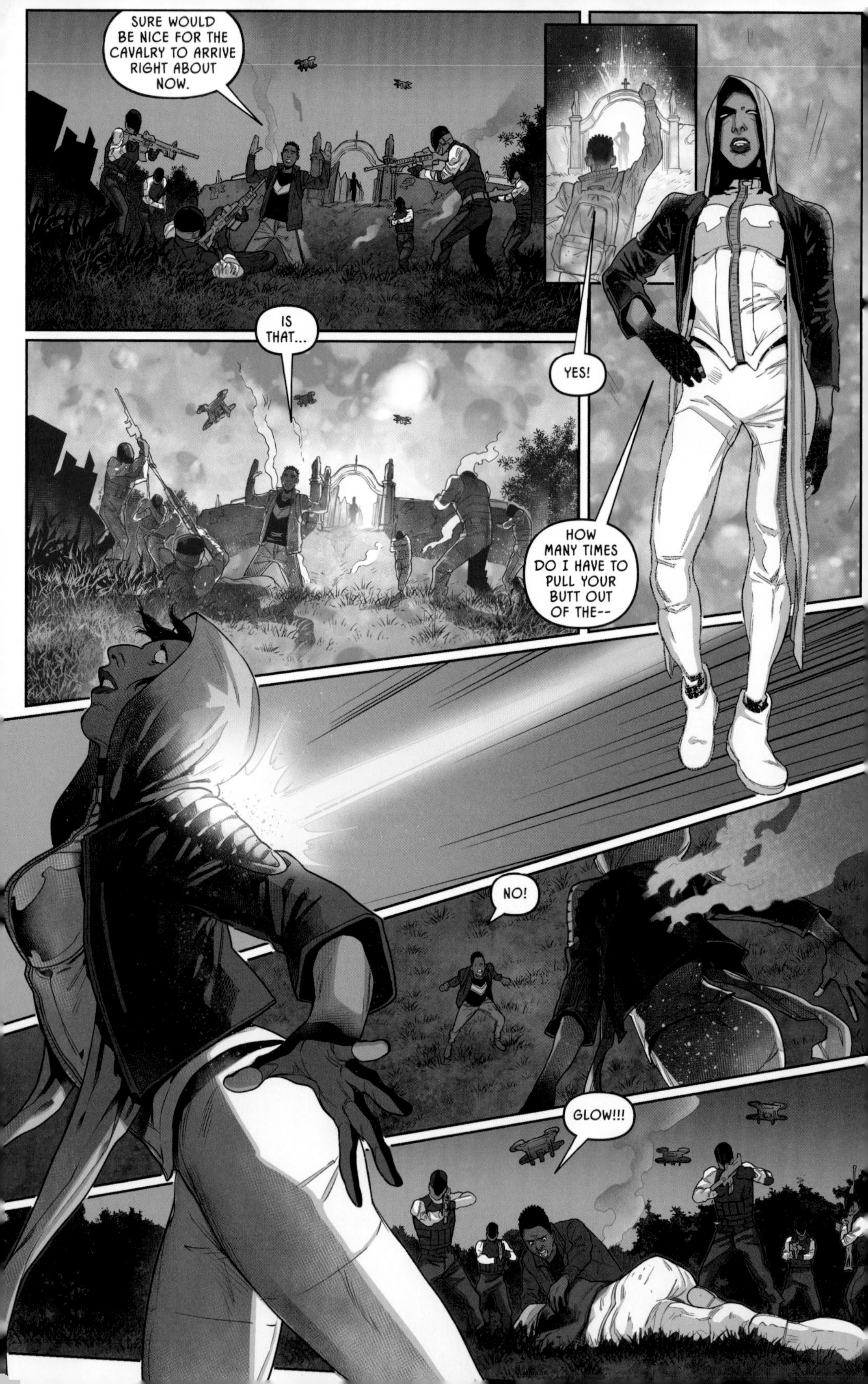
SURE WOULD BE NICE FOR THE CAVALRY TO ARRIVE RIGHT ABOUT NOW.
YES!
HOW MANY TIMES DO I HAVE TO PULL YOUR BUTT OUT OF THE--
IS THAT...
NO!
GLOW!!!

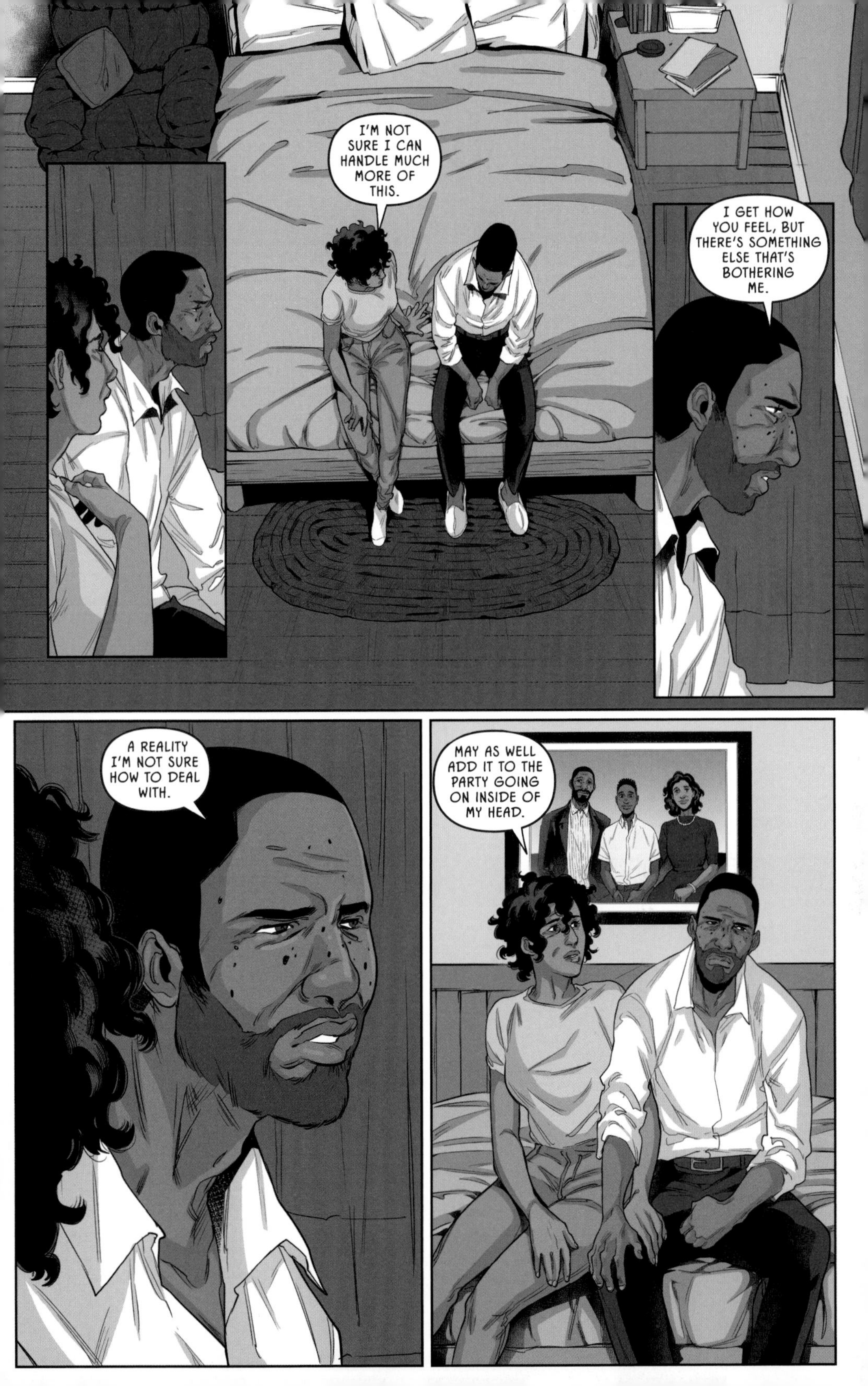
I'M NOT SURE I CAN HANDLE MUCH MORE OF THIS.
I GET HOW YOU FEEL, BUT THERE'S SOMETHING ELSE THAT'S BOTHERING ME.
A REALITY I'M NOT SURE HOW TO DEAL WITH.
MAY AS WELL ADD IT TO THE PARTY GOING ON INSIDE OF MY HEAD.

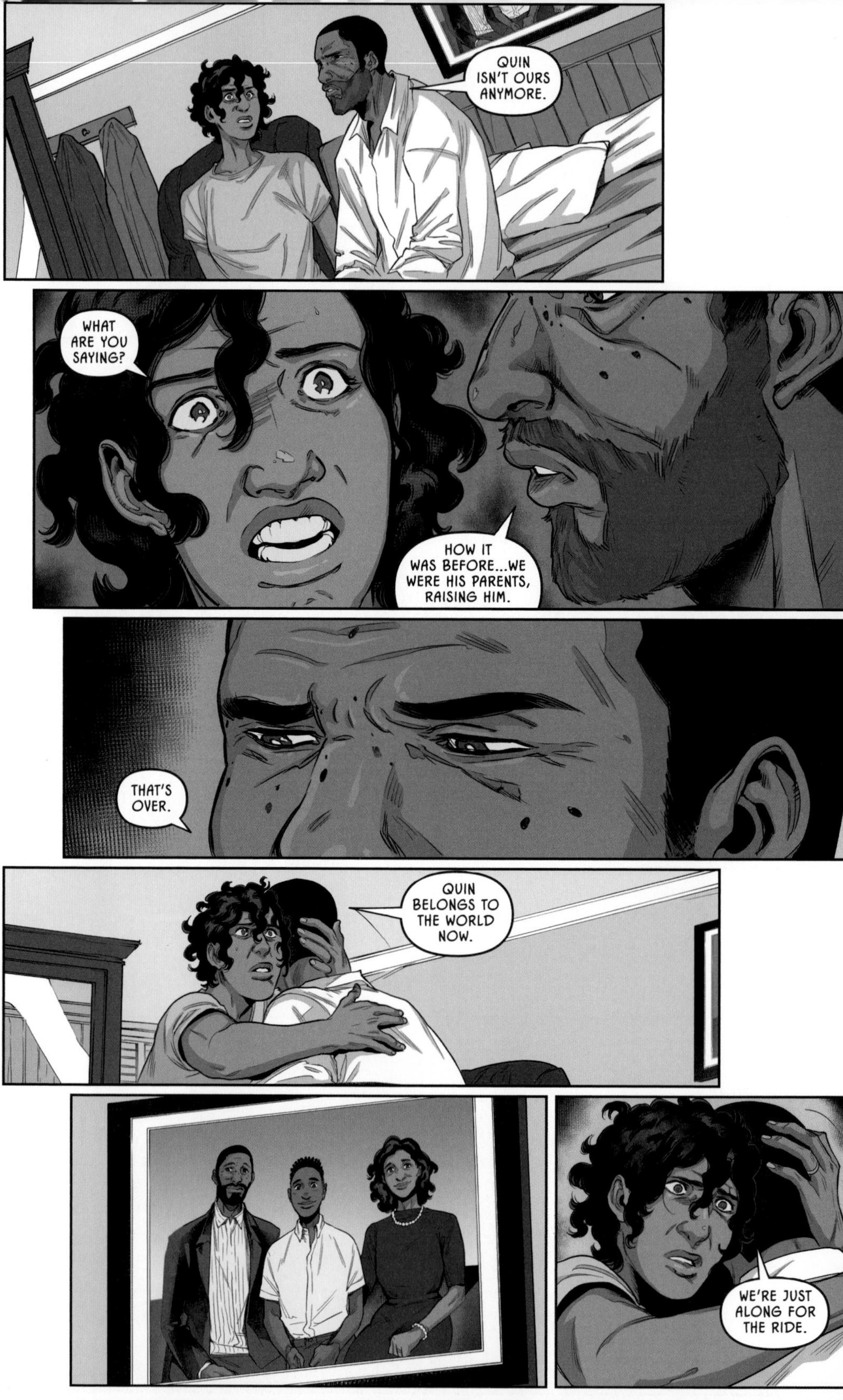
QUIN ISN'T OURS ANYMORE.
WHAT ARE YOU SAYING?
HOW IT WAS BEFORE...WE WERE HIS PARENTS, RAISING HIM.
THAT'S OVER.
QUIN BELONGS TO THE WORLD NOW.
WE'RE JUST ALONG FOR THE RIDE.

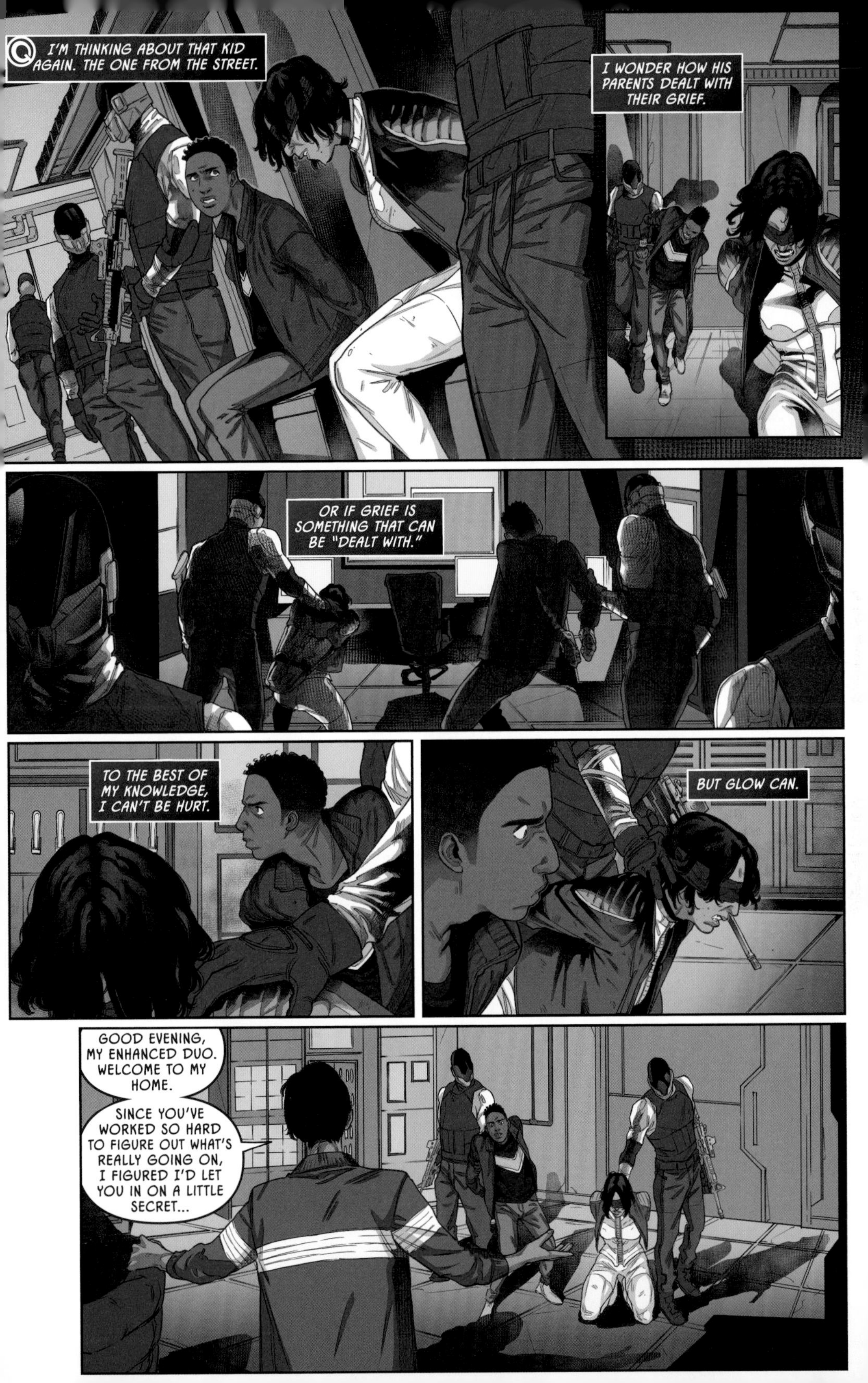
I'M THINKING ABOUT THAT KID AGAIN. THE ONE FROM THE STREET.
I WONDER HOW HIS PARENTS DEALT WITH THEIR GRIEF.
OR IF GRIEF IS SOMETHING THAT CAN BE "DEALT WITH."
TO THE BEST OF MY KNOWLEDGE, I CAN'T BE HURT.
BUT GLOW CAN.
GOOD EVENING, MY ENHANCED DUO. WELCOME TO MY HOME.
SINCE YOU'VE WORKED SO HARD TO FIGURE OUT WHAT'S REALLY GOING ON, I FIGURED I'D LET YOU IN ON A LITTLE SECRET...

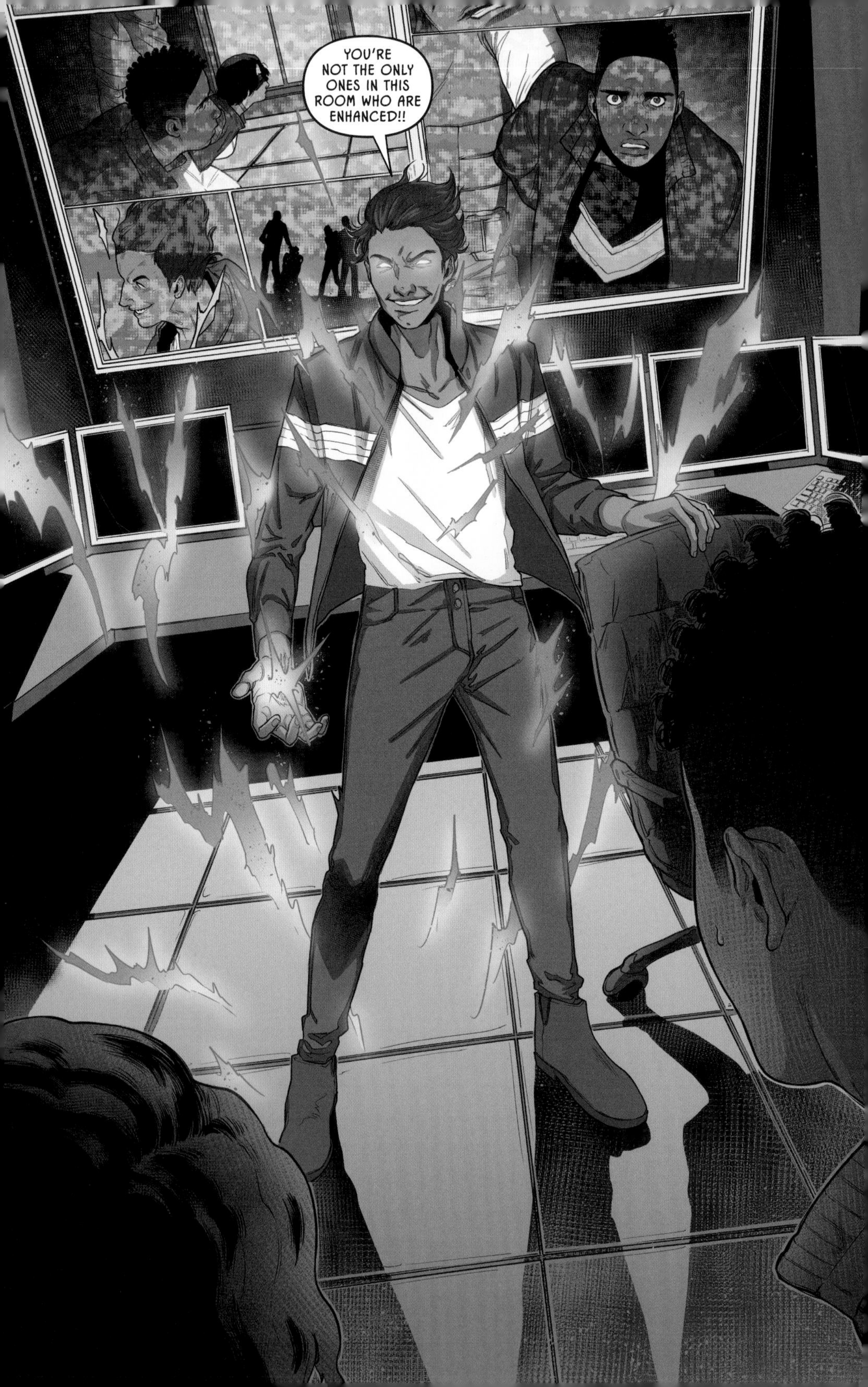
YOU'RE NOT THE ONLY ONES IN THIS ROOM WHO ARE ENHANCED!!

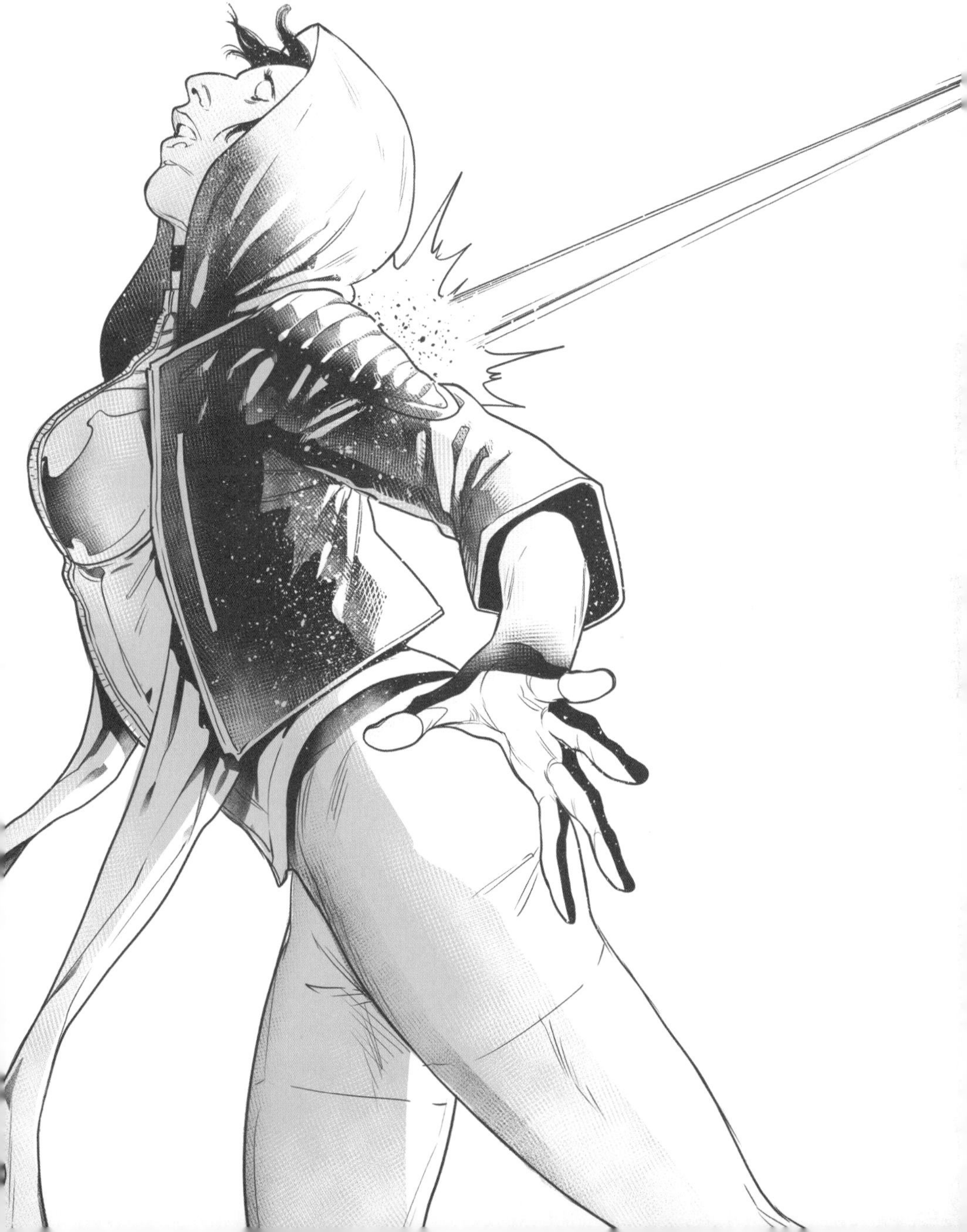

CHAPTER FOUR

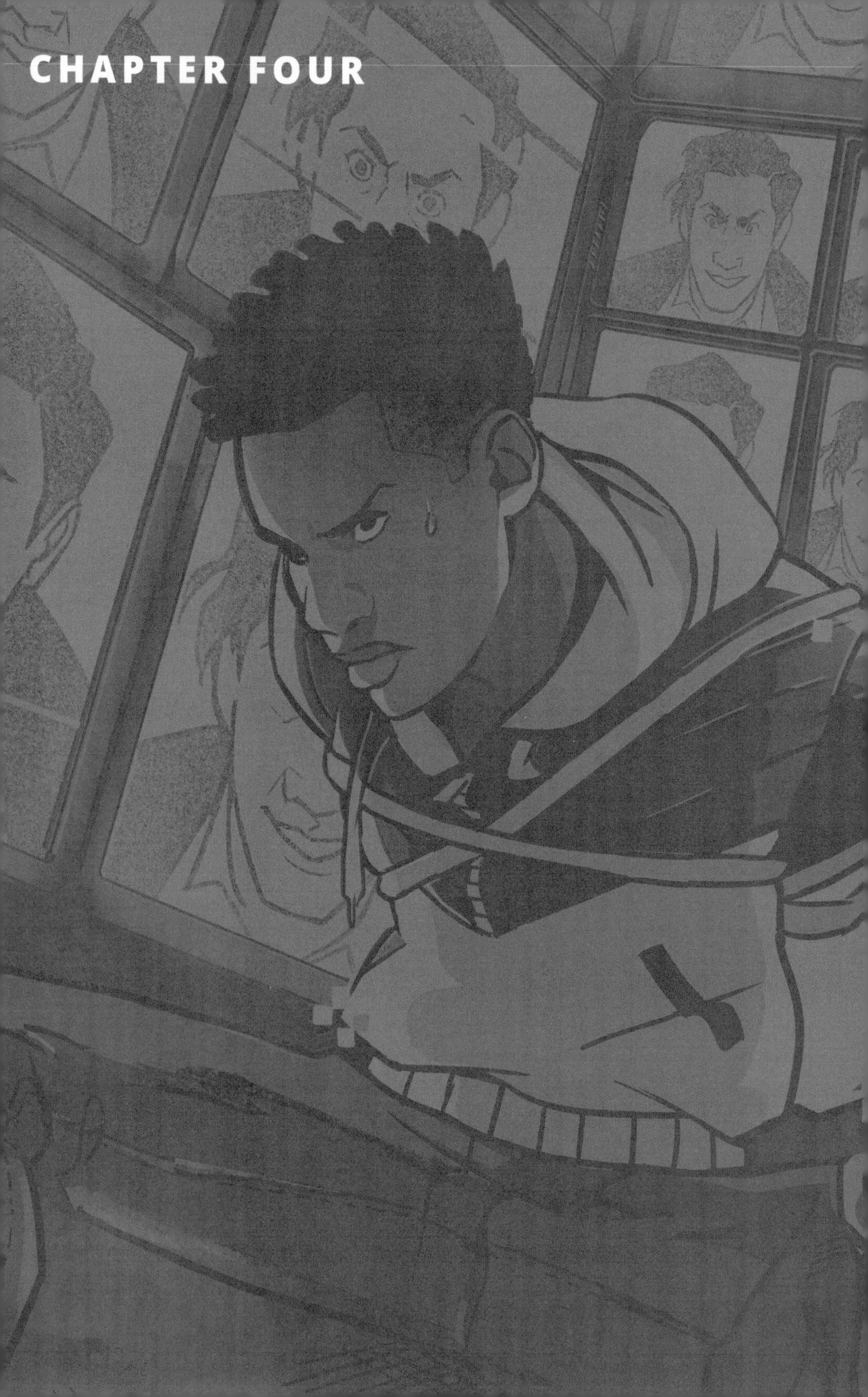

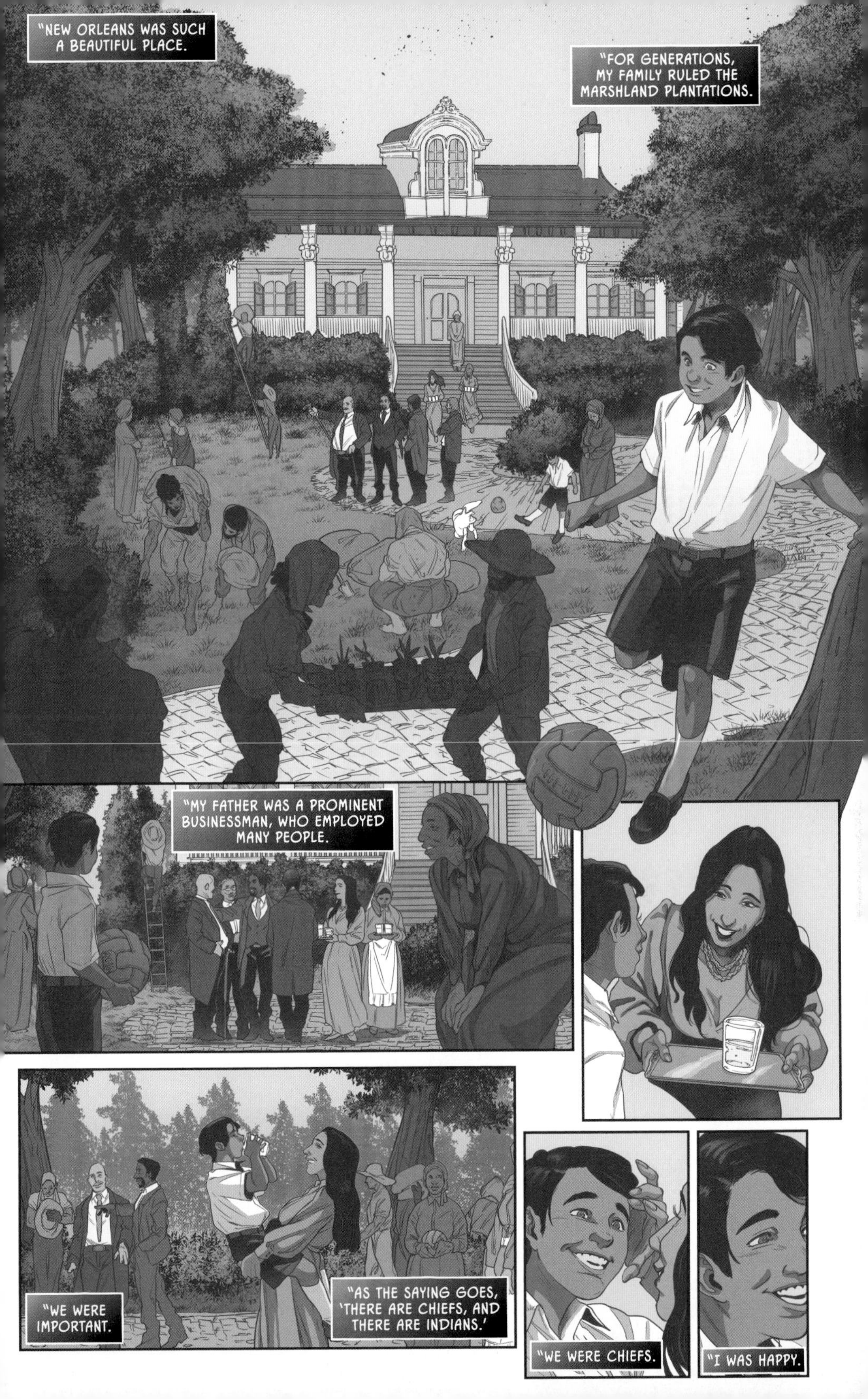
"NEW ORLEANS WAS SUCH A BEAUTIFUL PLACE.
"FOR GENERATIONS, MY FAMILY RULED THE MARSHLAND PLANTATIONS.
"MY FATHER WAS A PROMINENT BUSINESSMAN, WHO EMPLOYED MANY PEOPLE.
"WE WERE IMPORTANT.
"AS THE SAYING GOES, 'THERE ARE CHIEFS, AND THERE ARE INDIANS.'
"WE WERE CHIEFS.
"I WAS HAPPY.

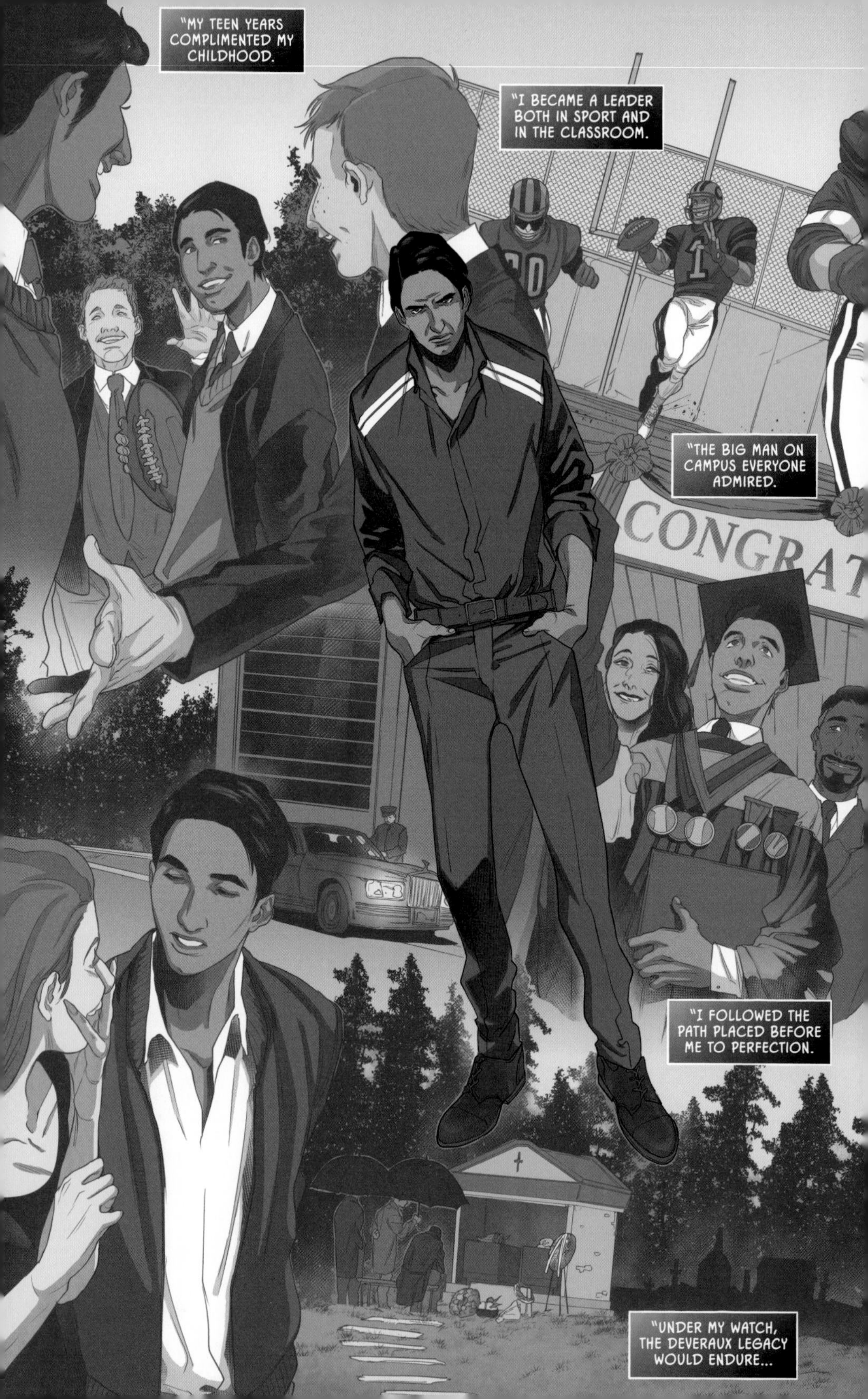
"MY TEEN YEARS COMPLIMENTED MY CHILDHOOD.
"I BECAME A LEADER BOTH IN SPORT AND IN THE CLASSROOM.
"THE BIG MAN ON CAMPUS EVERYONE ADMIRED.
CONGRAT
"I FOLLOWED THE PATH PLACED BEFORE ME TO PERFECTION.
"UNDER MY WATCH, THE DEVERAUX LEGACY WOULD ENDURE...

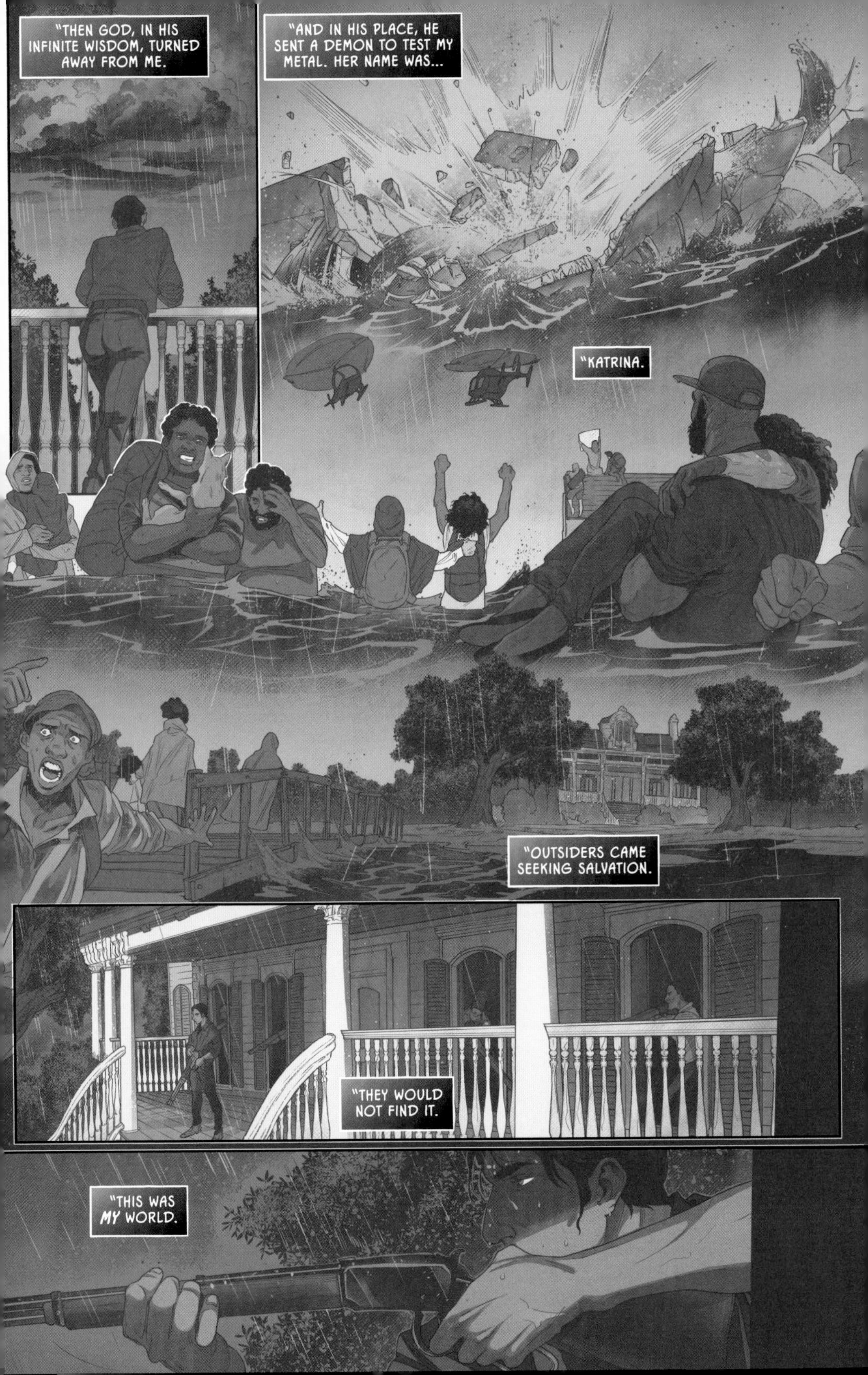
"THEN GOD, IN HIS INFINITE WISDOM, TURNED AWAY FROM ME.
"AND IN HIS PLACE, HE SENT A DEMON TO TEST MY METAL. HER NAME WAS...
"KATRINA.
"OUTSIDERS CAME SEEKING SALVATION.
"THEY WOULD NOT FIND IT.
"THIS WAS *MY* WORLD.

"MINE ALONE.

"BUT KATRINA HAD OPENED A DOOR.

"ONE THAT ASKED QUESTIONS ABOUT CIVILITY AND ORDER.

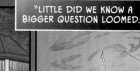

"LITTLE DID WE KNOW A BIGGER QUESTION LOOMED.

"ONE THAT WOULD CHANGE *EVERYTHING*.

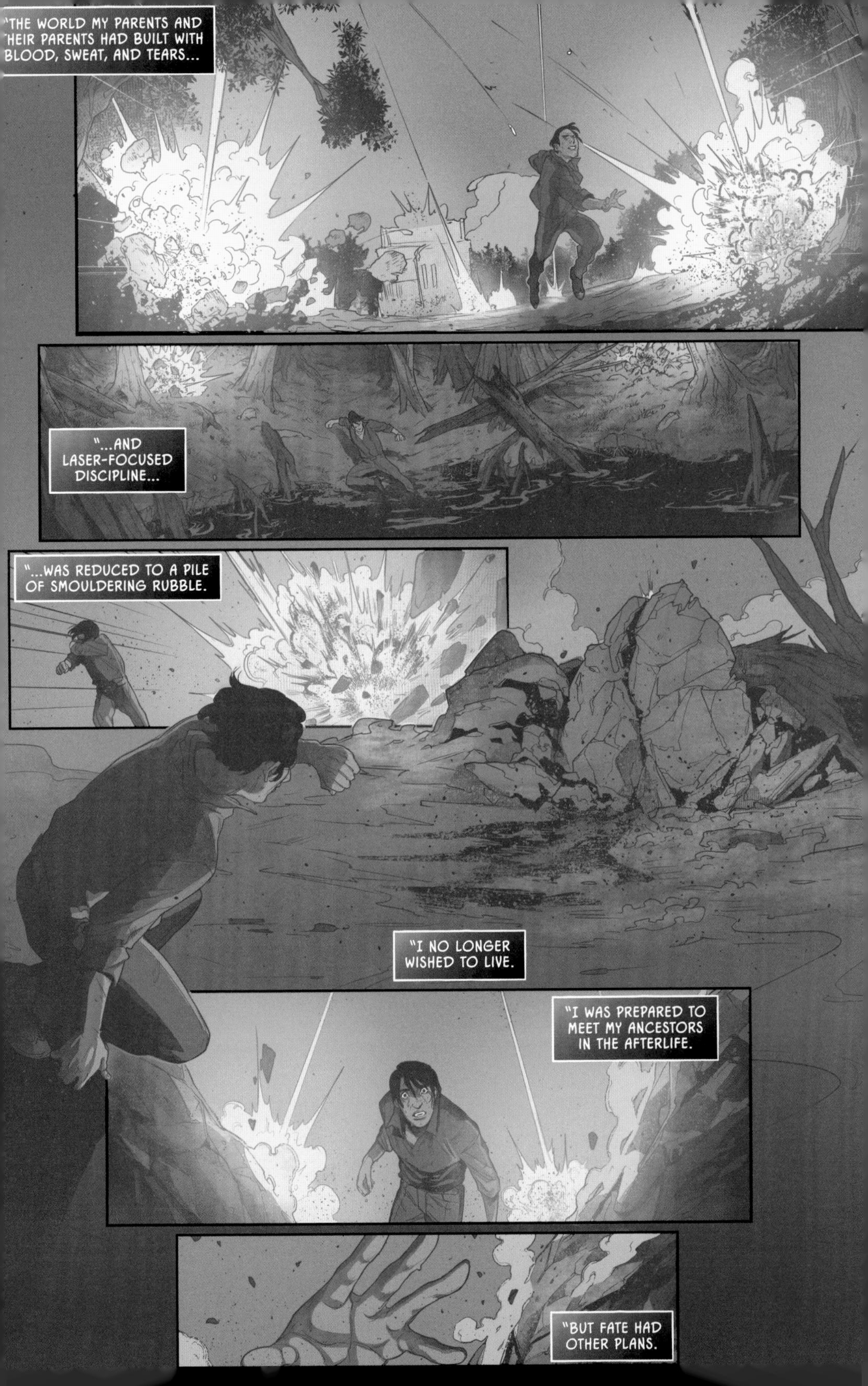
"THE WORLD MY PARENTS AND THEIR PARENTS HAD BUILT WITH BLOOD, SWEAT, AND TEARS...
"...AND LASER-FOCUSED DISCIPLINE...
"...WAS REDUCED TO A PILE OF SMOULDERING RUBBLE.
"I NO LONGER WISHED TO LIVE.
"I WAS PREPARED TO MEET MY ANCESTORS IN THE AFTERLIFE.
"BUT FATE HAD OTHER PLANS.

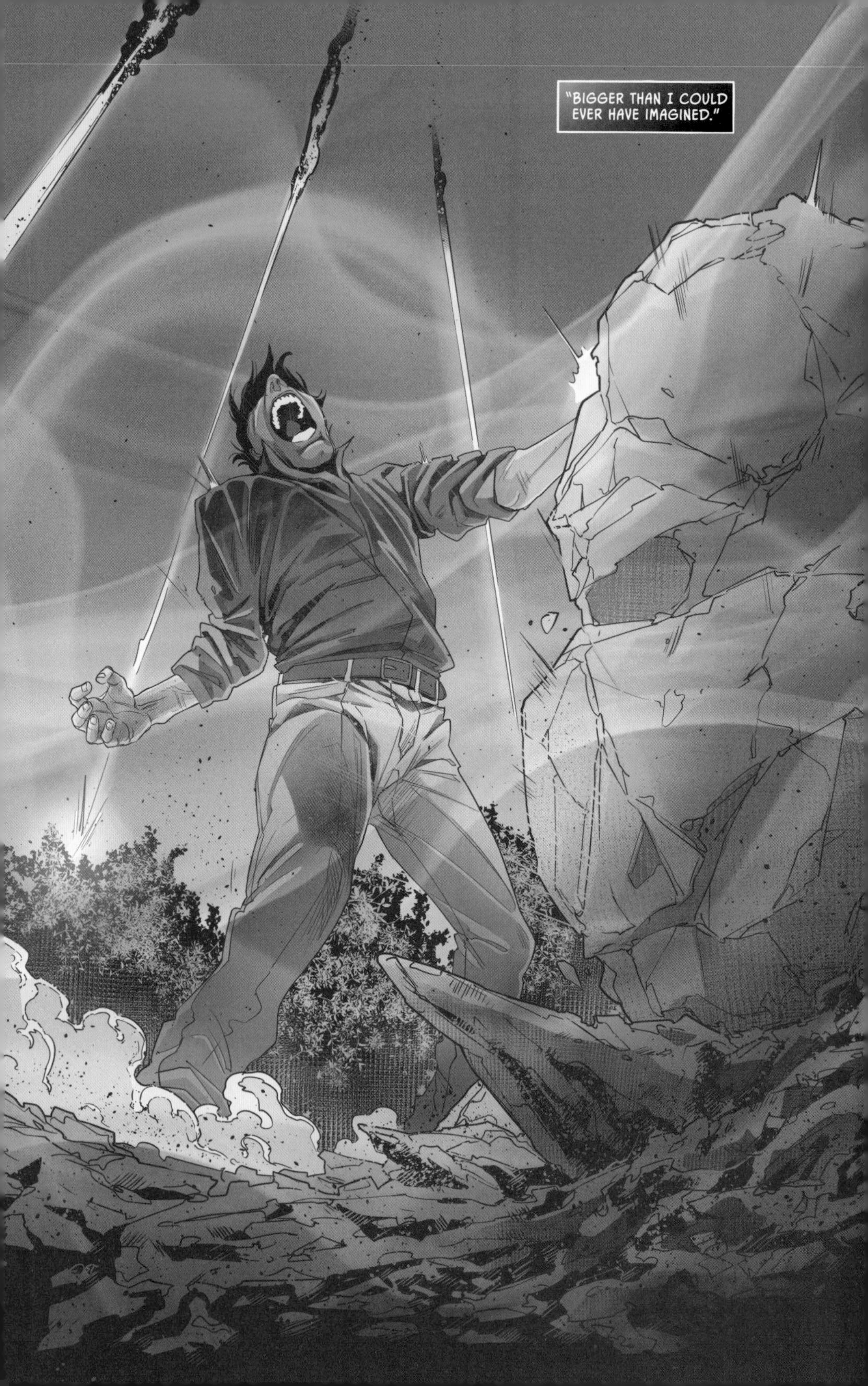
"BIGGER THAN I COULD EVER HAVE IMAGINED."

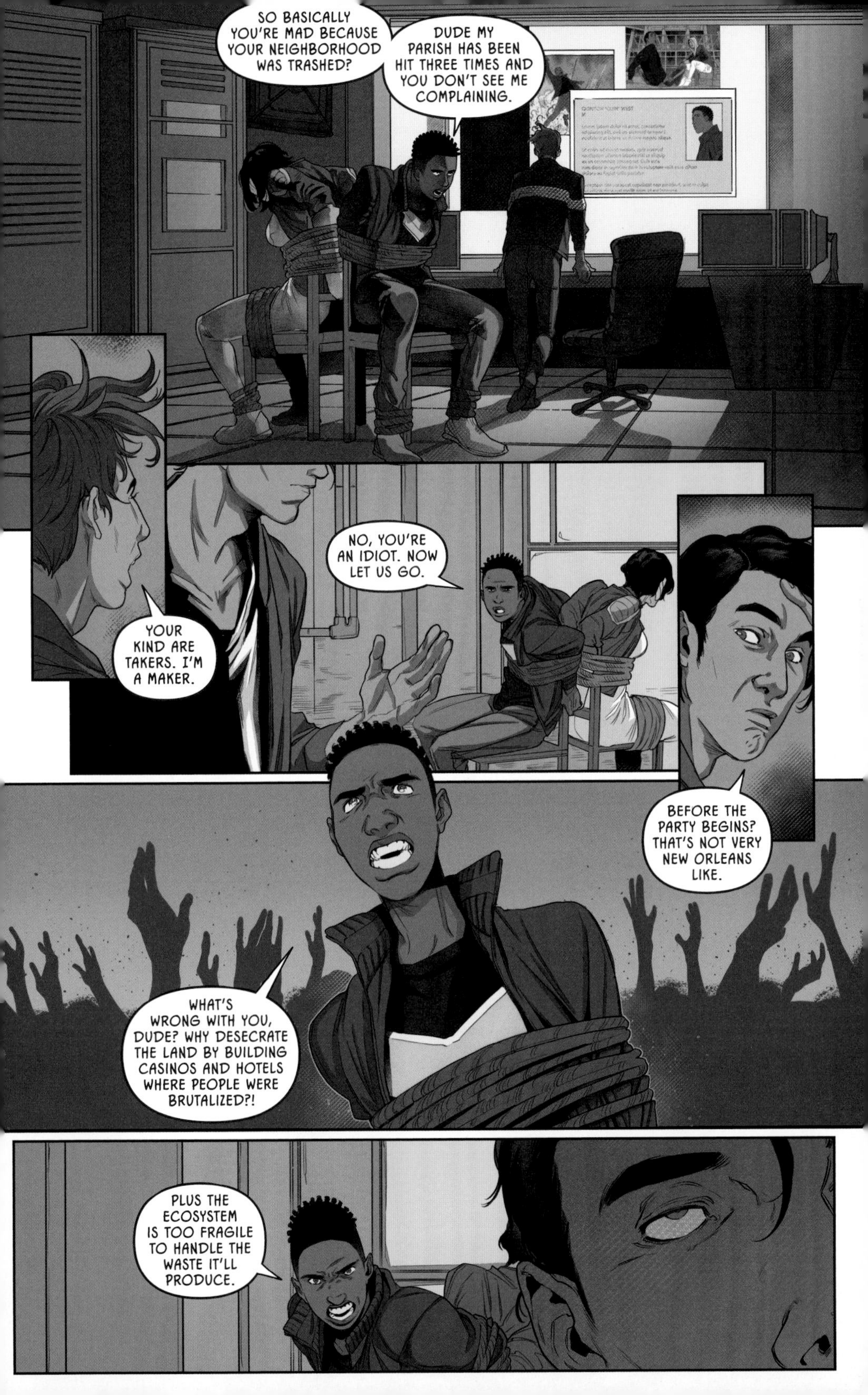
SO BASICALLY YOU'RE MAD BECAUSE YOUR NEIGHBORHOOD WAS TRASHED?
DUDE MY PARISH HAS BEEN HIT THREE TIMES AND YOU DON'T SEE ME COMPLAINING.
YOUR KIND ARE TAKERS. I'M A MAKER.
NO, YOU'RE AN IDIOT. NOW LET US GO.
BEFORE THE PARTY BEGINS? THAT'S NOT VERY NEW ORLEANS LIKE.
WHAT'S WRONG WITH YOU, DUDE? WHY DESECRATE THE LAND BY BUILDING CASINOS AND HOTELS WHERE PEOPLE WERE BRUTALIZED?!
PLUS THE ECOSYSTEM IS TOO FRAGILE TO HANDLE THE WASTE IT'LL PRODUCE.

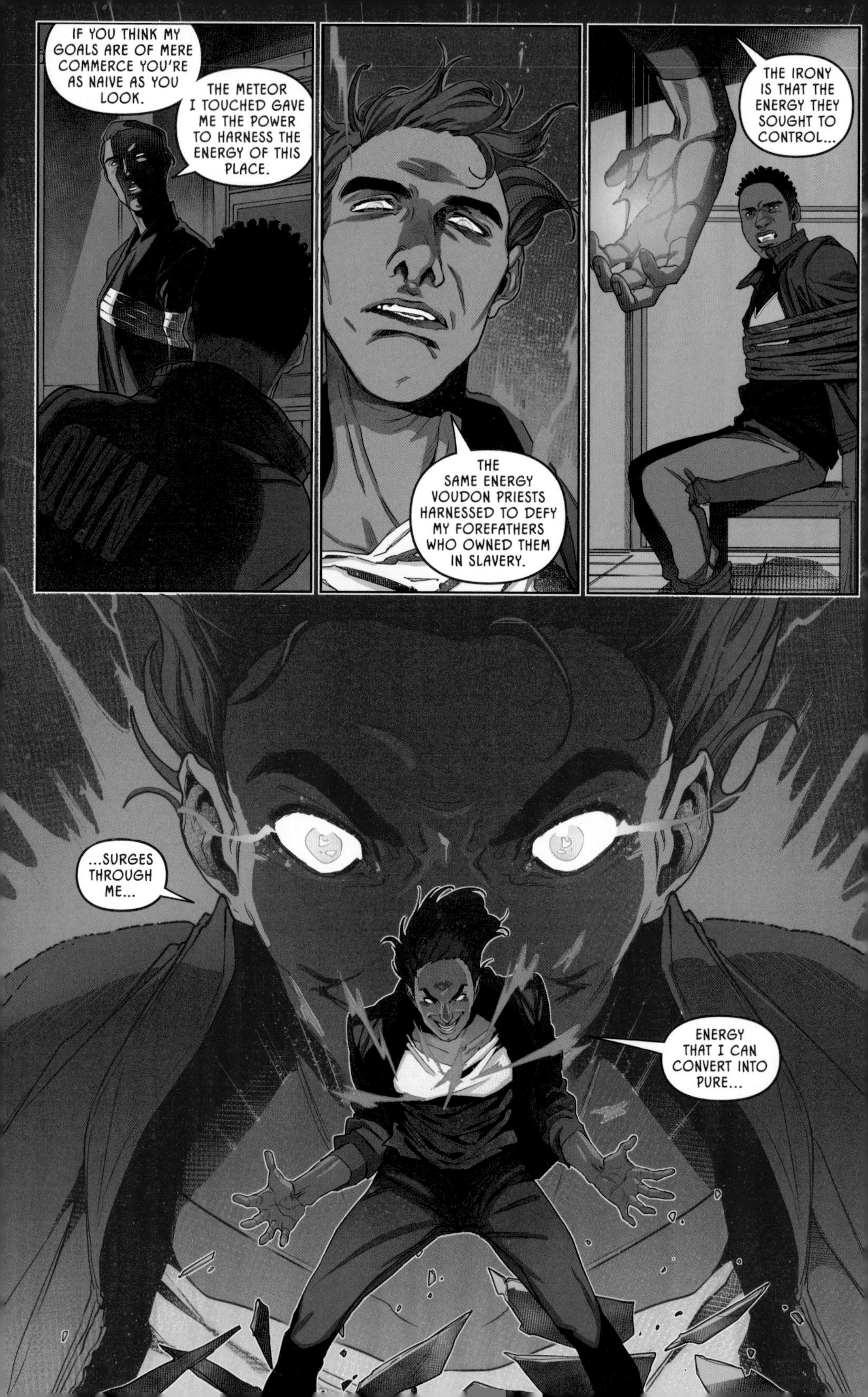
IF YOU THINK MY GOALS ARE OF MERE COMMERCE YOU'RE AS NAIVE AS YOU LOOK.
THE METEOR I TOUCHED GAVE ME THE POWER TO HARNESS THE ENERGY OF THIS PLACE.
THE SAME ENERGY VOUDON PRIESTS HARNESSED TO DEFY MY FOREFATHERS WHO OWNED THEM IN SLAVERY.
THE IRONY IS THAT THE ENERGY THEY SOUGHT TO CONTROL...
...SURGES THROUGH ME...
ENERGY THAT I CAN CONVERT INTO PURE...

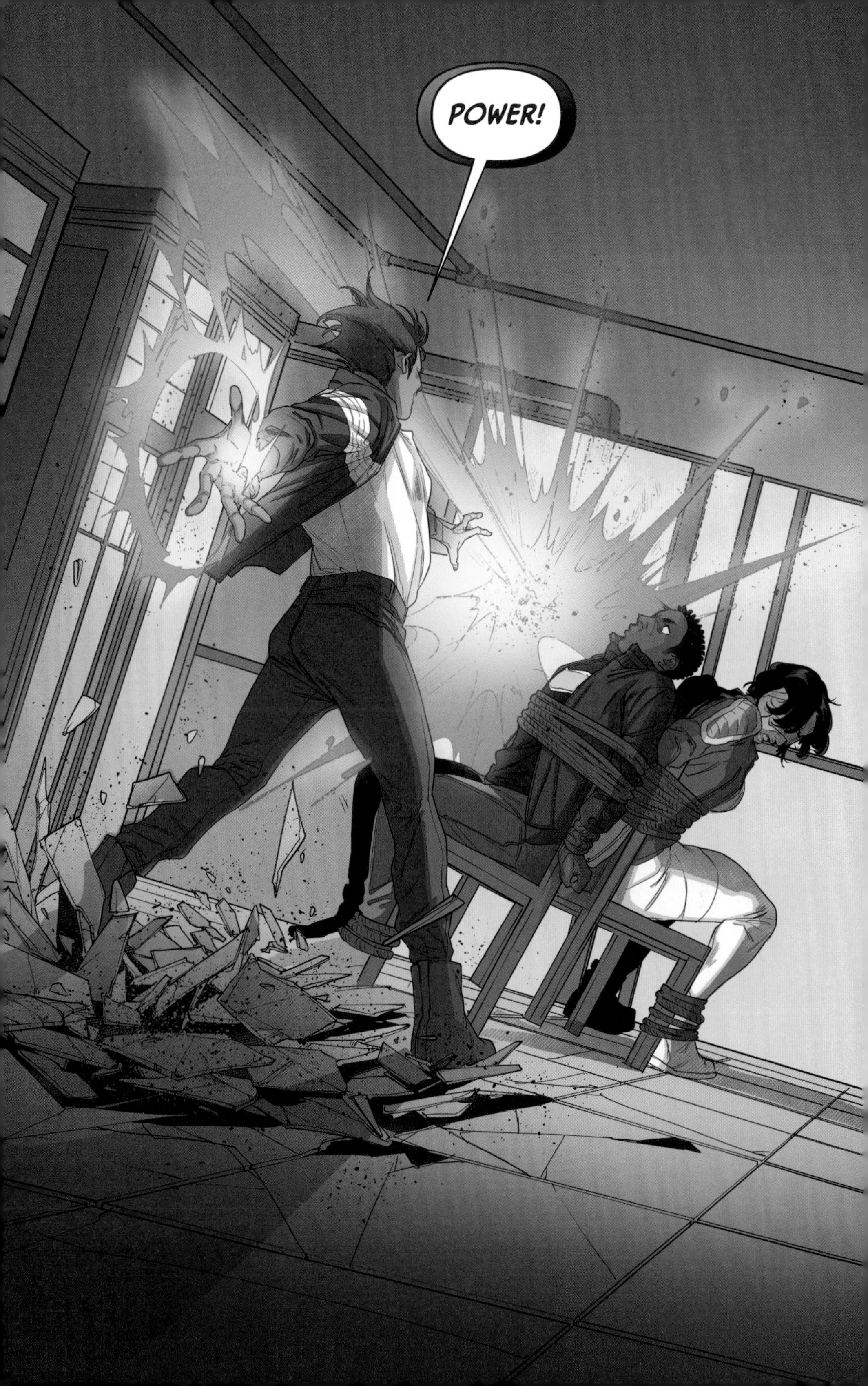
POWER!

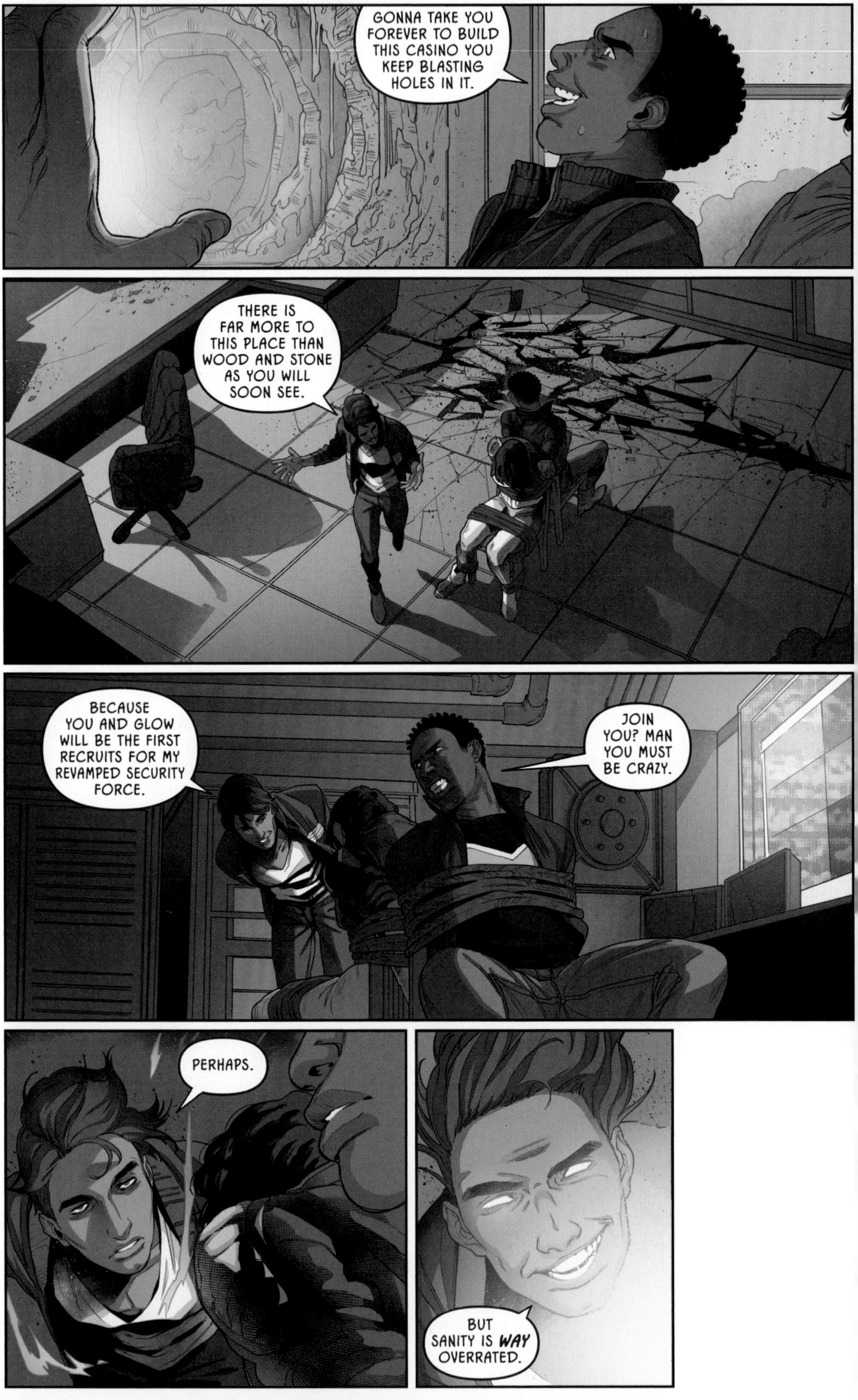
GONNA TAKE YOU FOREVER TO BUILD THIS CASINO YOU KEEP BLASTING HOLES IN IT.
THERE IS FAR MORE TO THIS PLACE THAN WOOD AND STONE AS YOU WILL SOON SEE.
BECAUSE YOU AND GLOW WILL BE THE FIRST RECRUITS FOR MY REVAMPED SECURITY FORCE.
JOIN YOU? MAN YOU MUST BE CRAZY.
PERHAPS.
BUT SANITY IS *WAY* OVERRATED.

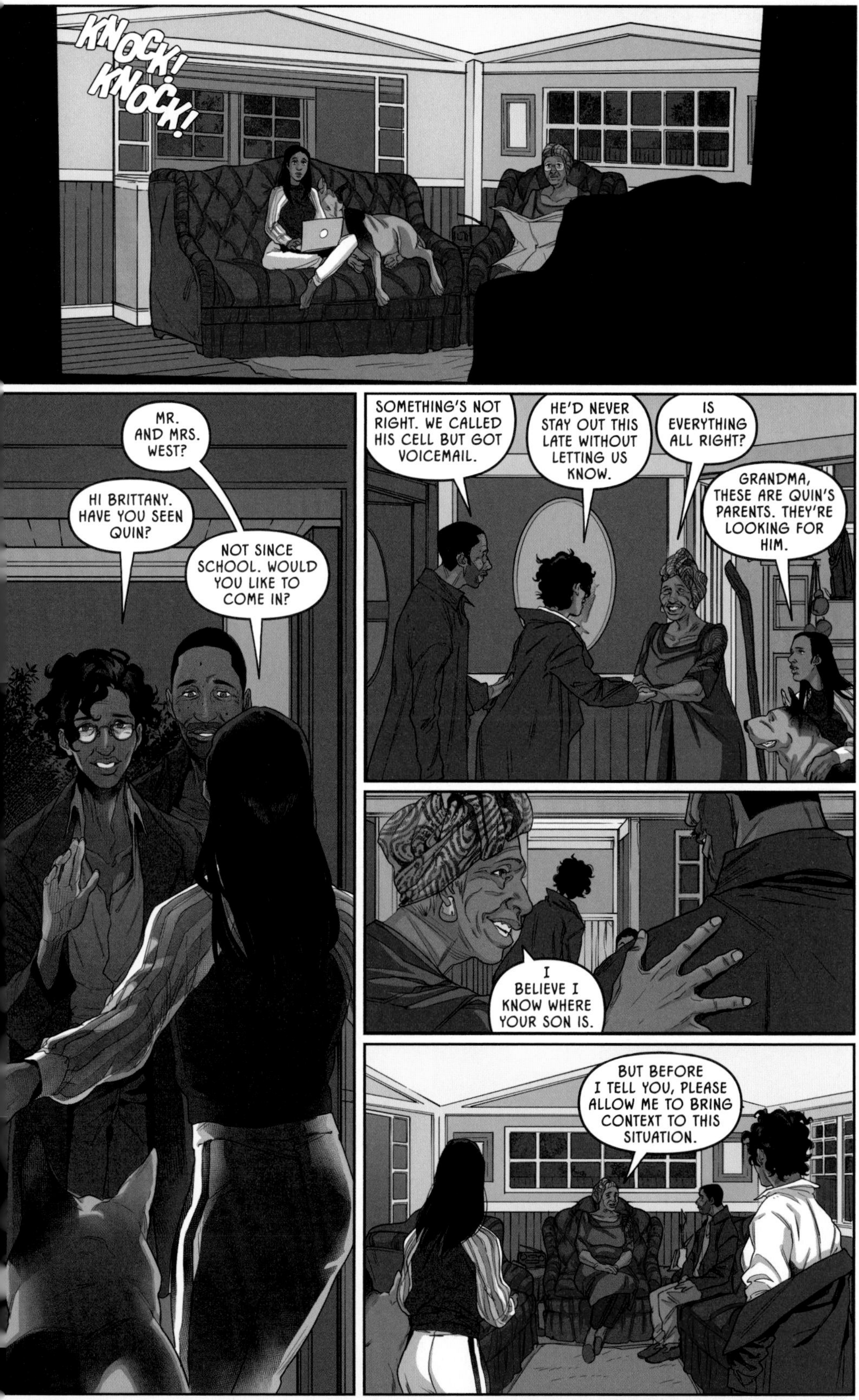
KNOCK! KNOCK!
MR. AND MRS. WEST?
HI BRITTANY. HAVE YOU SEEN QUIN?
NOT SINCE SCHOOL. WOULD YOU LIKE TO COME IN?
SOMETHING'S NOT RIGHT. WE CALLED HIS CELL BUT GOT VOICEMAIL.
HE'D NEVER STAY OUT THIS LATE WITHOUT LETTING US KNOW.
IS EVERYTHING ALL RIGHT?
GRANDMA, THESE ARE QUIN'S PARENTS. THEY'RE LOOKING FOR HIM.
I BELIEVE I KNOW WHERE YOUR SON IS.
BUT BEFORE I TELL YOU, PLEASE ALLOW ME TO BRING CONTEXT TO THIS SITUATION.

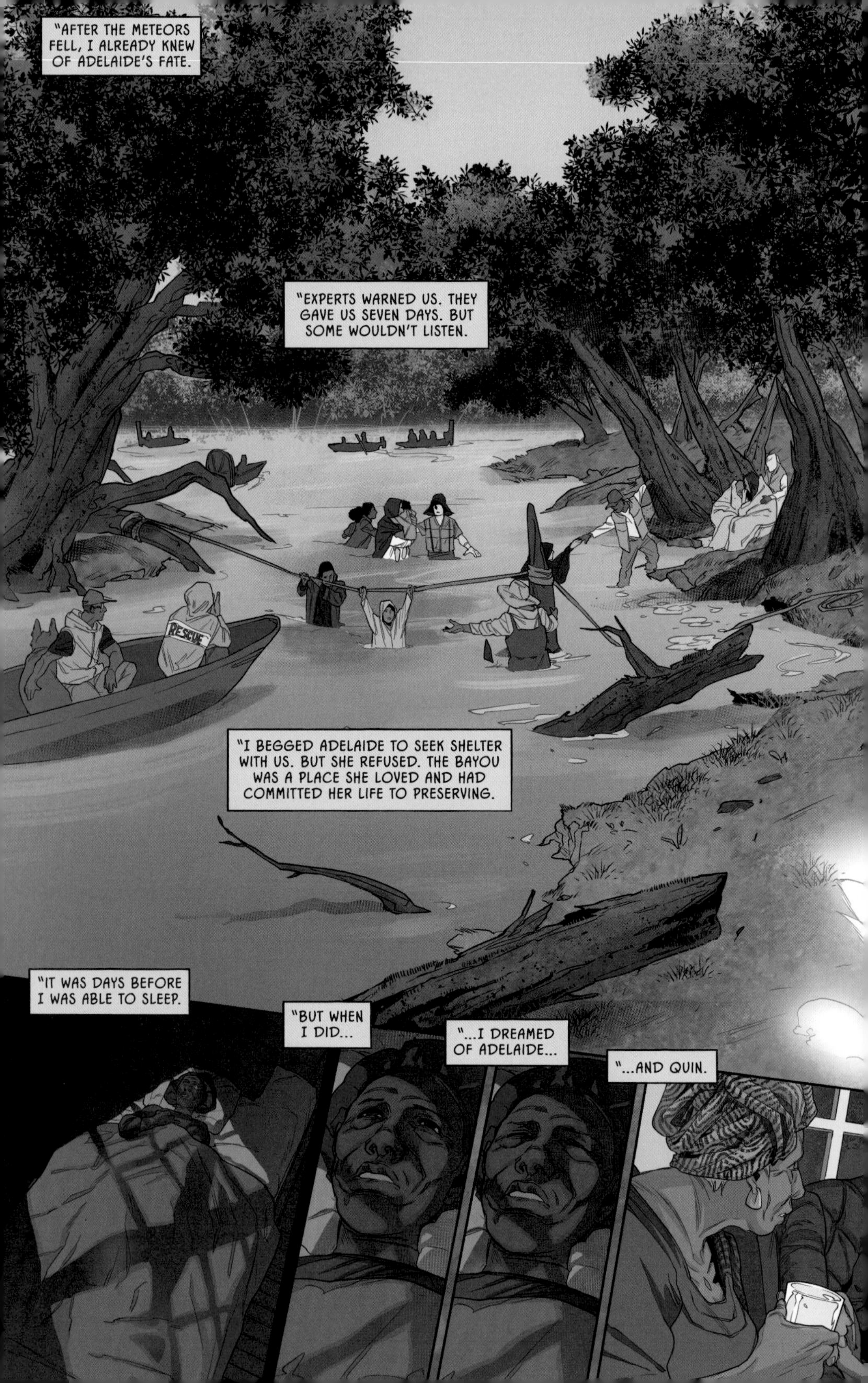
"AFTER THE METEORS FELL, I ALREADY KNEW OF ADELAIDE'S FATE.
"EXPERTS WARNED US. THEY GAVE US SEVEN DAYS. BUT SOME WOULDN'T LISTEN.
RESCUE
"I BEGGED ADELAIDE TO SEEK SHELTER WITH US. BUT SHE REFUSED. THE BAYOU WAS A PLACE SHE LOVED AND HAD COMMITTED HER LIFE TO PRESERVING.
"IT WAS DAYS BEFORE I WAS ABLE TO SLEEP.
"BUT WHEN I DID...
"...I DREAMED OF ADELAIDE...
"...AND QUIN.

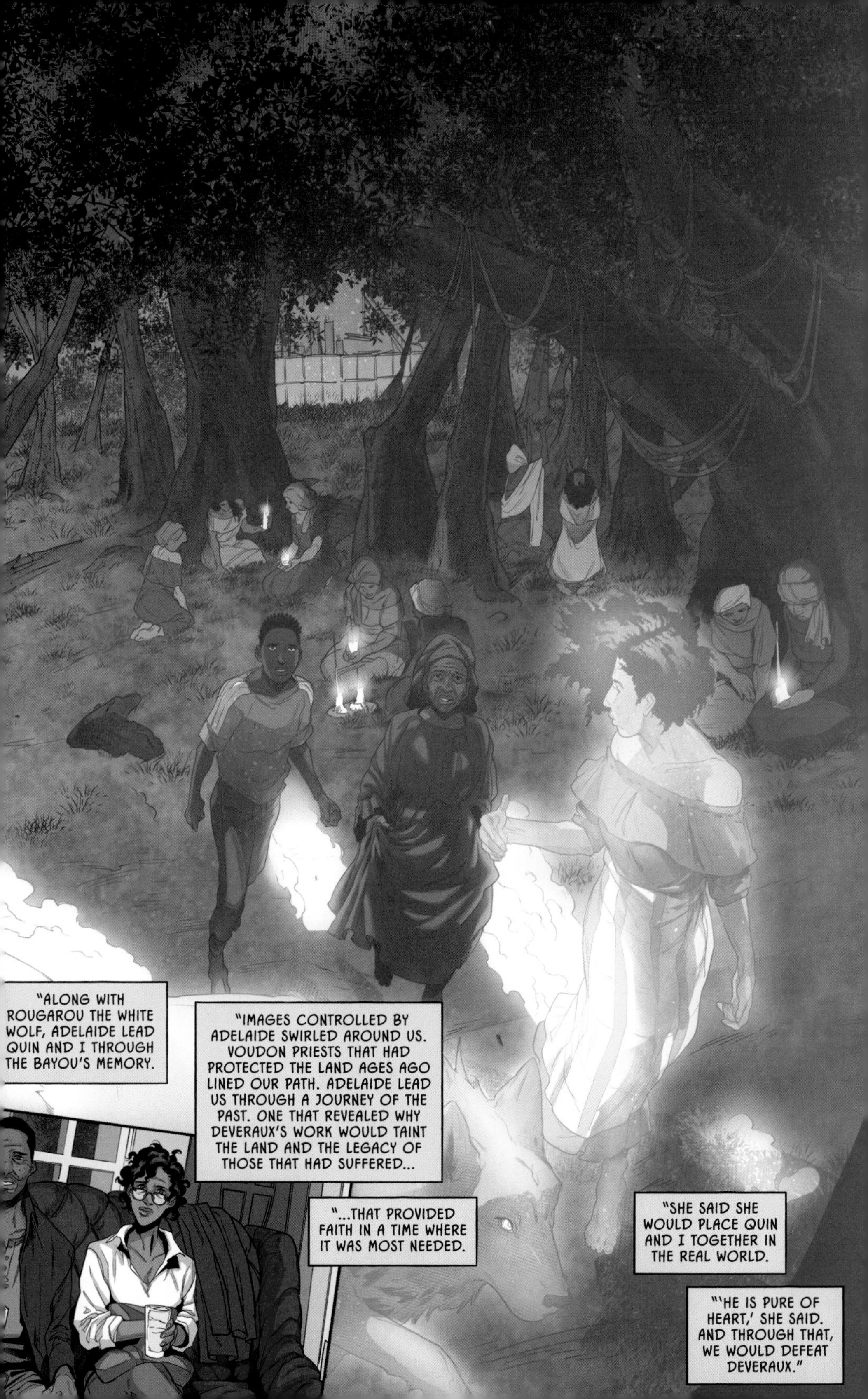
"ALONG WITH ROUGAROU THE WHITE WOLF, ADELAIDE LEAD QUIN AND I THROUGH THE BAYOU'S MEMORY.
"IMAGES CONTROLLED BY ADELAIDE SWIRLED AROUND US. VOUDON PRIESTS THAT HAD PROTECTED THE LAND AGES AGO LINED OUR PATH. ADELAIDE LEAD US THROUGH A JOURNEY OF THE PAST. ONE THAT REVEALED WHY DEVERAUX'S WORK WOULD TAINT THE LAND AND THE LEGACY OF THOSE THAT HAD SUFFERED...
"...THAT PROVIDED FAITH IN A TIME WHERE IT WAS MOST NEEDED.
"SHE SAID SHE WOULD PLACE QUIN AND I TOGETHER IN THE REAL WORLD.
"'HE IS PURE OF HEART,' SHE SAID. AND THROUGH THAT, WE WOULD DEFEAT DEVERAUX."

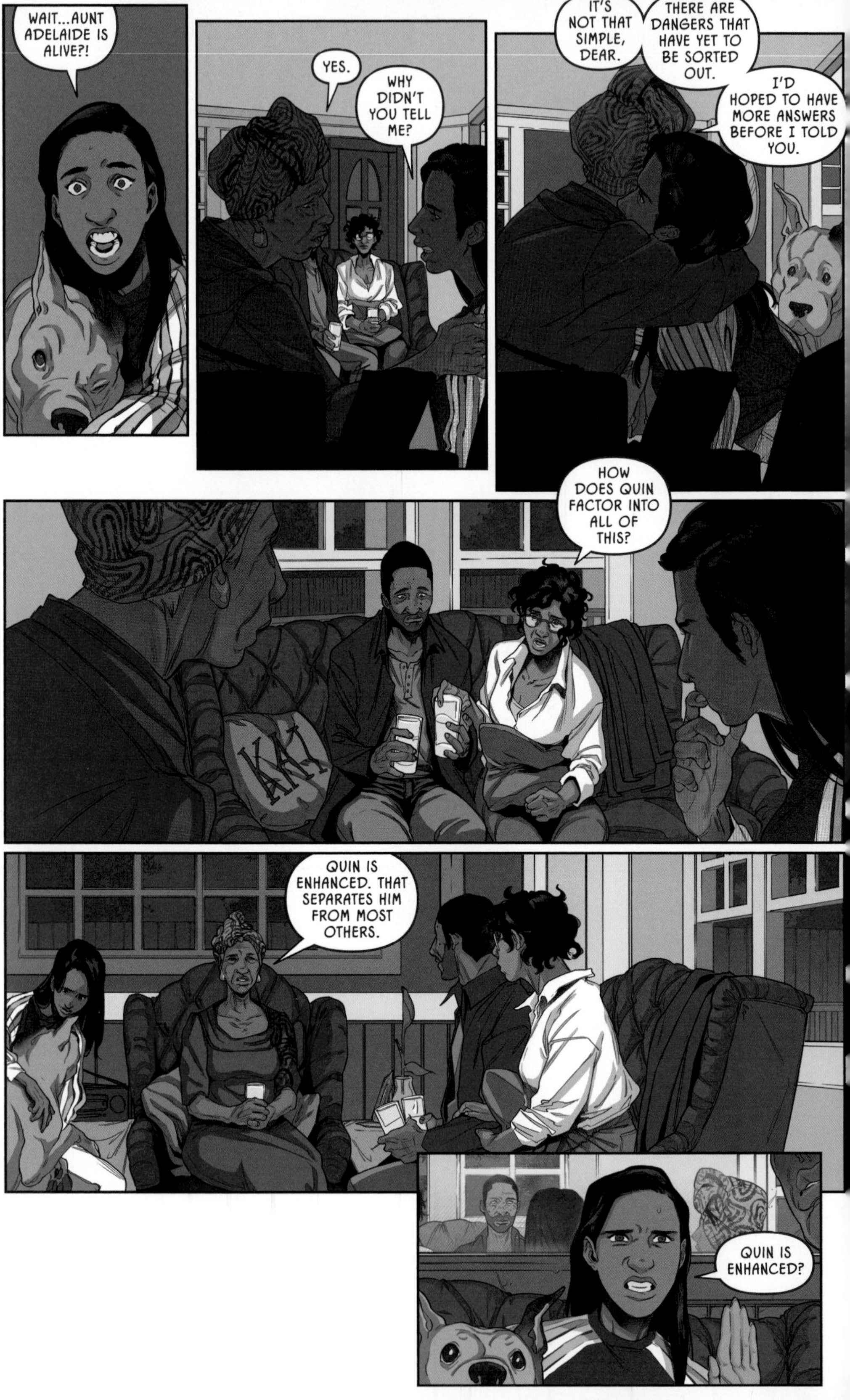
WAIT...AUNT ADELAIDE IS ALIVE?!
YES.
WHY DIDN'T YOU TELL ME?
IT'S NOT THAT SIMPLE, DEAR.
THERE ARE DANGERS THAT HAVE YET TO BE SORTED OUT.
I'D HOPED TO HAVE MORE ANSWERS BEFORE I TOLD YOU.
HOW DOES QUIN FACTOR INTO ALL OF THIS?
KAI
QUIN IS ENHANCED. THAT SEPARATES HIM FROM MOST OTHERS.
QUIN IS ENHANCED?

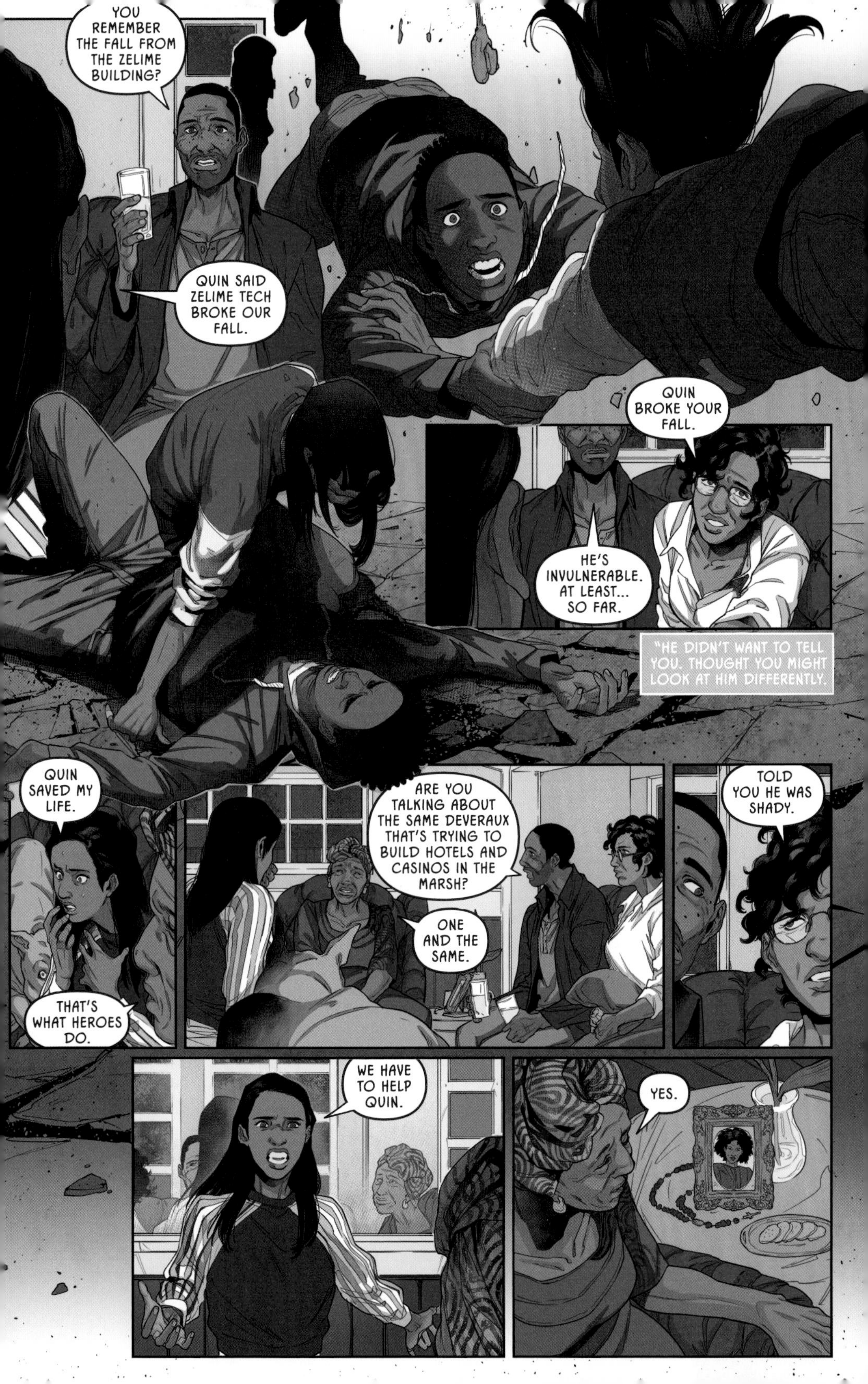

YOU REMEMBER THE FALL FROM THE ZELIME BUILDING?
QUIN SAID ZELIME TECH BROKE OUR FALL.
QUIN BROKE YOUR FALL.
HE'S INVULNERABLE. AT LEAST... SO FAR.
"HE DIDN'T WANT TO TELL YOU. THOUGHT YOU MIGHT LOOK AT HIM DIFFERENTLY.
QUIN SAVED MY LIFE.
THAT'S WHAT HEROES DO.
ARE YOU TALKING ABOUT THE SAME DEVERAUX THAT'S TRYING TO BUILD HOTELS AND CASINOS IN THE MARSH?
ONE AND THE SAME.
TOLD YOU HE WAS SHADY.
WE HAVE TO HELP QUIN.
YES.

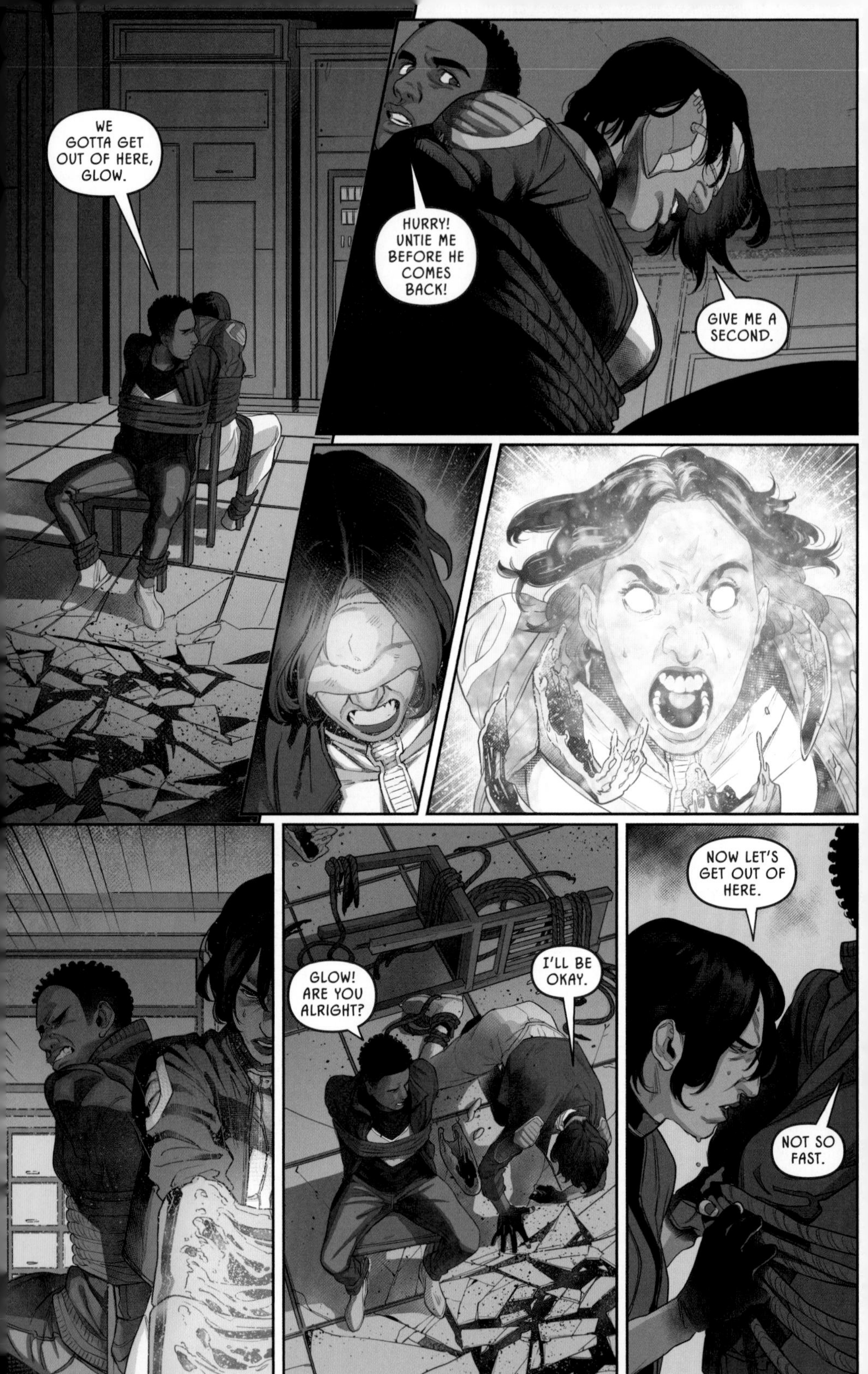
WE GOTTA GET OUT OF HERE, GLOW.
HURRY! UNTIE ME BEFORE HE COMES BACK!
GIVE ME A SECOND.
GLOW! ARE YOU ALRIGHT?
I'LL BE OKAY.
NOW LET'S GET OUT OF HERE.
NOT SO FAST.

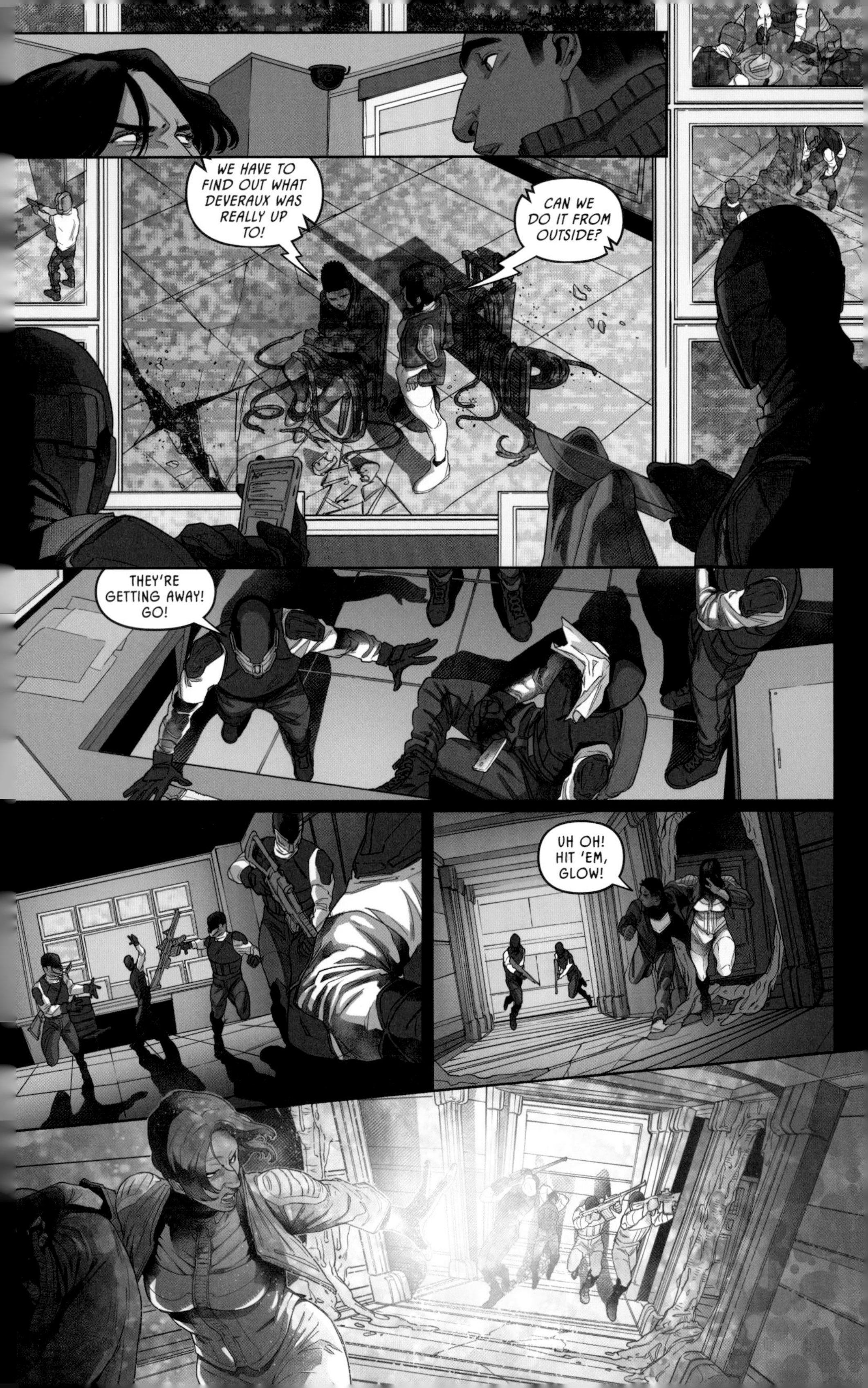
WE HAVE TO FIND OUT WHAT DEVERAUX WAS REALLY UP TO!
CAN WE DO IT FROM OUTSIDE?
THEY'RE GETTING AWAY! GO!
UH OH! HIT 'EM, GLOW!

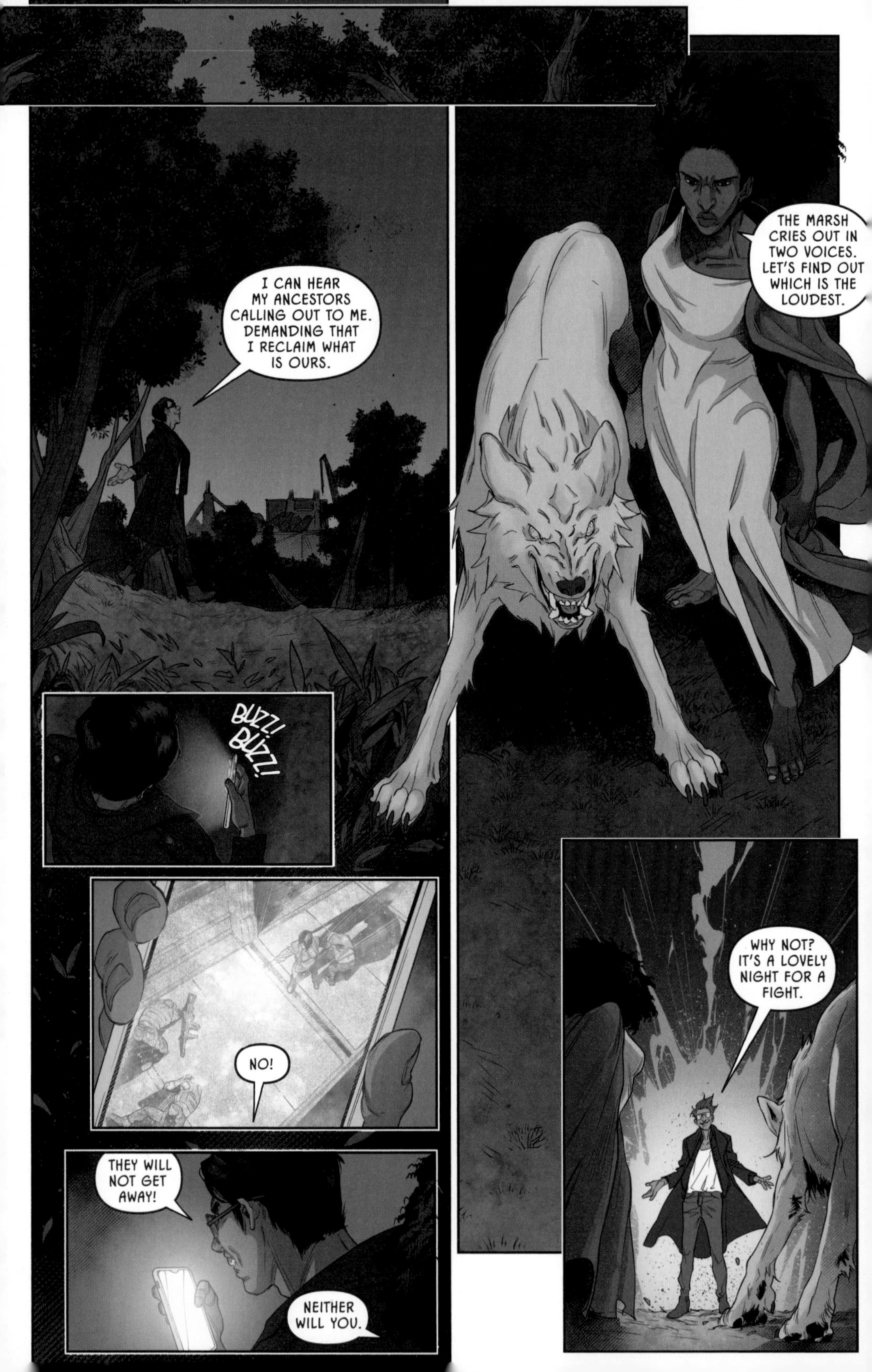
I CAN HEAR MY ANCESTORS CALLING OUT TO ME. DEMANDING THAT I RECLAIM WHAT IS OURS.
THE MARSH CRIES OUT IN TWO VOICES. LET'S FIND OUT WHICH IS THE LOUDEST.
BUZZ! BUZZ!
NO!
THEY WILL NOT GET AWAY!
NEITHER WILL YOU.
WHY NOT? IT'S A LOVELY NIGHT FOR A FIGHT.

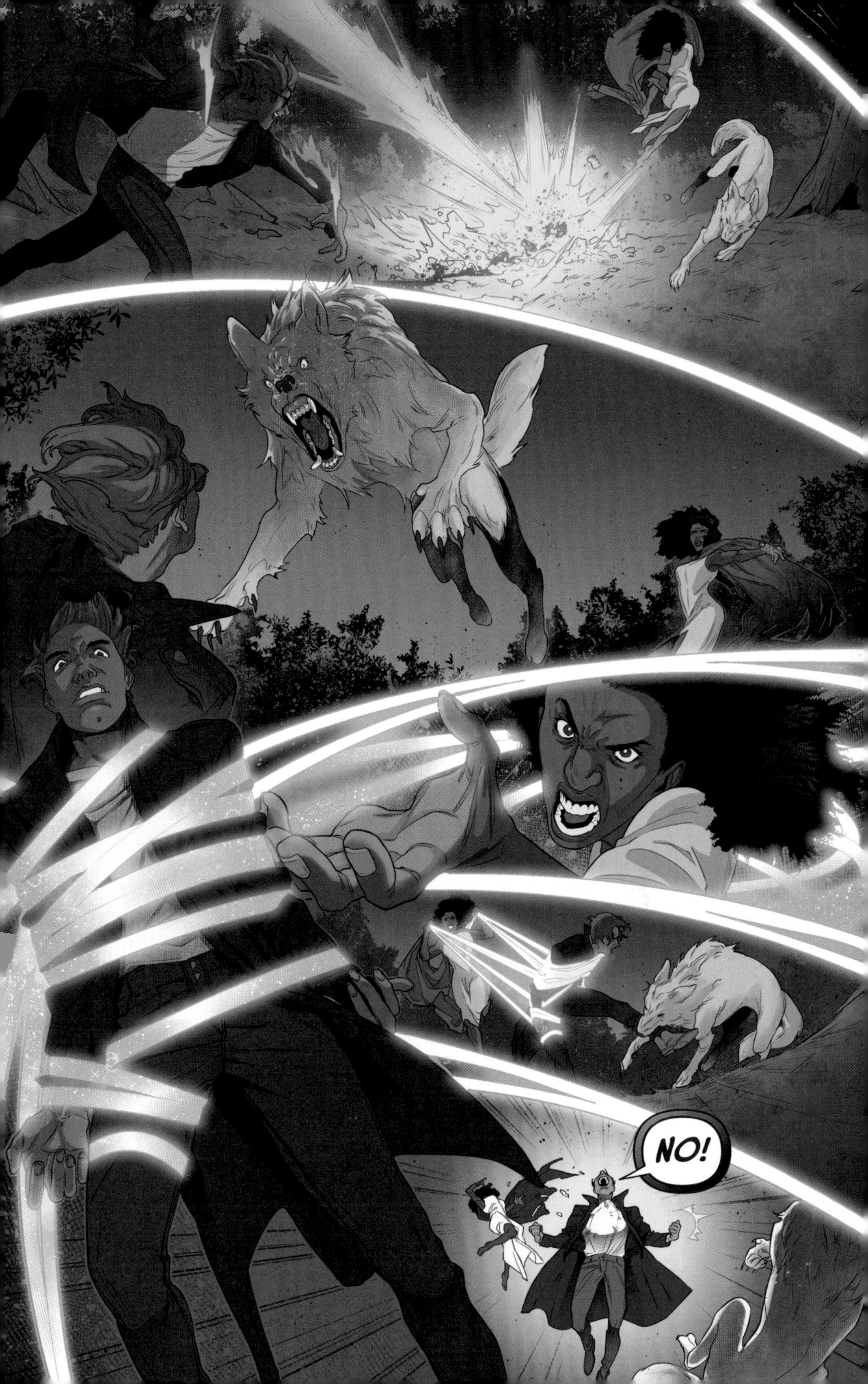
NO!

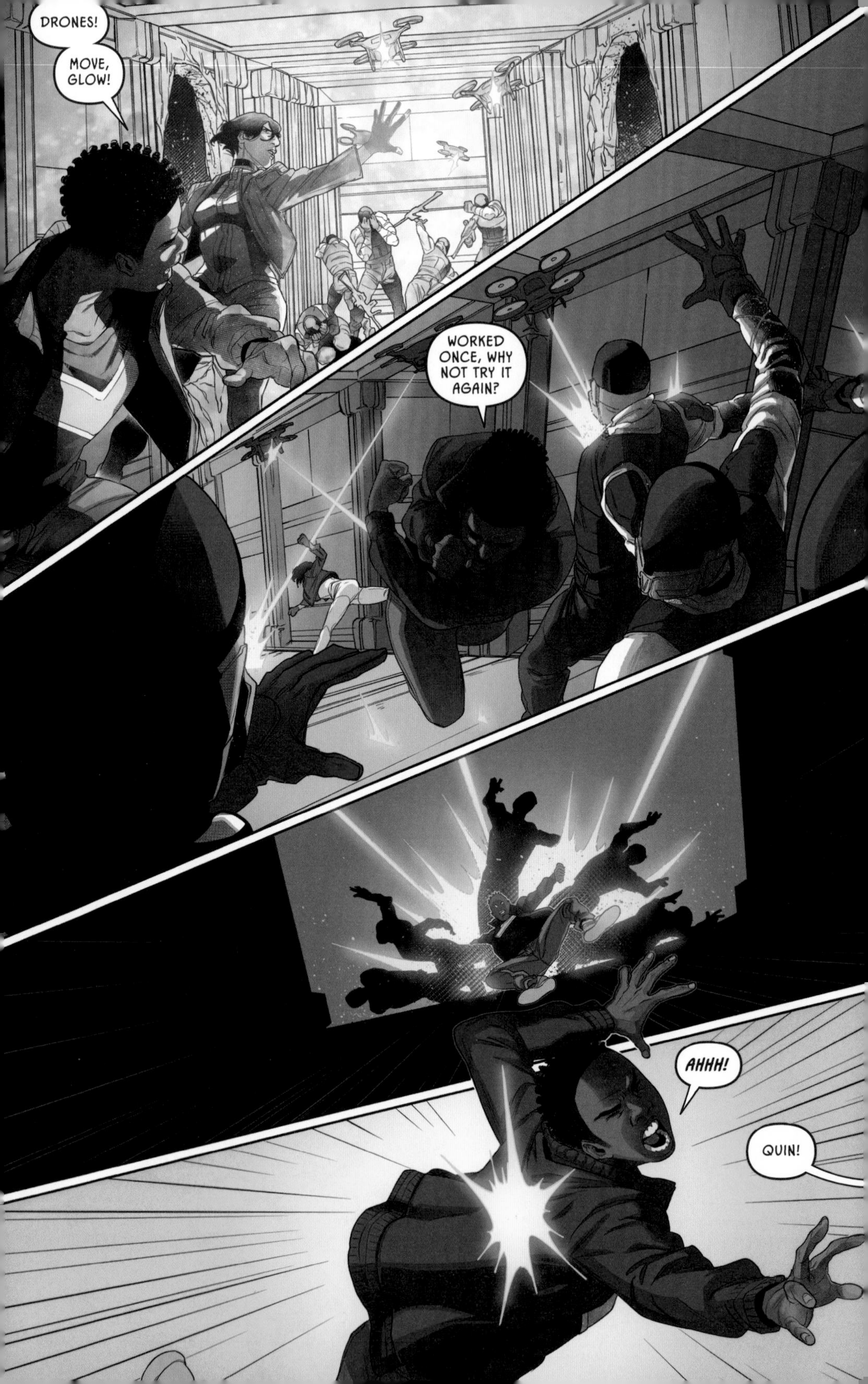
DRONES!
MOVE, GLOW!
WORKED ONCE, WHY NOT TRY IT AGAIN?
AHHH!
QUIN!

THESE BLASTS MAY NOT KILL ME BUT THEY'RE PAINFUL AF.

WHAT WOULD I DO WITHOUT YOU?

YOU'D FIND A WAY.

C'MON!

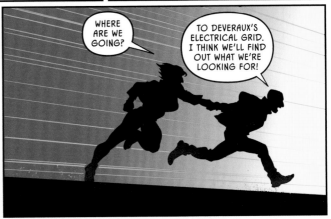

WHERE ARE WE GOING?

TO DEVERAUX'S ELECTRICAL GRID. I THINK WE'LL FIND OUT WHAT WE'RE LOOKING FOR!

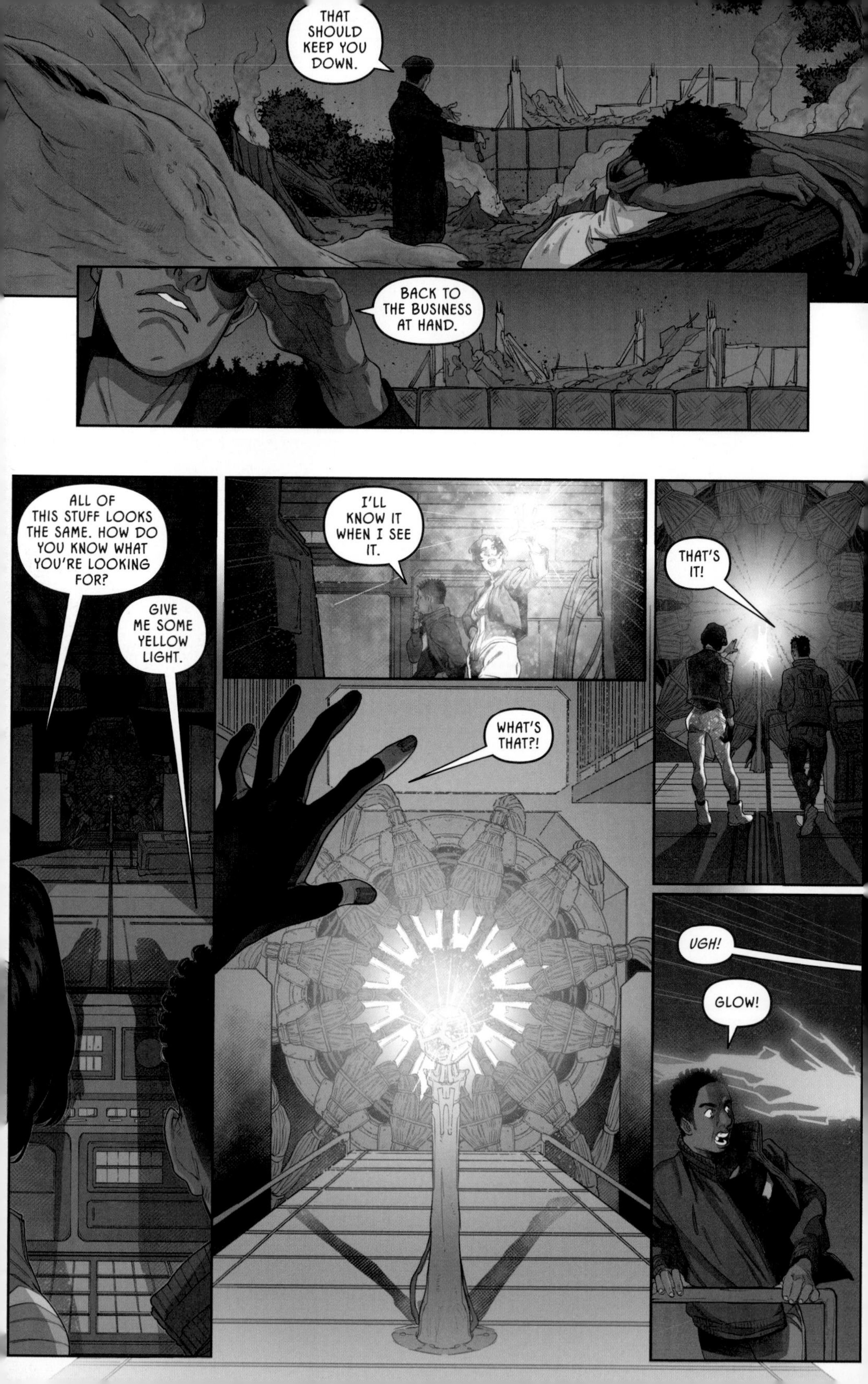
THAT SHOULD KEEP YOU DOWN.
BACK TO THE BUSINESS AT HAND.
ALL OF THIS STUFF LOOKS THE SAME. HOW DO YOU KNOW WHAT YOU'RE LOOKING FOR?
GIVE ME SOME YELLOW LIGHT.
I'LL KNOW IT WHEN I SEE IT.
THAT'S IT!
WHAT'S THAT?!
UGH!
GLOW!

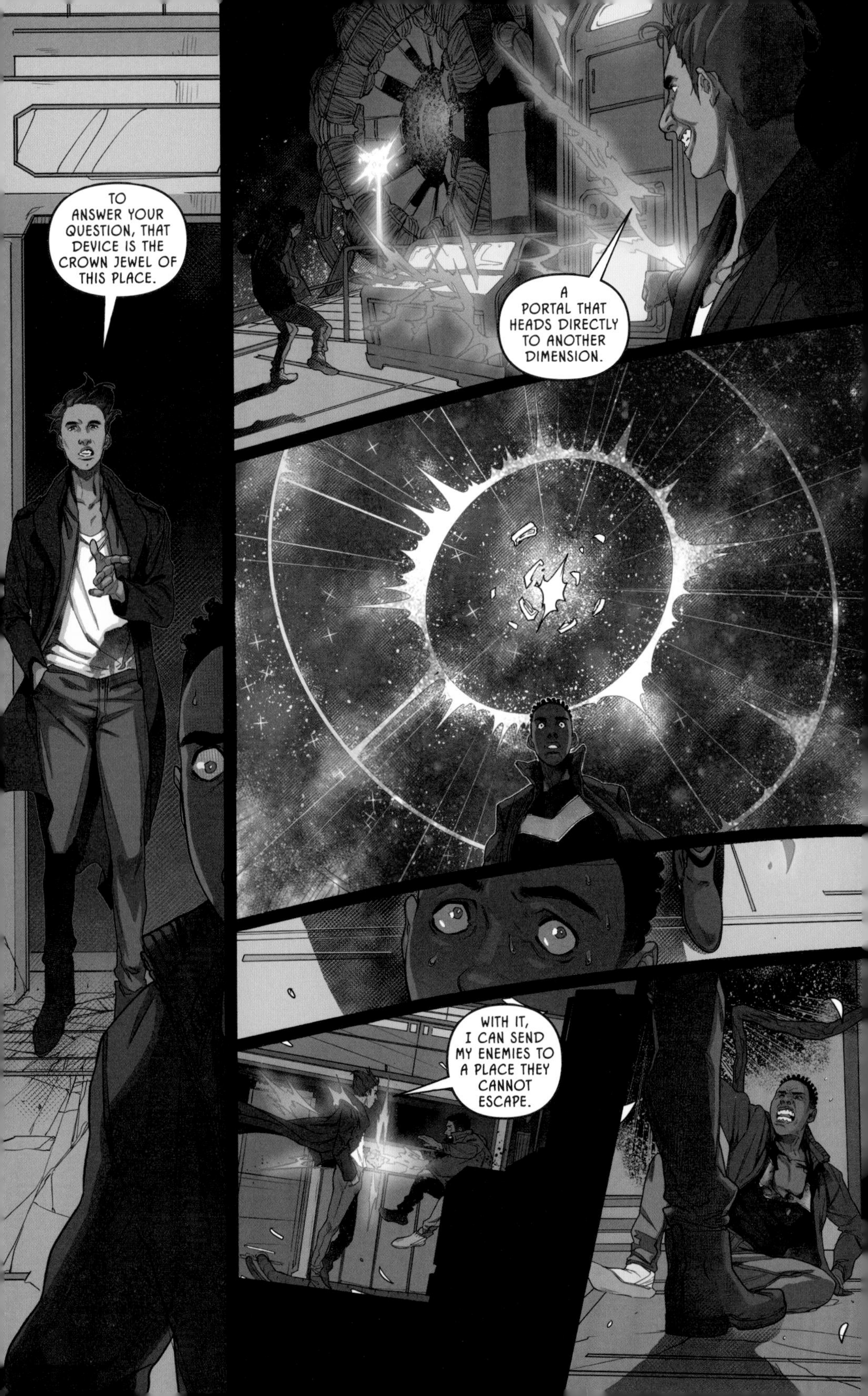
TO ANSWER YOUR QUESTION, THAT DEVICE IS THE CROWN JEWEL OF THIS PLACE.
A PORTAL THAT HEADS DIRECTLY TO ANOTHER DIMENSION.
WITH IT, I CAN SEND MY ENEMIES TO A PLACE THEY CANNOT ESCAPE.

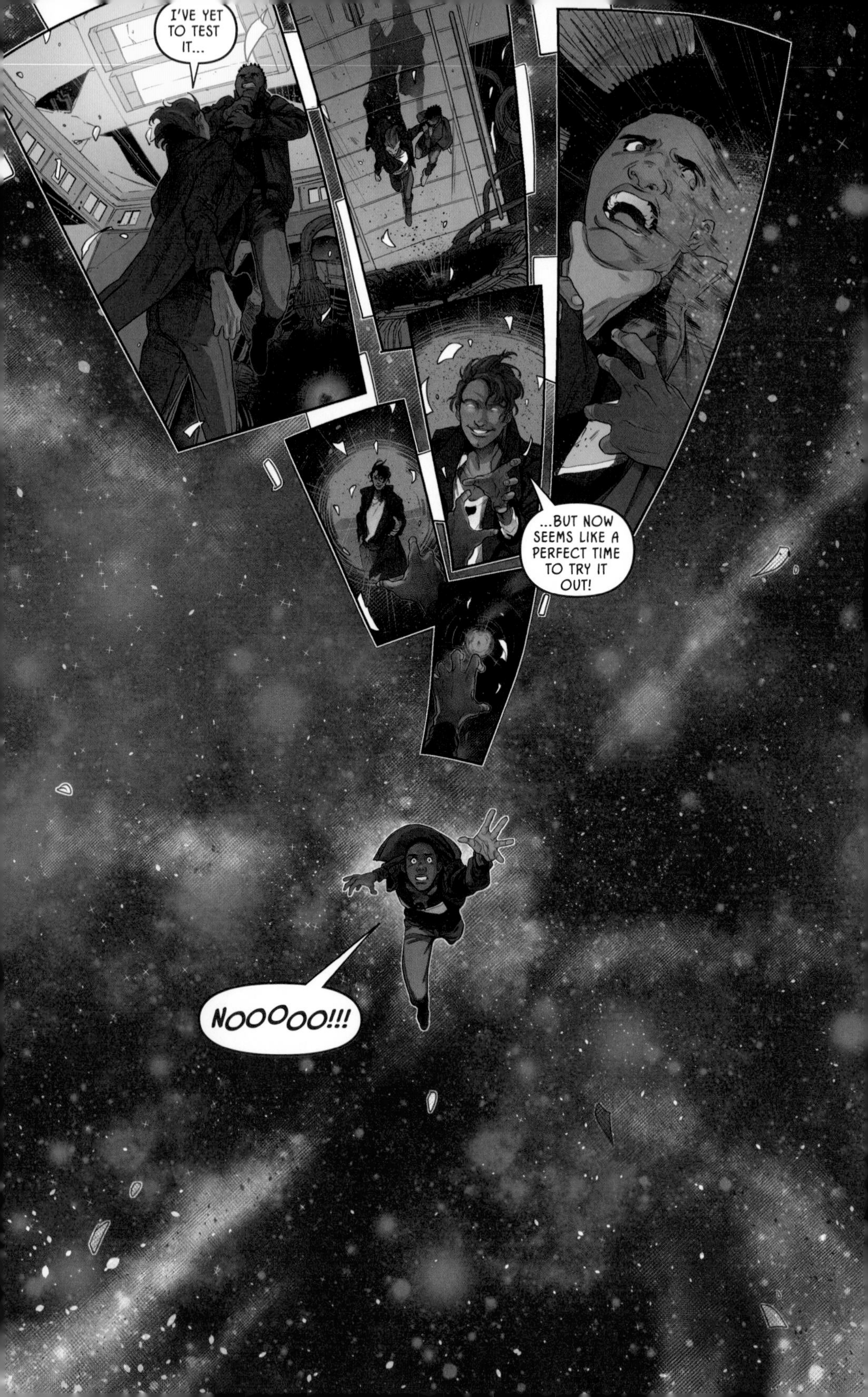
I'VE YET TO TEST IT...
...BUT NOW SEEMS LIKE A PERFECT TIME TO TRY IT OUT!
NOOOOO!!!

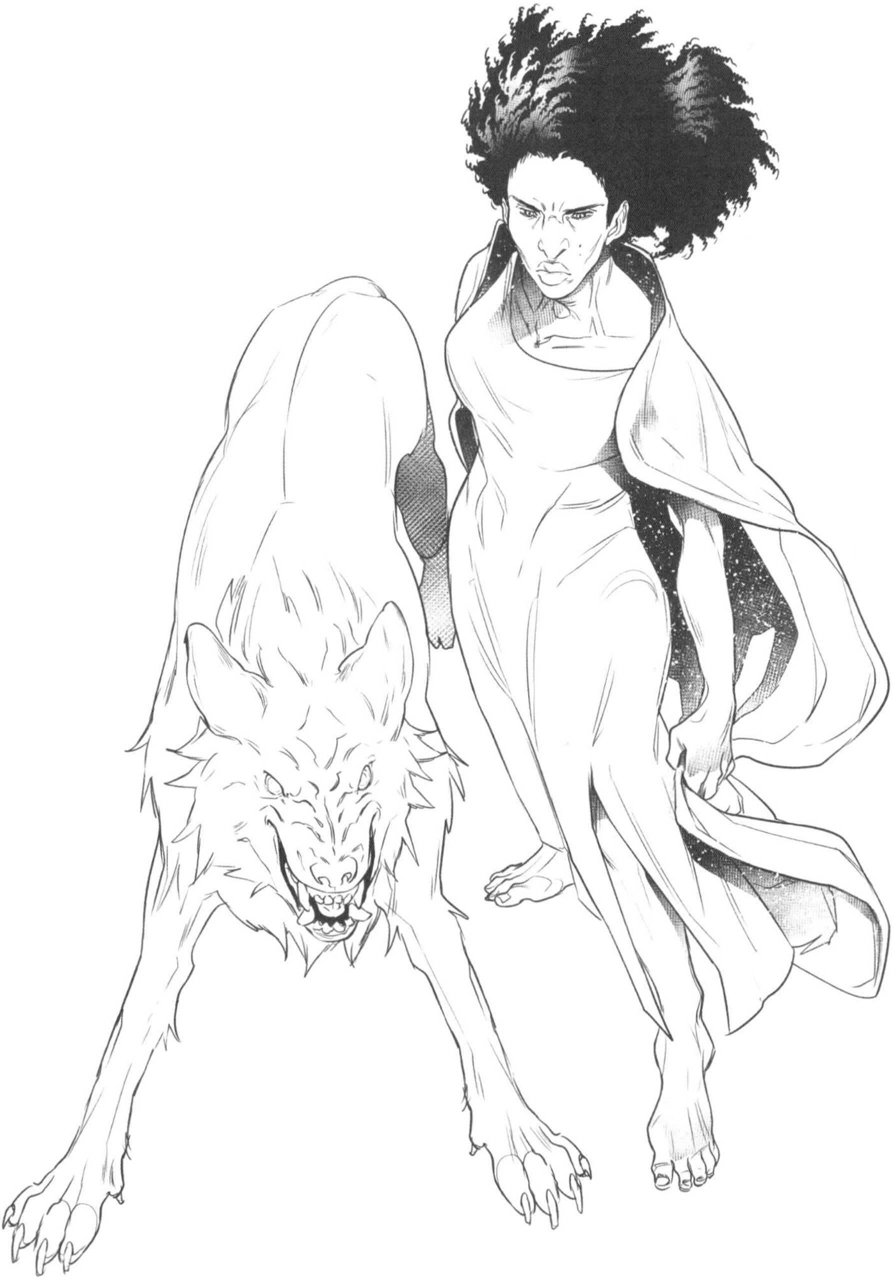

CHAPTER FIVE

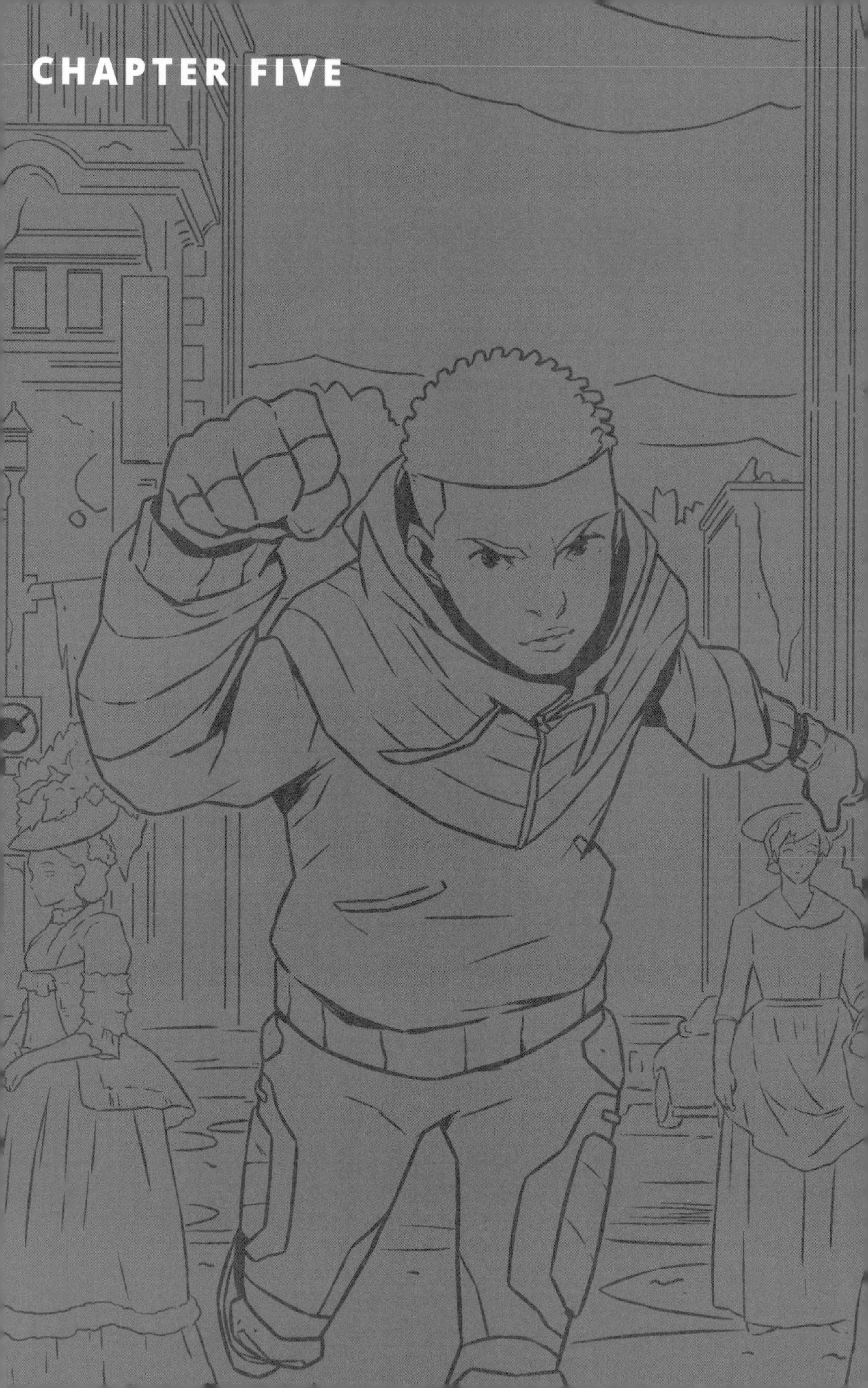

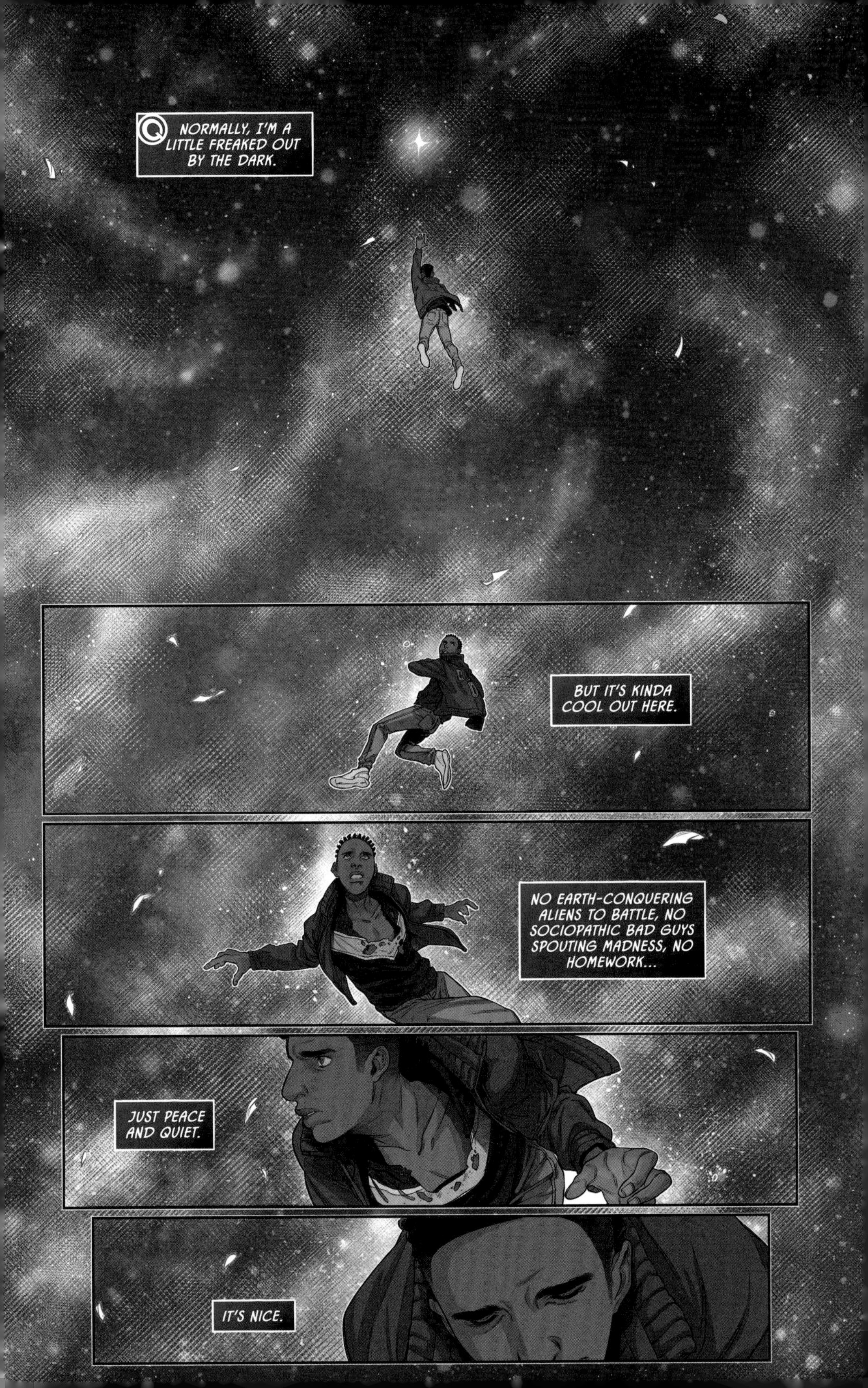
NORMALLY, I'M A LITTLE FREAKED OUT BY THE DARK.
BUT IT'S KINDA COOL OUT HERE.
NO EARTH-CONQUERING ALIENS TO BATTLE, NO SOCIOPATHIC BAD GUYS SPOUTING MADNESS, NO HOMEWORK...
JUST PEACE AND QUIET.
IT'S NICE.

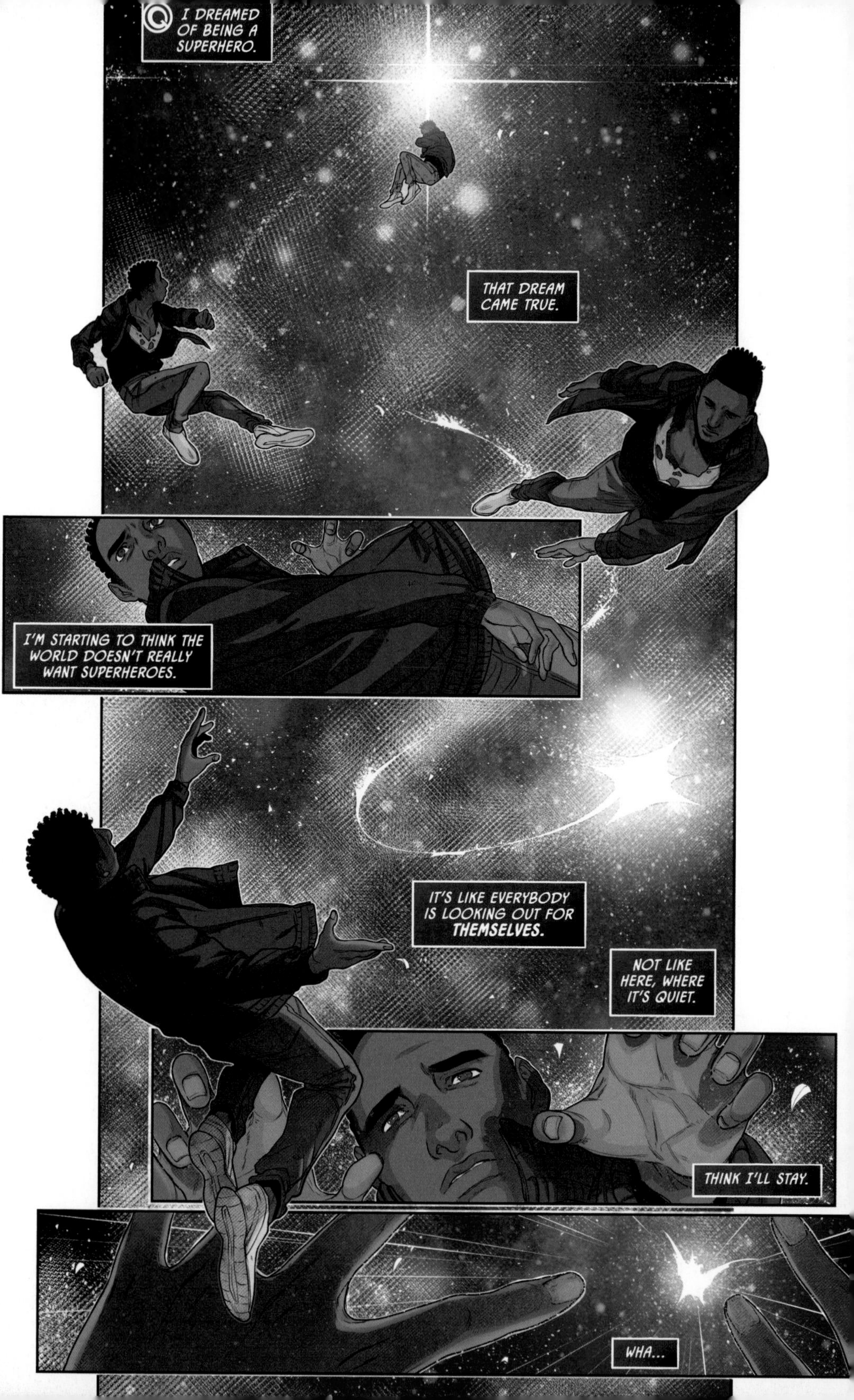
I DREAMED OF BEING A SUPERHERO.
THAT DREAM CAME TRUE.
I'M STARTING TO THINK THE WORLD DOESN'T REALLY WANT SUPERHEROES.
IT'S LIKE EVERYBODY IS LOOKING OUT FOR THEMSELVES.
NOT LIKE HERE, WHERE IT'S QUIET.
THINK I'LL STAY.
WHA...

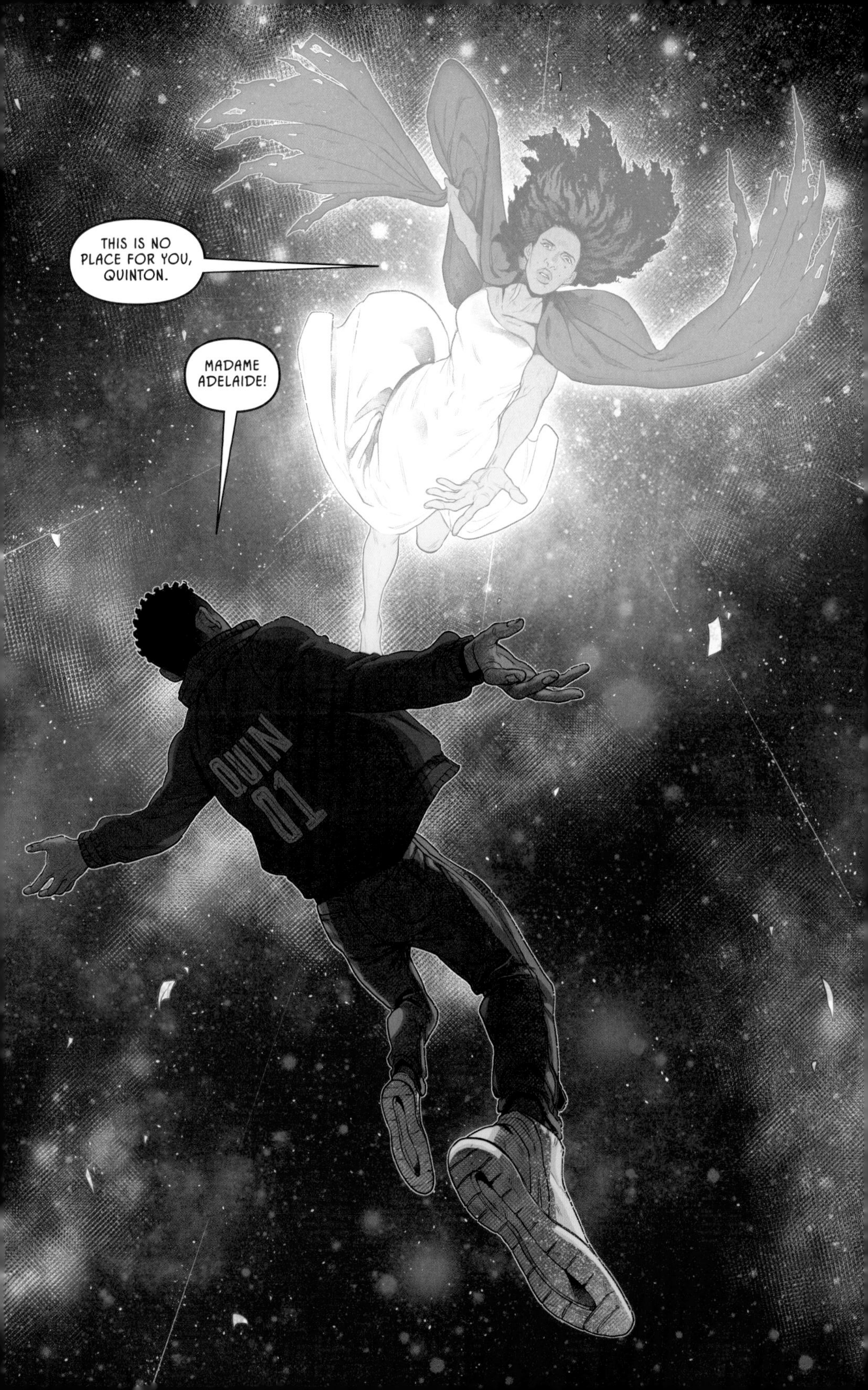
THIS IS NO PLACE FOR YOU, QUINTON.
MADAME ADELAIDE!
QUIN 01

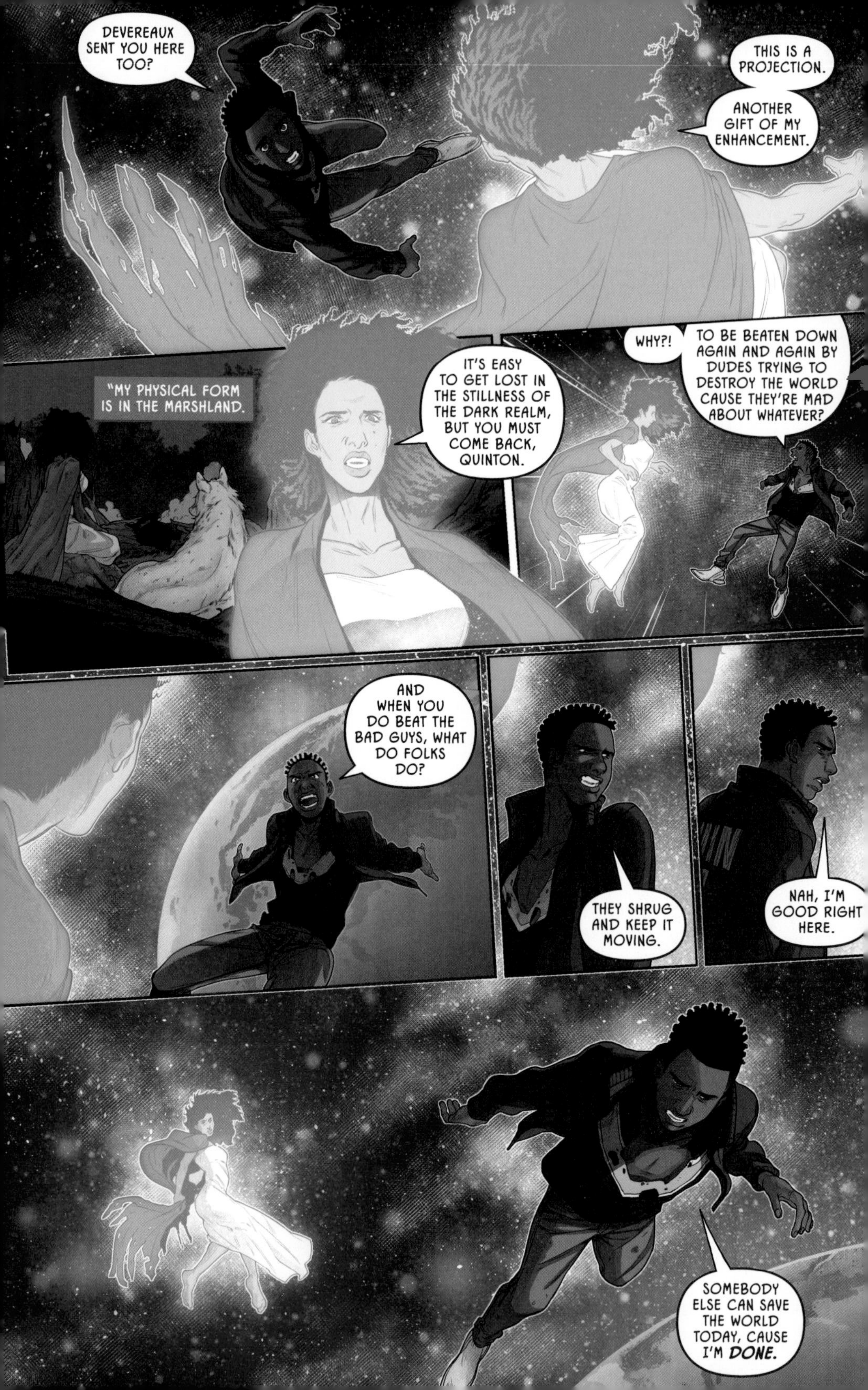

DEVEREAUX SENT YOU HERE TOO?
THIS IS A PROJECTION.
ANOTHER GIFT OF MY ENHANCEMENT.
"MY PHYSICAL FORM IS IN THE MARSHLAND.
IT'S EASY TO GET LOST IN THE STILLNESS OF THE DARK REALM, BUT YOU MUST COME BACK, QUINTON.
WHY?!
TO BE BEATEN DOWN AGAIN AND AGAIN BY DUDES TRYING TO DESTROY THE WORLD CAUSE THEY'RE MAD ABOUT WHATEVER?
AND WHEN YOU DO BEAT THE BAD GUYS, WHAT DO FOLKS DO?
THEY SHRUG AND KEEP IT MOVING.
NAH, I'M GOOD RIGHT HERE.
SOMEBODY ELSE CAN SAVE THE WORLD TODAY, CAUSE I'M ***DONE.***

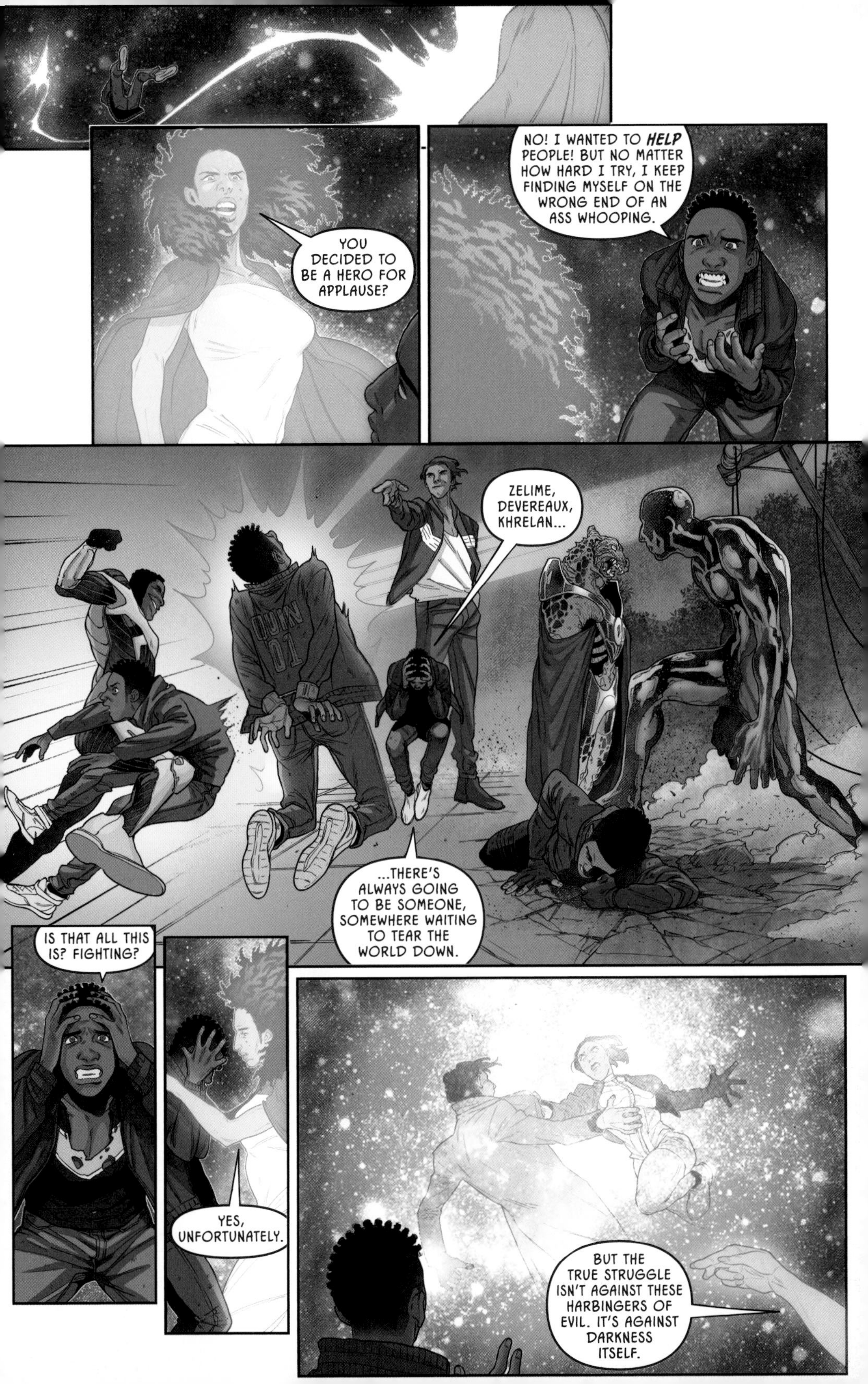

YOU DECIDED TO BE A HERO FOR APPLAUSE?
NO! I WANTED TO HELP PEOPLE! BUT NO MATTER HOW HARD I TRY, I KEEP FINDING MYSELF ON THE WRONG END OF AN ASS WHOOPING.
ZELIME, DEVEREAUX, KHRELAN...
...THERE'S ALWAYS GOING TO BE SOMEONE, SOMEWHERE WAITING TO TEAR THE WORLD DOWN.
IS THAT ALL THIS IS? FIGHTING?
YES, UNFORTUNATELY.
BUT THE TRUE STRUGGLE ISN'T AGAINST THESE HARBINGERS OF EVIL. IT'S AGAINST DARKNESS ITSELF.

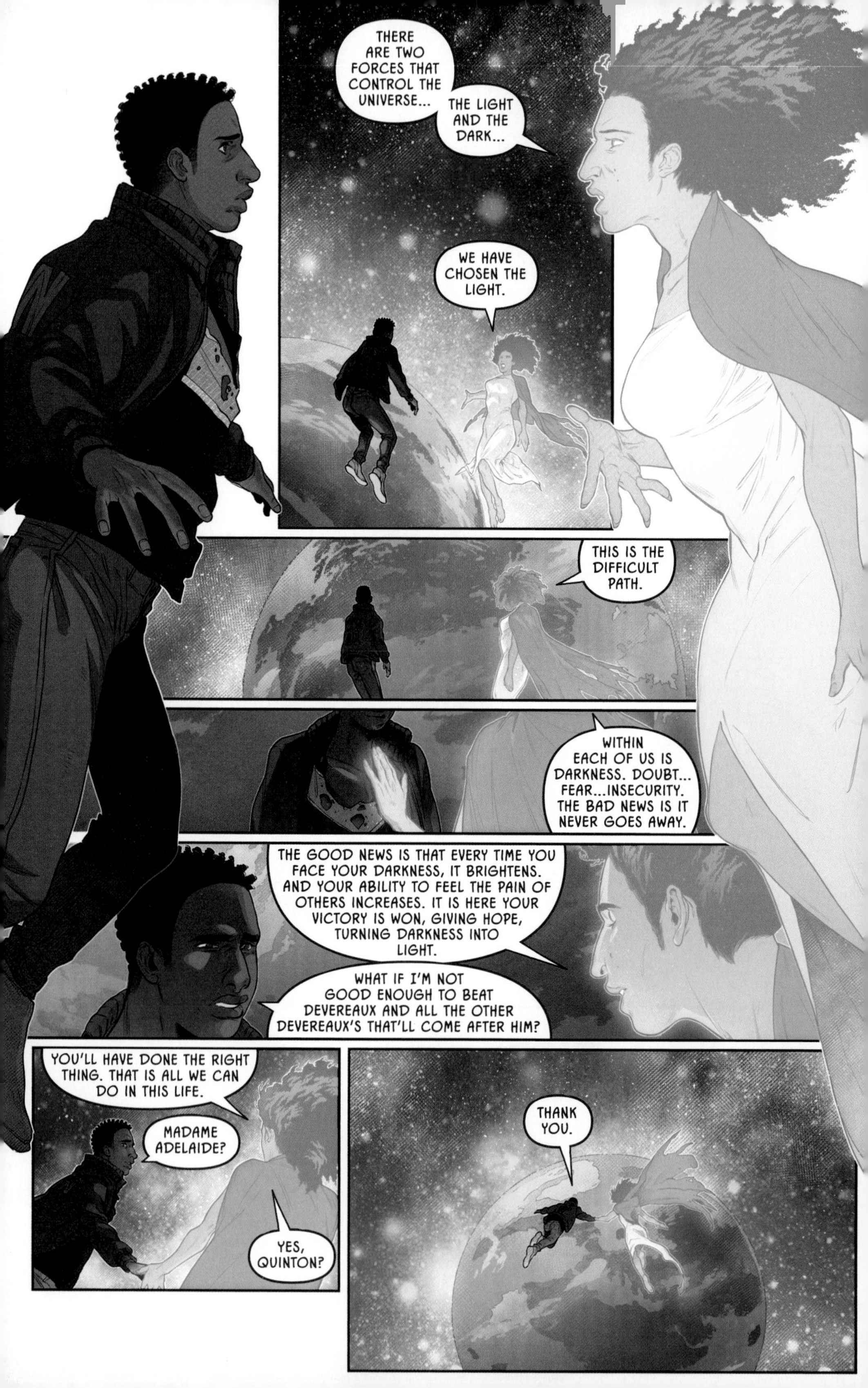
THERE ARE TWO FORCES THAT CONTROL THE UNIVERSE...
THE LIGHT AND THE DARK...
WE HAVE CHOSEN THE LIGHT.
THIS IS THE DIFFICULT PATH.
WITHIN EACH OF US IS DARKNESS. DOUBT... FEAR...INSECURITY. THE BAD NEWS IS IT NEVER GOES AWAY.
THE GOOD NEWS IS THAT EVERY TIME YOU FACE YOUR DARKNESS, IT BRIGHTENS. AND YOUR ABILITY TO FEEL THE PAIN OF OTHERS INCREASES. IT IS HERE YOUR VICTORY IS WON, GIVING HOPE, TURNING DARKNESS INTO LIGHT.
WHAT IF I'M NOT GOOD ENOUGH TO BEAT DEVEREAUX AND ALL THE OTHER DEVEREAUX'S THAT'LL COME AFTER HIM?
YOU'LL HAVE DONE THE RIGHT THING. THAT IS ALL WE CAN DO IN THIS LIFE.
MADAME ADELAIDE?
YES, QUINTON?
THANK YOU.

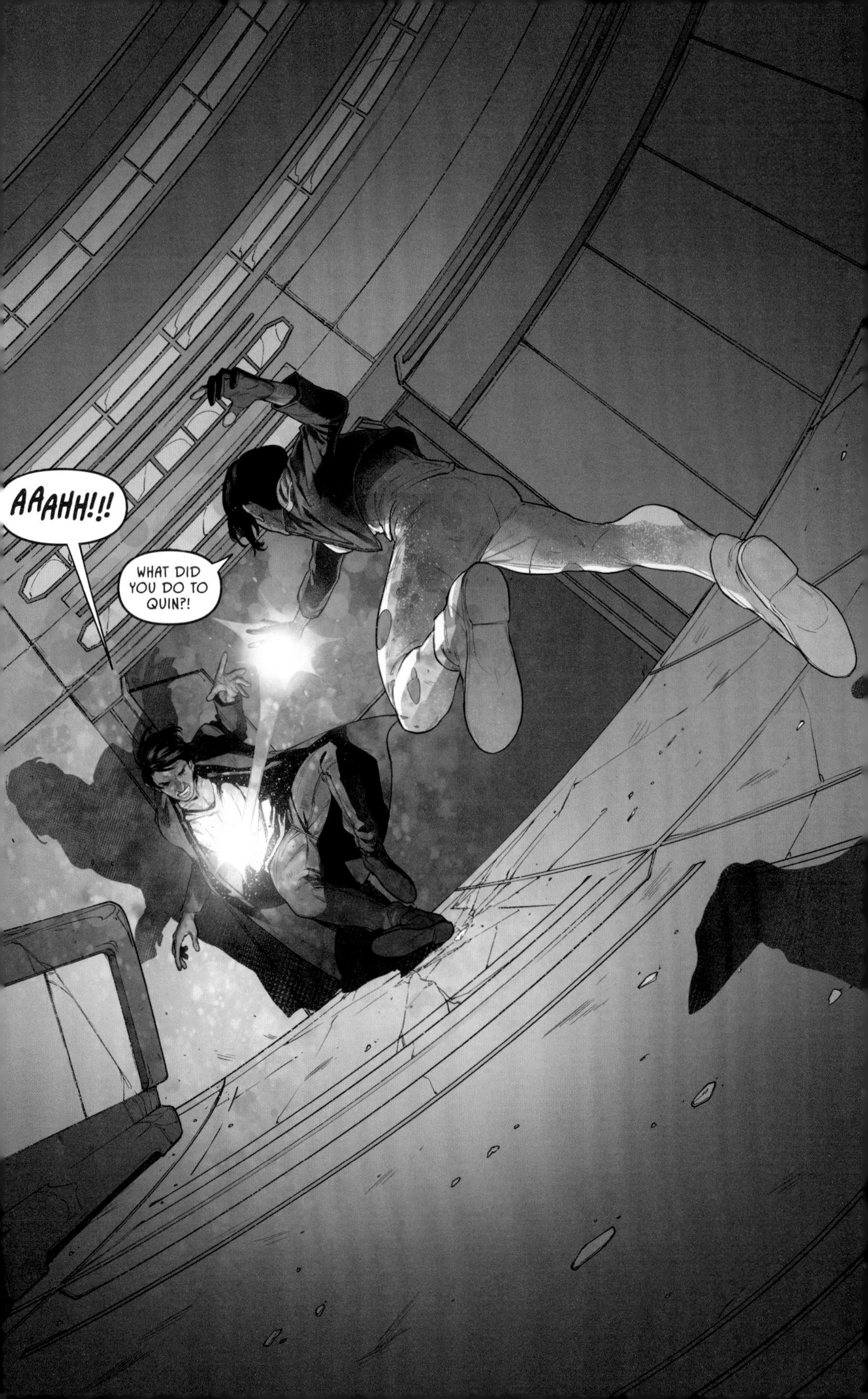
AAAHH!!!
WHAT DID YOU DO TO QUIN?!

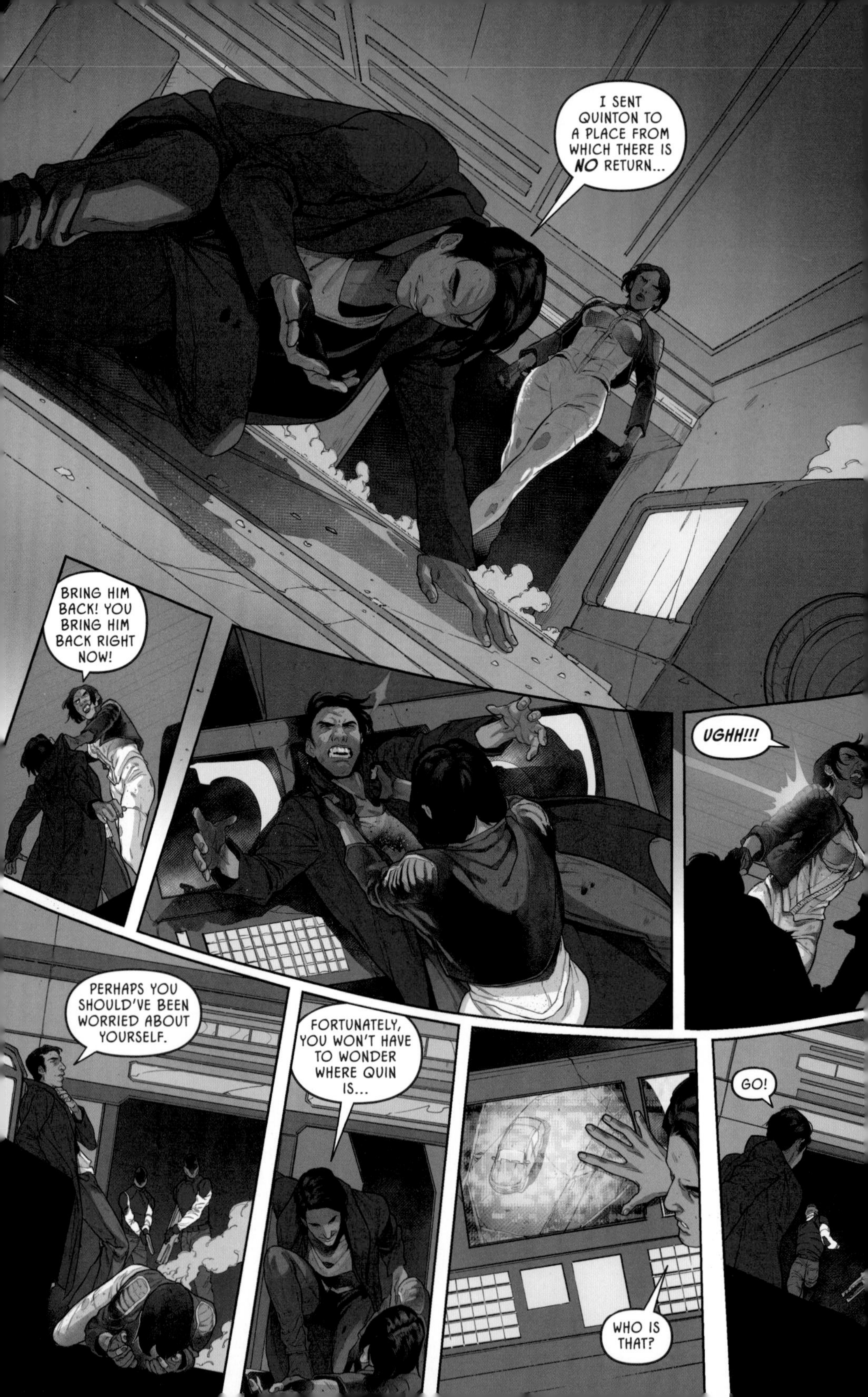
I SENT QUINTON TO A PLACE FROM WHICH THERE IS **NO** RETURN...
BRING HIM BACK! YOU BRING HIM BACK RIGHT NOW!
UGHH!!!
PERHAPS YOU SHOULD'VE BEEN WORRIED ABOUT YOURSELF.
FORTUNATELY, YOU WON'T HAVE TO WONDER WHERE QUIN IS...
WHO IS THAT?
GO!

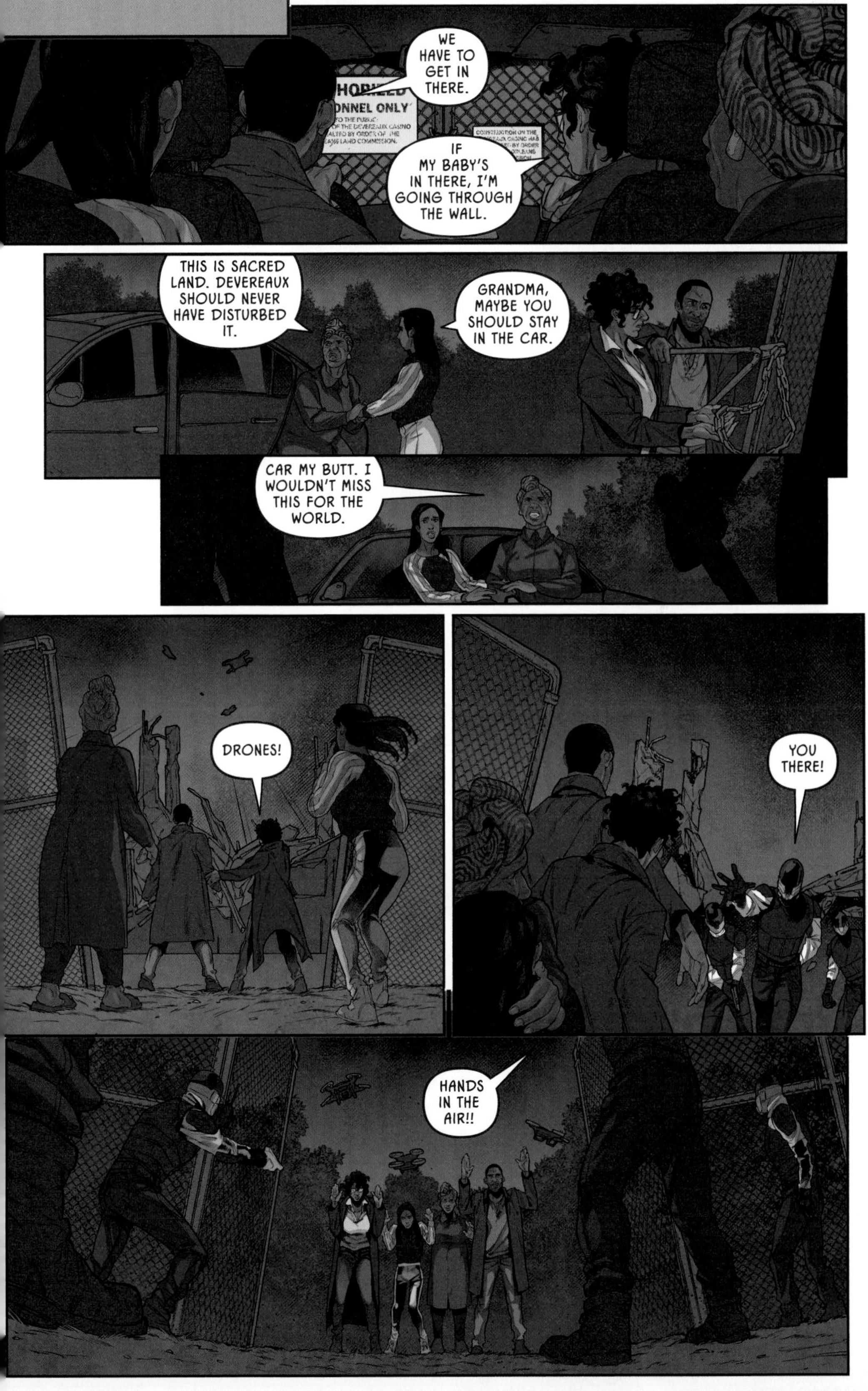
WE HAVE TO GET IN THERE.
IF MY BABY'S IN THERE, I'M GOING THROUGH THE WALL.
THIS IS SACRED LAND. DEVEREAUX SHOULD NEVER HAVE DISTURBED IT.
GRANDMA, MAYBE YOU SHOULD STAY IN THE CAR.
CAR MY BUTT. I WOULDN'T MISS THIS FOR THE WORLD.
DRONES!
YOU THERE!
HANDS IN THE AIR!!

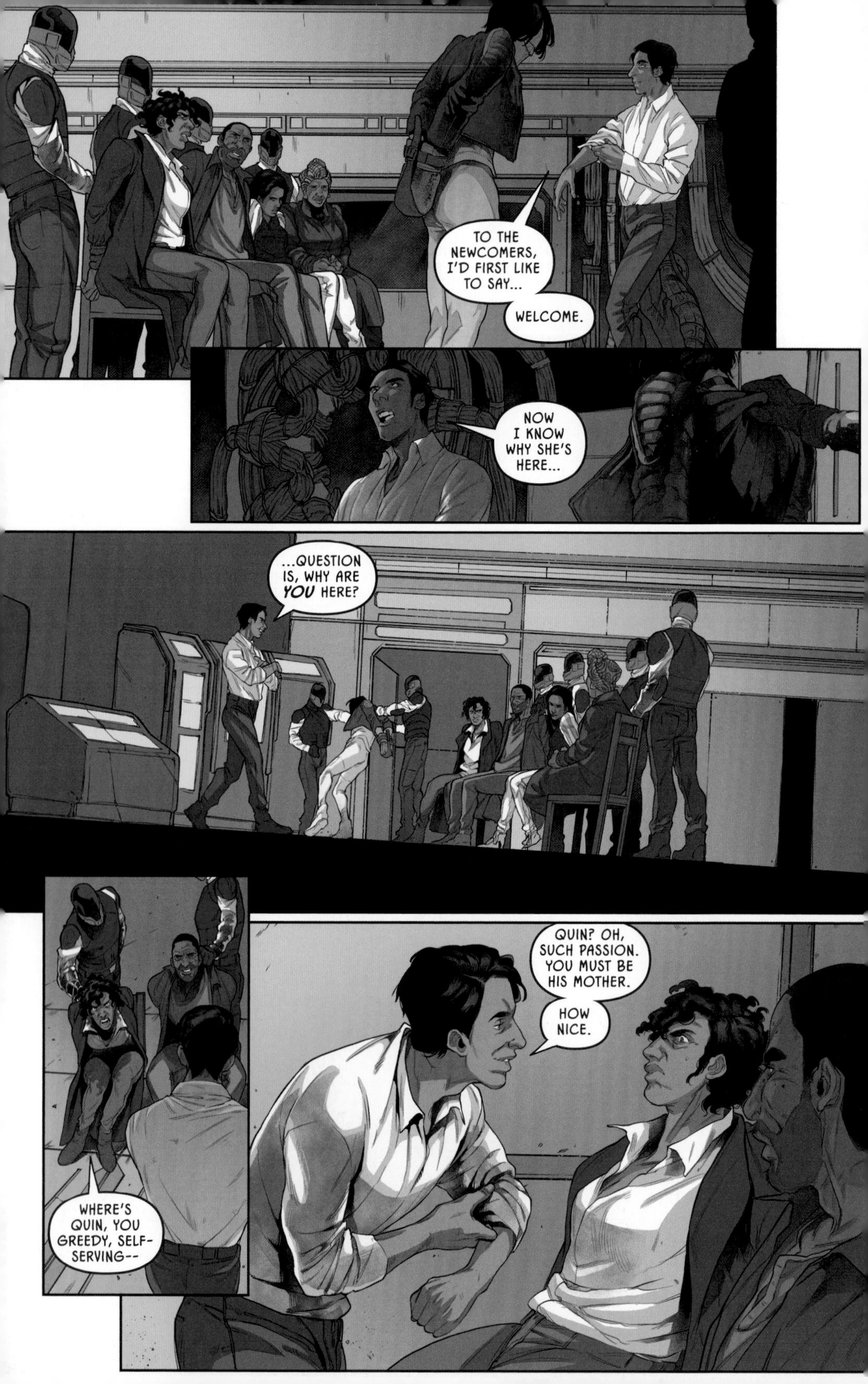
TO THE NEWCOMERS, I'D FIRST LIKE TO SAY...
WELCOME.
NOW I KNOW WHY SHE'S HERE...
...QUESTION IS, WHY ARE *YOU* HERE?
WHERE'S QUIN, YOU GREEDY, SELF-SERVING--
QUIN? OH, SUCH PASSION. YOU MUST BE HIS MOTHER.
HOW NICE.

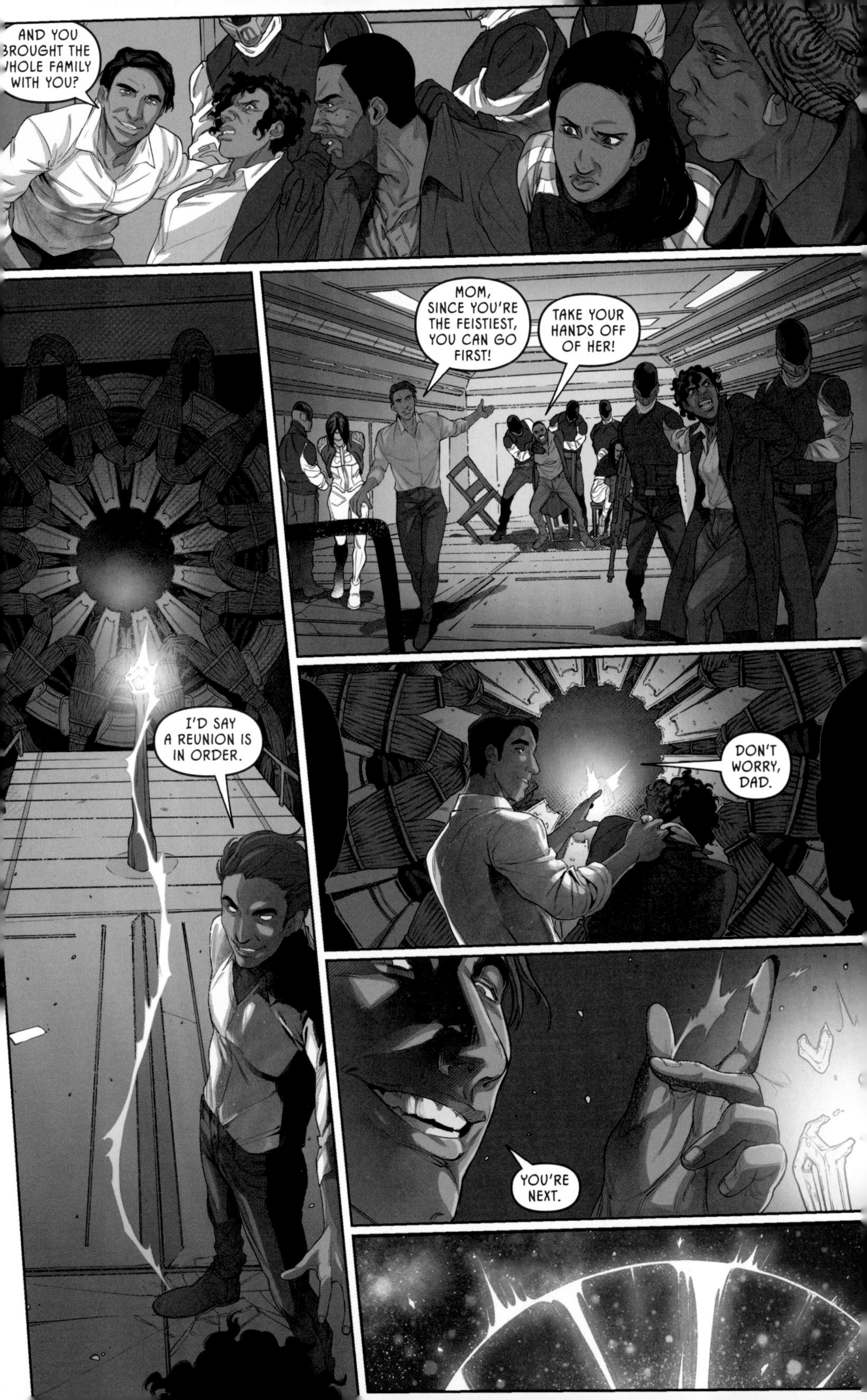
AND YOU BROUGHT THE WHOLE FAMILY WITH YOU?
MOM, SINCE YOU'RE THE FEISTIEST, YOU CAN GO FIRST!
TAKE YOUR HANDS OFF OF HER!
I'D SAY A REUNION IS IN ORDER.
DON'T WORRY, DAD.
YOU'RE NEXT.

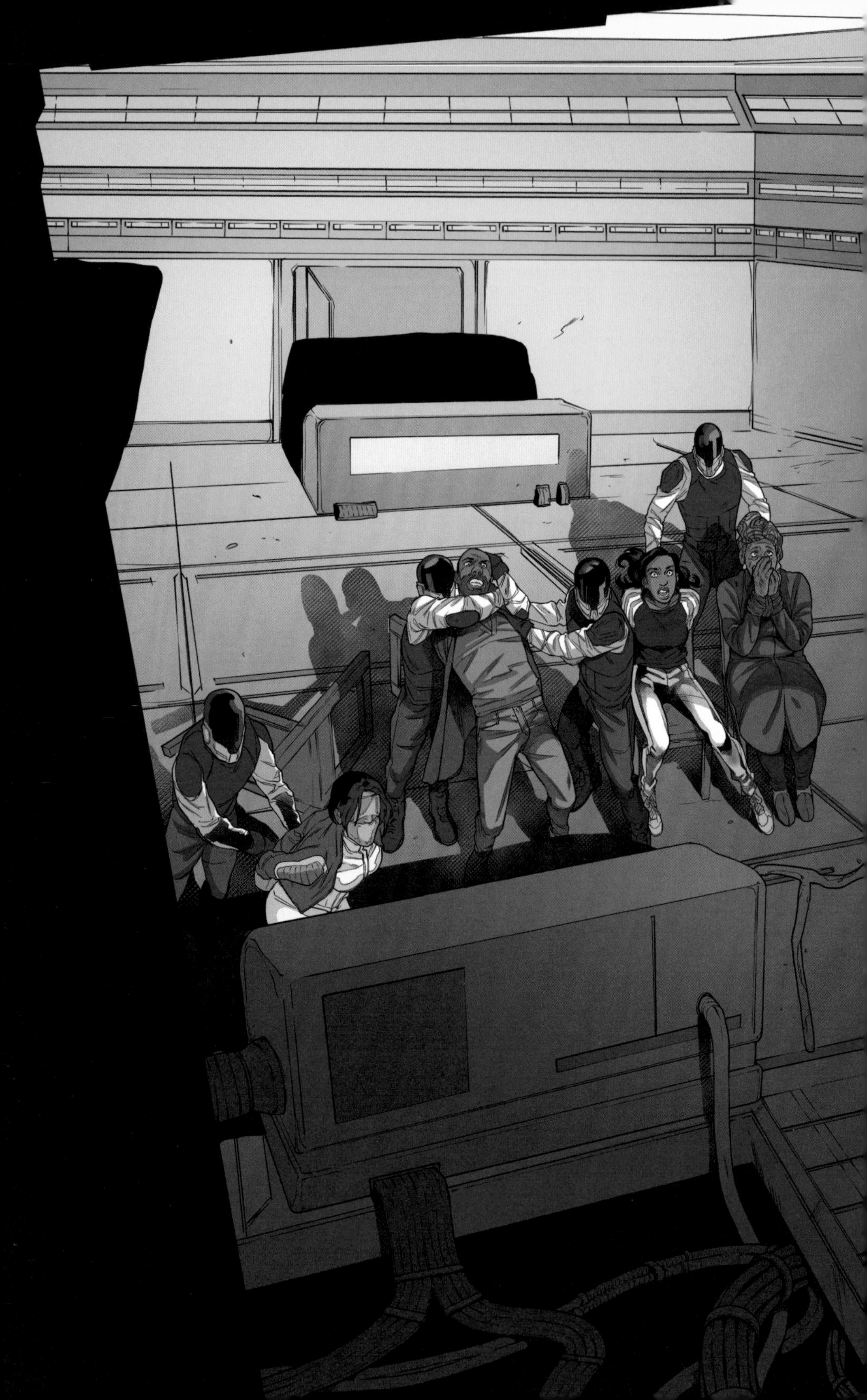

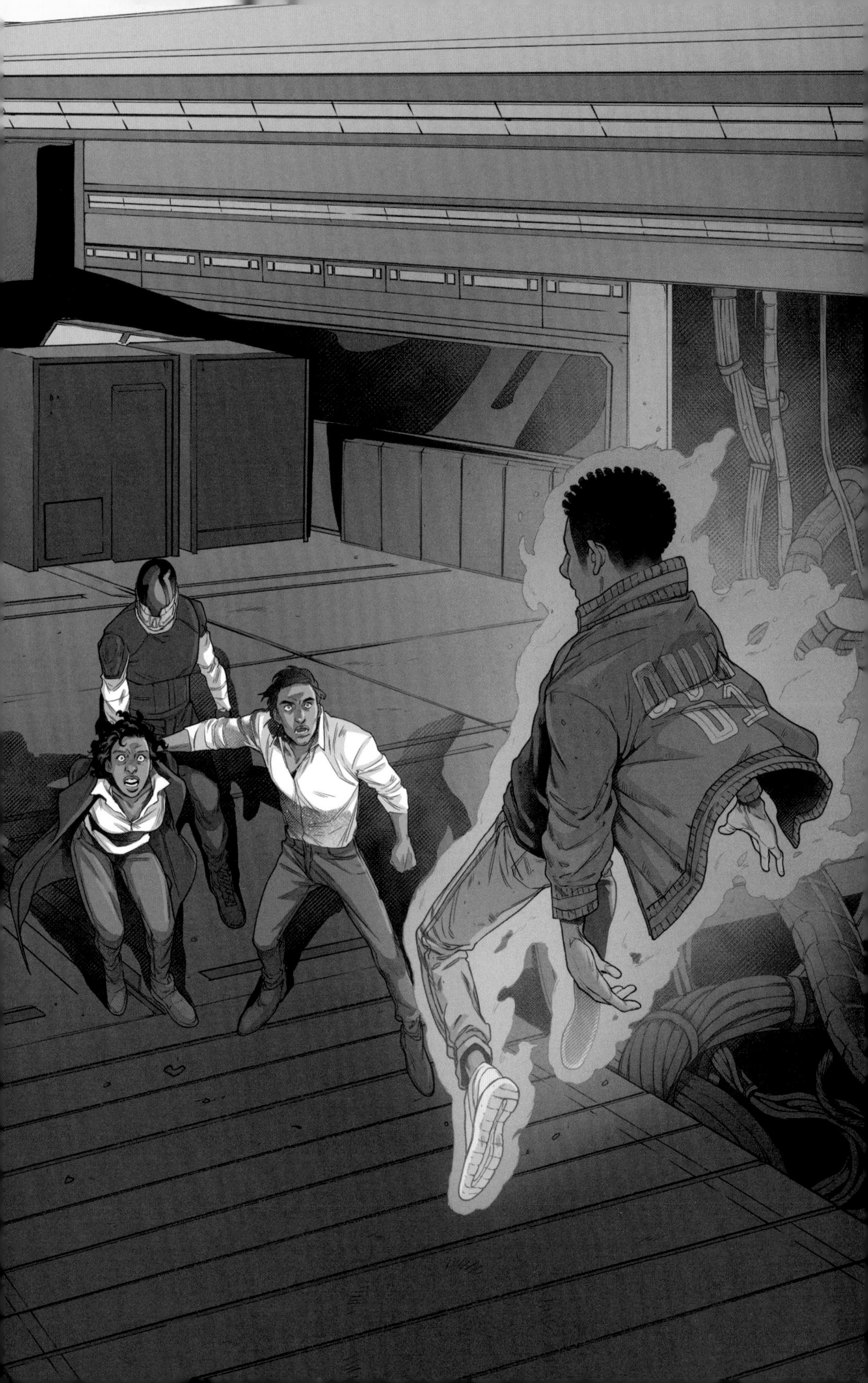

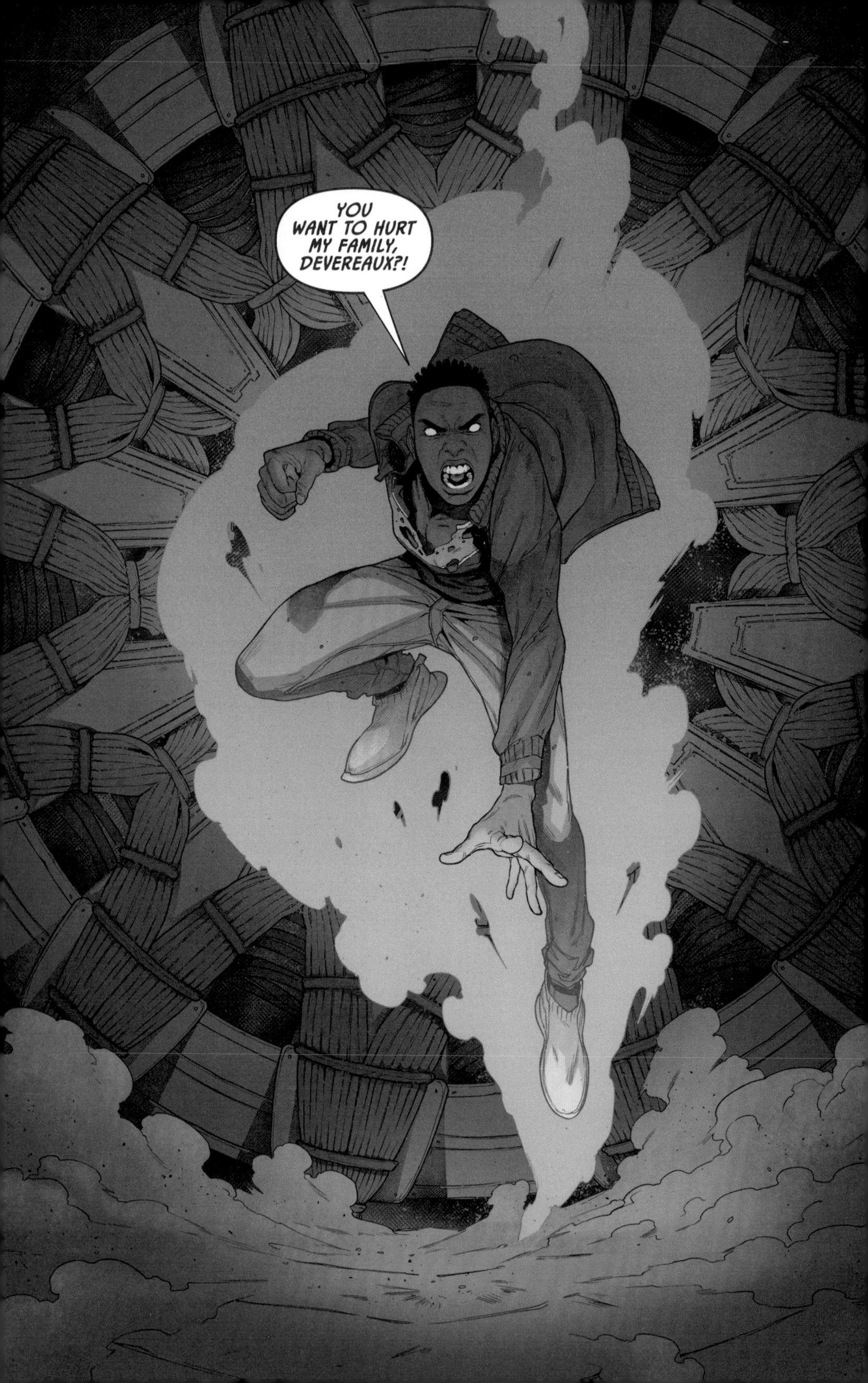
YOU WANT TO HURT MY FAMILY, DEVEREAUX?!

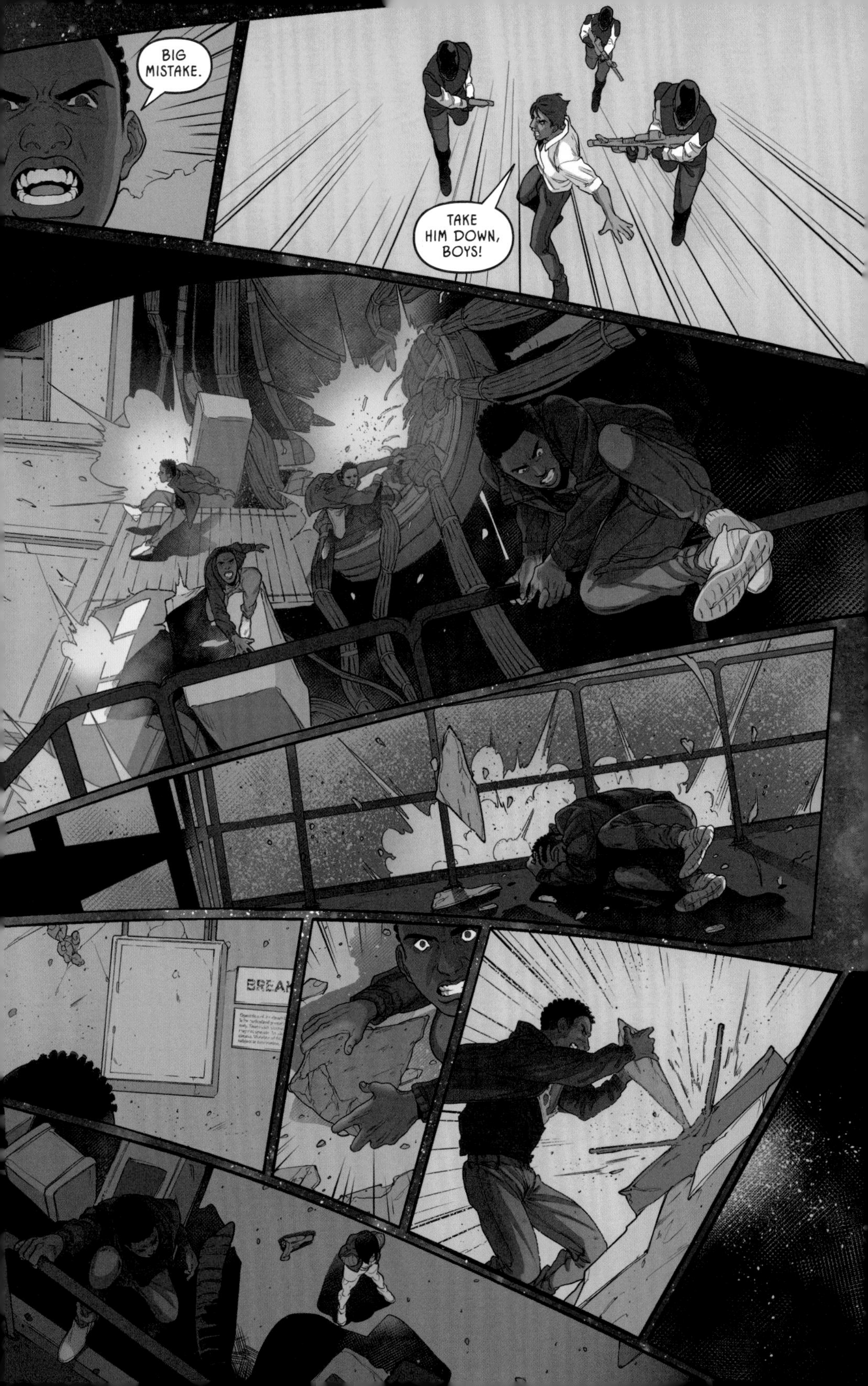
BIG MISTAKE.
TAKE HIM DOWN, BOYS!
BREA

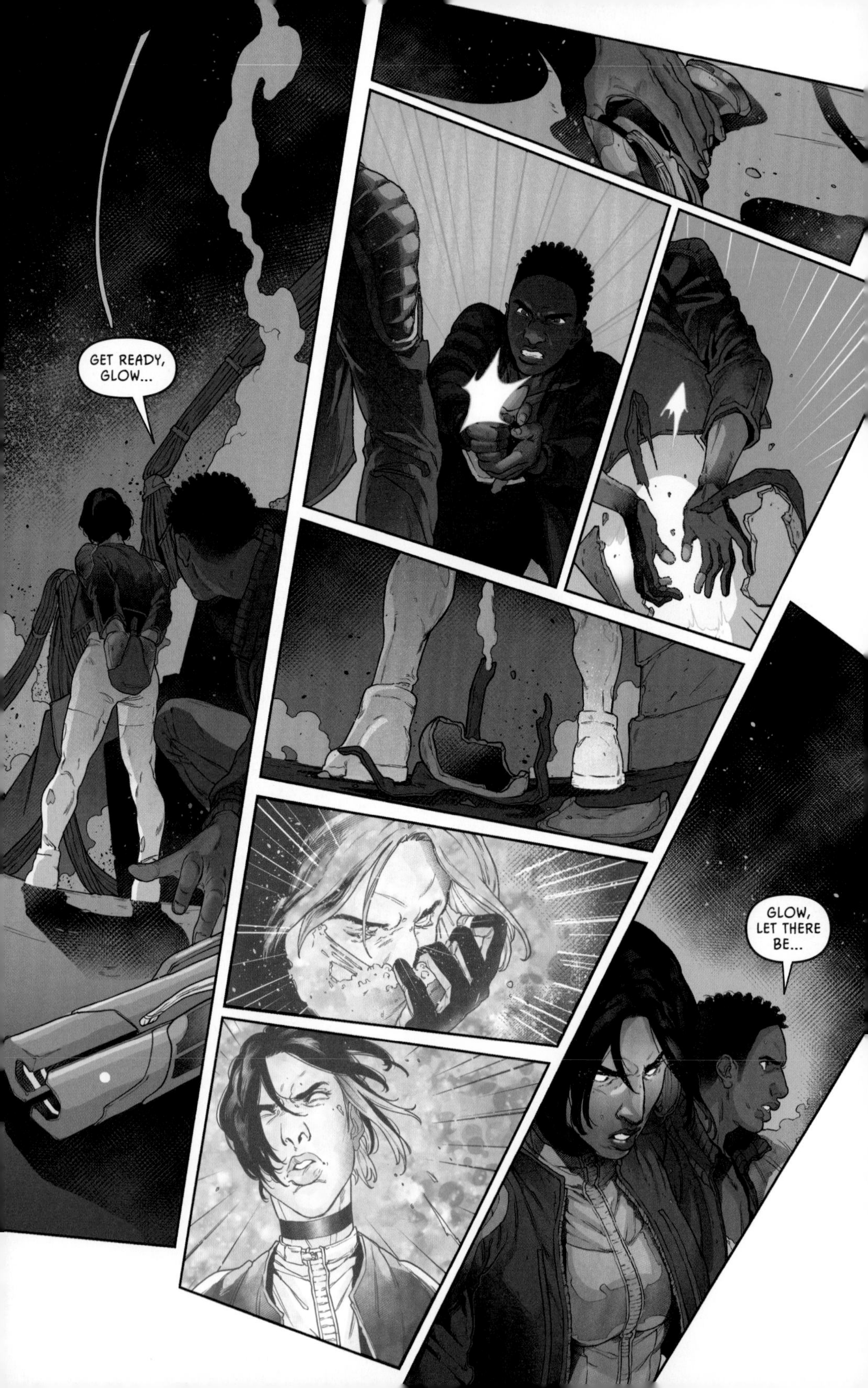
GET READY, GLOW...
GLOW, LET THERE BE...

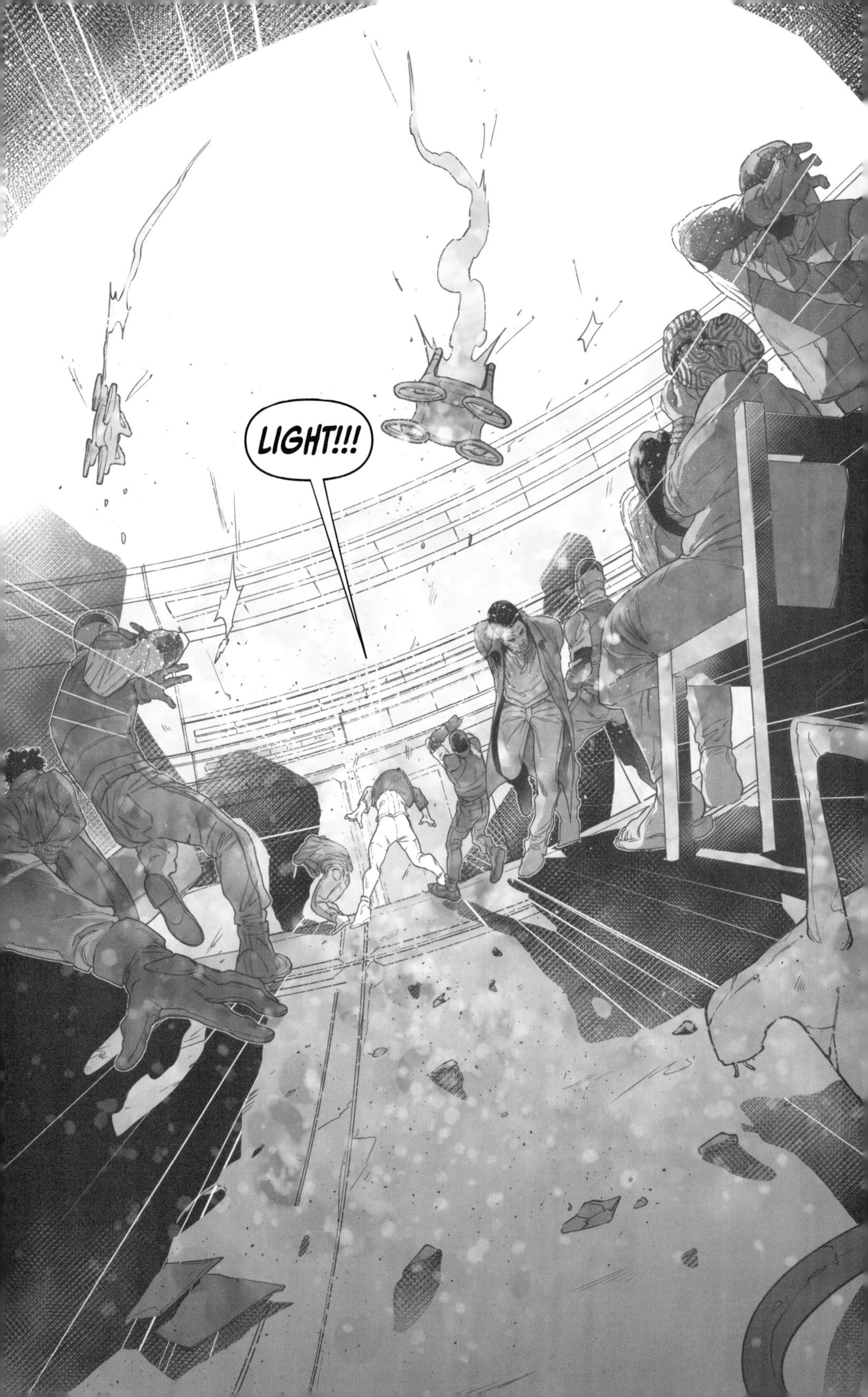
LIGHT!!!

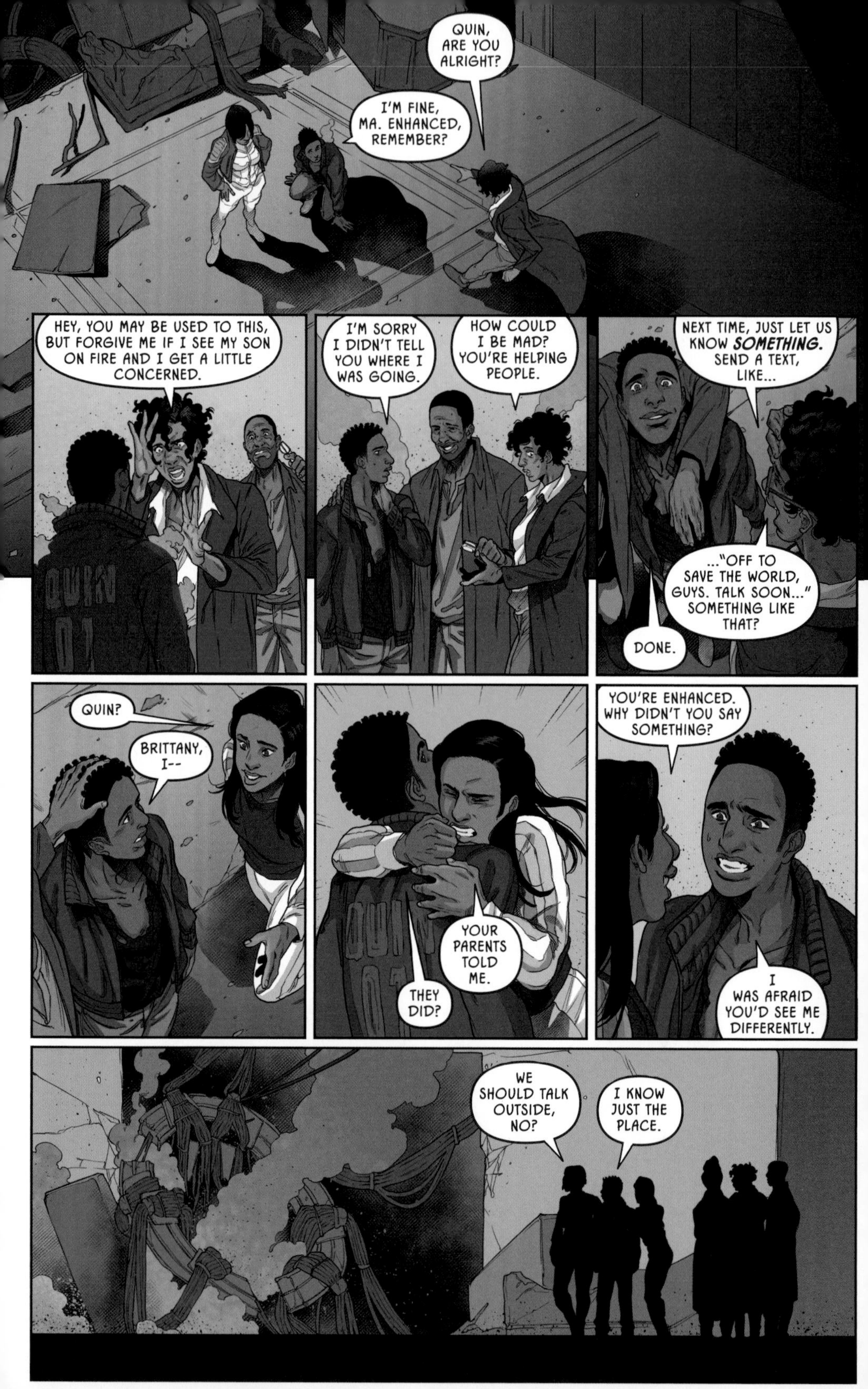
QUIN, ARE YOU ALRIGHT?
I'M FINE, MA. ENHANCED, REMEMBER?
HEY, YOU MAY BE USED TO THIS, BUT FORGIVE ME IF I SEE MY SON ON FIRE AND I GET A LITTLE CONCERNED.
I'M SORRY I DIDN'T TELL YOU WHERE I WAS GOING.
HOW COULD I BE MAD? YOU'RE HELPING PEOPLE.
NEXT TIME, JUST LET US KNOW SOMETHING. SEND A TEXT, LIKE...
..."OFF TO SAVE THE WORLD, GUYS. TALK SOON..." SOMETHING LIKE THAT?
DONE.
QUIN?
BRITTANY, I--
YOUR PARENTS TOLD ME.
THEY DID?
YOU'RE ENHANCED. WHY DIDN'T YOU SAY SOMETHING?
I WAS AFRAID YOU'D SEE ME DIFFERENTLY.
WE SHOULD TALK OUTSIDE, NO?
I KNOW JUST THE PLACE.

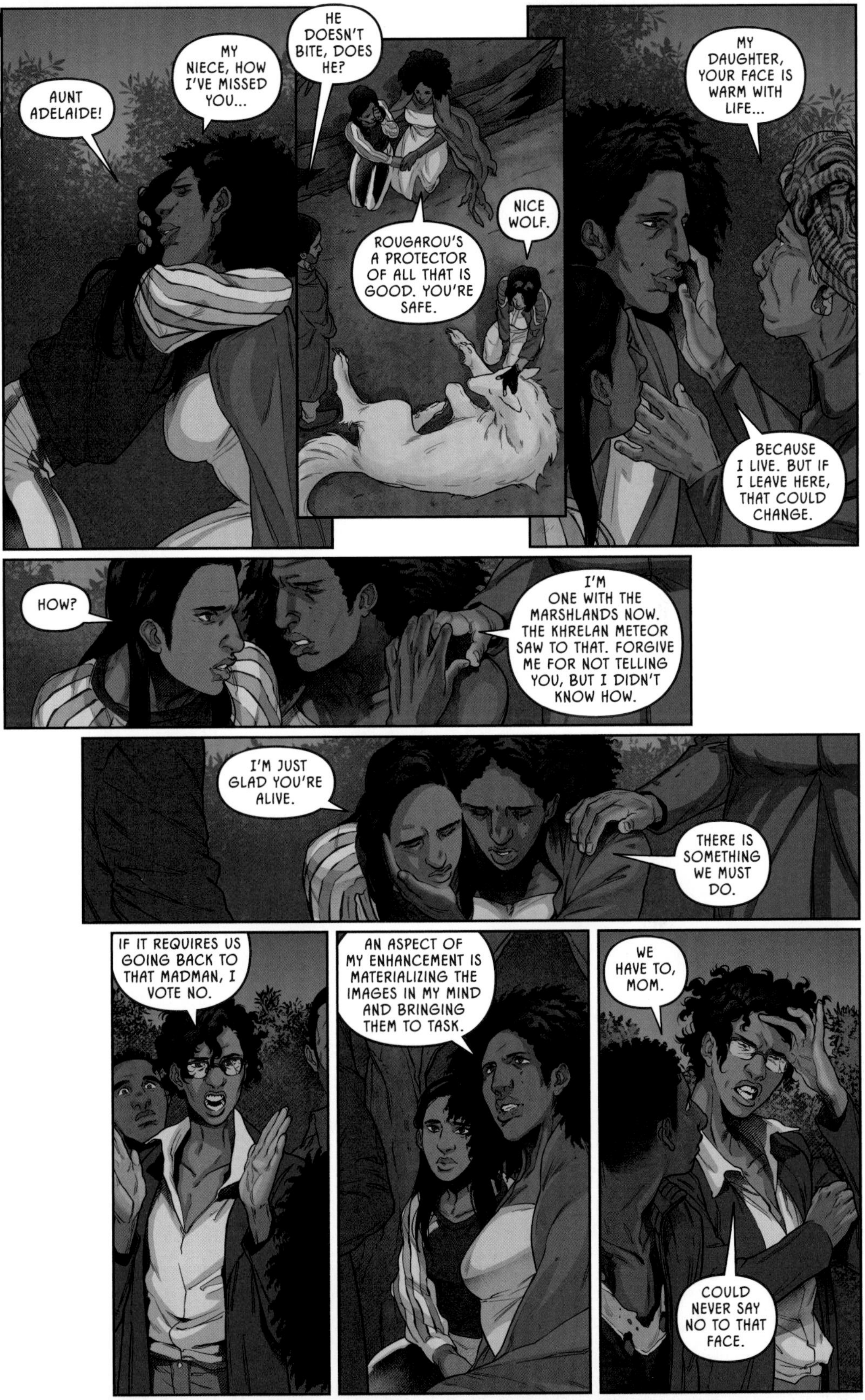
AUNT ADELAIDE!
MY NIECE, HOW I'VE MISSED YOU...
HE DOESN'T BITE, DOES HE?
ROUGAROU'S A PROTECTOR OF ALL THAT IS GOOD. YOU'RE SAFE.
NICE WOLF.
MY DAUGHTER, YOUR FACE IS WARM WITH LIFE...
BECAUSE I LIVE. BUT IF I LEAVE HERE, THAT COULD CHANGE.
HOW?
I'M ONE WITH THE MARSHLANDS NOW. THE KHRELAN METEOR SAW TO THAT. FORGIVE ME FOR NOT TELLING YOU, BUT I DIDN'T KNOW HOW.
I'M JUST GLAD YOU'RE ALIVE.
THERE IS SOMETHING WE MUST DO.
IF IT REQUIRES US GOING BACK TO THAT MADMAN, I VOTE NO.
AN ASPECT OF MY ENHANCEMENT IS MATERIALIZING THE IMAGES IN MY MIND AND BRINGING THEM TO TASK.
WE HAVE TO, MOM.
COULD NEVER SAY NO TO THAT FACE.

MOTHER, TO HONOR THE PAST, WOULD YOU PLEASE LEAD US IN THE OLD WAY?

YES, MY DEAR. EVERYONE PLEASE SIT.

WHAT'S GOING ON?

I'LL EXPLAIN LATER. JUST GO WITH IT.

CLOSE YOUR EYES.

TONIGHT, WE HONOR THE PAST. OUR BATTLE WILL BE IN THE NAME OF THOSE WHO IN THEIR TIME WERE UNABLE TO FIGHT FOR THEMSELVES.

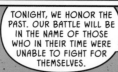

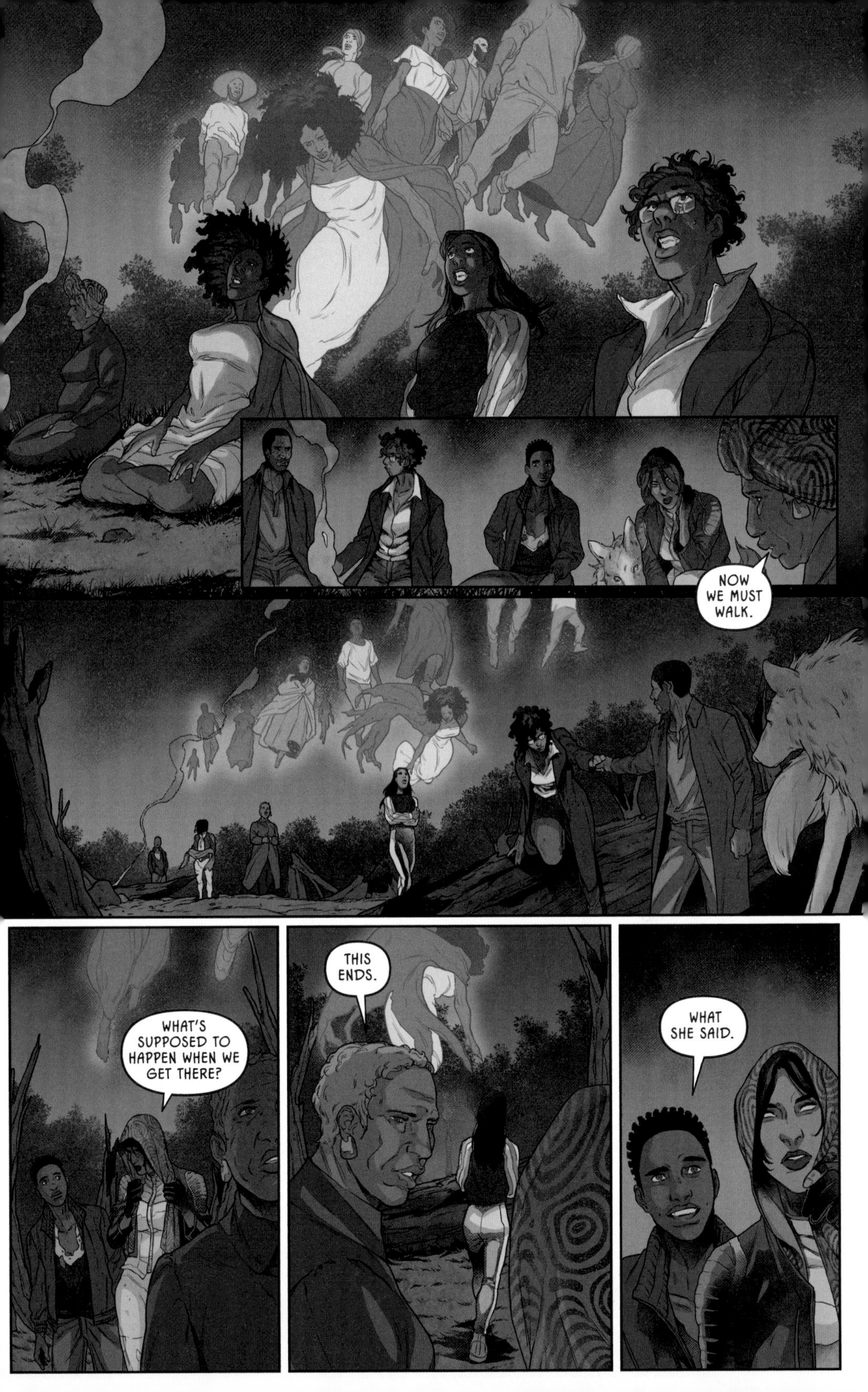
NOW WE MUST WALK.
WHAT'S SUPPOSED TO HAPPEN WHEN WE GET THERE?
THIS ENDS.
WHAT SHE SAID.

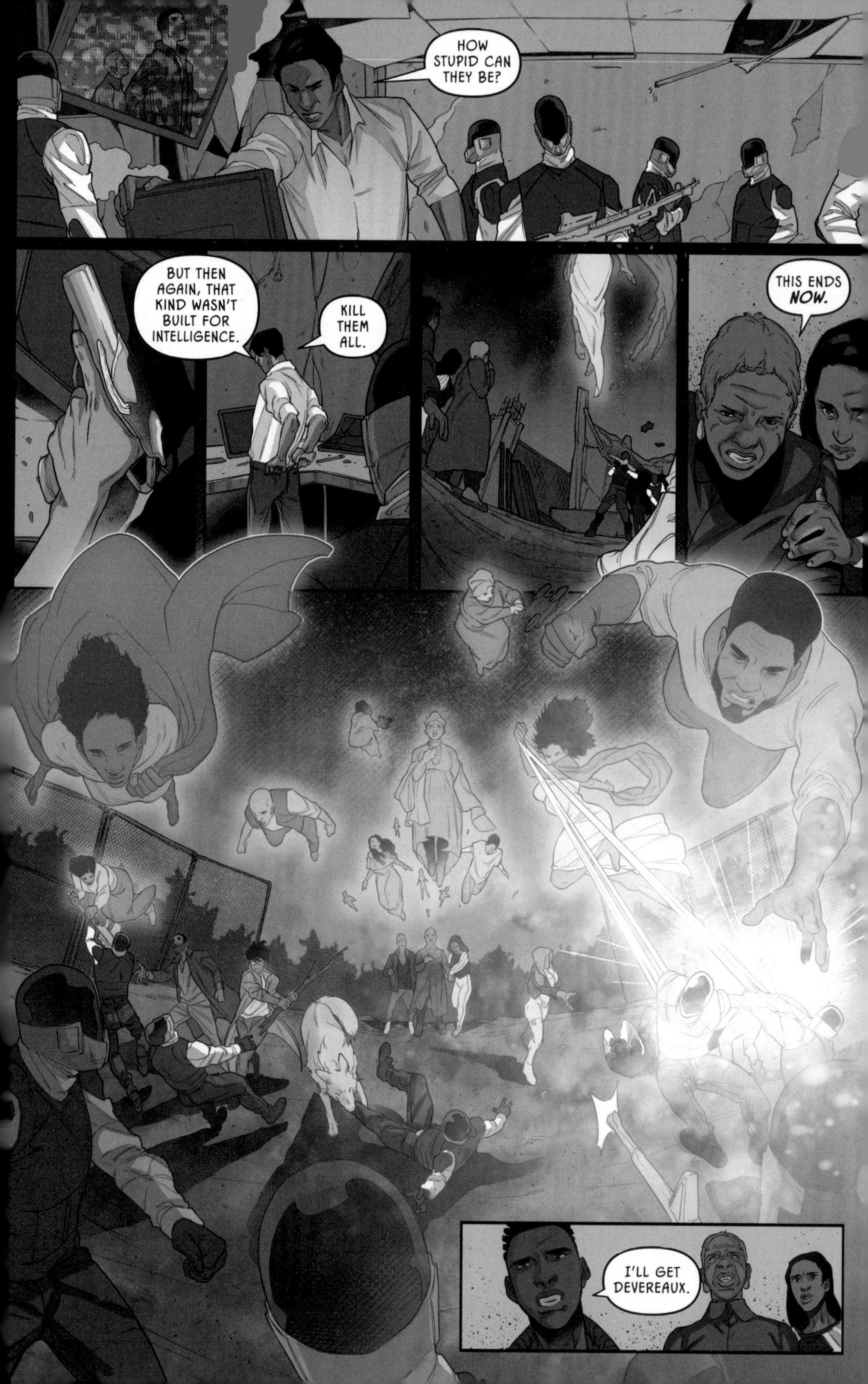
HOW STUPID CAN THEY BE?
BUT THEN AGAIN, THAT KIND WASN'T BUILT FOR INTELLIGENCE.
KILL THEM ALL.
THIS ENDS NOW.
I'LL GET DEVEREAUX.

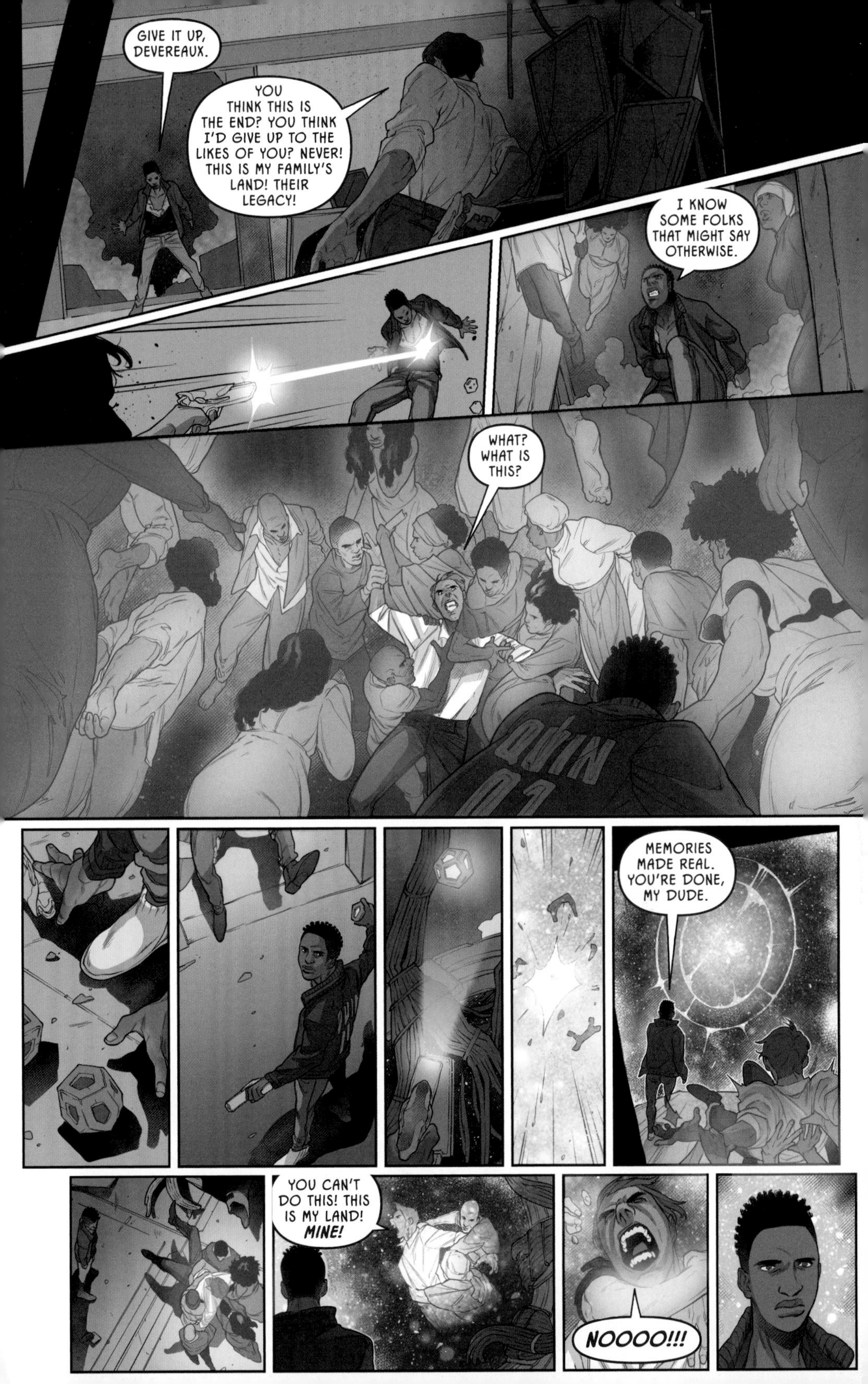
GIVE IT UP, DEVEREAUX.
YOU THINK THIS IS THE END? YOU THINK I'D GIVE UP TO THE LIKES OF YOU? NEVER! THIS IS MY FAMILY'S LAND! THEIR LEGACY!
I KNOW SOME FOLKS THAT MIGHT SAY OTHERWISE.
WHAT? WHAT IS THIS?
MEMORIES MADE REAL. YOU'RE DONE, MY DUDE.
YOU CAN'T DO THIS! THIS IS MY LAND! *MINE!*
NOOOO!!!

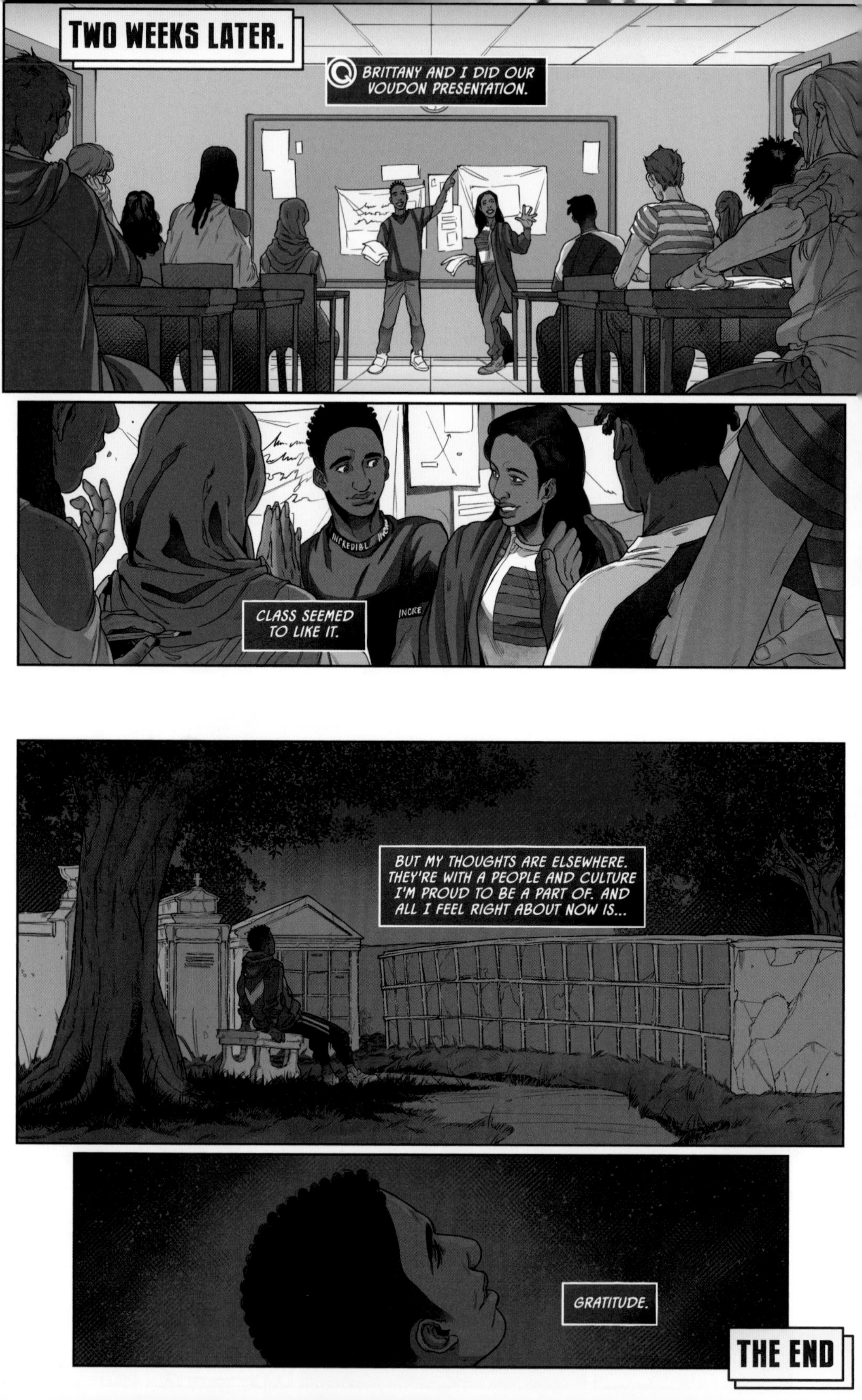
TWO WEEKS LATER.
BRITTANY AND I DID OUR VOUDON PRESENTATION.
CLASS SEEMED TO LIKE IT.
BUT MY THOUGHTS ARE ELSEWHERE. THEY'RE WITH A PEOPLE AND CULTURE I'M PROUD TO BE A PART OF. AND ALL I FEEL RIGHT ABOUT NOW IS...
GRATITUDE.
THE END

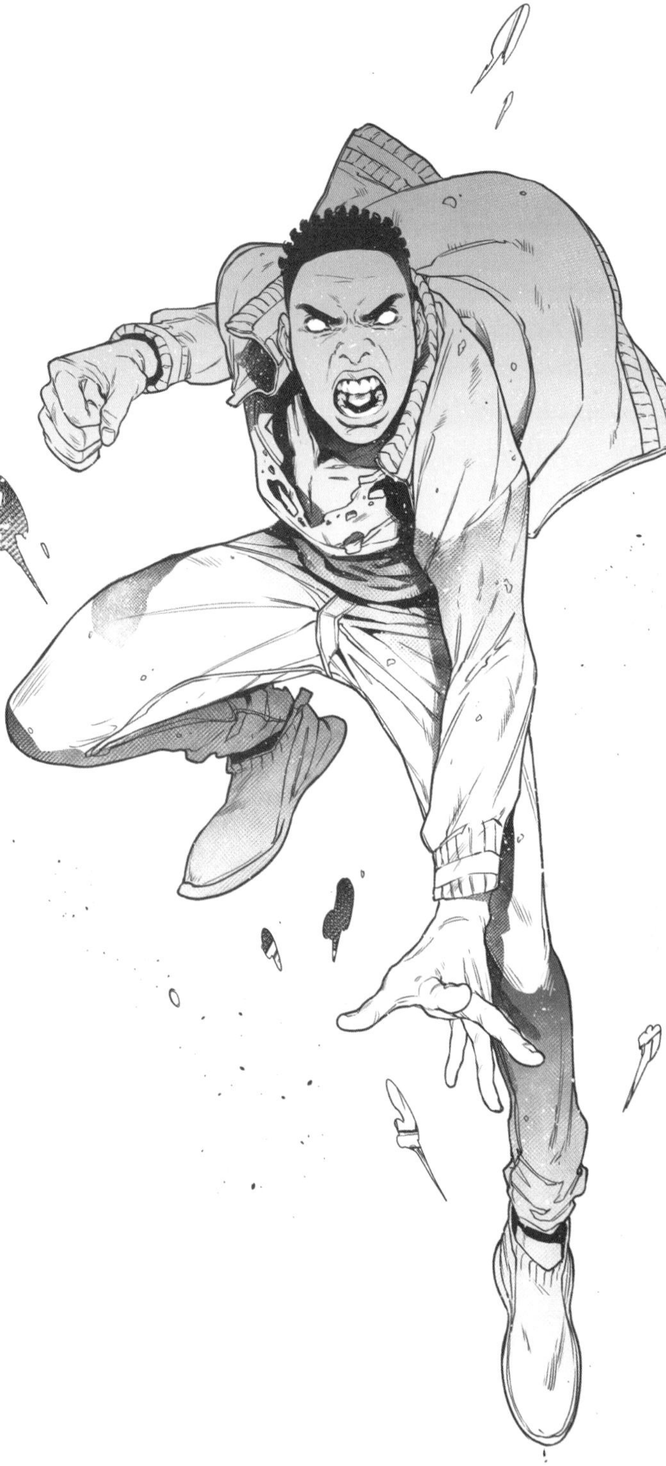

PIN UP GALLERY

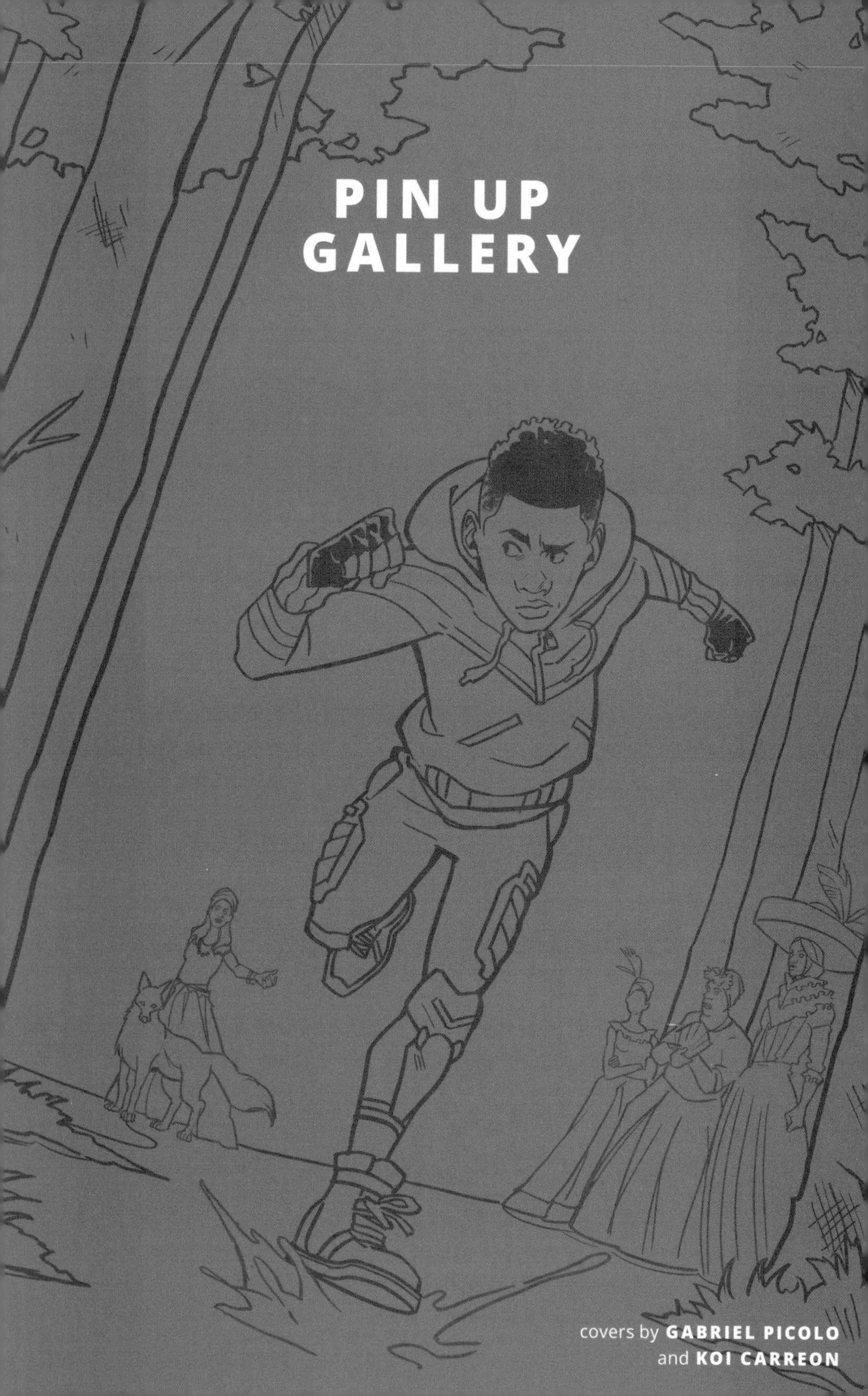

covers by **GABRIEL PICOLO**
and **KOI CARREON**

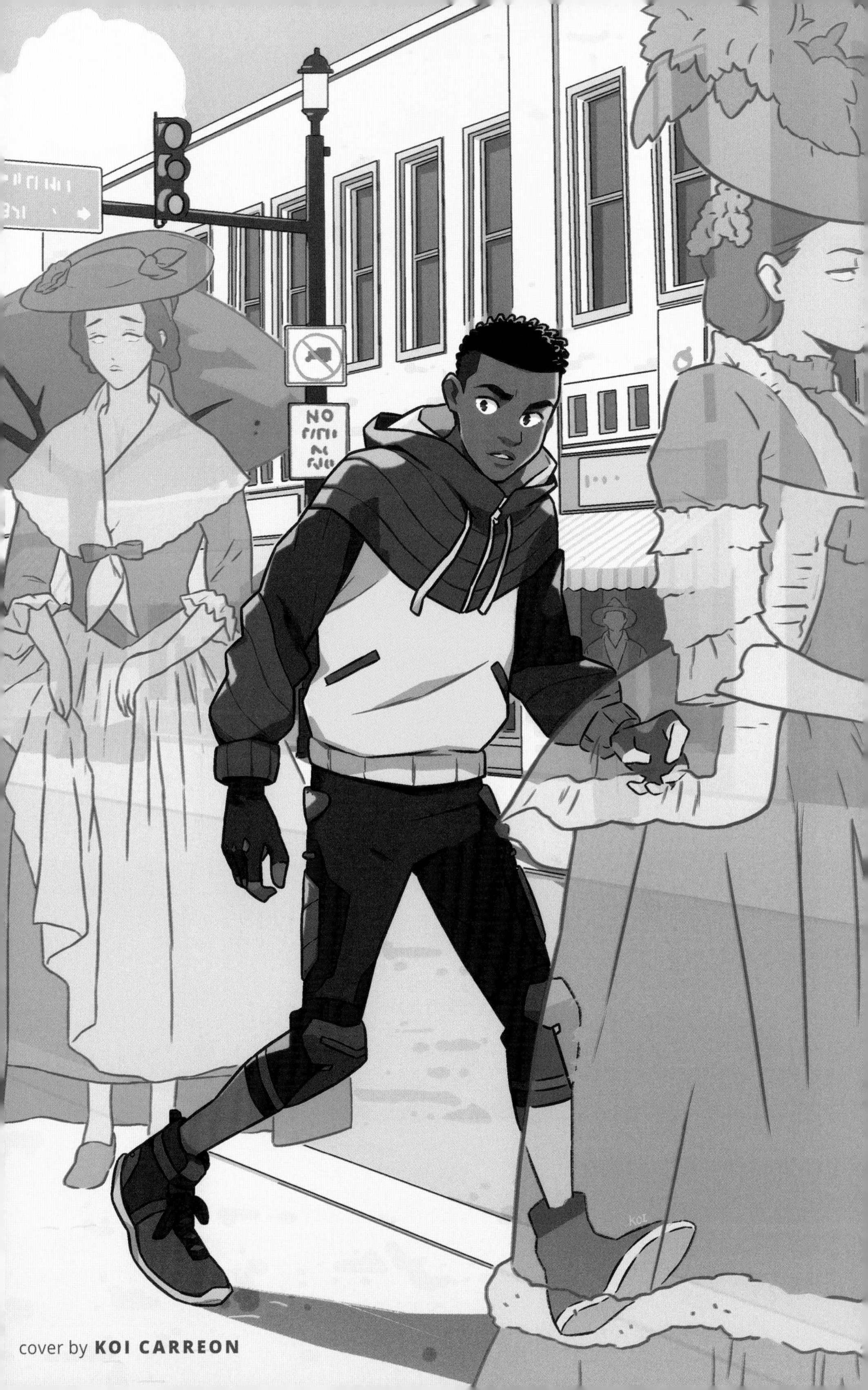
NO

cover by **KOI CARREON**

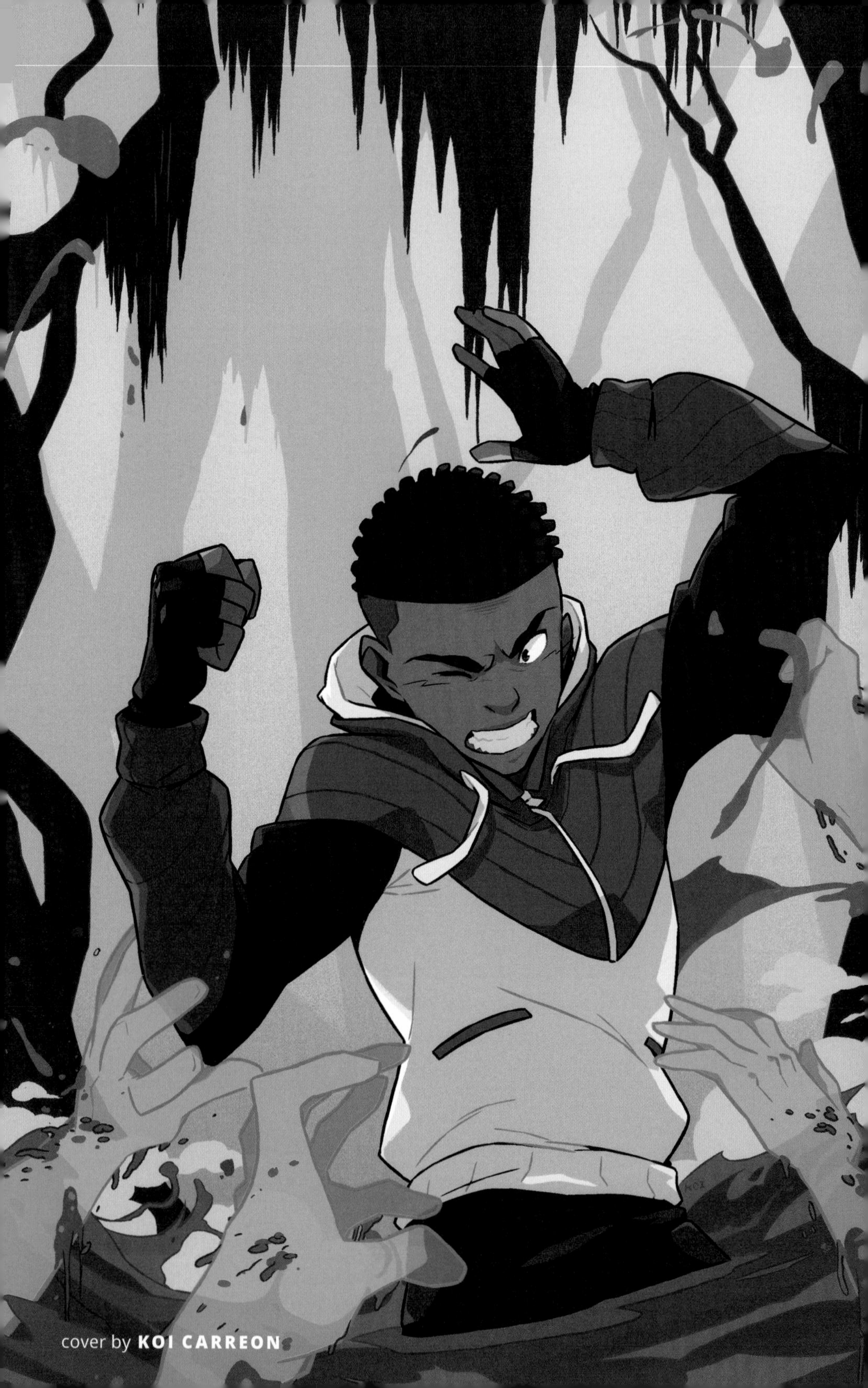

cover by **KOI CARREON**

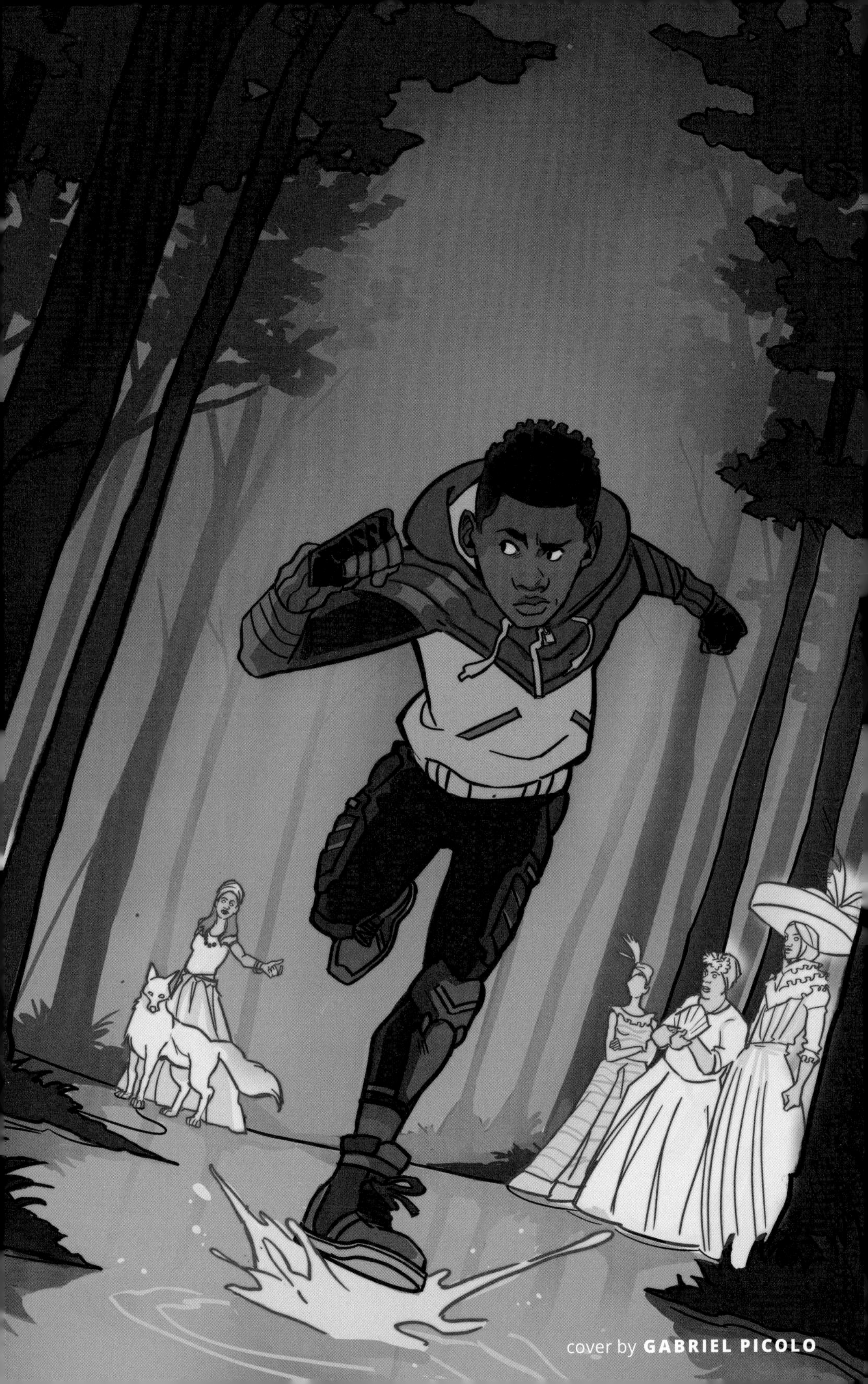

cover by **GABRIEL PICOLO**

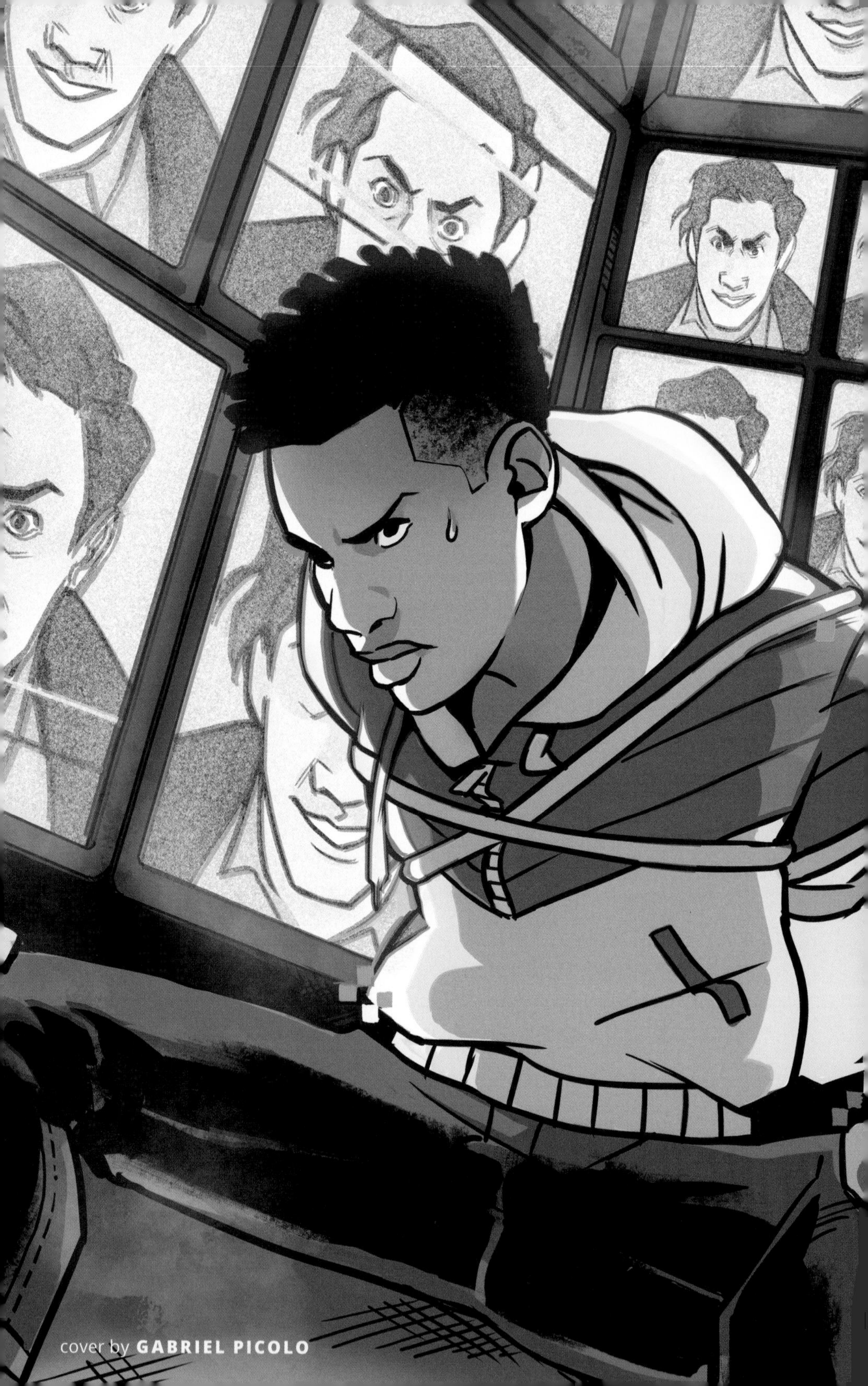
cover by **GABRIEL PICOLO**

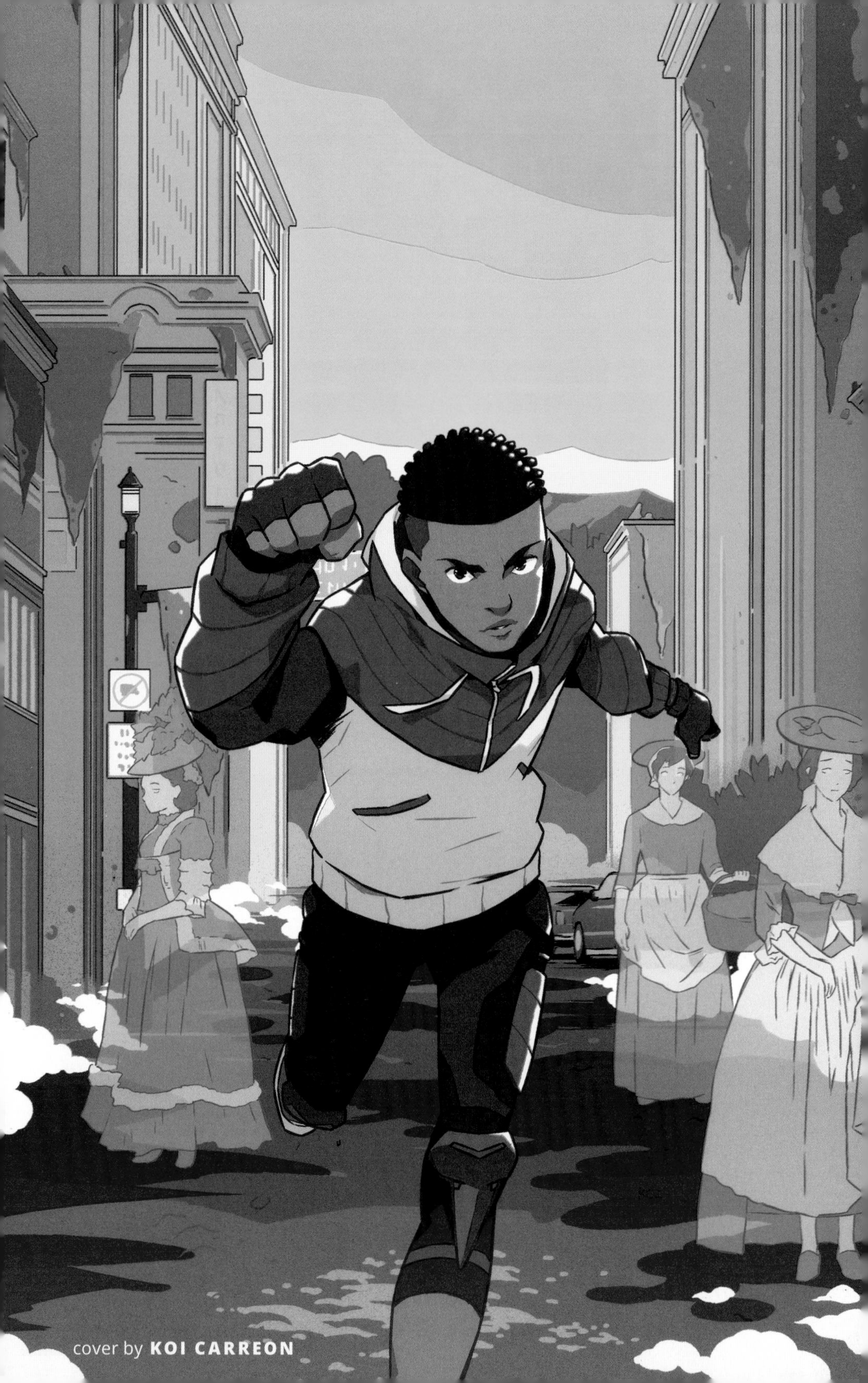

cover by **KOI CARREON**

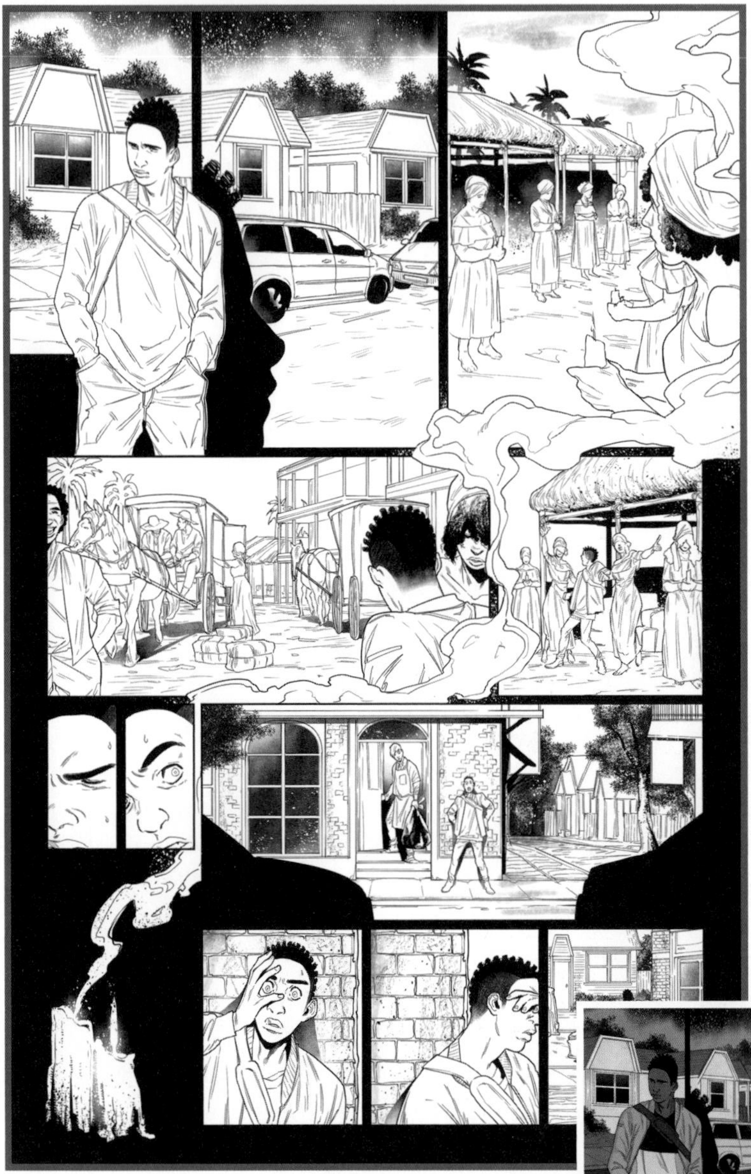

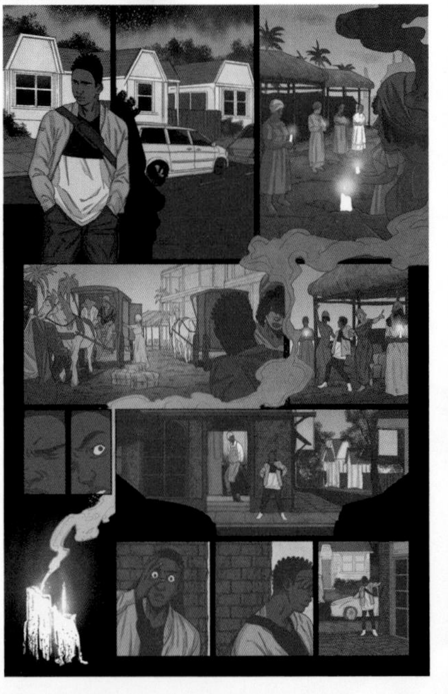

Illustrated by **SELINA ESPIRITU,**
Colored by **KELLY FITZPATRICK**

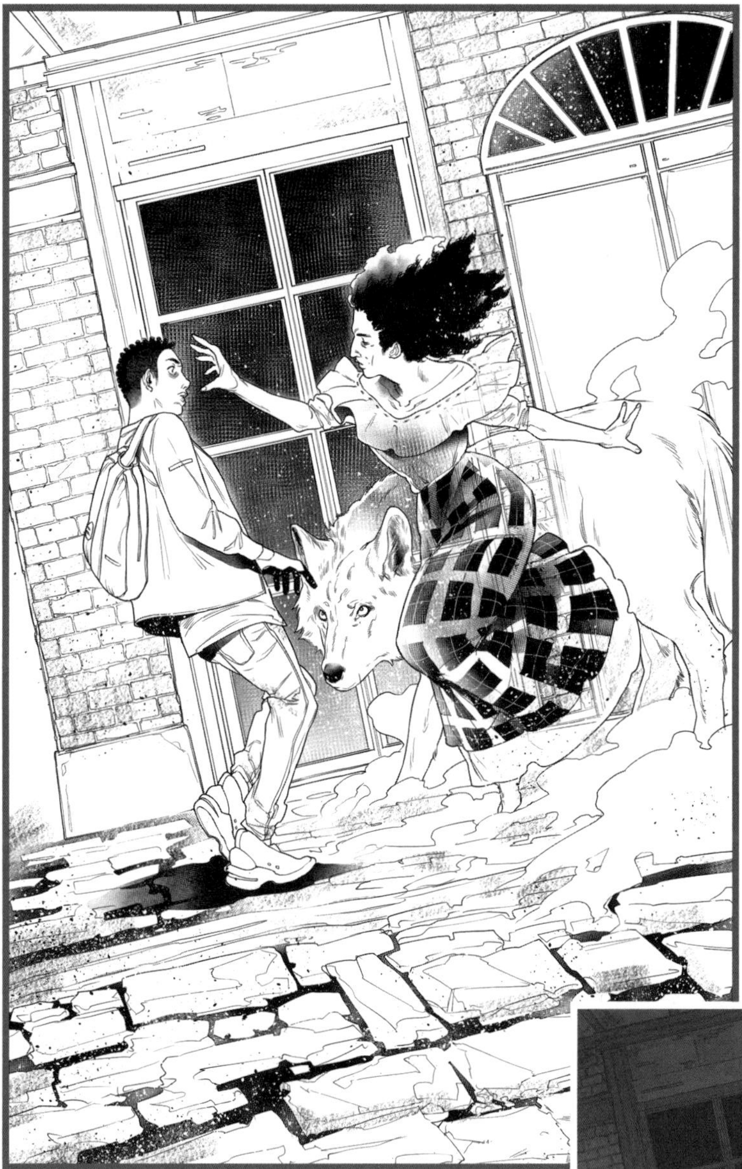

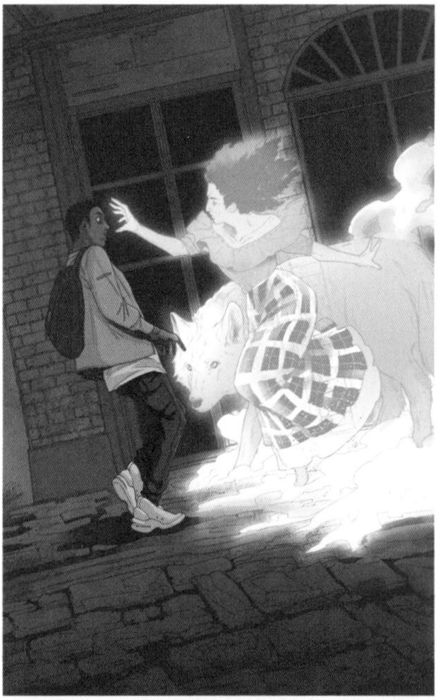

Illustrated by **SELINA ESPIRITU,**
Colored by **KELLY FITZPATRICK**

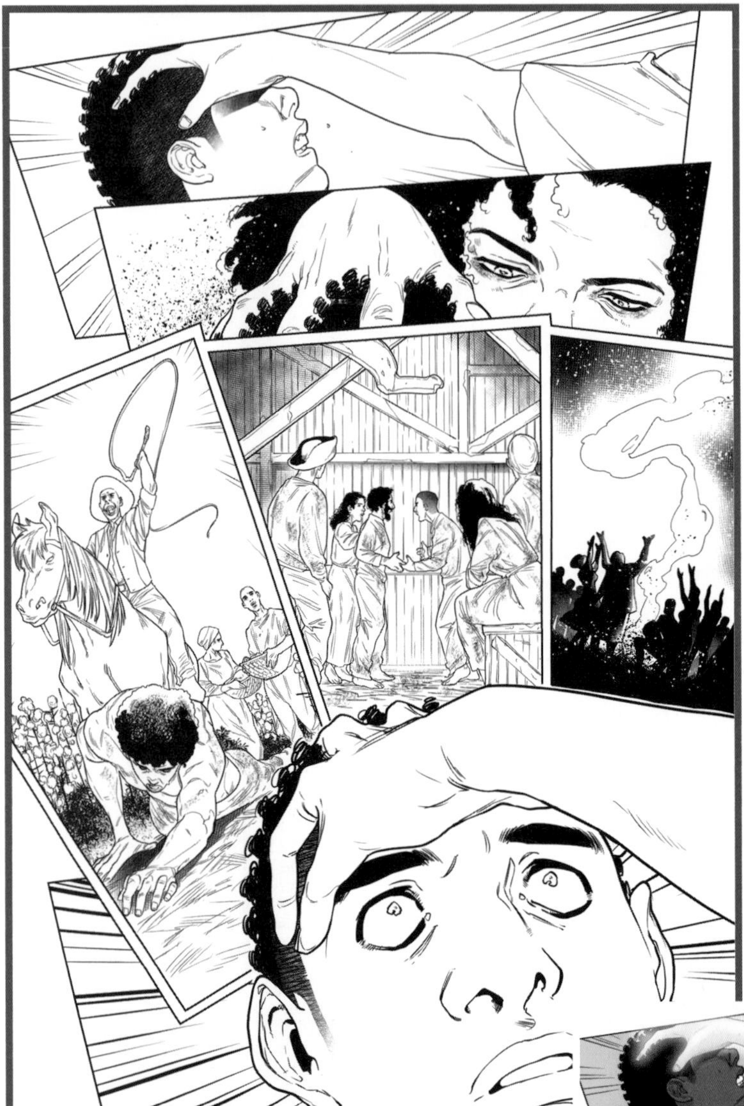

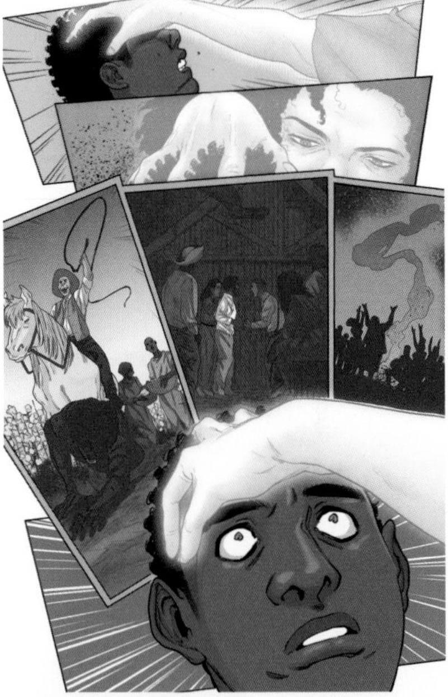

Illustrated by **SELINA ESPIRITU,**
Colored by **KELLY FITZPATRICK**

CREATOR BIOS

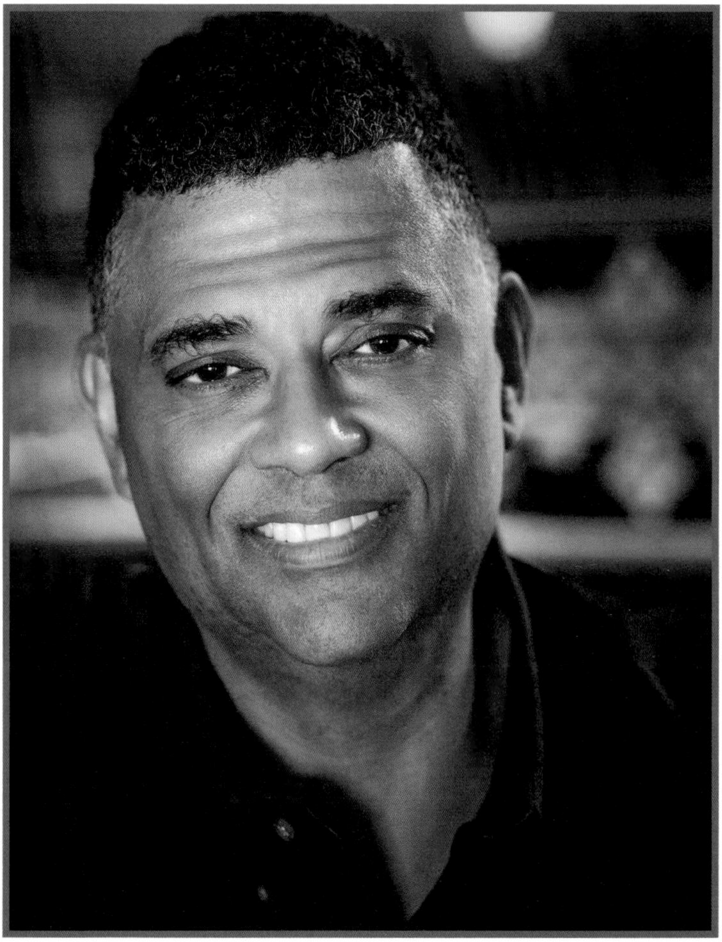

RODNEY BARNES is the award-winning writer/producer of HBO's Showtime, Hulu's *Wu-Tang: An American Saga*, Marvel's *Runaways*, Starz's *American Gods*, and a host of other television programs and films. He has also authored graphic novels for Lion Forge's *Quincredible* and *Star Wars - Lando: Double or Nothing*, as well as *Falcon* for Marvel Comics. He is now writing *Killadelphia* for Image Comics. Rodney resides in Los Angeles.

Twitter: **@THERODNEYBARNES**

CREATOR BIOS

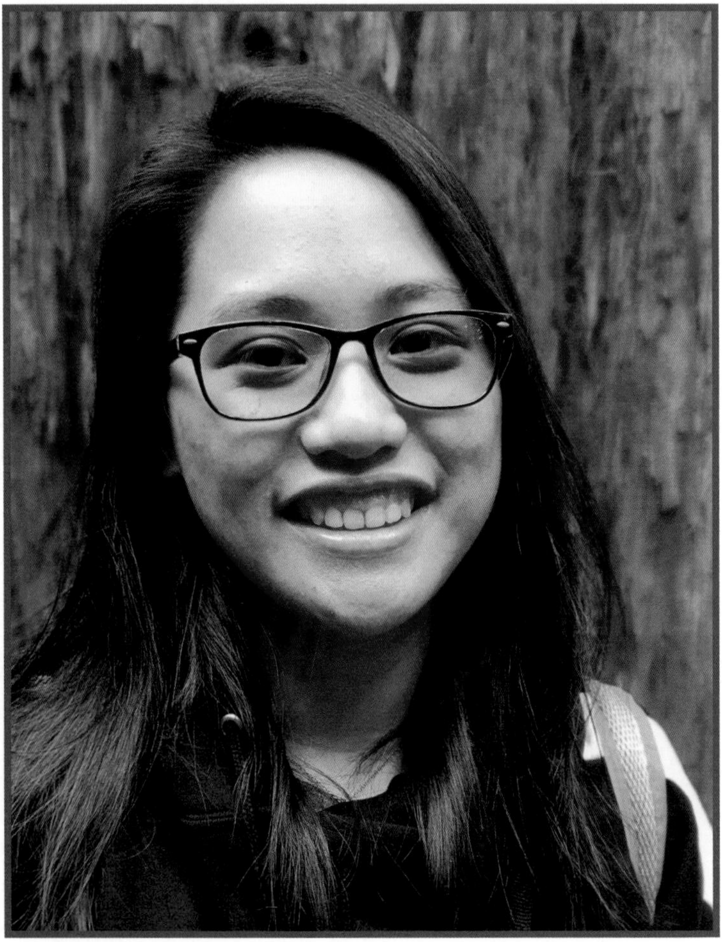

SELINA ESPIRITU is a freelance illustrator working from the Philippines with an enthusiasm for dogs and storytelling. She has worked on titles such as *QUINCREDIBLE*, published by Lion Forge, and *BRAVE CHEF BRIANNA*, by BOOM! Studios. Outside of comics, Espiritu's freelance work revolves around cover illustration and character design, for which she possesses a particular passion for. Otherwise, she amuses herself with her dogs, history books, and her work as an emergency medical technician.

Twitter: **@SIRIUSDRAWS**